Praise for the
Rekke and Vargas series by David Lagercrantz

"A classic mystery.... One Holmes himself would have loved to solve."
—*The Independent*

"This book kept me up half the night.... It works brilliantly.... David Lagercrantz knows his craft." —*Expressen*

"A terrifically well-wrought book that grabs readers and tugs them through a dangerous deductive adventure."
—*The Wall Street Journal*

"Rekke [is a] gem of a character.... Kudos to Lagercrantz and translator Giles for a compelling read." —*Kirkus Reviews* (starred review)

"David Lagercrantz, who inherited Stieg Larsson's mismatched investigators in his sequels to the Millennium series, introduces an odd couple of his own.... It has a cosmopolitan collection of oddball characters, and themes as diverse as classical music and Sweden's anti-terrorist policies." —*The Sunday Times* (London)

"A must-read.... Another writer might have gotten lost in a swamp of clichés. But not David Lagercrantz.... Lagercrantz skillfully navigates a complex plot." —*Smålandsposten*

"A rich, engrossing novel." —*Literary Review*

"Very entertaining. . . . The depiction of this duo's friendship is finely tuned and poignant, and I have only good things to say about the suspense." —*Svenska Dagbladet*

"We are without a doubt dealing with a dynamic duo. . . . Both affecting and engaging." —*Göteborgs-Posten*

"Complex and dark." —*Irish Independent*

"Lagercrantz really captures readers. . . . We like Rekke and Vargas—both as partners and as individuals." —*Kulturnytt*, Sveriges Radio

"Fans of dark Swedish crime will love this moody thriller." —*The Sun*

David Lagercrantz

# FATAL GAMBIT

David Lagercrantz is an acclaimed author and journalist. His continuation of Stieg Larsson's Millennium Trilogy—*The Girl in the Spider's Web*, *The Girl Who Takes an Eye for an Eye*, and *The Girl Who Lived Twice*—are worldwide bestsellers. He is also the author of *I Am Zlatan Ibrahimović*, *Fall of Man in Wilmslow*, and *Dark Music*. He lives in Stockholm.

REKKE AND VARGAS INVESTIGATIONS

*Dark Music*

THE MILLENNIUM SERIES BY DAVID LAGERCRANTZ

*The Girl in the Spider's Web*
*The Girl Who Takes an Eye for an Eye*
*The Girl Who Lived Twice*

ALSO BY DAVID LAGERCRANTZ IN ENGLISH TRANSLATION

*I Am Zlatan Ibrahimović: My Story On and Off the Field*
*Fall of Man in Wilmslow*

# FATAL GAMBIT

A MYSTERY

## David Lagercrantz

*Translated from the Swedish by Ian Giles*

VINTAGE CRIME/BLACK LIZARD
VINTAGE BOOKS
A DIVISION OF PENGUIN RANDOM HOUSE LLC
NEW YORK

FIRST VINTAGE CRIME/BLACK LIZARD EDITION 2025

*English translation copyright © 2024 by Ian Giles*

Penguin Random House values and supports copyright. Copyright fuels creativity, encourages diverse voices, promotes free speech, and creates a vibrant culture. Thank you for buying an authorized edition of this book and for complying with copyright laws by not reproducing, scanning, or distributing any part of it in any form without permission. You are supporting writers and allowing Penguin Random House to continue to publish books for every reader. Please note that no part of this book may be used or reproduced in any manner for the purpose of training artificial intelligence technologies or systems.

Published by Vintage Books, a division of Penguin Random House LLC, 1745 Broadway, New York, NY 10019. Originally published in Sweden as *Memoria* by Norstedts Forlag, Stockholm, in 2023. Copyright © 2023 by David Lagercrantz. This translation originally published in hardcover in Great Britain by MacLehose Press, an imprint of Quercus Editions Limited, London, and in the United States by Alfred A. Knopf, a division of Penguin Random House LLC, New York, in 2024. Published by arrangement with Quercus Editions Limited.

Vintage is a registered trademark and Vintage Crime/Black Lizard and colophon are trademarks of Penguin Random House LLC.

The Library of Congress has cataloged the Knopf edition as follows:
Names: Lagercrantz, David, author.
Title: Fatal gambit / David Lagercrantz.
Description: First edition. | New York: Alfred A. Knopf, 2024.
Identifiers: LCCN 2024939672 (print)
LC record available at https://lccn.loc.gov/2024939672

**Vintage Crime/Black Lizard Trade Paperback ISBN:** 978-0-593-31293-3
**eBook ISBN:** 978-0-593-31924-6

*Book design by M. Kristen Bearse*

penguinrandomhouse.com | vintagebooks.com

Printed in the United States of America
10 9 8 7 6 5 4 3 2 1

The authorized representative in the EU for product safety and compliance is Penguin Random House Ireland, Morrison Chambers, 32 Nassau Street, Dublin D02 YH68, Ireland, https://eu-contact.penguin.ie.

# FATAL GAMBIT

# PROLOGUE

On June 1, 2004, a Hungarian businessman with uncommonly strong powers of deduction received a call to his desk landline. The conversation fell into a familiar category—analysis of the surrounding world—and no-one could have foreseen that anything important or decisive would be discussed. However, since the analyst who called that day had an optimistic outlook on the world at large—aside from the situation in Iraq—he prattled on about all sorts of things and happened to mention Professor Hans Rekke.

"I hear Rekke is taking an interest in the death of Claire Lidman."

That was all, but it was enough to make the Hungarian businessman feel that the whole world was changing hue.

Though of course, the story had begun much earlier.

# ONE

Hans Rekke was only twelve years old at the time.

The snow was falling very heavily when the doorbell rang in the grand house in Vienna. Dr. Brandt, his mathematics teacher, stepped inside wearing a vastly oversized fur hat. With him was a boy of Rekke's age with curly hair and dark, intense eyes. Dr. Brandt introduced him as Gabor, and Hans proffered his hand.

It lingered alone in mid-air, the boy slipping by sinuous as a cat. There was something threatening about him, and Hans could not understand what was going on. The boy's gaze shone green, and in every one of his movements there was a vigilance, a readiness. The two of them were placed at the large desk beside the bookshelf with the Beethoven bust, and only then did things become a little clearer.

The boy was evidently a talent of some kind, and the idea was for them to compete and measure themselves against each other. Dr. Brandt issued them their tasks—on Cantor's mathematical proof of infinities—and at once an intense tension arose. The boy—Gabor—was trembling with eagerness and set to work immediately. Hans, however, remained still, staring at the contours of the boy's shoulder muscles.

"Why are you not writing?" Dr. Brandt asked.

"I'm going to," he said.

But he was wrapped up in his thoughts, consumed by a riddle that was more alluring than mathematics; and he watched in amazement as the boy performed calculations at lightning speed—a virtuoso, almost. Hans decided to let him win. *What do I care?* Nevertheless, something within him wanted to fight back, and he slowly worked his way into the task. Afterward, he thought it had gone quite well—not brilliantly, but decently enough—but when he looked up again, Gabor's eyes were shining with triumph.

"I'm impressed, boys. Why don't you take a twenty-minute break so you can get to know each other?" Dr. Brandt said, obviously pleased. So Hans and Gabor dressed to go out into the garden, their footsteps creaking against the frozen ground.

The snow was falling in large flakes. It was a cold day and Hans suddenly made out a faint wheeze—a high, four-times-accented G—audible on every third or fourth exhalation. It was a kind of vulnerability that contrasted with the fiery nature of the boy's aura.

"What are you training in?" Hans said.

Gabor appeared to pause for thought.

"Self-defence."

That was too vague for Hans.

"In what way?" he said.

"I can show you."

Gabor's body tensed and the faint wheeze of his breathing came down a semitone to an F sharp, which made Hans inattentive. That was part of his curse over the course of those years: when the soundscape changed he would compulsively analyse the notes in his surroundings. That was why he was not on his guard when Gabor grabbed hold of him.

It was as if he had fallen into a trap. He was spun around with violent force and struck the ground, and for a few seconds he saw nothing. Then he sensed Gabor's eyes above him, replete and satisfied, as if they belonged to a predator that had gotten what it wanted.

Then he was gone. Rekke lay there with a shooting pain in the back of his head, and only after the third or fourth attempt did he manage to get to his feet and stagger into the house. His hair was sticky and wet, and he stood in front of the bathtub on the ground floor for a long time trying to stop the flow of blood. By the time he returned to the library, some fifteen or twenty minutes had elapsed.

Dr. Brandt, still at the desk, indicated with exaggerated gestures and a look of deep disappointment that Gabor had gone home. He never noticed that Rekke was injured and pale. Nor, indeed, did Rekke's mother. She was preoccupied the whole evening, searching for a couple of pieces of jewellery that had suddenly gone missing.

# TWO

Police Constable Micaela Vargas from Husby had moved in with Professor Hans Rekke of Grevgatan in Stockholm's most refined neighbourhood, something which had gotten everyone around her all worked up and had set them to gossiping. But now she wanted out.

Rekke was depressed and hopeless, and he barely emerged from the bedroom. As soon as he had pulled himself together just a little, she would head over there to pack up her stuff. But first of all, she wanted to bring to a close the case they had embarked upon. It was to do with a woman who had been declared dead, but who had possibly made an appearance in a recently taken holiday snap in Venice, and while Micaela didn't really believe in any of that, there was something about the story that titillated her.

That was why she had come to the police station on Bergsgatan to meet Inspector Kaj Lindroos, who had investigated the incident almost fourteen years earlier. But Kaj Lindroos was taking his time, which didn't surprise her. He had sounded recalcitrant and grumpy on the phone, and she was standing a little listlessly in reception on the ground floor, staring out at the street. A truck drove by with a pack of screeching sixth-formers celebrating their graduation in the back. It was June 5, 2004, a glorious summer's day, and she was on the brink of chucking it in and leaving when she heard a voice behind her.

"My private investigator colleague, I presume?"

She turned around and shook his hand. He was younger than she had imagined—barely fifty—with big brown eyes and back-combed blond hair, but he was also seedier. He looked at her as if it were five to three in the morning. She tugged her denim jacket closer to her body.

"I'm grateful you agreed to see me," she said.

"Claire Lidman's dead," Kaj Lindroos said.

"Probably. But I still think this is somewhat interesting," she said, touching her inside pocket. "I promise to be brief."

Inspector Lindroos continued to eye her body.

"You can be as brief as you like but I still don't believe it."

Micaela wished she had something to ram down his throat.

"Maybe you could take a look at the picture before you make up your mind," she said, following him into the elevator.

Of course Kaj Lindroos was going to take a look at the photo, and it was obviously downright ridiculous to be bugged by the fact that the girl was so young, and an immigrant to boot. On the other hand, it wasn't that easy to fend off one's prejudices, especially where the Lidman investigation was concerned. It was the gaping wound of his career, and there was most definitely something peculiar about the whole business. A beautiful, well-educated woman who had negotiated with business high-flyers for a living had disappeared without trace fourteen years ago—only to turn up a few months later burned to a crisp in a petrol-tanker crash in Spain. Of course, he had pondered it all a thousand times since then. Then again . . . fuck it. That was all history, and it was a Friday afternoon. He really should be off home soon to get drunk and maybe even have a crack at the wife. It had to be worth a try at the least.

"So you work in youth crime?" he said.

"I try to do other stuff in my free time."

"I bet you do. I like your denim jacket," he said, but he actually meant her tits, and he scrutinised her from head to toe again.

Her legs could have done with being longer, and it wouldn't have hurt for her to smile a bit more. But it would be churlish to complain.

They stepped into his office, and he shuffled some papers out of the way on his desk. Outside the open window, the sixth-formers were screaming away as the parade of trucks passed by. He was tempted to say something scornful about them, but he didn't want to come across as out of touch.

"What a party," he said. "Almost makes you wish you were down there."

"Almost," she said.

"Did you scream when they let you out for the last time?"

"For all I was worth."

"Can't have been that long ago, I suppose?" he said, regretting it immediately.

The same irritation again, the same unconscious way of saying that she was too young and inexperienced to put forward strange theories suggesting that Claire had risen from the dead. But that couldn't be helped.

"Did you mean something by that?" she said.

"No, no," he said. "But back in my day everyone thought those white caps were right wing. Now, all of a sudden, everyone wants them."

"Is that right?" she said, uninterested.

"Apparently being a rebel is out again."

"Is it?"

"Do you like Ulf Lundell?"

"Who?"

These goddamn chicks from the hood didn't know diddly-squat about Sweden.

"Well, what do you say? Might as well get it over with," he said in a tone that failed to entirely mask his irritation, and she nodded. She slipped her hand into her inside pocket and pulled out a plastic-covered photograph.

For a moment he was frightened. He couldn't understand why. No, he reassured himself—it was impossible. There was a death certificate. DNA samples. He'd seen the body himself. Claire Lidman was most definitely not roaming the world again dressed in an elegant red coat.

# THREE

Hans Rekke was playing the adagio in *Pathétique* on the grand piano. He stopped after just a few minutes. The piece no longer spoke to him, though it probably wasn't Beethoven's fault. Nothing spoke to him any longer. He stood up wondering where to turn. Left or right?

His life at present consisted of these kinds of decisions. Should he lie down or stay seated? There was a car alarm wailing outside and his wall clock was ticking—*tick tick tick tick tick*—as if to show how many seconds were being wasted on meaninglessness.

Where had Micaela got to? He hadn't seen her in a week. Perhaps she had moved back home—and who could blame her? He probably made for dreadful company—but it still hurt. He decided to go to the kitchen and drink a glass of wine; he was in such a poor state that he regarded even that as a sign of enterprise. But he didn't succeed in that either. Instead, he diverted to the bathroom and opened the medicine cabinet. Close it again, he chided. Leave. But his hands had a life of their own, and he helped himself to the new pills he had been given by Freddie, his doctor from hell.

They were called OxyContin, and were hardly addictive at all, according to Freddie. Rogue, he thought, as he sank onto the toilet seat and let the memories wash over him—of course, there were no good memories, just anguished nonsense, like those distant days in Vienna when the snow had kept falling and falling. Would those recollections never fade? He stood up, listening. Was that a sound? Most definitely. Footsteps in the stairwell. Familiar footsteps.

His daughter Julia's heels clicking as briskly as ever. Well, actually . . . he listened more carefully . . . perhaps not *as ever*. The footsteps slowed, deprived of their spring and their youthful insolence, and he was reminded that Julia had looked troubled of late. But the old memories were like a haze across his thoughts and he could not recall whether she had mentioned anything.

He tidied his hair and made for the door. He was never called upon to open it—Julia usually let herself in—and now he scrutinised her, his thoughts still not clear. She wore jeans with holes at the knees, a leather jacket from a vintage store, and a pair of black shoes with absurdly high heels, and she was overly made up. She tugged her jacket close around her, as if cold.

"Hello, sweetheart. Is it snowing?" he said, peering at her shoulder as though he had just discovered a couple of snowflakes.

"Was that a joke?"

"Yes," he said in embarrassment. "Of course."

He extended his arms to embrace her, but she walked straight past him.

"It's summer, Pappa."

"Naturally."

"Or perhaps it's snowing somewhere in your thoughts?" she said, which unfortunately hit the nail on the head, but right now he needed to return to the present. His little girl was here. He subjected her to even closer inspection. She had definitely lost weight, and he didn't like that. Chastisement of the body ran in the family. Of course, his mother considered it a virtue—a sign of elegance and class—but he knew that it sometimes masked a dread, a deadly addiction. It was the only thing he knew that strived for a dearth, an absence.

"Sweetheart," he said. "Let's have some lunch."

"You're cooking, are you?"

There was a prickliness in her voice, a tension of sorts in her slender arms.

"Definitely," he said, going to the kitchen and opening the fridge. "My clumsiness usually amuses you. Otherwise, I dare say Mrs. Hansson will have prepared something. See here." He peered into a bowl on the middle shelf. "Definitely risotto," he said, sniffing it. "With white wine, vegetable broth and Parmesan. And take a look here." He perked up. "Fried champignons and arugula—quite a feast."

"No, I've got to get going."

"But you've only just arrived. I'll heat it up in the microwave. I can even offer you a glass of wine—you did turn nineteen recently, if I'm not mistaken?"

He beamed, pretending to be more scatterbrained than he was, but he got nothing in return.

"I'm only here to say one thing," said Julia, as he stood there with the risotto in his hands and a premonition that he was going to hear something disturbing.

But perhaps it was just the memory of that winter obtruding on him. He did his best to look like a calm, reassuring father—as if he hadn't just gulped down a bunch of opiates.

# FOUR

I shouldn't have come, Micaela thought. I shouldn't have let myself get dragged into this business.

She knew precisely when it had happened. At exactly half past eight in the evening on the tenth of May, when Samuel Lidman—the widower—had come to see them at Grevgatan and had slapped a photograph down onto the coffee table. It had been an agonising experience. Samuel Lidman had been breathing heavily and sweating profusely at his brow and shirtfront. He was wearing a brown corduroy suit and polished cowboy boots, and while he was an imposing figure from the neck down—as if carved from stone—his face was flushed red, his eyes downcast. It hadn't been hard to feel sorry for him.

"You have to look carefully," he said. "I've got other pictures with me. Look at the ear, the nose, the lips. It's absolutely astounding."

It was no small thing that he was seeking to prove. His wife had been dead for thirteen and a half years—not dead as in missing and never found, but dead as in identified by her dental records and buried in the Roman Catholic Cemetery in Solna. It was—as Rekke put it—a rather ambitious project to bring her back to life. But Samuel was evidently eager to try, by pointing to a beautiful woman in a red coat captured in a holiday snap taken in Venice.

"Do you see? Do you?" he said.

"Absolutely; let us examine it," Rekke said.

Micaela guessed he would dismiss the discovery as gently as possible. When all was said and done, he was a gentleman who disliked hurting others, and Samuel looked as if his whole life was at stake.

Their guest was without doubt a man who had suffered greatly. He had been head over heels in love and newly wed when Claire had left him without any warning or words of farewell. That had been a long time ago—in the autumn of 1990. But the wound had been torn open time and time again, and it really was true that the story didn't add up. Claire was a beautiful and talented woman who had enjoyed a meteoric career. She had been the Chief Analyst at one of Sweden's largest banks—Nordbanken—reporting directly to the CEO, William Fors. At that time—during the early days of the financial crisis in the nineties that had seen the Swedish housing bubble burst—she had been responsible for the recovery of loans and secured lines of credit from precarious major corporations and financiers. She was under pressure, Samuel told them, but she liked that. She was a fighter and a gambler, and their marriage had been happy, he reassured them. Rock solid, as he put it.

But one evening Claire went to post a letter to her sister in London and never came back. She disappeared without trace. The police initiated strenuous efforts the very next day. Those weeks were terrible, according to Samuel. Nonetheless, he said he longed for that time because then he still had his past. The time he'd had with Claire was still beautiful and unbesmirched. But that, too, would be taken away from him. When the police operation was at its most intensive, word had arrived from her—not a long letter like the one she had written to her sister but just a postcard depicting a Cézanne—to the effect that she'd left him and couldn't take it anymore.

That had hurt more than her dying, he said, and not long afterward he had gone travelling. He described it as a pilgrimage, and for several weeks he had been unreachable. When he eventually called home from Bombay, he found out that Claire had died in an explosion caused by a petrol tanker in San Sebastián, and there was apparently time for him to make it to the funeral at Solna Church and see her one last time.

But he hadn't wanted to.

"It wasn't really her anymore," he said. It hadn't helped matters that he'd been told the body was badly burned. He decided to ignore it all and continue travelling.

"That was the biggest mistake of my life," he said. "They were able to fool me."

It wasn't straightforward to follow his logic. The sister, mother and Inspector Kaj Lindroos had all identified the body, but Samuel had become increasingly obsessed with the idea that Claire might still be alive. This was obviously related to the fact that he hadn't been able to say goodbye, and that Claire must have had help leaving Sweden since she would otherwise have left traces in her wake rather than vanishing in a puff of smoke. Micaela recalled how Samuel strained his muscular body and sweated even more as Rekke examined the photograph. It wasn't much of a photo, either—it was about as far from proof of resurrection as you could get. Nevertheless, Rekke picked up the print with a grave expression and stared at it—out of politeness, Micaela thought—alongside the old photographs of Claire that Samuel had brought with him.

"Fascinating," he said.

"You do see it, don't you? It's her . . ."

"I don't know," Rekke said. "The focus is not altogether sharp, is it? I'm not prepared to say anything with certainty except that Claire and this woman have the same charisma. *Where I go, life goes*, as I was once told by a haughty violinist. But I do wonder . . . wait a moment . . ."

He didn't say any more, and it didn't matter how much Samuel Lidman went on about the similarities between Claire and this woman, Rekke couldn't hear him. He was deep in one of his trance-like states.

"She's a little anxious, is she not?" he said at last. "Appears to be looking for someone?"

"Perhaps."

Samuel Lidman contemplated Rekke tensely.

"But above all..."

"Yes?"

"There is something particular about her gait. She is lunging forward, but a little asymmetrically. Had Claire injured her right knee?"

Samuel Lidman looked astonished.

"Yes, absolutely," he said. "Why do you ask? She tore her ligaments while skiing."

"Because this woman's gait has compensatory features. The left foot and hip, well, do you see... They are tilted slightly and taking her weight, which could be temporary, as the result of a sudden imbalance. But at the same time, there is nothing defensive about her—there is no sense that something has been disturbed or twinged."

"What are you getting at?"

"That compensatory way of turning her body is something she has practised to perfection, and it may be that one cannot even tell she is doing it. Perhaps it is necessary to freeze the image to see it. Of course, it might have its origins in an old fracture in the lower leg or thigh, but injuries there do not usually trouble us for such a long time. Rather, I would guess that something in the meniscus never properly healed."

Samuel Lidman leaped from his chair and paced back and forth across the kitchen, growing more agitated with each passing minute.

He managed to create a febrile atmosphere—as if they were actually on to something—and for half an hour or so Micaela devoted herself mostly to calming him down. That was why it had taken her a while to notice that Rekke had fallen silent. He needed to be alone, he said, and only the next day did she realise that he had begun to doubt his conclusion.

That was typical of Rekke. His brain noted a series of details with lightning speed and formed them into a picture—an observation. But afterward, he would spend more time doubting the conclusion than it had taken to reach it, and on this particular occasion he was particularly ashamed of himself. He had raised the hopes of an unhappy man. "I am a fool," he said, and perhaps that had been the beginning of his crisis—his descent into darkness.

But it didn't matter how ashamed he was—Samuel Lidman was already off his head and didn't care one jot that Rekke had changed his mind. He just kept on at them, and in the end Micaela had promised to get to the bottom of it, which was why she had turned up to see Inspector Kaj Lindroos clutching the photograph. But it was also why she had no strength of conviction either way, and now as she laid the picture on Lindroos's cluttered desk it seemed insignificant and paltry.

"There we have it then," said Kaj Lindroos, picking it up.

But he didn't seem to have it in him to look for long. He turned his gaze toward the window, as if hoping to hear the graduating sixth-formers again.

"You probably should look a little closer."

He fidgeted.

"You don't feel like a drink, do you? Maybe somewhere down by the water? I could tell you a thing or two."

He looked at her with a new attentiveness, unconsciously unfastening one of his shirt buttons as if he had already begun undressing ahead of the date.

"Huh? No, sorry," she said. "I've got to get home."

She felt uneasy.

"Are you sure? It *is* Friday and all that, and the sun is shining."

"I'm seeing my mother," she said.

"Oh right, I see. Okay, okay," he said, his body language demonstrating that he now intended to devote even less attention to this silly photograph. She wondered whether she should add a couple of softening words to her refusal along the lines of "maybe another time" but that would only have been stupid and cowardly. She decided to concentrate on the photo.

"Do you see?" she said. "The ear and nose in particular are significantly alike."

"Are they?" he said with a snort, buttoning his shirt back up again. "But Samuel Lidman found the photograph at his neighbour's."

He was giving as good as he got—that much was clear—and she became defensive.

"A friend of Samuel Lidman's found it at *their* neighbour's," she said, correcting him.

"It's just—it's a bit strange isn't it?" he said, and she had to admit it was.

It would have felt better if the photograph had been found after a long and methodical search process, rather than randomly turning up in the holiday album of an acquaintance. But things were the way they were, and soon she would hopefully be able to leave here and forget all about it.

"Does it really matter how it was found? It's either her or it's not."

"Hmm, yes, of course," Lindroos said, picking up the photograph again as Micaela closed her eyes and wished she could be like the woman in the picture. She would very much like to be able to glide about and shine with such natural entitlement.

# FIVE

Rekke noted everything he had seen in his daughter: the pallor and slight emaciation, but also a new kind of defiant happiness in her gaze.

He searched for more clues with sudden fervour, as if his concern for his little girl had brought him back to life, and at first he saw nothing except more signs that she had lost weight. Then he spotted a red mark on her right wrist—the fading imprint of a tight grip.

Was that something she had consented to? A game? The hand of a lover? Or had someone attacked her? No, he thought to himself. She seemed otherwise well, and his brain was always conjuring up awful scenarios. That was part of *his* crisis, and there was probably nothing to worry about. He just needed to get her to eat better.

"Don't hold back, sweetheart," he said. "What's happened?"

"I've broken up with Christian," she said, which he supposed was good news of a sort.

He had never really been able to bear Christian. He was one of those self-assured boys who thought too highly of himself and talked a lot of nonsense about things he didn't understand.

"Oh dear. I'm sorry," he said.

"No, you're not. You've never liked him."

"That's not true; he's a fine boy," he said, wondering whether he did, indeed, think that—or if he should, at least.

After all, it was not easy being young. It took time for those kinds of boys to realise that they were not that much better than anyone else. *Nescit occasum.* It knows no decline. Life needs to leave its marks first. On the other hand, that wasn't the issue at hand. Someone else had taken his place. He could see that clearly now.

"You're so full of bullshit, Pappa."

"Perhaps," he said. "But you've met someone new, haven't you?"

"How do you know?"

I can see it by the marks on your wrist, he thought to himself. A new, more powerful hand is gripping you now, and touching you more forcefully than before.

"I'm merely guessing, my dear. Who is the lucky person?"

She was looking at him critically—that was clear—but also nervously. Although she wanted to ignore his opinion, she wasn't doing so, which gave him a little hope, at least. She was still a child—a girl who didn't know how to tear herself free—and he leaned forward to hug her. She pulled away. The movement made her look even thinner.

"No-one you know."

"No, of course not. But what's he like? What makes you like him?"

"You wouldn't understand," she said.

He wondered whether she really believed that.

He had a thousand shortcomings and had just been popping opiates like a junkie, but he understood the powers of attraction, both good and destructive, and if it was the case—which he assumed it was, given her reaction—that she had met someone who did not correspond with the family's expectations or was possibly even the antithesis of them, then that was certainly not shocking to him. He had himself longed to follow all manner of siren songs. He would understand, and he believed she knew that.

"Yes, yes," he said under his breath. "But perhaps you can tell me something about him. What does he do? Is he studying?"

"Does it matter what the hell he does?"

"Well, it matters a little, but I'm most interested in whether he's kind."

"He's not kind in some boring Djursholm way."

"I see," he said, uncomfortably affected. "But you will be careful, won't you? Nothing can happen to you. No-one can . . ." He glanced back at her wrist. "Hurt you. Not even a little."

"Why would anyone hurt me?"

"No, why would they?" he said, thinking, But if someone does then I will come for them. If only you knew, sweetheart, if only you knew.

And in that moment, he recalled once again that winter in Vienna when the snow had kept falling and falling.

# SIX

The photograph depicted St. Mark's Square in Venice, but the Basilica itself had been cut in half and there was no-one in particular in the foreground—only a group of Japanese in late middle age who didn't seem to have seen the camera. The main characters in the scene were in fact the pigeons, which were everywhere, and the birds were also the reason the photo had been taken at all. The photographer, Erik Lundberg, had wanted to show that Venice was infested with both tourists and pigeons and "might as well fall into the sea."

But without Erik Lundberg noticing, a woman in a red coat had stepped into the right-hand corner of the shot, counteracting the picture's very purpose, which had been to show something ugly and ruined. The woman was forty or perhaps forty-five years old, dark-haired and luminescent—and not just because of her red coat. Something in her stride and her aura drew your gaze to her, and while she was turning her head as if to glance over her shoulder, her features were quite visible.

"Of course Samuel wants that to be Claire. I'd like her to be my missus too," said Kaj Lindroos.

Micaela looked down at her hands self-consciously.

"There are strong similarities and the age also lines up fairly well. I've got old pictures you can compare it with," she said.

Kaj Lindroos made a dismissive gesture. Still, he took it seriously enough to produce a pair of reading glasses from his inside pocket—why on earth hadn't he been wearing them from the start?

"You can tell from the twist of her body and the way she's placing her foot that this woman has a damaged meniscus," Micaela said.

Lindroos looked at her as if unable to tell whether she was joking or serious.

"You what?" he said.

"If you look here . . ." she said, leaning forward and pointing to the woman's hip and left leg, but then she could feel how little she believed in it herself, and she didn't bother to complete her sentence, possibly because her own uncertainty made her think of her brother, Lucas.

Lucas was constantly popping up in her thoughts nowadays, and sometimes—like now—she would feel unexpectedly frightened. She remembered when she'd seen him press a pistol against a young guy's Adam's apple in the woods by Järvafältet. It had been such a shock that she had begun to see her whole life in a new way. Since then, she had been feeding her colleagues in Narcotics with information on him, and she knew Lucas had found out. There was something ominous about the whole situation, but the strength of her fear still astounded her.

It was as if she had been transported out of the room she was in. And so she didn't notice that Kaj Lindroos had frozen as if he had seen a ghost. In fact, she thought he was just annoyed at their non-existent date, since when he raised his gaze again, he looked self-conscious and then he pulled out his phone.

"Something's come up, I take it?" she said.

"What . . . no, no, just got a proper job I need to do too."

He began to type something on his phone and indicated she should remain silent, allowing him to concentrate.

"As I said," he said at last, "Samuel's barking up the wrong tree again. And by the way . . ."

"Yes?"

He held the photo close to his eyes. A bitter, yet slightly self-righteous smile spread across his lips.

"What's that in the woman's hand?"

"A book," Micaela said.

"It says something on it, doesn't it?"

"We think it says *Love*. There appears to be a line above it too, but it's not visible."

"Some kind of romance novel then?"

"Probably—judging by the colour. But it's not a particularly common book. I haven't been able to find it."

Kaj Lindroos smiled with relief, as if he had discovered something that liberated him from a burden.

"Claire Lidman would never read chick lit."

"No?" she said.

"*Never*. She had an agenda, and she would never lose herself in something imaginary or sentimental."

"That's not exactly what I've heard."

"Of course it isn't," he said with a snort.

"Then what makes you say that?"

"Because it took us a long time to understand her. But that woman didn't waste any time on fiction or other shit like that. She was always two steps ahead, and that's why she was able to lean on a financier like Axel Larsson. There was always a plan ticking away inside her."

"She might have changed."

"She's dead," he said, looking back at his mobile and seemingly rereading what he had just written.

"Yet here you are with me."

He looked at her with an injured expression. "I suppose I'm like any other ambitious son of a bitch out there. I don't close any doors."

"Even though you've seen the body."

"The body was burned to a crisp—you know that—and I'm not so blind that I can't see the oddities in this case, but that doesn't mean I'll buy any old garbage."

Micaela reached out to take back the holiday snap, but Lindroos stopped her with a gesture.

"I heard you're working with some professor Stanford sacked."

"I think Stanford would have liked to keep him."

"Well, who was it who kicked him out then?"

The CIA, she thought to herself.

"It's complicated. But he's got an incredible eye for detail."

"A little too good, from what I hear," Lindroos said, pointedly tucking the photograph into his top desk drawer.

"Can I have the picture back?" she said.

"I'll be hanging on to it," he said.

"You can't do that."

"This is where we keep all the crap Samuel Lidman brings in. One of these days we'll have to put a stop to it. He's upsetting the family and . . ."

He didn't have time to finish his sentence. There was a knock at the door and an older, balding man in a turtleneck with small, critical eyes stepped in. The man seemed stressed and worried as he apologised for interrupting. Micaela knew she should have put up more of a fight about the photograph. But she was sick of it, and if she was honest, had she ever really been convinced herself? Hadn't she engaged with it mainly because she'd dreamed of working with Rekke again? But that had been in May, when he'd still had his dizzying eye for detail.

Now he couldn't even make out the chair legs and other obstacles in his way whenever he happened to get out of bed and stumble to the bathroom. She was being drained by him, dragged down into the maw of his depression. I need to be far away from him, she told herself as she nodded to Lindroos and the man in the turtleneck before leaving the room. She was determined to forget Claire Lidman and take charge of her own life instead.

# SEVEN

Julia departed and Rekke wondered what kind of embrace awaited her.

He dismissed his concerns. He needed to lie down. He wasn't up to doing anything these days. He lay or sat slumped, not even making it into the stairwell outside his front door. But right now, he had stopped by the grand piano. Was he going to play? No, the keys sneered at him and he murmured: "Cartaphilus." *Cartaphilus.* That was the word that had set it all in motion.

He had picked it up by chance while Micaela had been on the phone around a week ago talking about the woman who had gone missing and been declared dead in Spain. The case did not particularly interest him. He regarded the entire business as tainted by deluded wishful thinking, and he was ashamed of his own semi-psychotic analysis of the holiday snapshot. But as he had made to leave, Micaela had said *that* word.

It turned out that the woman, Claire, had been dealing with Cartaphilus just before she vanished into thin air, and that was worrying in itself.

Cartaphilus was a Hungarian investment company that had formerly been allied with the KGB and organised crime in the Soviet Union. But that hadn't been the thing that had made him stiffen. The word had taken him back to those snowy days in Vienna. He had gone out and walked restlessly for hours.

By the time he returned, Micaela had left and he hadn't seen her since. He really should have called and told her what he knew, but he simply couldn't bear to dig into it. Good God... why wouldn't the past release its grip on him?

His childhood was such a dreary stream of uniform days. In the mornings he would be at home with his mother playing his scales, arpeggios and études. Only in the afternoon did the other tutors—like Dr. Brandt—arrive, and occasionally pupils brought to show off—like Gabor with his whistling F-sharp exhalation and that grasp that had hurled him to the ground. Rekke could still recall the blood on his fingers and the stains on his pillow the next morning.

He remembered getting up with the feeling that the world had been recast in a new, sharper light and that all the movements in his orbit were more threatening and angular. Somehow, it had seemed he was in two places at once—both the present and the past, when the attack had taken place in the snow.

Gabor's throw had kept on running through his head, over and over. At first, he thought it was just his brain's way of tormenting him or preparing him for the fact that he might be attacked again at any moment, but gradually he realised that his memories also served another purpose, and the next day he went to the library.

"I want all the books you have on martial arts," he had said, and afterward he had sat in a corner at the back of the reading room, overencumbered with books and turning their pages feverishly.

By a quarter past five that day he had found it. The throw was known as *osotagari*, and it was one of the forty original moves of judo as set down by Jigoro Kano. It was described in a number of books. Rekke was able to follow it step-by-step through the illustrations, grasping with even greater clarity how he had been thrown to the ground. He was able to freeze each second of the attack, and afterward a sense of how long it was possible to stay in the transient moment had lingered in him. It was possible to remain in a second for hours. But it wasn't just an understanding of the course of events that he had sought. He wanted to develop a defence—a way to respond to the throw. He sat there for a long time as if in a trance. In the end it came to him as a revelation.

He realised he should have moved his left leg back, braced himself and reversed the grip. He saw an immediate beauty in his solution—a symmetry akin to a dance—and he stayed there for a long time as he performed it in theory, fighting in his thoughts. Then he stood up with a new posture, and on the walk home the grip had entered his body. He had begun to walk in a new way, and he would practise in his room with every spare moment he had—and not just his own throw. He imagined other lunges and attacks, and came to understand with ever-greater clarity the very heart of the philosophy he was mastering—it was possible to defeat one who was stronger.

It was all just a matter of following the movement being directed at one until its inevitable breaking point, and there—at exactly that moment—finding one's own foundation to strike back. *Fortitudo hostium amicus est.* Your enemy's strength is your friend. Hour after hour, he kept going, and in the end he could no longer contain himself. He needed to get it out of his system, so he asked his mother:

"Could Gabor come around again?"

"Dr. Brandt said you didn't seem to much care for each other," she said with a look of concern.

"But he stimulated me," he said—these were always the magic words.

As soon as something stimulated him, his mother was in favour of it, and one afternoon when it was once again snowing—or at least it was in his memory—Gabor showed up. On that day, the family cat, Ahasuerus, was rubbing itself against their shins. The cat stayed close, jumping onto the table when they did their mathematics, as if he sensed something in the air. Afterward, they went out into the garden just like they had the time before, and Rekke made an effort to seem as lost as he had then. He wanted to strike as the underdog, and almost submissively asked:

"Can you show me that grip again?"

Gabor didn't seem prepared for those words. It was as if he couldn't understand how Rekke could be so stupid. Still, he agreed within a second and smiled scornfully as the faint whistle of his exhalation came down a semitone to F sharp. Then he went for Rekke, but using an entirely different throw, and for the first few seconds Hans was convinced that he was going to be humiliated just like the last time. But then his synapses connected more quickly, and he took a step back and followed Gabor's movements intently.

He saw them as if illuminated by a surgical lamp, and when he sensed a moment of instability he stepped forward and grabbed Gabor, forcing them into the same position as the time before. He then bent backwards, and Gabor might have thought he had regained the upper hand. But that was precisely the illusion that Rekke sought to foster.

He used Gabor's own strength like a lever to cast him to the ground with numbing force, surprised by his own absence of emotion. Without having planned it, he pulled him back up and repeated the throw, and this time, when Gabor's head struck the ground, Rekke experienced a rush in his chest. Then something happened that he would never forget.

He saw Gabor's face and gasped. The face was suddenly naked, as if all the regal self-confidence had been swept away and replaced by something helpless, and Rekke realised instinctively that he would pay for what he had seen. Gabor was not a boy who tolerated being humiliated. He was someone who always had to get his own back and win, though at that time Rekke was incapable of imagining how ruthlessly Gabor would take revenge.

He simply stood there in the snow, watching Gabor retreat like a threat of things to come, as Dr. Brandt rushed out of the house, waving his hands.

# EIGHT

Micaela was walking toward Rådhusparken, lost in her thoughts. Why had Lindroos kept the photograph if he had completely dismissed it? She didn't understand. Although perhaps it wasn't that strange after all, she reflected. The whole business was messed up... Well, she didn't care.

She was on leave—not voluntarily, but nonetheless—and she had a hundred things to be getting on with. While she would have preferred to take a longer period of leave in July, they had said they needed her in high summer, so she had taken two weeks now at the beginning of June and would take the rest in September. She worked on juvenile crime in the suburbs around Järvafältet, which wasn't exactly what she had dreamed of when she had finished sixth form and had been standing on her own truck bed shouting for all she was worth. But it had the advantage that she could study the flow of drugs into the city neighbourhoods up close, which was yet another reason she had begun to see her brother in a different light.

She was now receiving her own information about the key figure he was in the drug trade out on the streets, but gathering evidence was tricky and, if she was honest, she had ended up becoming a little obsessed, which was probably not healthy. Tongues were wagging, she was on the receiving end of gibes and veiled threats, and—sometimes, like with Lindroos earlier—she felt downright uneasy. A white bus drove past, and at that moment her mobile rang. It was Vanessa, her best friend, more or less.

"Hi," said Vanessa. "How are things?"

"Up and down. I'm thinking about buying some new shoes."

"Just make sure they're not white sneakers."

Micaela looked down at her feet—she effectively wore nothing but white sneakers. One of these days she'd change that.

"I'd rather die," she said.

"Right."

"What are *you* doing?"

"I've just had my hair dyed by a guy with barely any hair of his own—well, except in his ears. Now I'm out of here to get laid. I feel like I'm about to explode."

"That'd be a pity."

"Wouldn't it just? By the way, Lucas is looking for you."

Micaela's reply was wry.

"Then why doesn't he call me?"

"He says he's tried a hundred times."

Three times, she thought to herself. Tops. But she hadn't felt like answering and it bothered her that Vanessa was running his errands. She supposed her friend was just like all the other suckers—attracted to and a little enchanted by Lucas.

"What's he want?"

"He's pretty cute if you ask me."

"Sure."

"Word is you're trying to put him away."

"He's a crook."

"It's not like he's the only one."

But he's the worst, Micaela thought to herself.

"That doesn't make it any better," she said.

"Who's that screaming?"

"High schoolers. Want to grab a beer?"

"I'm heading out with Malika. Is it to do with Jojje?"

It was partly to do with Jojje, but that wasn't something she wanted to discuss with Vanessa, and she searched for something else to say. Anything. Further along the sidewalk a round-shouldered man lit a cigarette. In the light, he looked sallow and haggard.

"Have you heard they're going to ban smoking in pubs?" she said.

"What you on about?"

"The Norwegians did it like yesterday."

"So it's like some religious thing?"

"Wouldn't it be kinda nice?" she said.

"Do you think Lucas scared the shit out of Jojje and his mum?"

She thought so, but she had no proof either—just a feeling that had been getting stronger over the last few months.

"I think you're being unfair on him," Vanessa said. "He only wants the best for you."

Micaela closed her eyes and once again sought new topics of conversation. "I'm going to move out," she said.

Vanessa fell silent, apparently shocked.

"Wha—? Are you kidding? Why?"

"I just feel like it."

"Has something happened?"

Micaela contemplated describing the situation at Grevgatan in further detail, explaining how Rekke was descending into his darkness again and how it was impossible to get a single sensible word out of him.

"Not exactly," she said.

"But it's not working out, huh?"

She heard a tone in Vanessa's voice that she didn't like—it wasn't exactly delight, but it was some kind of restrained triumph. A what-did-I-tell-you.

"It's no big deal," she said defensively. "I just want some peace and quiet again."

"Hun, I get it. I get it. Do you want to meet up? I can cancel on Malika. I'll take care of you."

Why had her voice suddenly become so smooth?

"It's not that bad."

"Of course it isn't. But honestly, maybe it's for the best that you figured this out now before . . . I dunno . . . you got hurt."

"Why would I get hurt?"

"Maybe it wasn't meant to be. You don't belong there, not really," Vanessa said, and that was admittedly true—she was so far removed from Rekke in many respects.

Still, she was annoyed and regretted mentioning the move. It wasn't definite yet—it was just a thought that had been gnawing away at her for a while.

"What would you know about where I belong?" she snapped.

"My God, chill out. All I mean is . . . I've missed you," Vanessa said, and it wasn't altogether impossible that Micaela had missed Vanessa and their daily chats too. But not as much, it struck her, as she missed Rekke as he had been over those days in spring when the world had seemingly been transparent to him.

"Sorry," she said.

"It's okay."

"If you bump into Lucas, tell him I'll call."

"You hanging up now?"

"Give my love to Malika," she said before actually hanging up unnecessarily brusquely. She suddenly felt alone and decided to pay her mother a visit in Husby, just like she'd told Lindroos.

In any case, her mother was someone who had definitely been in favour of the move to Grevgatan, even if it was partly because she thought it was fancy.

Kaj Lindroos had been due to end his Friday with Superintendent Lars Hellner, but he'd texted to ask him to come earlier so he could get that damn Latino chick out of his office sooner—something he now regretted. It wasn't that he was dismayed by the girl's departure; she was welcome to do a permanent bunk back to her mum in the hood.

But he would have liked to be alone with his thoughts for a while, even if those thoughts were probably just crazy and stupid, because it couldn't be Claire in the picture. It was just as impossible as his own late father suddenly being glimpsed at a hog roast in Majorca. God he needed a drink.

"You're looking tense today," Hellner said.

"Just a little tired." He wondered if he simply should get the photo out and show it to Hellner to be reassured once and for all.

But he had no desire to drag anyone else into this business, especially not Hellner, who had taken over the case from him and shut him out. Probably he should tear the picture into a thousand pieces and forget all about it and focus instead on the new investigation Hellner had for him. But he couldn't: memories were intruding. He remembered when he had first heard about the accident in San Sebastián. It had been late in the evening thirteen and a half years ago, and he had still been at the office. A Spanish policeman—Comisario Antonio Rivera—had called and informed him about various circumstances that initially seemed unrelated. A petrol tanker had gone off the road, or perhaps it was an off-ramp somewhere up in the mountains, and it had crashed down onto a street where people had been making their way home from a choral performance, before catching fire.

Sixteen people were dead, many burned beyond recognition. But that wasn't the real reason for his call. What Comisario Rivera actually wanted to talk about was a woman with dual citizenship—British and Swedish—who had checked into the city's Grand Hotel two days earlier. This woman had deposited her passport with reception and gone out for a long walk, never to return.

"Her name is Claire Lidman," Comisario Rivera had said. "And we believe she is one of the victims in the accident."

Lindroos recalled his reaction when the news had sunk in. He had been deeply disappointed. Not because Claire Lidman had potentially died—he'd never met the woman—but because the investigation had lost its heft. If it was Claire who had died, then it had been in an accident and nothing else. No-one—not even an evil genius—could orchestrate a disaster like that while also ensuring Claire Lidman was on the scene.

There were too many random coefficients and parameters, and he had been far too slow in getting away to Spain. There had been no flights until the next day, and by the time he and his colleague Roffe Sandell had arrived in San Sebastián the following afternoon, Claire's sister and mother were already there. They were standing outside the mortuary smoking and looking trashy, or so he'd thought, about as far from the general impression he'd gained of Claire as was possible. But he knew that she had undertaken her own class journey. He greeted them politely and deferentially, and had been struck by how collected they were—perhaps even grimly satisfied, as if they had always known it would end that way.

He had reflected that they were probably jealous of her, begrudging her every damn ounce of her success. "How terrible to meet under these circumstances," he had said. The sister, Linda, replied: "Thanks. Claire was the best of us—it's so awful," or something along those lines, something impeccable and touching that didn't sound entirely genuine, and he remembered making an effort not to look at her inappropriately.

There was something provocative about the sister, he had thought, something almost vulgar, not helped by her ill-fitting skirt. She was a big woman with narrow eyes, voluminous curves and a complexion that suggested she'd been chain smoking and living it up since the age of thirteen. He remembered holding the door open for her and following her into the mortuary, his shoes creaking. The sister's bra straps were visible through her black blouse, and he'd found himself trying to guess her cup size, which was perhaps not the most dignified use of his time at that moment. Then again, mankind was what it was, and death was supposedly an aphrodisiac. He'd smelled it from a distance. It was worse than he had imagined: thick, sweet, sickening. It wasn't just the skin that had burned but the fat, muscles, blood too, and on top of it all was the stink of burnt oil and rubber. It was unbearable. He'd recoiled, on the brink of throwing up, and felt an instantaneous sense of disbelief.

Surely that couldn't be Claire, he'd thought to himself. It was unthinkable. But he assumed that was a natural response of sorts. No-one expected to see a human being so utterly destroyed, especially not a woman like her, and he couldn't fathom how the mother and sister were so calm and collected. It was a terrible sight: a red, scorched, evil-smelling, wounded, partially blackened creature lying there before him. Impossible to relate to. How had the others been able to stand there looking at it so nonchalantly? It was incomprehensible. Later on, he had realised that the mother and sister had already seen her and were ready for the sight of it—maybe they had just shut down.

Together with Comisario Rivera, they had moved along the body from the burned feet up to the crown where there was no hair left and barely a face either. All the characteristics he was already familiar with were pointed out—the gap between the front teeth, the old fracture to her collarbone. "It's her," the mother had said. "It's her." Why should he have doubted that, given the gap between the teeth and all the rest of it?

Yet afterward he'd had the feeling something wasn't right, even if it wasn't a feeling he had acted upon or indeed taken seriously. But it had been there, and perhaps it was because of Comisario Rivera.

The Comisario had seemed too handsome a figure to be loitering in a mortuary. His English was perfect. He was stationed in Madrid, his deportment was that of the officer class, and he completely lacked the deferential respect for doctors and the erudite that Kaj had grown up with as a boy. He had bossed the medical examiner about a little, and he'd kept taking the initiative, explaining that all the relevant laboratory tests would be run. The results had turned up with surprising speed.

The fingerprints had been burned off, but the dental records confirmed the identification. It seemed there was no doubt, and yet . . . There had been something gnawing away at him, and just like with the holiday snap in his desk drawer, he wanted to return to it and push it away at the same time. To remember and forget.

"Have you been listening to a single word I've said?"

Lindroos was torn away from his thoughts. Hellner was looking at him in concern in his brown, rather sharp eyes that always seemed to be sceptical and disapproving.

"Absolutely," he said. "I'm just a little . . ."

"What, Kaj . . . ?"

"Unfocused," he said, once again tempted to show Hellner the photograph and share his misgivings, but as more memories welled up, the prospect of that became even more remote.

"Is it to do with the girl who was here?" Hellner said.

"Maybe a bit," he said.

"How so?"

"Oh, she was rabbiting on about Claire Lidman, that's all," he said, regretting it immediately.

Hellner visibly reacted to the name and became uncomfortably attentive.

"What did she say?"

"Oh, you know, just the usual—that Claire was alive and wandering about somewhere in expensive coats."

"And where was it this time?"

"I'm not sure I remember. It was complete bollocks," he said, not at all happy about his own tone of voice.

It was obvious that his nonchalance was feigned, and Hellner fixed his steely gaze on him even more closely.

"So there's nothing more specific you can tell me?"

"No, not really," he said.

"She looked familiar. Is she police?"

"In a way," he said, hoping he wouldn't have to say her name. It was coursing through his whole body, the feeling that he didn't want anyone else poking their nose into the case again. He did his best to change the subject and ramble on about whatever he could think of, while completely ignoring the fact that Lars Hellner had seen through him from the very first moment and was far more interested in the young woman than in anything else he had to say.

# NINE

Rekke stood up from the piano stool with a premonition that something terrible was going to happen. But it was probably just old memories playing tricks on him again. Nothing ever happened in his life these days—bar Mrs. Hansson occasionally popping in to check if he was behaving himself, which he wasn't.

He was a wreck, but what was he actually doing? He was thinking about an old cat—and by the by, hadn't it been idiotic to name it Ahasuerus? But he had been a little boy fascinated by the topic, possibly for the straightforward reason that there was quite a lot about it in his parents' library. Goethe had written about Ahasuerus, as had Schlegel, Hamerling and even Hans Christian Andersen, Fröding and Pär Lagerkvist.

In their depictions of him, especially those of Lagerkvist, Ahasuerus was often a decent person, a perfectly ordinary man enjoying a quiet life with his family but living a little inappropriately. The condemned passed by in the street outside—poor wretches carrying their crosses on their backs on the way to Calvary—and one day one of them stopped to rest on his doorstep. Ahasuerus would gladly have let him—he was not without heart—but he didn't want problems with the authorities, so he drove the man away and for this he was cursed to wander forever as a lost soul. There had been something about that story that had so captivated Rekke at the time. The fate of Ahasuerus was described not only as a curse but also as something of a dark gift.

It was said that, after rejecting Jesus of Nazareth, Ahasuerus was no longer able to rejoice or be affected like the rest of us. Ashes fell upon all that he beheld. Yet he could not be dazzled either. He saw emptiness where others saw greatness, affectation where others made obeisance and preened, and when Hans had given the name to his cat on a whim, the animal had taken on a kind of gloomy majesty. Hans had loved that cursed cat and identified with it very strongly. Thus he was immediately worried when—not long after Gabor Morovia's visit—Ahasuerus went missing.

He was nowhere to be found in the house, and it was no weather for a cat to be out in. Below freezing. With snow falling, a storm on the way, Rekke wandered around the neighbourhood calling out: "Suerus, Suerus." But he hadn't found him, and as he made his way home late in the evening and engrossed in his thoughts, there was a rustle in the bushes. For a moment or two it had filled him with hope.

Then he'd tensed up as he saw something by the mailbox that he thought was Dr. Brandt's fur hat. The doctor always wore it pushed up his brow. Perhaps it had been blown off by a gust. But then it suddenly flared up. The fur crackled in the cold. It smelled of petrol and something else even worse. Suddenly it broke out with a dreadful cry and Rekke rushed over to smother the fire with his coat, burning his shoulder and chest.

He had looked into Ahasuerus's eyes while the cat was still alive, skinless and scorched, as if it were losing more than its life, and he wasn't even sure what he had done with the body.

Perhaps he'd fled the scene, leaving Mrs. Hansson to bury it. However, he knew for sure that he'd sworn many dramatic oaths that night, and that he had practised his Japanese martial art moves day in, day out, as if it might save him from sinking. On the other hand . . . it was only a cat, and it was a long time ago. Nonsense, he muttered, going to sit down at the desk to look up Gabor Morovia and Cartaphilus. As he reviewed his search results, he realised how poorly informed he was, which was partly because Morovia had probably expunged almost all information about himself from the internet, but also because he hadn't researched the matter with his usual energy. As much as Morovia had remained a threatening shadow in his life, he must have avoided the subject, which was clearly a mistake. *Nosce hostem*. Know your enemy. But Magnus, his brother, that schemer, he probably knew all about it, and he'd also been around back when Nordbanken had cracked Axel Larsson, with Cartaphilus apparently lurking in the wings. Did he have it in him to talk to his brother? Hardly! Every conversation with Magnus gave rise to the queasy feeling that people were shares that went up and down in value in line with their status and usefulness. But then again . . . talking to the schemer might offer some clarity.

Rekke shook his head, got out his mobile and took care to sound just as miserable and drugged as he felt, thinking that it might cheer Magnus up. If he hadn't had any particular successes in the global political arena of late, then there was always his brother's depression to gloat over.

The weakness of others provided comfort to every little Machiavelli.

# TEN

Micaela got off the Tunnelbana at Husby and walked toward her mother's place on Trondheimsgatan. There were quite a lot of people out and about: market traders hawking their wares, the odd group of graduating kids sauntering by with yellow pennants in their hands, two raucous teenage boys, a teenage girl in a hoodie and with purple hair who greeted her with a "S'up pig."

Business as usual. To the right-hand side of one of the plazas, a group of young boys were playing soccer like always. Yet it felt different. She couldn't put her finger on it, but she was on the receiving end of suspicious glances and there weren't as many smiles as usual. A man she recognised was approaching her in the distance wearing a beanie in the summer heat.

Hugo Pérez was only a couple of years older than her: macho, cocksure but also flirtatious, constantly grinning as if the whole world was nothing but a big joke. Now—she could already see from afar—he had puffed up his chest. What nonsense was this?

"Hi, Hugo. What's up?"

He didn't reply.

"Nice trousers."

Hugo ignored that too and passed her by with consummate studied indifference.

"Although you might like to pull them up a bit," she added, and she meant it.

His trousers—a faded pair of jeans—were halfway down his ass and why on earth was he wearing a beanie in the middle of summer? "Muppet," she said under her breath. Not that it helped much. Hugo's cold shoulder bothered her and suddenly she felt like a stranger in her own neighbourhood. Obviously, it could be because she'd been living in Östermalm for a while, but she knew that it didn't have anything to do with Rekke and Grevgatan.

It was about Lucas, and there was a certain logic behind it. If her perception of Lucas was changing, then Husby should be changing with him. Throughout her childhood, he had been the strong big brother who protected her from all ills, but nowadays, when she received information about his criminality on an almost daily basis, he was more of a threat.

It was abundantly clear that Husby couldn't stay the same after that, and it was hardly a surprise that guys like Hugo regarded her as a traitor. She was digging into things that were best left alone, but she couldn't help it. She had to know.

"Micaela!"

She had reached Trondheimsgatan and now she looked around in bewilderment. It was her own mother calling to her, but no matter where she looked around the plaza she couldn't see her.

"Where have you got to?"

"Aquí, estúpida!"

Mamá was standing behind the swings in the playground, beating carpets. She wore checked harem trousers and a loose-fitting cotton top with a red heart across the chest. She had her hair down and it had been recently dyed. On her feet she wore sandals with heels.

"Vas a ir a una fiesta?"

"Huh? No." Mamá tugged theatrically at her attire. "This old thing's well past it. But if you knew what these carpets weighed . . ." she said, giving one a wallop.

"Isn't it just as easy to vacuum them?"

"I wanted to beat the bastards—they deserve it," Mamá said with a grin, and then she became serious again, as if reminded of something sobering.

She scrutinised Micaela from head to toe, evidently not wholly satisfied. She took hold of her denim jacket and tugged at it, then pulled back her hair and stared into her daughter's eyes, disappointed in some way.

"I've heard your professor wants you to move out."

"He definitely doesn't want that."

"No? I just spoke to Dolores." Dolores was Vanessa's mother. "She says you're moving out. I can't fathom how you blew it so quickly, Micaela. It's the best thing to happen to you since . . ."

Mamá didn't seem to be able to think of anything else good that had happened to her, and Micaela wondered for the umpteenth time if she should point out that she was a lodger rather than a girlfriend. She didn't feel like it. She was furious that the news had travelled so fast—well, not only travelled, but also been distorted before it had been received.

"Nothing's been decided yet," she said. "But I'm tired of him. He's depressed and he takes too many pills."

"You find it even in the best of families," Mamá said, and there was no doubt which she was referring to. Simón, Micaela's other brother, had barely been clean since he was fourteen.

"You take it so lightly," said Micaela.

"Lightly? Me? After everything I've been through? Are you out of your mind? But you know, you should stand by him and help him. And why on earth don't you tidy yourself up a bit? Put on a dress, show your curves and stop brushing your bangs down and hiding behind them. Why don't you try a pair of shoes with some heels? Those white sneakers make you look squat."

"Mamá, I can't be bothered."

"A woman has to—"

"Didn't you claim to be a feminist recently?" she interjected.

"I'm a socialist, my dear, a socialist. And I believe in helping others, and my God, a man like him! A man of the world. You have to take care of someone like that. By the by, you must introduce us before it's too late. I think he'd like me—I've always been interested in psychology. You do know I met Erich Fromm once, don't you?"

"More like you almost met him."

"Yes, well, that's as may be. But I *have* read him. I would have plenty of insightful things to say."

"Sure," Micaela said, feeling it was time to leave. It had been a stupid idea to come here.

"Are you going?"

"I've got loads to do."

"Far too much, if Lucas is to be believed."

Micaela glared at her irritably.

"What do you mean by that?"

"Nothing! Nothing at all. I'm just saying what Lucas says. He thinks you're just causing yourself trouble."

"Maybe trouble's what I want."

"Pfft, now you sound like your papá."

"Would that be such a bad thing?"

"Lucas only wants the best for you. If you knew how wonderful he's been lately! Natali is such a good influence on him, and it wouldn't surprise me in the least if they're thinking about having kids and making me a grandmother, no matter how unlikely that sounds," she said, coquettishly adjusting her hair.

"Stop it," said Micaela.

"Stop what? I think you're being unfair on him. I have to say that. Apparently, you're poking around asking all sorts of unpleasant questions."

Micaela looked up at the building and at the external walkway her father had fallen from some sixteen years before.

"It doesn't feel like you're on my side anymore," she said.

Mamá propped her carpet beater against the clothes rack and came toward her with her arms extended.

"Oh sweetheart. How can you say that? I'm always on your side. I just don't want you to get in trouble. Lucas and I are worried about you."

"Worried about yourselves, more like," Micaela said quietly as she withdrew from the embrace, reflecting that she belonged neither here nor at Rekke's.

# ELEVEN

Undersecretary Magnus Rekke was in his walk-in closet at his home on Ulrikagatan. He'd packed a black suit into a Huntsman & Sons carrier and was now trying on his dinner jacket and tying a bow tie. He was bound for the village of Arromanches in Normandy for a ceremony to mark the sixtieth anniversary of D-Day, which did not particularly interest him.

The Second World War was not only ancient history, it had been done to death. He knew just about every battle in it. That aside, the ceremony was like Christmas morning for him. Everyone would be there: Bush, Blair, Chirac, Schröder and Schröder's secret pal Putin. For goodness' sake, Queen Elizabeth was coming, as well as a lot of éminences grises, and he was not going to waste a single second.

The jacket was damn tight. It had fit perfectly at the Polar Music Prize—surely he couldn't have put on weight since then? Well . . . naturally he should stop drinking beer and take up with wine again. Just so long as he didn't have to go sober, God help him. His mobile rang. Where the hell had it got to? He rummaged frantically through his knitwear and shirts and eventually found it in the trouser pocket of the grey suit he had just tried on. By then the phone had fallen silent, which was probably for the best, although . . . good God. It was Hans. Had he risen from the dead—from his shadow kingdom? Magnus called him back.

"So you're alive then?" he said.

*"Morituri te salutant,"* Hans said.

"There's a car waiting outside to take me to Arlanda, so you'll have to be quick," he said, feeling satisfied that he sounded busy when the shining light of the family, mother's little genius, was listlessly idling in his narcotic fog at Grevgatan.

"In that case I shall call another time," Hans said defensively.

Magnus felt nothing but contempt.

*Have you also begun to kowtow to me?*

"I can give you five minutes if you'll play nicely."

"Kind of you," Hans said with barely any sarcasm detectable at all. "I don't suppose you've heard anything about Julia's new boyfriend?"

Ah, a family matter, Magnus thought to himself.

"Only that it would appear he does not hail from any of the customary noble families," he said. "But I have no other details, and I doubt Lovisa does either."

"I see," Hans said, still docile and possibly genuinely worried, but then he changed tack. "Recently, I happened to remember how you and the Ministry of Finance crushed Axel Larsson in the early nineties."

"So you're enquiring after my old brutality."

"More what drove it."

"Axel Larsson deserved to be crushed."

"Is that so?" Hans said acidly, which bothered Magnus too. Surely his brother wasn't going to start defending Axel Larsson?

"You must remember what he got up to in the eighties? Buying up real estate, art and arms shares like he was Croesus reborn. But when we took over Nordbanken in the spring of 1990, it was revealed that he was up to his ears in debt. And do you remember the old saying back in those days?"

"No, what was the saying?"

"If you've borrowed a million then that's your problem. If you've borrowed a hundred million then it's the bank that's in trouble. If you've borrowed billions then it's the state that's screwed. And that's the position we were in. Nordbanken was being bled dry by bad loans. We had to turn the screws on him and I'm not ashamed to admit I took some pleasure from it. Axel came into the boardroom turned out like a dandy with pomade in his hair and big eighties shoulder pads, thinking he was in full control, but we were well prepared and we issued an ultimatum: either we take over your portfolio of properties and shareholdings, or we make you personally bankrupt. He went pale and bawled and waved his arms about, but in the end, he gave in. He seemed to have shrunk by several inches by the time he left."

"That must have delighted you."

"Just a little, as I said. But above all, I felt like a good civil servant. We gave something back to the taxpayer."

"Hmm, but the bank went bankrupt anyway."

"It was revived in a new form, as you know, and if you're worrying about Axel Larsson, then you can stop right away. I gather he's at Riche these days with his young blondes, ordering bottles of Dom Pérignon. Why are you interested in any of this?"

"Because it wasn't just the state that took over Larsson's assets, was it? Am I not right in recalling that you worked alongside a certain Hungarian investment company?"

Magnus unbuttoned his trousers.

"What are you getting at?"

"I have happened upon something you should have told me fourteen years ago."

"What?" he said uneasily.

"That you allied yourselves with Gabor Morovia's company—Cartaphilus."

Sweat began to break out under Magnus's shirt and he grimaced at his reflection in the mirror. Damn it. But then he roused himself and managed to achieve a tone of gentle mockery.

"Is this about your old cat?"

"In a way," said Hans.

"I'm not entirely familiar with the law," Magnus said. "But surely the crime of *burning a gloomy cat* has passed the statute of limitations by now?"

"Don't talk drivel."

"Or would you assert with the authority of your expertise that he who burns animals as a child invades Poland as an adult?"

"Perhaps somewhat. But above all, I am interested in the facts of the matter. Gabor hated our family—with some justification, I am regrettably forced to add. How did you come to work together as bosom buddies?"

"I might rather categorise it as wolves fighting over the same prey, and if I'm honest I never met him. He mostly stays in the shadows."

"But when he emerges from them, someone gets hurt."

"Oh, come off it," Magnus said. "Wasn't it you who said that the truly intelligent psychopaths pass best? They know it isn't worth chopping off horses' heads in the long run. Gabor is a pragmatic, shrewd businessman these days and nothing else," he added, well aware that this was not entirely true.

"How reassuring, dear brother of mine," Hans said.

"Indeed. Now, I apologise . . . but I really must be going."

He checked his wristwatch as if to reinforce his own words to himself.

"Do you remember Claire Lidman?" said Hans.

"No, I don't think so," Magnus said, lying again.

"I'm guessing she designed the scheme that you clobbered Axel Larsson with."

"Oh yes," he said, pretending to remember. "Didn't she die in an explosion in San Sebastián?" Burned to ashes like your cat, he thought, although he kept that to himself.

"Exactly," said Hans. "Interesting personality, although I can't quite grasp which side she was on."

"Our side, naturally. My side."

"Naturally."

"Or are you implying something?"

"It would never occur to me. Now run along, dear brother of mine. I apologise for making you nervous."

"I'm not nervous," Magnus said nervously.

But by then Hans had already hung up and Magnus was left standing in front of the mirror in his dinner jacket wondering how Hans could possibly have risen from the underworld only to immediately put his finger on his most tender spot. Although there was probably a logic to it. Only the worst stories could wake the dead.

# TWELVE

Good God, but things had been dire, Julia thought.

Mamma had been the worst. She had nagged her until her head was splitting about how Lydia had gotten a place at Yale, and it didn't stop at Lydia either. A whole bunch of her friends had gotten onto good courses or just been generally fantastic while Julia—needless to say—did nothing, took the odd art history class and drifted around without any ambition whatsoever.

It was a disgrace in every possible way. Well, actually, no it wasn't. According to Pappa, it was spot on. First you obtained a general knowledge of the humanities, then you began to specialise.

But . . . Mamma and Mormor and her stupid uncle at the Ministry for Foreign Affairs were all in her face, and the same old questions had resurfaced: Would she turn out a disappointment? She didn't have a great high school diploma. She was effectively doomed to mediocrity—and was she even that bright? Did she have an ounce of her father's outlook on the world? Maybe all she had inherited were his demons—and if that were true then all that remained to be said was Congratulations, Julia! First prize.

Her face was admittedly quite nice, which was an asset. But her thighs ... Good God. They were too fat, and as for her tummy, come on! Positively distended. It was high time she gave up frivolities such as breakfast, which incidentally made her think of Christian. Did he do anything other than eat and talk bullshit? He watched porn online, she supposed. And when was the last time he'd complimented her?

A hundred years ago. She would have left him anyway, but the process had now been accelerated. She'd broken up with him on Monday, but in practice their relationship had already died by ten a.m. the preceding Tuesday, a day that had started like most others.

She had been strolling along Storgatan all alone, feeling like a failure. What was more, she had been worried about Pappa. Her father was in a hopeless state, and the only good thing to have happened to him lately—Micaela Vargas moving in—was about to end. Micaela couldn't hack it any longer, which was entirely understandable. Although ... surely she could have a little patience? Not everyone was that strong. Not everyone was raised with the knowledge that you had to fight or perish. It had been overcast and drizzly that morning. There was a demonstration on Strandvägen—something about Israel, she thought. Both her head and stomach ached, and there was nothing else to suggest that something incredible was going to happen, but as she passed the Eriks Bakficka restaurant she heard a voice behind her:

"Sorry, excuse me."

She had turned around and seen a man of about thirty-five wearing grey chinos and a blue shirt. A pair of Ray-Bans were pushed up over his close-cropped hair, and he was muscular and most definitely cool—she could tell as much right away. Nevertheless, his smile was cautious, almost shy, and she returned it with her own.

"Yes?"

"I thought I'd buy some curtains," he said.

"Curtains?" she said, feeling immediately that they had formed a bond. There was something slightly comical about these curtains. They didn't fit with his image, and the two of them both knew it, as if they were sharing a joke.

"I thought I'd try and get things sorted in my pad," he said.

"If you're looking for the haberdasher's then it's on the other side of Narvavägen, and I don't think it's open yet."

"What am I like? I'm all over the place," he said, smiling again. She took a step toward him and immediately felt uncomfortable that she was taller. She hated feeling big. However, she quickly forgot about it. His presence registered like a jolt in her chest, and she was seized with a sudden self-confidence. It was like a gift from his gaze.

"Nice shades," she said.

He pulled them down over his eyes and made a silly face, as if mimicking an action hero. She giggled and looked at him more closely. Good God, even just the way he held out his hand made Christian seem weak and boyish by comparison.

"Do you know something?" he said, delaying his next statement as if he'd suddenly been overcome by nerves.

"No, what?" she said.

"You're absolutely gorgeous."

She wasn't ready for that. The words were like a shock to her body, and while a part of her had wanted to dismiss the man as a playboy playing the tough guy, there was a hesitant, uncertain look on his face that made her feel safe. He was vaguely familiar too, as if she had seen him before—or at least someone who resembled him, someone who was a good person.

"Thanks," she said, suddenly struck by an impulse to look away.

She hoped to God she wasn't blushing.

"Maybe it was stupid to just blurt it out like that."

She tried to think of a fitting rejoinder.

"I wish more people were that stupid."

He laughed.

"Then I'll happily continue—being stupid, that is."

She looked down at her legs and her scuffed ballerinas.

"My shoes could do with a bit of encouragement."

"Coolest kicks in town."

"Although they could do with some heels."

"That can be arranged," he said, as if ready to buy a new pair for her right away.

She couldn't quite remember what happened next. She hadn't made it to university that day. Instead, she'd gone for a walk with him. In the evening, he'd taken her for dinner at Riche, where it had become even clearer that he wasn't like Christian. He didn't just talk about himself.

He was genuinely interested in her and he didn't give a damn that she wasn't at some posh college. He asked what *she* wanted, and it didn't matter one jot to him that she was a *Rekke*. It seemed he hadn't even heard of the family. He saw only her—not her ancestry—and when he leaned forward and said, "Sorry, I just have to interrupt, you're absolutely wonderful," something tingled inside her that she hadn't felt in a long time. It was a hint of happiness.

With his charm—his way of giving her his full attention—he made her realise how joyless her life had been for so long, while she had stayed silent as Christian waffled on and on as if the words would never end. Since then, the days had flown by, and she often found herself dancing along the streets. Not that it was always easy. She was still eating too much and her thighs were still too fat, but she felt special again and not at all a disappointment.

At last, someone who sees me for who I am, she thought to herself.

Micaela was already quite far away by the time she heard her mother's footsteps behind her. She was hoping for a "sorry, I was stupid." But something in her mother's expression made Micaela doubt she was going to get an apology.

"Cariña," her mother said.

"Yes, Mamá. What is it?"

"Did you hear that they put up the rent? And the dishwasher needs replacing. There's a white film over everything, and that monstrosity of a coffee maker that Lucas bought . . ."

Micaela made a gesture that indicated she need hear no more and took out her wallet. There were two five-hundred-kronor notes in it. She gave one to her mother.

"Muchas gracias. But it's really not easy, honey," her mother continued. "And I don't have to paint, not really. But it means a lot to me, and I do have a talent. Everyone's saying so, and those paints that I need... You would not believe your ears if you heard what they cost."

Micaela sighed and gave her the other five hundred. Afterward, she swore silently. Couldn't Lucas even do this one thing? He had money—dirty money, and he didn't hesitate to brag about it either. *Damn moron.* He called himself a businessman. Drug dealer, more like—the kind that rammed a pistol into the throats of people who didn't bow down before him.

She was feeling more and more overwrought, and it wasn't just that she was the sister of a career criminal. It was the whole thing of being alone in the family and her circle of friends in wanting to know not just what Lucas was up to these days but also who he had been throughout her childhood.

Mamá, Vanessa and Simón—her equally hopeless but far weaker younger brother who lived on the crumbs Lucas threw in his direction—and all those others in Husby, wanted nothing more than to turn a blind eye and move on. They didn't get the whole truth thing if it happened to interfere with their lives. But she wasn't going to give in just because people were looking askance at her.

She was going to find out exactly what Lucas was up to, and ideally she'd find people who were prepared to testify at a trial. There'd be one hell of an argument of course. Nothing short of outright war in the family. But perhaps that was what she was longing for? She wasn't just a police officer who hated crime and was even less inclined to put up with it when it was being committed by her brother.

She wanted trouble too, just as she'd told her mother. She wanted things to happen and she wanted change, even if it came at a cost, and perhaps that was why she was so furious with Rekke. He provoked her with his passivity. It was like seeing a thoroughbred lying on the grass refusing to move. It was an indecent waste, and yet... how different it had been. There had been times—not so long ago—when it wasn't just that he could see with rare clarity. Sometimes his whole gangly body had looked unexpectedly alert—as though he were under attack. He would stiffen in a defensive position that seemed peculiarly ingrained, and there was something about it that didn't tally with her perception of him.

It felt like he was preparing for violent close combat, but surely that couldn't be right? He was a pianist and Professor of Psychology, a fragile intellectual. He was no taekwondo master. And yet... something occasionally began to tick away in him, a kind of dormant explosivity. She would ask about it when he was back to himself again. She went down into the Tunnelbana station, where there were posters advertising the new Harry Potter film on the walls. A voice on the other side of the escalator called out.

"Stop digging dirt on your brother, you piece of cop shit."

It sounded like Hugo, but she wasn't sure, and she didn't turn to look. Her mobile rang and she gratefully turned her attention to it, hoping it was Rekke in slightly better shape, but it turned out to be an older and slightly austere-sounding woman who introduced herself as Rebecka Wahlin. Micaela was unable to place her. Then she remembered that the woman had worked with Claire Lidman at Nordbanken. They had spoken briefly before, and the woman hadn't wanted to say anything at the time, just like so many other banking bigwigs. It was as if the runaway financial crisis of that era had brought out behaviour they were all eager to repress.

"Am I disturbing you?" Wahlin said.

"No."

"There's something I didn't tell you."

"And what's that?"

"Claire met a man not long before she went missing—I think he scared her."

"Who?"

"I'd prefer not to say on the phone. Could you pop by? I live on Linnégatan in Östermalm," Wahlin said.

Micaela reflected that while she might have let go of the Claire Lidman investigation, it couldn't hurt to see what the woman had to say, and it wasn't as if she had anything else to do, even if she should have been having Friday night off to mark the end of her first week of leave. But her life was what it was—stuck in a limbo of sorts.

She said she would be there in forty minutes and got onto a train without noticing the hostile eyes that followed her.

# THIRTEEN

It was apparent that Magnus had lied to him, but Rekke could not tell to what extent. He was too affected by his pills and in all honesty he didn't care all that much. It had been a fit of curiosity, nothing more, or so he thought, and if there was anything he was worried about it was Julia. He called his ex-wife, Lovisa.

She picked up after two rings and when he heard her voice he realised how little he had missed her. The one he was missing was Micaela, and as Lovisa prattled on about the house at Djursholm and some heat pump or other that needed replacing, he wondered whether it was perhaps worth pulling himself together. He missed Micaela, didn't he?

"Is Mrs. Hansson taking care of you?" Lovisa said.

"In exemplary fashion," he said. "I was just wondering . . . Hasn't Julia become worryingly thin?"

"On the contrary—I think she's looking unusually beautiful. She's being careful with her figure—thank goodness—and she's got a new boyfriend."

"Do you know who?"

"She doesn't want to introduce him, and I would guess his parents aren't exactly from our circles. But I can't say I'm worried. She's a sensible girl and he seems very supportive. It's been a long time since I've seen her radiant like this."

You read people like a blind woman, he said to himself, and *careful with her figure* . . . Good grief.

"I'll call Dr. Richter," he said. "He can have a talk with her."

"Weren't you like that at that age? Drawn to all sorts."

"Is there any particular sort you have in mind?"

"That Ida Aminoff woman, for instance."

Veins became visible on the back of his hand.

"She died," he said.

"I know she died. But she was dragging you into ruin, wasn't she?"

Half a world fluttered by.

"Perhaps," he said quietly.

"You've always been hopeless, Hans."

"Well, it's nice that you've been there all along as the great role model."

"By the way, how are things going with that domestic helper you've got together with?"

He put a hand to his brow.

"She's not a domestic helper, and we haven't got together."

"You must be devastated. But at least you don't have to worry about disquieting thinness with her. Magnus gave me a most vivid description. I gather she's of southern extraction too. Perhaps even part American Indian."

"I wonder . . ." he said, ensuring he sounded almost calm.

"What is it that you wonder?"

"Whether you have always been so contemptuous and thick-skulled, or whether it's something you have picked up since you were liberated from my bad influence?"

As he ended the call, he regretted his words, at least for a brief moment. Then, perversely, he became even angrier and wanted to call her again to say that Micaela was a better person than Lovisa and all her friends put together, but to do so would be childish, and in any case other thoughts soon intruded.

It wasn't just Ida Aminoff, the great love of his youth—well, more than that, his life's great insanity—who was standing quite clearly before him for the first time in a long while. It was Magnus and what he had said and not said about Gabor Morovia. A whole series of recollections and reflections gushed forth as if a dam had burst, and suddenly he had an idea triggered by his rage. His first enterprising idea in ages, which was a minor miracle in itself—and all credit to Lovisa.

He would meet no-one less than the disgraced financier himself, Axel Larsson, and perhaps have a glass of champagne to boot. One had to celebrate one's crises and divorces, and who made better company for that than a flamboyant rogue?

Micaela got off the Tunnelbana at Karlaplan thinking about everything and nothing—but above all Lucas. There was so much she had misinterpreted during her childhood: money he'd said he'd earned as a bouncer in the city; young boys looking at him with admiration but presumably also fear; shootings that rocked the neighbourhood and men coming up afterward to whisper in his ear.

Some were connected directly to her, like Jojje Moreno's accident.

Jojje had been in the same year as her at school and was regarded as a bit of a loser, although she had seen something touching in his desperate desire to be liked, and he was definitely not stupid. He was good at maths and knew everything there was to know about whales and dolphins, and while he might have had a stutter and struggled to look people in the eye, he could be incredibly talkative in the right company. They had hung out sometimes, although it hadn't been serious. She'd never been in love or even attracted to him. What she had felt was a closeness and an impulse to help. One Friday or Saturday night when they were sixteen, Jojje had dragged her along to Lofotengatan after a few drinks. He said there was something he wanted to show her, but once they reached the street there was nothing there, and Jojje began to behave differently and pressed her up against the wall of a building.

When she told him to cool it, things got out of hand. His gaze had darkened and he'd broken the button on her jeans and torn her panties. She kneed him and ran off, taking a nasty fall because her trousers hadn't stayed in place. Limping, she made her way home. It hadn't really been a big deal and Jojje had even called after her, "I'm sorry, Micaela! I fucked up."

But she should have taken herself to the hospital when the pain in her hip didn't go away, and she most definitely should not have told Lucas about it. "No-one does stuff like that to you," he said, and at first it had felt good, just like it did every time back then when he took care of her. But a few days later, Jojje turned up in a plaster cast and on crutches, with one black eye. He said he'd fallen off the roof of the lock-ups on Bergengatan, and she'd believed that to begin with. Everyone had, or they'd pretended to.

You know how clumsy he is, they'd said. Fucking loser. But slowly there had been a change. No more boys coming up to her and wanting to make out at the weekends. They kept their distance. Not long after that, Jojje and his mother had moved away from Husby. It had hurt more than she had wanted to admit, and she should have acknowledged it and looked him up later, but she had probably been fooling herself—as she so often did during those years—and only subconsciously did she understand.

Her brother, her guardian spirit, her substitute father, had kicked the shit out of Jojje and scared his family witless, and he'd doubtless done worse things on flimsier grounds than that. She put her hand to her hip as it twinged—whether it was for real or phantom pain she didn't know. Then she turned right onto Linnégatan and tried, without much success, to shake off the discomfort of her visit to Husby.

Feeling that she was being followed, she glanced back as she strolled at an exaggerated pace toward the home of Rebecka Wahlin.

# FOURTEEN

Axel Larsson couldn't believe it. Some damn chancer by the name of Rekke wanted to buy him a drink. The name alone made him see red. Are you out of your mind? he'd wanted to scream. I'd rather sup with the devil himself. But the man—the brother of the Undersecretary of State—claimed they might share common interests, and that had piqued his curiosity. Of course it had. You never know. Even brothers can become enemies. So now he was on his way to the Hotel Diplomat.

He was due to dine there at seven o'clock with the CFO of Carnegie anyway, so there was no harm warming up with a couple of drinks with this Rekke twat. By the by, hadn't the man sounded high? Whatever. He quite fancied getting a little tipsy himself. He'd just bought a major stake in Nokia and the only way for a holding like that was up. The deal made his lifeblood crackle, a little like in the old days, and he gazed greedily toward the shops on Strandvägen and at the young women passing him in the street.

Don't I deserve an adventure? A little madness? Well, then, into the lion's den. He set a course toward the hotel. The commissionaire received him with a bow and indicated a table by the window, where a gentleman in a black shirt sat waiting with a hawkish look on his face.

"Mr. Rekke, I presume," said Axel Larsson.

"Quite so. What an honour." A hand was proffered in his direction.

"Don't mention it," he said generously, sitting down and taking a closer look at the man.

He was tall and lanky with oddly long fingers and sharp, slightly pointed features, and he looked tired, as if he hadn't slept for a week. His eyes were glazed, and he hadn't exactly made much of an effort—his hair was dishevelled, and it looked as if he hadn't even got the buttons properly aligned on his shirt. Why in God's name was he, Axel, meeting this failure of a man? Hang it all, he thought to himself. He would just have to consider it charity work.

"Hans, right?" he said.

"Yes, indeed."

The man squinted at him as if he had just woken up and ran a hand through his straggling hair.

"Are you well?" Axel said, already bored.

"Not too bad, all things considered," the man said. "It's not every day I have a drink with a financial institution—a legend in his own way. Let me get you something extravagant."

Flattery, flattery, Axel thought, surveying the restaurant for women to his taste: preferably blonde and young, with a streak of the gold-digger in them, so they didn't hesitate at the prospect of a rich man of his age.

"How about two glasses of 1986 Roederer Cristal?" the man said.

"Sounds good."

"I gather you've just done a big deal."

Axel Larsson looked at him in surprise.

"Why do you say that?" he said.

"I can see it in your pupils and your posture and your slightly voracious, hormone-fuelled way of looking at the world. Additionally, your fingers are drumming in triple time, like racehorses that want to reach the finishing line in triumph. What have you bought?"

"That's confidential."

"Is it, indeed? Isn't it actually a good thing if we less well-informed mortals pile in now to drive up the share price for you?"

"Amateurs should stay away," Axel said.

"By all means, even if some of us amateurs are wise enough to know that we don't know anything."

"You mean that the future is uncertain?"

"Not just uncertain, unknown. But naturally I bow to your expertise."

"That's probably for the best. Though I gather you are a connoisseur of champagne."

"Not at all," Rekke said. "I'm merely pretending, and I mostly want to calm my nerves. But let's get straight to the point."

"You said we have common interests?"

"We both want to get at the Hungarian investment company Cartaphilus, don't we?"

Axel Larsson did a double take. A series of unpleasant memories flashed through his head.

"That's not a company you take on lightly."

"Why not?" the man said, smiling so innocently that Axel wanted to punch him on the jaw.

"They crush you."

"That's definitely not something you want to experience. By the way, did you ever meet Gabor Morovia?"

Axel glanced nervously toward the street and muttered something in reply.

"Sorry?" said Rekke.

"I was on the brink of ruin back then."

"What do you mean by that?"

"That Gabor Morovia was hardly going to take the time to meet someone like me."

"Is he that stuck-up?"

"Ask your brother. He and Gabor are best mates."

The champagne arrived and the man—Hans—clinked glasses with him and suddenly no longer seemed naive, or even flattering. In fact, his gaze seemed to see straight through Axel.

"I doubt it," he said. "Our father—his name was Harald, though I'm sure you know that—ran a shipping line. I would like to take the chance to say a few kind words about him at this juncture, but I fear they wouldn't be wholly truthful. My father was tough and unscrupulous, and in the sixties he managed—by means of bribery and cartels—to break a competitor called Morovia Shipping. The owner, Sandor Morovia, became insolvent—a little like you—and was simultaneously beset by other misfortunes. His wife ran off and he was left alone with his son Gabor. He was forced to return to communist Hungary, which he hated, and only by the grace of God did he manage to secure a posting at the country's embassy in Vienna. Our family remained happily ignorant of this story for a long time. But we understood soon enough—the hard way, you might say. Gabor hated us with all his fervour."

"I dare say your brother wouldn't rule out a covenant with the devil himself if it suited his interests."

Rekke smiled almost sadly now.

"You have a point there. But dear Magnus is also complex, and he has a heart in there somewhere, a loyalty that extends further than the next victory, and he and Gabor would hardly build a long-term relationship. At least I hope that is the case. What do you know about him, by the way?"

"Morovia?"

The man nodded.

"That you shouldn't be his enemy."

"True. But, unfortunately, I already am. I met him once after a concert I gave in Bern."

"You're a musician?"

"I was a pianist once upon a time, and Gabor came to my dressing room. He was quite charming. At the time, he had recently received his doctorate in mathematics at Trinity College, Cambridge—at a record young age, of course—and he was lecturing on valuation methods applicable to derivatives at the London School of Economics. As you know, he was a bit of a whizz-kid, and surprisingly amiable."

"Really?"

"Unfortunately, I didn't respond in the same elegant manner, and when he handed me his card I rather elaborately ripped it to pieces. So, my question is quite simple: how do I reach him?"

Axel Larsson looked at the man and wondered whether he was serious. Did he really want to challenge Gabor Morovia, or did he have other plans in mind?

"I would advise you to leave him alone."

"I'm afraid I must insist."

"He has a contact here in Stockholm. A corporate lawyer by the name of Alicia Kovács. You'll find her at the Adler law firm not far from here."

"A friend, perhaps, of the late Claire Lidman?"

"I don't think so," he said.

"By the way, when did you last see Claire Lidman?"

"I don't remember," Axel said, and without being aware of it he began to drum his fingers at a new, anxious tempo that Professor Rekke was able to read like a seismograph.

# FIFTEEN

Rebecka Wahlin had a large apartment with books everywhere, which immediately made Micaela more positively disposed toward her. During the first, good part of her childhood—when Papá was still alive—their home had been one big library. But after Papá had taken his tumble from the external walkway, Lucas had purged the books one by one, even if Mamá had protested as best she could.

"How do you find anything?" Micaela said.

Rebecka Wahlin was tall and slender, around sixty years old, with short, back-combed hair. She was wearing a tartan skirt and a black jacket. Despite her wholly Swedish name, she looked East Asian with her dark eyes and jet-black hair, and she was conspicuously used to being in charge. There was an authority in her movements.

"I sort by subject," she said. "Political biographies are over there, business books are here on the left, and those are the novels. I've got a shelf of crime fiction too, and here . . ." She took a few steps toward the living room. "Here are my chess books."

"Chess books?" said Micaela.

"Oh yes," Rebecka said. "I've been interested my whole life. I sometimes played against Claire, and, of course, I always lost."

"Why *of course*?"

Rebecka laughed and made for the two white armchairs in the living room, positioned in front of a painting depicting a colourful seascape. Micaela lingered, examining the bookshelf with the chess texts. There was something about it that kept her there.

"Because one lost to Claire. That's how it was. She was elevated above us mere mortals, but she was a good winner and I forgave her most of the time."

Micaela tore herself away from the chess books and sat down opposite Rebecka. It wasn't easy for her to maintain her focus—something was trying to draw her back to the shelf.

"Can I offer you anything?" Rebecka said.

"No thanks, I'm fine," she said. "You mentioned . . ." She didn't quite know what to say, and after all she had largely dropped the Claire Lidman investigation. "A man that scared her," she managed finally.

"That's right. It's something I haven't talked about fully—not even with the police."

Micaela looked up.

"You mean you withheld information?"

"It was more that I didn't understand it all, and after her death it didn't seem to matter anymore. And I suppose I wanted to spare Samuel."

"Spare him from what?"

"Even more suffering. They were a slightly odd couple. Many people couldn't get their heads around why Claire fell for him in the first place. There was such an obvious disparity between them: Claire had the money, the looks, the brains, the career—while he . . ."

"Yes, what did he have?"

Rebecka Wahlin laughed again, but this time more warmly.

"Physique. He had his body, his muscles and his kind eyes. He was tremendously attractive. I felt that myself, if I'm honest. He was also caring and just so lovely with her. He cooked, he cleaned, he handled all the practicalities, and he was a superb carpenter. But above all . . ." She hesitated.

"Yes?"

"Claire probably needed a kind man, given her experiences."

"Which experiences?"

"That's what I was going to tell you about."

"So you don't think she got bored of him?" Micaela said.

"I'm sure she could have, and it's entirely possible that he was smothering her—or however you want to put it. But I don't think that's why she left. Look, what do you say?" Rebecka made to stand up. "Don't you think we should have a drink or two? It's Friday night and abstinence won't grease the wheels."

"Sure," said Micaela. "What are you drinking?"

"Red wine—preferably a light Bordeaux."

"That sounds fine," she said.

Rebecka Wahlin hastened away across the herringbone parquet. Micaela wondered whether to take another look at the bookcase. She dismissed it as an irrational impulse.

"Tell me," she said, once Rebecka Wahlin had returned with a bottle and two glasses. "Why do *you* think she left?"

Julia was lying naked on the bed in her flat on Karlaplan, her eyes closed. She was happy—how long since she had last felt that way? A thousand years. It was as if all her old problems had just blown away—okay, okay, she still needed to eat a little less and not be so staid and respectable. But she was working on it. She opened her eyes and said to him:

"I'm a bit boring, aren't I?"

He laughed in just the right way, as if that was the last thing she was, and she wrapped herself around him in gratitude.

"I'd like to be crazier," she said.

"What's stopping you?"

Well, what is? she asked herself, wondering whether to launch into a bout of craziness—maybe she'd straddle him, pretend to bite his neck like a vampire and seduce him in a totally unboring way. But she stayed lying close to him, studying his ribcage. He looked so experienced and masculine, with his clearly drawn features and chiselled muscles, that she found herself embarrassed and felt an impulse to pull up the covers to hide herself.

But she didn't want to seem a prude, least of all now that she was meant to be crazy, so she caressed him tentatively on his stomach. He smiled back—looking just as calm and stable as ever—and then she winced as his body tensed. His mobile phone had beeped and it occurred to her that he must have had it turned off on the previous occasions they had seen each other. She had never heard that sound before, and she stared at his back, absorbed, as he reached toward the bedside table.

There were scratches high on his shoulder blade. Were they from her nails? Surely they were.

His head moved forward in a tense motion.

"Is something the matter?" she said.

He didn't reply. He turned toward her with absent eyes and she once again resisted the temptation to pull up the covers to hide, but that was the best she could do. She needed words of kindness—she'd become addicted to his compliments.

"Do you think I'm thin enough?" she said.

He didn't seem to hear her. He was still engrossed in what he had read on his phone, and she had to repeat the question before he lit up in that way that she loved.

"You're perfect."

He lay down next to her and caressed her from her navel up to her throat until the movement stopped and he pressed his finger between her collarbones. She gasped. Something primitive and primal was awakened in her, something that was instantly attractive and a little terrifying.

"Have you ever . . . ?" she said.

She didn't quite know what she wanted to ask, but she thought about his back. The back had wanted to tell her something.

"Hurt anyone?" she said, surprised at her own words.

"I guess everyone has," he said, moving his hand to her throat and looking her in the eyes with a gaze that shone—she saw it in a sudden moment of lucidity—with something boundless that she hadn't seen in anyone else she knew.

"I haven't," she said.

"No?" he said. "How's Christian doing right now?"

"Not great, I guess."

"There you go."

She thought it over, thinking that she wanted to say something philosophical that would demonstrate that she wasn't like the other girls he'd been with.

"Do we have to hurt in order to be free?"

He smiled as if it were a thought that had never occurred to him, which was precisely why it amused him.

"Maybe," he said, stroking her hair gently. She wanted to ask whether he could stay the night, but whenever she did, he always had to go, so she kept quiet. Instead, she pressed herself against his chest and wrapped her arms around him. She didn't want him to ever leave her.

# SIXTEEN

Rebecka Wahlin sat in the armchair with her wine glass and looked to be daydreaming, as if she wanted to postpone her story or talk about something else altogether.

"Tell me," Micaela said again.

"Axel Larsson," said Rebecka. "How familiar are you with him?"

"Pretty familiar."

"But you're too young to remember him in his glory days, aren't you?"

"I suppose so."

"He was a regular at Studio 54 in New York and had a penchant for buying Matisses and Picassos. He was the epitome of the yuppie, the whizz-kid living the good life. In the late eighties he was good for seven or eight billion kronor. But the whole equation was based on real estate and art prices skyrocketing. When the market crashed in the autumn of 1990 he was in a tight corner. Unfortunately, he wasn't alone."

"The banks were going under too."

"Especially Nordbanken. Interest rates were high and we'd made so much on our loans that we'd lost all perspective, and now we risked being taken down by credit losses, so we were pushing hard to secure as much as we could. But our efforts were never enough and that spring we were nationalised. A little naively we believed that we were smart and tough while the civil servants from the Ministry of Finance were nothing more than wimpy intellectuals. Goodness me, how wrong we were. Magnus Rekke, of all people, turned up to one of our management meetings."

Micaela started.

"Really?" she said.

She thought about when Magnus Rekke had trudged into Grevgatan and mistaken her for a cleaner and looked at her like she was worthless.

"Of course, Magnus was quite young back then and not yet associated with the Ministry of Foreign Affairs and Kleeberger," Rebecka said. "But he was already a significant force in the Government Offices who got wheeled out when ministers didn't want to get their hands dirty."

"I can imagine," she said.

"Magnus had been contacted by a colleague in Bonn, I think, and heard that Axel Larsson had borrowed at least the same again from a Hungarian investment bank called . . ."

"Cartaphilus," Micaela said.

"Exactly. Cartaphilus. A strange name. But it turned out they were a major player."

"I've gathered as much," she said, remembering when Rekke had asked about it.

It had been one of the few times lately when he had seemed alert again. He had looked at her a little ominously and asked for the details, but soon after that he had withdrawn, becoming just as gloomy as before.

"Axel had borrowed just as much from Cartaphilus as he had from us," Rebecka said, sipping her wine. "And it didn't add up. What little respect we still had for Axel vanished. He wasn't just a venture capitalist, he seemed to have no limits, as if he'd wanted to dig his own grave from the very beginning. We later came to revise that outlook too. He turned out to have hidden assets in Nobel Industries, Saab and Airbus, and we agreed that we would work with Cartaphilus to restructure these investments—or to take them over, to put it more bluntly."

"And Claire was cast in the leading role?"

"You might say that. From the off, Magnus Rekke turned primarily to her."

"Why was that, do you think?"

"For all sorts of reasons, I would guess, but most probably because she had knowledge about Cartaphilus that the rest of us lacked, and perhaps because the rest of us wanted to remain as uninvolved as possible. That's why, in the end, the responsibility fell to Claire and the CEO of Nordbanken, William Fors. Wille, as we used to call him. He and Claire were meant to meet with Cartaphilus's representatives for an initial discussion. That's actually what I called you about," Rebecka Wahlin said, draining her glass.

Rekke emerged from the Hotel Diplomat, squinting in the evening sunlight. Had there been any point to that meeting? Probably not... Then again, he'd secured a name, a contact, and who knew? Perhaps that would lead somewhere...

He had met Gabor Morovia later as an adult—well, Rekke hadn't been that much of an adult really. He hadn't been much older than Julia was now, and he had been fatally infatuated with Ida Aminoff at the time. He had been in his dressing room after playing Ravel's Piano Concerto in Bern when the message came that a young man wanted to meet him.

He had said no—he wasn't up to it. But the young man had come anyway and suddenly he was standing there in the doorway with a bunch of flowers saying that he'd never heard Ravel played with such expression and melancholy. Rekke had thanked him and asked whom he had the honour of addressing.

He didn't have to wait for the answer. The dark-haired man, who was dressed in a grey double-breasted suit with an expensive red scarf around his neck, took a couple of steps forward. A faint wheeze was audible in his exhalation: a G falling to an F sharp. Rekke leaped up as if to fend off a new judo move. Gabor Morovia, however, didn't seem to notice. He handed him the flowers and proffered his hand, and Rekke saw no option but to take it.

"This is an unexpected visit," he said.

"I've been thinking that you and I should let bygones be bygones and become friends."

"Have you indeed?"

"I've heard that not only do you play beautifully," Gabor said, making a sweeping gesture toward his eyes, "you're apparently able to observe rather than seeing blindly like everyone else."

"I don't know about that," Rekke said, quickly scanning the room.

"It's said you can read people and places," Gabor said.

"You, on the other hand, are the master of numbers."

Gabor took another step forward and there was no doubt that his aura was just as explosive now as it had been in the past. It felt as if it might transform into something aggressive and agile in the space of a second.

"I'm interested in patterns, disquieting signs—the kind that precede dramatic changes," he said.

Rekke put down the flowers to free up his hands.

"That sounds like a valuable area of study," he said.

"Above all, it is profitable. He who foresees sudden movements owns the future."

"Is that so?" Rekke said, taking a couple of steps back and picking up a water carafe that stood next to the mirror without fully knowing what he was going to do with it. But then he poured two glasses, offering one to Morovia.

"I'm afraid I haven't much to offer."

"I'm just glad to be here. Here is my card. I've started a company, and a little bird told me that you have grown tired of life as a concert pianist."

Rekke took the card, contemplating Gabor's hands and the position of his legs and upper body. Almost automatically, as if out of some survival instinct, he pictured a whole series of close-combat scenarios.

"Is that so?" he said.

"I heard you said that music lacks *claritas* and that you want to move on. Perhaps we might work together."

Rekke's gaze wandered from the contours of Gabor's shoulder muscles to the lines above his brow.

"The problem is, I don't forget that easily," he said. "It's a character flaw. Things stay, they etch themselves in."

"The curse of aptitude."

"It could be a kind of inertia too. A difficulty in moving forward."

"I doubt that."

Rekke looked down at the business card in his hand and spotted the company name. He winced with discomfort.

"This name?" he said under his breath.

"Yes—it just came to me," Gabor said, at which point Rekke lost it.

He grabbed Gabor and pushed him against the wall with a force and speed that surprised even himself. Gabor's face lit up as if he had been thrust into a heightened state of being.

"It was just a cat, my friend. A cat. I can make up for it handsomely."

"Out," Rekke snapped, grabbing Gabor by the lapels and tugging so hard the fabric tore.

Then he threw him out in two or three rapid movements that he must have been subconsciously preparing for. Gabor staggered away, just about keeping his feet, seemingly without losing his composure. Nevertheless, he was changed. He seemed to grow, and just like the last time they had met, his eyes changed colour from green to something almost akin to black.

"Get out of here," Rekke said.

"If you insist. I heard you've bagged Ida Aminoff—what a catch! Quite a few of us have been dreaming of her."

Rekke took a step closer, ready to go at him if that was what it took.

"And?" he said.

"I just wanted to offer my congratulations," Gabor said. "And remind you to take care of her."

"What do you mean by that?"

"Nothing. Simply that she is a young woman who likes drugs and heights. It would be a pity if anything were to happen to her."

"If you touch her . . ."

"Then what?" said Gabor, with that unpleasant air that gave the impression he was in full control and enjoying himself.

But when Rekke hadn't answered but had merely glowered back at him furiously, Gabor had nodded and disappeared with footsteps that remained forever imprinted on Rekke's memory. Now—long after the fact, as he stood there on Strandvägen—it came back to him as a prelude to impending disaster. What was he to do?

Nothing, he concluded. I have a daughter, I have friends, I have something that might actually be a life. I shall leave that devil alone. Then he walked back to Grevgatan, thinking about Micaela and the light in her eyes that made him want to be a better person.

# SEVENTEEN

Rebecka Wahlin poured another glass of red wine and stared out of the window.

"Claire met a representative of the company," she said. "Alicia Kovács. She's from Hungary, though she's lived in Stockholm for many years. I know her slightly and I like her. She's a lawyer and an economist, pure quality and nothing less. It's therefore somewhat surprising that she works for this company, which is increasingly associated with organised crime. But she must be worth her weight in gold to them—a respectable public face. She seemed to know Claire already and suggested that she meet with the company's owner. That was a big deal right away."

"How so?"

"We didn't know who he was at the time. The company was owned by a trust in Switzerland and the owner's name wasn't a matter of public record. But when we started looking into it, we realised there were all sorts of rumours circulating about him. He supposedly had an almost hypnotic power over people and was an infernally skilful negotiator, so you can understand that we were worried. Given the sums involved, it was extremely important that we didn't back down, and

William Fors, our CEO, insisted he join the meeting. Apparently, that was out of the question. The owner would see Claire alone or no-one at all, and we spent a fair while weighing that up, but in the end we agreed that it was good to establish contact and Claire was hardly the worst person we could have sent. So we prepared her well and did our homework and it was my lot to make sure she looked a million dollars. After all, it wouldn't hurt if she made an impression in every possible way. Claire and I went out shopping. I suppose I thought it would be a bit of an adventure, but I noticed right away that Claire had changed. She seemed ill at ease and I was worried. 'Have you met the owner before?' I asked. Claire didn't answer, and I remember wondering about the company name. I mean . . . who names their company after a man who was condemned by God?"

"Condemned by God?"

"I'd looked it up and found that Cartaphilus was a name used over the centuries in place of Ahasuerus—the man who, according to myth, wouldn't let Jesus rest on his doorstep."

"That's a bit weird."

"Yes, definitely shady. But do you know what Claire said? 'He's evil,' she said. *Evil*. It sounded so . . . I don't know. Anachronistic. I tried to laugh it off, but she refused to play along and changed the subject. She said she was going to cycle to the meeting."

"Cycle?"

"She always cycled everywhere and she didn't want to be driven there in the bank's limousine as we'd planned."

"When was this?"

"Six or seven weeks before she disappeared. It was a Thursday, I think. She insisted that none of us were to come over for a final briefing. She wanted to prepare alone and the rest of us never even found out where the meeting was held. All evening and all night I waited for her to call and tell me how it had gone, but she never did. I only saw her the next day. She was wearing a long-sleeved top and she seemed to be struggling to walk."

"She was struggling to *walk*?"

"Well, at any rate, there was something strained about her movements."

"What had happened?"

"She said she'd had too much to drink and fallen off her bike, that there was nothing to worry about, but I didn't really believe her. She was completely focused on presenting the restructuring plan she and the owner had agreed on, and there was a lot of fuss about that. It subsumed everything else, and there were people shouting that she'd pulled a fast one, but a lot of that was jealousy and bullshit, and what we achieved would go on to represent a huge shift in Swedish business. It was an aggressive, elegant set-up. We worked intensively to hammer out the details of the agreement that William Fors and Magnus Rekke would put to Axel Larsson, and I—"

"But this is a big deal," Micaela said, interjecting. "Had she been assaulted? What do you think?"

Rebecka Wahlin drank from her glass, suddenly looking uncomfortable.

"Hmm, no . . . I don't know. Claire played it down afterward, and she recovered pretty quickly."

"You said on the phone that she was scared."

"That was my feeling, yes."

Micaela thought back to Samuel Lidman's story. He hadn't said a word about Claire seeming scared in the final weeks. Just that she'd had a stomach ache and locked herself in the bathroom.

"Did you tell the police?"

"I said I thought she'd been subjected to something unpleasant in her meeting with the owner of Cartaphilus, but I didn't have any details and it didn't feel like Lindroos saw much in it."

"Moron," Micaela muttered.

"I dare say he was."

"Did you find out who the owner was later, then?"

"Yes, we did."

Rebecka looked troubled again.

"And are you able to tell me?"

"His name was Gabor Morovia."

"Is it uncomfortable to tell me that?"

Rebecka laughed nervously.

"Yes, perhaps."

"So he *was* a bit evil?"

"I suppose that's stretching it. He's a major, serious player with powerful friends all over the world."

"That's not exactly evidence to the contrary."

"No, perhaps not, and sometimes I do wonder. There aren't many pictures of him around and there's not much information online either. But William Fors, our CEO, once played a recording of his voice. I think he'd made it himself over the phone, and I've got to say that it made me shudder. It's impossible to understand how you could say no to a voice like that."

"How do you mean?"

"I'm not quite sure I can say," Rebecka Wahlin said. "The voice touched me—it was as if it wanted to lead me into a dark room."

"Gosh, that sounds dramatic."

"I might be over-egging it."

Micaela paused for thought and leaned forward.

"So there's nothing else you can tell me about whatever it was that happened to Claire?"

Rebecka pondered.

"Not really," she said.

"That's not a good answer to a police officer," Micaela said.

"Okay, well there's one thing I haven't said to anyone because I suspect it was just my imagination."

"I'm listening."

"Claire's figure just before she disappeared. I got it into my head that she looked pregnant."

"Are you kidding?"

"No, no. She'd said that Samuel wanted kids and that she was thinking about coming off the pill, so I was rather forward one evening when we were working late. 'Are congratulations in order?' I asked her, pointing to her belly. She took it badly, and I thought I'd offended her. Though afterward I did wonder..."

"Whether she hadn't in fact been pregnant after all?"

"I suppose so."

"But the father wasn't Samuel?"

"Yes, possibly, and I couldn't help but think about her Catholic upbringing. I wondered whether she'd actually be able to go through with an abortion in a situation like that."

Micaela nodded and stood up as if she was suddenly in a rush. "One might speculate that it was from..." she began, but she failed to complete her sentence.

"A rape?"

"Maybe," she said. "Have you spoken to Samuel about it?"

"No," said Rebecka. "I haven't had the heart to."

Damn it, Micaela thought to herself. She offered her thanks and left. As she descended the stairs, she dialled Samuel Lidman's number.

# EIGHTEEN

Samuel Lidman was chalking his hands and tightening his weight-lifting belt when his mobile rang.

He was at the gym on Hälsingegatan—his home turf, one might say. He'd been there back in the days when there had been no women's changing room, though there had been a sign over the entrance that read "Go for a bad girl" and pictures of Arnold Schwarzenegger and Frank Zane all over the place.

It was the world of men, and in that world Samuel was king.

People stared at him entranced as he curved his back inwards on the bench and did eight reps at one hundred and sixty kilos. Afterward, the puny boys gazed at him in admiration as he posed in the changing room and applied liniment to his injuries. It wasn't anything like the world outside, where feelings of inferiority ached within him and it didn't matter one bit that he was ninety kilos of hench muscle. He invariably felt like a nobody. But here he was in his natural element. He pulled the phone out of his bag and answered it, not caring that he was talking too loudly.

Then he lowered his voice and went into the hallway. It was Micaela Vargas calling—the police officer who lived with Professor Rekke—

and she asked him a question that immediately unsettled him. Could Claire have been assaulted during her meeting with the owner of Cartaphilus? He said no, he didn't think so. But it was something he had asked himself nonetheless, and he did remember that night. He had lain there waiting for her. It had been apparent beforehand that it was an important, perhaps even fateful meeting, but he hadn't known much about it—Claire had always hidden herself behind a veil of confidentiality. He remembered the door opening at around one or half past one. She had crept in ever so quietly before locking herself in the bathroom. He heard her sobbing in there and went to the door and asked: "Are you okay, sweetheart?" She replied: "I'm fine, I just fell off my bike. My skirt was too wide," which seemed to make sense.

She always rode her bike, even in her high heels and glad rags, and in the morning he saw for himself the wonky wheel and broken spokes. There was nothing to indicate that anyone had harmed her—not then, not in the first few days. But later on, he had wondered, that much was true. She didn't let him come close for a week or so, and she seemed to have a stomach ache, which didn't tally with a bicycle accident. One evening, when she returned after an unusually long visit to the loo, she mumbled an apology that worried him a little.

"Sorry for what?" he said.

"Sorry I went to that meeting."

But no matter how much he pressed her, she wouldn't say anything more about it. Shortly after that, it seemed to have been forgotten and their days together were as bright as ever, right up until disaster struck.

"Why do you ask?" said Samuel.

"I just want to know if anything serious happened to Claire before she went missing," Micaela Vargas said.

"Have you heard anything more about the photo?"

Vargas was silent for a moment.

"No," she said, adding: "Did you ever try to contact him?"

"Who?"

"The owner of Cartaphilus."

"I did early on, but I was told to forget about it. Everyone said he had nothing to do with it."

"Who was everyone?"

"The police and Claire's bosses."

"Strange that they were so sure of themselves."

Micaela hung up and emerged onto the street, lost in thought—it wasn't just Claire's encounter with Morovia that preoccupied her. Something she had seen or sensed in Rebecka Wahlin's apartment, something that lay across her eyes like an irritating veil, but she still couldn't fathom what it was, and the only really clear feeling she had was that she was hungry. What should she do? Sit down to eat somewhere and think it all over? That sounded reasonable. She turned right and spotted a limousine on Ulrikagatan, its engine idling. Behind her, a black Porsche pulled out of the parking lot opposite Oscarskyrkan.

What a neighbourhood, she thought to herself. Vanessa was right—she didn't belong in Östermalm. These surroundings galled her. She thought about Jonas Beijer, her old colleague from the murder squad in Solna. He wouldn't have been out of place in this world, but he would have immediately recognised how uncomfortable she was and made her feel better. Should she call him to get it off her chest? That wasn't a bad idea; she felt in slightly better spirits at the prospect. Someone shouted:

"Micaela!"

She peered down toward Narvavägen and spotted a familiar figure. It was Julia—beautiful young Julia—racing toward her with something new and sweeping in her movements. She wore holey jeans and a waist-length leather jacket and didn't look one bit the good girl anymore. Well, she *did*, but she looked like a good girl trying to come across as tough and decadent while not quite succeeding, and one who had dressed in a hurry to boot. Her hair was untidy, as if she had just been asleep, or otherwise occupied in bed. Her blouse wasn't tucked into her trousers either—and now Micaela came to think about it, hadn't she got thinner?

Micaela had always envied more or less everything about Julia: her class; her beauty; the breeding passed to her in her mother's milk; the fine-limbed nature of her figure; and the wakeful gaze that was so reminiscent of her father. But now she seemed different, and for the first time Micaela asked herself: was she okay? She pushed the thought away. Someone like Julia was the last person she should be worrying about. She extended her arms and hugged her.

"How are you?" she asked.

"Good," Julia said.

Micaela looked her in the eyes.

"You're glowing."

Or at least you want to glow, she thought to herself.

"I guess," Julia said, blushing slightly.

"Are you in love?"

"Something like that."

"Nice," Micaela said, though not with much enthusiasm—possibly because she had caught a momentary glimpse of what the lucky man was like.

She sensed him in Julia's new look and in her gaze, and she reflected that she had known boys like that—cool guys who took one look at you and instantly made you want to be someone else, someone you thought they would love a little bit more.

"Who is it?"

"It's kinda new. I'll tell you later. But I was wondering something," Julia said, gazing intently at Micaela as if she'd just had an unexpected thought.

"What?" Micaela said.

"If a guy suddenly legs it—like, in a split second—and says he'll be back really soon, what might that mean?"

Micaela looked back at her, surprised by the question, and surprised that Julia—who was usually able to draw conclusions better than most— was asking it of someone who knew nothing about the circumstances.

"I suppose it might mean just about anything."

Julia appeared to consider this.

"Of course. Sorry. Dumb question."

"No, not at all. Where are you headed?"

"I was just going to take a walk and think a bit," Julia said.

Micaela wondered whether she should offer to accompany her, but something was still gnawing at her and she wanted to be alone with her thoughts.

"What about you?" Julia said. "Going up to see Pappa?"

She shook her head.

Julia looked toward Strandvägen.

"You haven't had enough of him, have you?" she said.

*I've definitely had enough.*

"I've just got other plans," Micaela said.

"He needs you."

"He'll manage."

"He's concocted all sorts of daft ideas. Everywhere he looks he sees dark threats. He even thinks my new boyfriend, who is soooo kind . . ."

Julia didn't finish her sentence.

"I'm worried," she said instead. "He needs help."

I'm not some fucking nurse, Micaela thought to herself.

"He's got Mrs. Hansson," she said.

"Sure, but you make Pappa pull himself together. You're good for him, and sometimes I think . . ."

"What do you think?"

"Nothing. You'll have to figure that out for yourself. But I'd really appreciate it if you looked in on him," Julia said.

"Another time," Micaela said sternly, but then she softened, hugged Julia again and told her she was sure it would work out with her new boyfriend.

Then she walked away, not knowing where she was going and without noticing the footsteps falling just ten metres behind her.

# NINETEEN

Rekke was at the computer, reading about Axel Larsson. Reading every damned word there was about him, reflecting that the old fox had seemed peculiarly anxious when Claire Lidman's name came up in conversation. It hadn't just been the neurotic drumming on the oak table, but an entire cascade of micro-expressions on his face: a hint of shame in the eyes that he wanted to suppress at any cost, but which had moved down toward his mouth in a rapid spasm. Could Axel Larsson have done something to her?

Possibly. But frankly, Rekke could no longer interpret people. His brain was mush. It had been bad enough on the opiates, but now the champagne, which had boosted him for a moment, had pulled him even further down. He went into the bathroom and splashed cold water on his face, which helped for a second, but no more than that.

The mist continued to linger over the world, and he closed his eyes and allowed random colours to dance before him until they settled into images. Then he pictured Micaela in front of him: Micaela, who had rushed toward him on a Tunnelbana station platform that night; Micaela, who looked at him as if he had deeply disappointed her.

He resolved to call her and apologise and say that he was feeling better. Damn it, he'd drunk champagne with an old billionaire and tried to elicit information about an enemy—that was as good a sign of enterprise as any. But no matter how much he searched, he couldn't find his mobile, nor his wallet either. He eventually began to aimlessly rip open pillows and duvets and he even resorted to opening the fridge and freezer and checking the garbage. Good God, what was wrong with him?

He was growing tired of himself—tired in general—and he sank down at the Steinway and on a whim played Liszt's *Un Sospiro*—a piece where his hands crossed over each other, which had amused him in his youth, and even though the first bar served as a way to settle his nerves, he soon forgot the outside world and lost himself in the recital. He allowed all his grief and weariness to find expression in the notes, becoming somewhat carried away and absorbed in it, his body rocking back and forth. That was why it took a while for him to notice that the doorbell was ringing, and though he was inclined to ignore it, he stood up and sidestepped. "Well, I'll be damned," he said quietly. Then he opened the door and for a few seconds he understood nothing.

Micaela was walking along Storgatan, oblivious of the city, but it was no longer Rekke or Julia she was thinking about. It wasn't even what Gabor Morovia might have done to Claire Lidman. It was Rebecka Wahlin's chess bookshelf. Micaela had sensed something there among the books. It was a feeling that had grown ever stronger, something had been blazing out at her from the rows of spines. She turned on her heel and that was when she caught sight of Hugo Pérez. What was he doing here?

They had only just crossed paths in Husby, and Östermalm was most definitely not Hugo's home turf. But she was so preoccupied with her own thoughts that she didn't fully register how strange it was for them to bump into each other again in a completely different part of the city. Ordinarily, she would have gone up to him to ask him what the hell he was playing at: what kind of joker didn't even say hello? Instead, she looked at him sullenly and spat out: "Idiot."

Hugo—the smirking clown of her childhood—reacted like a hormonal smackhead. He leaped at her and pressed her against the wall and in the same movement slammed his fist into her lip and chin. She lost it and yanked herself free and at that moment Hugo spluttered something.

She asked him to repeat himself.

"Stop digging dirt on your brother. Ain't no-one gonna testify anyway. You're just messing things up for your family," he said.

"What the hell's it got to do with you?"

"If you don't stop then someone you like might get hurt."

"What?"

"It's the truth. Things can happen," he muttered. She shoved him toward the street, but then she spotted a man in his forties not far away who seemed about to intervene.

"It's cool," she said. "Just some loser kicking up a storm."

She turned back to Hugo, who now looked more his old self—he wasn't quite grinning, but he no longer looked menacing.

"You do know I'm a cop, right? You're threatening me and my loved ones. I'll arrest the fuck out of you."

"I'm just saying," he said, which bothered her even more. She pushed him again. He staggered.

"Why can't Lucas tell me himself?" she snapped.

"He doesn't know anything."

"Do you think I'm thick or what? He'd murder you if you pulled a stunt like this without his say-so."

"I'm just saying you should leave us alone."

"Us?" she said furiously. "It's *us*, is it? Fuck you all. You think this is going to stop me? I'm coming at you with everything I've got," she said, thumping his shoulder and then turning away to head back toward Karlaplan.

She could hardly believe it. Had that pathetic dickhead really followed her, and who was he referring to? *Someone you like...* It couldn't be Mamá, let alone Simón, who was already completely beholden to Lucas and at his beck and call. Nor could it be Vanessa or Malika, who were both basically in love with him. Anyway, it was probably all bullshit, a power play, but still... She suddenly felt nauseous. How far might he go? Maybe he had no limits at all—not when it came to his life, which it sort of did...

She had to talk to Lucas—that was the first thing she needed to do. She pulled out her mobile and called but he didn't pick up. Probably too much of a coward. She looked around and swore out loud.

The whole neighbourhood was so provocatively calm and peaceful with all its decent inhabitants in their shirts and dresses—it made her want to scream. She might as well be in another century. There wasn't a building anywhere in the vicinity that had been built in the last hundred years, and looming over all of it was Oscarskyrkan with its green and black spire and Gothic windows. Adjoining Narvavägen there were well-trimmed avenues, where resplendent hags and neat-looking girls wandered about with their lapdogs and designer handbags. Micaela was as far from Husby as she could get, and she had no idea where she was going. She had been on her way back to Rebecka Wahlin's to take another look at her bookshelf, but now the rage and fear were boiling within her and she didn't give a flying fuck about Claire Lidman. She was history.

The woman was dead. Anything else was just a widower's wishful thinking, and all that mattered was Hugo's muttered warning: *Someone you like might get hurt.* She stopped abruptly. Surely it couldn't be Rekke? No—that was impossible. Wasn't it? It was one thing to mess with people in the hood, but going after someone like Rekke, with his network of contacts and his position... Surely they'd never dare. She was certain of it.

Yet she kept wanting to turn on her heel and go to his apartment to check. But she didn't. She settled for calling him instead. He didn't answer—on either his mobile or the landline. He's probably sleeping off his pill high, she thought to herself as she reached Linnégatan. A young man in a pale-blue suit gazed at her with something verging on horror. "What are you looking at?" she snapped, touching her lip.

Blood came away on her fingers. Who cared? The lip wasn't the problem, let alone what the snobs in this neck of the woods thought about her. The important thing was the threat, and once again she pictured Lucas: Lucas drawing his weapon in the woods, Lucas making people back away simply by looking at them. He was genuinely vile—that was it, wasn't it? Even if it had taken her a while to realise . . .

She found herself back outside the door to Rebecka Wahlin's stairwell. The grand-looking main door was adorned with carved wooden soldiers at the top. Was she going back up? She pressed the buzzer.

"Hello?" Rebecka Wahlin said over the intercom.

"It's Micaela Vargas again," she said. "There was something I forgot to ask you. Do you mind if I come up?"

"Oh, really? Of course," Rebecka Wahlin said, letting her in.

At that very moment, Lucas called. His voice was silky-smooth, as if he only wanted the best for her in this world.

# TWENTY

Rekke opened the door and squinted in the light from the landing. He supposed he had been expecting someone else entirely, because he was briefly unable to comprehend what he was seeing. Standing on the threshold was a dark-haired, elegant woman of around forty-five years of age, wearing a blue tailored suit. She was, if not eye-catching, then certainly interesting, with a nervous, delicate smile and lively brown eyes that were shiny with tears, giving a contradictory impression.

He couldn't tell whether the woman had been in an accident and wanted help, or had come on more hostile business. Perhaps the latter, upon reflection. She straightened her back. She was quite clearly highly educated, and he could tell from her purposeful and efficient movements that she was of the managerial class—responsible for hiring and firing.

A woman with power and influence, but this particular matter moved her, he thought to himself.

"Professor Rekke, I presume," she said, proffering a hand.

"A poor version of him, alas," he said.

"I think he looks as impressive as he is rumoured to be. I must apologise for turning up unannounced. I have tried calling. My name is Alicia Kovács."

"My telephone is gone, along with my good sense. Your name sounds familiar," he said.

"I represent Cartaphilus. I heard from Axel Larsson that you are looking for my principal," she said. At that point he realised he needed to be alert, but in that instant it seemed impossible, so he asked her to wait outside a moment.

He needed to drink some water and wash his face again, and he disappeared to do so. Upon his return, he smiled as best he could and stood up straight.

"My apologies," he said. "Although I am honoured, of course. Especially by the urgency. The expeditiousness."

"I live by the principle of not putting things off."

"Indeed," he said absent-mindedly. "A virtue, of course, although it's not one I always practise. *In dubio non est agendum.* In dubious cases, you should not act. But nevertheless, I bid you welcome—and I fear I shall have to disappoint you. As an enemy, I do not currently pose much of a challenge."

He gave the woman another look, trying to understand what she might want. His best guess was that she had come to deliver a subtle threat. Her shoulders and hands were tensed, and the teary eyes that indicated that she was shaken or affected were cool. He was clearly facing a complex intelligence both in thought and emotion.

"Enemy? No, no. My principal—"

"My apologies *again*," he said. "I have some difficulty with the legalese. Might we not say *Gabor* instead? Or perhaps Professor Morovia? Whichever suits. Principal has such a tedious, bureaucratic ring to it."

"Most certainly," she said. "Professor Morovia emphasises that you are an exceptional person. Apparently, you see things no-one else can."

"Very much like the psychotic patient."

"For goodness' sake, please don't misunderstand me. There is no-one whom he speaks of with such respect, and just now when I heard you play—Liszt, if I'm not much mistaken?—I simply wanted to sink down and disappear into the music. It was unspeakably beautiful."

"Most kind. And do send my regards to Gabor in return. I have so many memories of him. Not least my burns."

He put a hand to his chest.

"You both have burns, but his are worse."

He didn't understand, and was tempted to ask what she meant. It bothered him that there was something fundamental that he didn't know, but he let it be and led Alicia Kovács into the kitchen.

Her heels echoed ominously—*dam, dom, dam*—G, C, G—and for the second or third time, she touched her jacket pocket. He guessed that she had something in it that she was afraid of losing, and he felt increasingly sure that she was not happy about her task, even if there had been a fervour—almost a pleasurable aggression—in the way she had spoken of the burns.

"You have a lovely home," she said.

"It would have fallen into disrepair long ago without the help of others. Unlike you, Madame, I put off everything—even the most minor of kitchen chores. But again, thank you. Might I offer you a glass of wine? I have a quite adequate Corton-Charlemagne in the wine chiller. Not that I'm a connoisseur—my brother considers me a barbarian in that field."

"I must decline. I will be brief. Professor Morovia asked me . . ."

She ran her hand down her throat. The tears were still visible in her eyes, and he was tempted to recommend that she change employer, but he guessed that Gabor was not so easy to free oneself from.

"What did he ask? Actually, first, please take a seat," he said, gesturing toward one of the kitchen chairs. "I must say I admire your courage. It has cost you to come here, has it not? I insist upon offering you something—if not wine then water."

He stood up and got a bottle of Ramlösa mineral water, pouring a glass for her.

"Thank you," she said, taking a sip. "And, of course, you are right. Sometimes the job isn't as easy as one might wish," she said, smiling again—a beautiful and melancholy smile, he thought.

"Then we share a burden, for it is not glad tidings that you bring, is it?" he said, also sitting down.

"No," she said. "You see . . . I have been tasked with a standing assignment by Professor Morovia. It has been entrusted to me for many years—ever since my first days with him."

"Out with it then," he said, meeting her gaze, and while he surely should be more worried for himself, he felt an impulse to comfort her.

"I promised Professor Morovia," she said, "that as soon as you made contact, or otherwise indicated that you wished to do so, I would hand an item over to you."

Rekke gazed at her intently, realising that something crucial was about to unfold.

"Why must he wait for my move?" he said. "He used to love taking the initiative."

"He thinks it more elegant to respond."

"Is he always so vain?"

"I believe he always wants to make it clear that challenging him comes at a price."

"Then let us see what toll must be paid."

Alicia Kovács put a hand into her jacket pocket and produced a pearl pendant on a gold necklace which she placed on the kitchen table, and for a moment Rekke dedicated his full attention to the object. Then it was as if he had lost his footing, and for a moment his vision darkened. That's not possible, he said to himself. Not possible.

Magnus Rekke was on board a government plane sipping a glass of red wine while engrossed in an intelligence report on counter-terrorism operations in the Stockholm suburbs. But the report was too speculative and wordy, and he gazed outside at the airport instead. A plane emblazoned with the Saudi flag took off beside them. They were waiting for the prime minister, who was late, and Magnus felt impatient and off balance. He turned to Kleeberger—the foreign minister—who was sitting opposite him reviewing the programme for the next day.

"My brother just called," he said.

Kleeberger raised his eyebrows. He became nervous whenever Hans came up.

"What did he want?"

"He was interested in some old business from my days at the Ministry of Finance. You remember Axel Larsson, don't you?"

"Who can forget Axel Larsson?"

Kleeberger continued to glance through his document. A flight attendant brought him a dinner tray and he muttered his thanks without looking up.

"Then you also know we didn't get as many of his assets as we hoped to. A Hungarian investment company with ties to the Kremlin grabbed the choicest morsels," Magnus said.

"Oh yes," Kleeberger said, raising his gaze again.

"We threw our lot in with this company and still ended up drawing the short straw."

"Certainly not ideal. But why is your brother interested in all this?"

Magnus wondered how much he should say—he really should keep his mouth shut given his own head was at stake, but he couldn't help himself.

"He may be asking himself whether the heat was turned up on us, or whether we got into bed with organised crime."

"Ouch."

"But mainly it's because he and the company proprietor are personal enemies. The owner's name is Gabor Morovia—he's a lapsed mathematician and womaniser."

Kleeberger suddenly looked frightened—or at least Magnus thought he did, because a moment later the look was gone.

"Is that so?" was all the foreign minister said.

"Do you know him?"

Kleeberger drained his glass.

"He's hard to overlook. Said to have a penchant for excessive acts of revenge and intellectual pursuits—particularly chess. A brilliant man, I gather?"

"Yes, possibly," Magnus said, as reluctant to give compliments as ever.

"What does your brother want with him?"

Magnus would have preferred to leave it at what he had already said, but now he had Kleeberger's interest he would have to accept the consequences.

"They crossed paths as children," he said. "But they also met later on when Hans was in his early twenties and courting Ida Aminoff."

"Ida," Kleeberger said dreamily.

"Did you know her too?"

"Oh yes, I was in those circles. Her father Werner was ambassador to Moscow and our parents were acquainted. Incredibly talented. I remember her paintings and the poems she read at some recital in town. Like everyone else, I was a little bit in love with her, even if she scared me."

"She scared our whole family," said Magnus. "It was as if she could only be induced to live if she risked something crucial."

"Yes, in a way," said Kleeberger.

"But Hans loved her. She was his great love. Lovisa was a marriage of convenience by comparison—and he worried about Ida constantly. In the midst of all that, he bumped into Gabor Morovia after a concert in Bern and received some kind of threat. Three or four weeks later, Ida was found dead—as I'm sure you know—in her father's apartment on Torstenssonsgatan."

"I actually met her on that last night in Stockholm," Kleeberger said.

"You were at the wedding reception on Djurgården?"

"Indeed. Everyone was. Maybe you were too?"

Magnus would have gladly denied it and claimed to have been on the other side of the planet, yet he nodded.

"And everyone was after her," Kleeberger said. "But she was just toying with the men, wasn't she?"

"She turned Wille Fors's head, among others," Magnus said rashly, against his better judgement.

Kleeberger looked surprised.

"The future CEO of Nordbanken?"

"Exactly."

"You mean the stories are connected?"

I shan't say a word on that, Magnus thought to himself, but by way of explanation he said:

"The same people were involved, and while Wille was nothing more than a spoiled brat back then, he had the same attitude toward money."

"It was there to be thrown around, you mean?"

"Oh yes, thrown around or burned if that elevated his status even a fraction among those fools. But on that particular evening, he lost his wallet and accused Ida of having stolen it. He followed her back toward town at dawn—both hoping to get it back and to go home with her."

"He wanted to sleep with the thief?"

"He was completely off-kilter."

Kleeberger looked at him with interest—a little too much interest for Magnus's liking.

"You're not suggesting that William Fors had anything to do with her death, are you?"

"No, no," Magnus said hastily. "But for Hans, Wille was a question mark. He never did accept the police findings and he threw himself into an investigation of his own. Sometimes I think . . ."

He hesitated.

"What do you think, Magnus?"

"That Hans's fascination with unsolved crime began right there."

"Yet he didn't find a solution, did he?"

"No, his detective career began with failure, and I fear it was one of life's educational and unexpected successes: failure cured him of all hubris and drove him on."

"But he must have found something. Hans has the eyes of a hawk."

"Naturally he found all sorts of things, but he was unable to put the jigsaw pieces together. Perhaps he was in such a bad state that he couldn't see clearly."

And thank God for that, Magnus thought.

"I still think about it often," he said.

"How so?"

"How strange it is that he let go of it. It was the great sorrow of his life, and he usually won't tolerate the unexplained. But in this case—the worst thing to ever happen to him—he put it behind him. I've been waiting for him to come back to it."

"And now he has?"

"Or perhaps it's something else. At worst, he's looking to take down Gabor Morovia personally, which can hardly end well."

Kleeberger looked at him, both worried and quizzical.

"For you or him?"

"For him," Magnus said, overcome by a sudden desire to pour his wine into Kleeberger's lap.

# TWENTY-ONE

Micaela stepped out of the elevator one floor short, so that Rebecka Wahlin wouldn't overhear her conversation. Lucas seemed strangely calm, which pissed her off even more.

"How can you?" she said.

"Calm down, baby sis."

"Don't call me that."

"Sure, Micaela, sure. But I haven't set anyone on you. I guess Hugo's just worried about himself. You know he's already got a suspended sentence."

"Fucking genius move to jump a cop."

"Who said anything about a genius? He's an idiot. Surely you remember that from school?"

"He'd never dare do something like that without your blessing."

"You think?"

"Never."

"Okay, listen up. I'm only going to say this once . . ."

He fell silent and the atmosphere changed in a second. A chill filled the silent void.

"I'm listening," she said.

"So here's the thing, sis. *You're* threatening me and I can't just duck. I have my own life. You gotta quit it. Otherwise things are gonna go south. You get me? *South.* We're family and we stick together. Simple as."

She lost her temper again.

"You're a crook, Lucas. You push drugs to kids and scare people shitless. You're the one messing things up," she snapped, realising that she was being even more provocative because they were doing this over the phone.

"Easy, sis. Easy," he said.

Then the call was over and it felt as if all the blood had drained from her body—or perhaps it was more like a blow to the stomach. When she had recovered and was breathing more normally, her first thought was that she wouldn't stand a chance against him. The chill in his voice and his dispassionate words made her want to simply give up. How the hell could she have put herself in this situation? But there was nothing to be done about it now. She would just have to bite the bullet and take things as they came.

She climbed the stairs to Rebecka Wahlin's apartment. A door slammed below her in the building. Smells of cleaning fluid and cooking were seeping out from somewhere, and she took a deep breath and rang the bell as old pictures of Lucas flickered before her mind's eye.

What was it that Gabor had said? A divine sensitivity in his touch. As if he made the keys come alive. *No-one plays like him, no-one.* As Alicia Kovács had stood in the stairwell and listened to the music, it had been as if she had separated from herself, wanting nothing more than to drop everything and weep over her life. But she was a professional, for God's sake, and she had pulled herself together and was now sitting before the man she had heard so much about.

He was so strangely attractive in all his brokenness, and she would have liked to ask him to play again or to explain why he had given up music, but now was hardly the time for that. He seemed to be completely beside himself, his trembling hands toying with the necklace she had given him.

The piece was even more beautiful in his long hands, and yet she had always loved it. For all those years it had lain in the safe on Strandvägen, and sometimes when she had gone to place other things in it—documents or tape recordings—she had picked it up and admired the craftsmanship and the sultry light of the stones.

At the bottom of the necklace there was a gold lemniscate, an infinity symbol comprising two perfect ellipses, and of course she knew that the piece had much to tell. It had belonged to a young woman who had been found dead in her bed after a long night partying in Stockholm, and she knew that Rekke had loved that woman and that Gabor had had something to do with her death. Still, she hadn't expected a shock of this magnitude.

"Are you alright?" she said.

It was as if Rekke were in another world. She was overcome by the impulse to grab his hands. But that wasn't why she was there, and she let him hold the necklace and mutter words she couldn't make out.

"Were you the one who gave it to her?" she said.

"What?" he said.

"Were you . . ." she repeated.

"I was young," he said.

He continued to touch the necklace, handling the pearls like a monk praying his rosary.

"The infinity symbol," she said, gently touching the gold pendant. "Were there any particular thoughts behind that?"

"Thoughts?"

"Yes."

"I don't know," he said. "Infinity fascinated me in those days. From an infinite perspective, everything that can happen does happen—even something as odd as me being alive and reflecting on it—and loving a woman with eyes so black that I almost lost my mind. I suppose I was thinking something along those lines—but I was also manic and in love. Sick, and doubly so, you might say."

"It looks incredibly expensive," she said.

"It cost as much as a house by the sea and there was something indecent about that—a recklessness that made me feel ashamed even then. It was a madness, a limitlessness that is really entirely alien to me, and now . . ."

He fell silent and hid his face in his hands. She saw no reason to ask him to continue, let alone to reply and meander on with his own philosophical reasoning, and in a way he seemed not to be talking to her but himself. Instead, she said in a professional tone:

"Professor Morovia wonders whether you have a message for him?"

The veins suddenly became prominent in Rekke's forearms and he turned toward her with shiny eyes and muttered something she didn't catch, but which she momentarily interpreted as: *Tell him I'm going to crush him.*

Though she must have misheard, because when she asked a second time he said:

"Send him my best wishes and my thanks. He has returned something to me."

"The necklace?"

"A sense of purpose, if anything," he said. "The power that makes us rise from the grave."

"I understand," she said, standing up. "I shall leave you to your thoughts. If you have anything else you wish to say to Professor Morovia, then you need only get in touch."

Rekke stood as well.

"Well," he said. "I'm simply wondering . . ."

She had difficulty looking him in the eye.

"What?" she said.

"If this was nothing more than a countermove at my invitation, or the beginning of a whole new game."

"I dare say time will tell," she said. "I am sincerely sorry if we have caused you suffering."

He took a step toward her.

"Don't be," he said. "If your gift has brought me the truth then I will gladly suffer, but I believe I must otherwise suppress my natural desire for openness."

She swallowed.

"What do you mean by that?"

"If this is indeed one of Gabor's games, then I should not reveal my moves in advance," he said. "For you are an evasive and interesting personage, Madame Kovács. You act as a friend but come bearing mortal tidings. Is that a tactic you frequently use? Caressing with a paw that conceals claws. *Ex ungue leonem*."

"I'm just acting as I must," she said, feeling that she wanted to leave quickly.

Yet she remained standing by the kitchen table while he brought out the bottle of Charlemagne he had mentioned and poured himself a glass.

"Might I offer you a glass of wine after all?" he said. "You too appear to be in need of a little pain relief, which is of course to your credit. For the guilty, there is always hope."

She averted her gaze.

"Thank you, but I must go."

"I understand," he said.

She held out her hand but then withdrew it and settled for a curt nod before making for the front door. She didn't get far—just a couple of steps. There was a crunching sound and she turned around. Blood and wine now covered Rekke's hand. The base of the glass was rolling among the shards on the floor. Rekke appeared not to have noticed.

"My God," she said.

"What?" he said indistinctly.

"Your hand," she said.

"Yes, sorry," he said, peering down at his damn fingers. "How careless of me. Glasses are so hopelessly thin these days. I must telephone them to complain. But I'll deal with it. Now run along and take some time off. I gather it is the weekend for the gainfully employed? I myself must..."

Once again she wanted to touch him, but she maintained her composure and nodded again before exiting into the stairwell. On her way down in the elevator she got it into her head that it was her hands—not Rekke's—that were bloody, but as she so often did when she doubted her task, she sought strength from the memory of Jan, her son. Then she hurried off to her car, which was parked on Riddargatan.

# TWENTY-TWO

Rebecka Wahlin opened the door and looked at Micaela searchingly, which annoyed her. What the hell's wrong with you, she wanted to snap. What are you looking at? But then she touched her lip again and understood.

"I bumped into some idiot. No big deal," she said.

She entered the apartment and went to the bookshelf and stood there without understanding what she was looking for. Rebecka Wahlin stood right beside her, clearly uncomfortable with the situation.

"You wanted to ask something else?" she said.

"What? No, not really," Micaela said, continuing to examine the bookshelf.

But no matter how long she looked, she saw only images of Lucas.

"I was wrong," she said quietly.

"About what?"

"I don't really know," she said, looking apologetically at Rebecka.

She saw that she had touched up her make-up and had put on a fresh blouse.

"Sorry, are you going out?"

"I was planning to have a drink with a girlfriend."

"I see," Micaela said, trying to regain her focus. "What you said about Claire possibly having been assaulted was interesting."

"I've no idea if it was an assault."

"But it was something? You said she looked scared."

"Well, scared and spiteful, I think. She seemed to loathe the owner of Cartaphilus."

"You don't know why?"

"Just that it goes back to her London School of Economics days. Morovia was a lecturer there and gathered a group of students around him. Claire and Alicia Kovács were among them. I think they admired him immensely before they realised that there were less savoury sides to him too."

"What kind of sides?"

"Bad ones, I'd guess. Ruthless ones."

"I see," Micaela said, surprised to be hearing this only now. "Do you know anyone else in that group that I might be able to speak to?"

"Claire mentioned a woman called Sofia from Spain."

"Not from San Sebastián perchance?"

"No, I don't think there's any connection like that, and it may be that I'm mixing things up. It might not be Spain either, but I'm fairly certain she was called Sofia."

"Isn't it a bit of a scandal that this Morovia angle hasn't been looked into more thoroughly?"

"It may have been looked into quite thoroughly."

"Just not by you at the bank?"

Rebecka shook her head.

And not by damn Lindroos either, Micaela said to herself, suddenly keen to leave. But she didn't get far before her gaze was drawn back to the bookshelf again. There was something there after all—a blue spine that called out to her.

It was the same spine that had gleamed away in her subconscious on her earlier visit, but now it was quite visible rather than just a point of irritation somewhere in her vision. She quickly pulled out the book and at first she didn't know what she was expecting. But when she saw the cover she understood, and she eagerly put her hand into her inside pocket to pull out the holiday snap—the photograph was, of course, no longer there.

And yet . . . She squinted with her full concentration at the cover, at the word *Love*, inscribed in large black letters on a blue and white background. It looked like the same *Love* visible on the woman's book in the photograph. The only difference was that Micaela could now see the whole front cover and the full title.

The book was called *Sicilian Love*. On the cover there was a slightly corpulent cartoon man with a prominent nose and curly hair wearing a long jacket or a coat. The layout implied he was the book's author rather than its fictional hero. Underneath it read: *Chess Tournament, Buenos Aires 1994*.

"What's this book about?" said Micaela.

"What . . . ?" said Rebecka. "Why are you interested in it?"

"Just tell me."

"What can I say?" Rebecka said. "I haven't read it in any great depth. It all went a bit over my head. It's by Lev Polugaevsky—the grandmaster. For many years, he was one of the best players in the world. He was a defensive master—especially the Sicilian Defence."

"Sorry," Micaela said. "I'm not much of a chess player."

"The Sicilian Defence is the best response to White's first move 1-e4. Polugaevsky was so good at it that, to celebrate his sixtieth birthday, they held a chess tournament in his honour in Buenos Aires where all openings were Sicilian. He wasn't able to participate. He was dying of a brain tumour, so I guess he didn't finish the book himself either."

"Is that something Claire would have read?"

"It was published after her death, so no. But apart from that . . . Oh yes. This book would be classic Claire."

"How so?"

"It's not just because she loved that kind of geeky nonsense—forgive me, Claire," Rebecka said, making a modest pleading gesture toward the heavens. "She often played the Sicilian opening with Black. She would have devoured it. Why do you ask?"

"Because..."

Micaela hesitated.

"Yes?"

"The woman who looks like Claire in that photo happens to have that book in her hand."

"Oh my," said Rebecka.

"Quite. But that still doesn't necessarily mean..."

Micaela looked down at her white sneakers.

"No, of course," Rebecka said slowly.

"Although the woman also had a knee injury and was wearing an elegant red coat."

"You mean it's all beginning to tip the scales?"

"Yes," she said, turning toward the front door. "I should talk to..." She cut herself short.

"I have to go," she said.

"No!" said Rebecka Wahlin. "You have to tell me what this is about. Do you really think Claire might be alive?"

"I don't know. Thank you for seeing me. Do you mind if I take the book with me?"

Rebecka Wahlin shrugged.

"Take whatever you like, as long as you let me know what you find out."

"I promise. But then you shouldn't"—she hesitated—"hide anything from me."

"I won't," Rebecka said, suddenly grave.

Micaela nodded and stepped onto the landing before quickly descending the stairs. This could only mean one thing: Claire Lidman was alive—no matter how unlikely that sounded. That was something she needed to discuss with Rekke. She suddenly saw him in a way she hadn't in a long time. What was she playing at, leaving him? He might be hopeless and depressed and a damn addict, but once he came to life—which he would have to now—there was no-one like him. Suddenly she couldn't get away quickly enough. On the street she began to run.

Everything seemed to have become urgent, and she wondered whether she should call Kaj Lindroos en route, but that moron had probably already knocked off for the weekend and would already be drunk by now. Instead, she made her way toward 2B Grevgatan, where she got into the elevator without noticing that there were traces of blood on the door handle. She was completely absorbed with staring at the book jacket and imagining everything she would say to Rekke.

# TWENTY-THREE

Axel Larsson was having dinner with the CEO of Carnegie, but he could barely focus on what the man was saying, and it wasn't just because he had effectively been inoculated against all sales patter around new flotations. He was all over the place. He had called Alicia Kovács. That was part of their old agreement: his serfdom, as he described it when he was feeling bitter.

Cartaphilus had put him back on his feet on the condition that he became the company's man, their ears in Sweden. Every rumour, every piece of gossip that might affect share prices or shine a critical light on the world of finance was to be forwarded, and he did so dutifully. But they rarely cared. Everything he sent them—even about mergers and acquisitions—was received with indifference. It was thus with hesitation that he had called. The information would probably not interest them, he had told himself, even if it was about Morovia himself.

On the contrary, as it transpired. He had delivered primed dynamite. Not that Alicia Kovács had openly said as much—she had merely listened and feigned her usual indifference—but she couldn't fool him.

She was clearly nervous, which was incomprehensible. Why should the company care about that loser Rekke? He couldn't even button up his shirt properly . . . Axel didn't get it. Yet he'd never met with a reaction like the one he'd just received for anything else he had told them, and now—he checked his mobile—she was calling again. He apologised: "I'm sorry. I have to take this."

He put the phone to his ear. "Hello," he said. There was some interference on the line and it crackled, but then she came through.

"Hello, Axel," she said. "I'm patching you through—Morovia wants to speak to you."

He froze. Morovia? He'd only spoken to him once before, and on that occasion he had hardly known what he was saying. It was ridiculous. He had been like a terrified child, and it wasn't as if he was usually a few bricks short of a load. Name the big shot he hadn't put in their place. But with Morovia it was different. In his presence, Axel was scared for real, and it was of little consolation that the same was true for many others. He had business associates who merely whispered his name, as if it were hazardous to say it too loudly.

"Well, fancy that—you turned out to be useful in the end."

The voice made him physically recoil—he stood up hastily and went outside to talk undisturbed.

"Oh right," he said. "That's good. I'm doing my best."

He didn't care if he sounded subservient. The only thing that mattered was that he got off the call unharmed and wasn't forced into doing anything.

"One of my interests in life is Professor Rekke," Morovia said.

"Really?" Axel said in surprise.

He couldn't understand how the man he had met deserved such attention.

"Indeed. One might regard it as a lifelong passion. Did you get any impression of what he wanted?"

"He wants to contact you. I think . . ." He hesitated before saying it, but then he felt an unexpected surge of bloodlust.

"He wants to take you down. He called you his enemy."

Morovia laughed.

"Was he that explicit? He tends to have a penchant for euphemism and Latin quotations."

"He mentioned Claire Lidman."

"I gather he's interested in her—I've already heard whispers to that effect."

"It felt like he was implying"—Axel Larsson hesitated—"that we did something to Claire."

Morovia was silent for a moment.

"I see," he then said. "Well, I'm sure the circumstances will become clearer to him soon."

Axel didn't understand which *circumstances* Morovia was referring to, but he didn't dare ask.

He limited himself to saying, "I suppose so."

"Quite, quite," Morovia said, as if talking to himself. "It's impossible to keep secrets from Rekke. That's one of the challenges with him. He sees right through them. Never gives in until he finds the innermost core. But as I said, Axel, it's excellent that you were finally able to provide some quality information. You take care of yourself."

Axel stiffened, afraid that he was being threatened. But when they rang off shortly afterward, he decided to regard it as a gesture of friendship, a sign that Morovia cared. They were obviously on the same side now—him and Morovia against those fucking Rekkes. He was in slightly higher spirits when he returned to the table.

When no-one responded to the doorbell, Micaela opened the unlocked door and went inside calling "Hans! Hans!" as she made her way to the kitchen. Mrs. Hansson had clearly dropped by. Everything had been cleaned and wiped down. One of the chairs, however, was carelessly tilted against the draining board—as if someone had stood up quickly or pushed it away. On the kitchen table she spotted an open wine bottle and half a glass of water. The red tablecloth was crumpled, and standing by the sink under the spice rack was a large bottle of mineral water. Next to that was a partly unravelled kitchen roll. Micaela took a few steps toward the cooker with its large metallic hood. Something crunched underfoot. It sounded alarming—as if she had stepped on something valuable.

It was a thin, fine shard from a wine glass. Crouching on the floor, she looked around and spotted bloodstains on the parquet. For a short while she stayed there, thinking. Then she rushed around the apartment searching everywhere, but Rekke wasn't there, so she called him.

His phone was buzzing somewhere inside the flat. She turned everything upside down and eventually found it under a sofa cushion in the living room, noticing at the same time that there was blood on the keys of the grand piano. Once again, she cursed herself for abandoning him. How could she have been so selfish? It was just that . . . he drove her crazy. What had happened?

She phoned Mrs. Hansson but she didn't know where he was either. Micaela hung up and went out, heading toward Djurgården—he liked to tear about the place whenever he was upset. There were lots of people out and about—it was a Friday night and all of them were merry—and down by the quay next to the bridge she spotted even more graduates with their white caps and their beaming faces.

She searched everywhere, but Rekke was nowhere to be seen. He was usually easy to spot in crowds, not least because of his height. Often it felt like he was walking at a different pace from everyone else, as if he were a misplaced character in a world where everyone but him was on their way somewhere. But now he was gone, and she was becoming increasingly anxious. Had he been abducted? Might Hugo's and Lucas's shitty henchmen have hurt him? No, she told herself. Dial it down. It's just a broken wine glass. She remembered that earlier she had been keen to have a beer with Jonas Beijer, her old colleague from Solna. Maybe she should discuss this with him?

She dialled and he picked up after one ring. Only briefly did she reflect that until very recently his cheerful opening line would have made her happy.

"Hello, my friend! It's been a long time. I've missed you."

She considered saying a few kind words in return but opted to cut to the chase.

"I'm worried something might have happened to Rekke."

This statement seemed to bother Jonas. Of course, he was just like the others. He felt threatened by her friendship with Rekke. It was as if they all believed that mere proximity to him would remove her from the ordinary world to which they themselves belonged.

"He's missing and there's blood on the floor," she said.

"You think we need to raise the alarm?"

"I don't know," she said, and she really didn't know, but a moment later she had something else to think about.

She had turned down Museistigen and reached the wooded area that led to Nobelgatan, and in the distance on a bench by the water she saw him. He was slumped there with his face in his hands.

"Maybe it's okay after all," she said to Jonas. "I'll call you back."

"Wait!" she heard him say before she ended the call and picked up her pace.

Rekke wore jeans and a battered old pair of Church's that Mrs. Hansson must have polished up for him, along with a black shirt that was hanging loosely outside his waistband. His hair was dishevelled and his face pale, and lying in his lap there was something that looked like a pearl necklace. Even though she was now very close, he hadn't looked up.

"I recognise those steps," was all he said.

"My old hip injury again?"

"No," he said. "It's the force and the rhythm—punctuated eighths."

She smiled cautiously—his voice was husky and agitated, but there was a playfulness to his words, at least, a touch of the good humour of his better days.

"Wasn't my pace different last time?"

"Your temperament affects it—the worries on your mind. You've been in the kitchen, I take it?"

"What makes you say that?"

"I thought . . ."

He removed his hands from his face. There were bloodstains on his cheek. She guessed they came from his right hand, which was bleeding. His eyes were anxious, but more alert now.

". . . that it sounded like you have a shard of glass in your left shoe," he said.

She lifted her foot and looked. She was unable to detect any glass.

"Doesn't seem like it," she said.

"I must have been imagining it."

"But I was there. What happened?"

He looked at her and wiped his cheek with a clumsy movement. Out on the water, a white swan glided past, seeming in that instant ominous in its majesty, as if it were part of a threat looming above them.

"I was just floored for a moment," Rekke said, smiling amiably as if he preferred not to trouble her with the details.

She felt a wave of unexpected tenderness and wanted to put an arm around him to make up for all the stupid things she'd thought.

"How's that then?" she asked.

He scrutinised her face.

"What's happened to *you*?" he said, countering her. Now it seemed as if it were he who wanted to reach out, but he didn't follow through either.

"Nothing," she said.

"No, of course not, my Spartan friend."

"Don't be silly. Now tell me: why were you floored?"

He held up the necklace, which glittered in the evening light. It was almost shockingly beautiful, but there was also something ill-fated about it.

"Once upon a time, long ago, I bought this necklace in a boutique on the Champs-Élysées in Paris," he said. "It was much too expensive and extravagant, but I was in a fit of mania, and that evening I hung it around the neck of a young woman with narrow shoulders and black eyes. I can still picture the scene. I already knew that she was nothing but trouble, but my love for her was blind and perhaps trouble was what I wanted back then."

"I was just saying something like that about me to my own mother."

"Were you?"

"But that's another story. Continue," said Micaela.

"The woman was named Ida Aminoff. She sang like an angel and wrote poetry that seemed to wrench my heart out of my chest, but she was also an abuser of amphetamines and alcohol and sedatives, and she was always eager to take me onto rooftops and balustrades, which scared me witless. But perhaps . . ."

"Was that attractive to you too?"

"Yes, unfortunately so. I suppose in a way I was prepared for the fact that something dreadful might happen to her, and I should have done more to help her. But if I'm honest . . . I simply couldn't at that time. I myself was drawn into her wake. She chaperoned me into my lifelong addiction." He pulled a blister pack of pills out of his trouser pocket as evidence of sorts. "But she was also the one who made me want to embrace life and finally start living."

"You were in love."

"Oh yes, head over heels crazy. I couldn't live without Ida, and I persuaded her to come on tour with me around Europe. She occasionally popped off on her own. When I played in Helsinki—her home city—she was in Stockholm to avoid running into her Finnish relatives who came to hear me play, and I missed her as much as if I had lost my own arm. I couldn't sleep that night. I kept reaching out for her with my hand as I tossed and turned in bed. There was a society wedding in Stockholm—a big wedding in a house right here on Djurgården. Everyone I knew was there. Ida called me in the middle of the party and said she was so sick of all the stupid speeches and the conceited fools that she wanted to do something scandalous. I told her to leave. 'I love you,' I said. 'I love you so much it scares me,' she replied. 'I almost feel like destroying it.'"

"What did she mean by that?"

"More or less what she said, I should say. She was always razing to the ground whatever she had achieved or gained. I had only bought this because she had thrown a diamond necklace given to her by her grandmother into the Seine. She constantly wanted to destroy and demolish—especially things that threatened to make her happy—and I had misgivings. In the morning, I couldn't get hold of her, and I called everyone she was close to. In the end her father picked up and said she was dead. She'd been found lifeless in his pied-à-terre on Torstenssonsgatan in Östermalm, and I went to pieces. I was on the brink of ending it all myself. But that's another story, as you would say."

"So I've gathered."

"Most evidence suggests she overdosed, which is also what the police investigation concluded. But there were suspicious circumstances. A small mark on her throat where her necklace had been, for instance."

"So she wasn't wearing it?"

"No, it was missing, and I suppose it was obvious someone had stolen it from her. But the wretched fools at the police—and I, the even bigger fool—believed she had thrown it away or shamelessly sold it for pennies just to be provocative. There was a witness statement to support that hypothesis. She had allegedly threatened to throw the necklace into the bay, and although I should have dismissed it—there were doubts about the statement—I accepted it. After all, it effectively confirmed my self-image."

"How so?"

"It was all so unfathomable that I got it into my head that she had not only died but also abandoned me in some more specific sense."

"Destroyed your love, like she said."

"Something like that, and I'm sure that contributed to the fact that I couldn't see as clearly as I should have," he said. "I just ran away from it. But now . . ."

"You've got the necklace back."

"Yes," he said.

"And that makes it even less likely she threw it into the sea."

He nodded and lowered his head, seemingly completely broken.

However, it only lasted a couple of seconds. When he raised his gaze, he seemed to be radiating determination.

"Do you think she was killed?"

"I do," he said, "and I'm fairly certain that the person who gave me the necklace wants me to think that too."

"Who are you talking about?"

"His name is Gabor Morovia. He owns and runs the company you mentioned—Cartaphilus."

Her body tensed.

"Are you serious?"

"Alas yes, I reacted when you mentioned it on the telephone, but I . . ."

He fell silent and ran his fingers over the necklace.

". . . doubted every truth you formulated," she said.

"Did I?"

"Yes, even your conclusion about the woman's knee injury in the picture."

"You mean I was right?"

"Answer me first. Why did you retract it?"

"I became convinced that Samuel Lidman had given a hint about that injury in his initial account. I believed that rather than having examined the photograph without prejudice, I had found what I was subconsciously looking for."

Micaela paused for thought. She examined her left sole again and found a truly tiny shard of glass, and while she wasn't certain that it came from Rekke's kitchen, she presented it as if it were a major discovery.

"See. You're right more often than you'd like to believe."

"Perhaps sometimes," he said, losing himself in thought, and it might have been wise to have let him finish talking about the necklace and Morovia, but she desperately wanted to talk about her own lead.

"I think it's definitely Claire Lidman in the photo."

"Risen from the dead."

"The book the woman is holding in her hand in the photo—the one that looks like a romance novel—was actually this," she said, handing over the book on chess.

He stared at it for a while.

"Lev Polugaevsky," he muttered. "I met him once in Prague, but I was never quite as interested in chess as people seemed to believe. I was always more fascinated by life away from the board. Why should this book make the woman Claire Lidman?"

"She was a passionate player and often played the Sicilian opening."

"I see," he said. "That's somewhat intriguing. You don't happen to have the picture with you?"

She hesitated for a second. "No," she said.

"No?"

He looked disappointed and she silently cursed Kaj Lindroos again.

"But this Gabor Morovia guy apparently met Claire and scared her," she said. "He might also have sexually assaulted her. It feels like he must have something to do with her disappearance."

Rekke looked at her anxiously, as if it were she rather than Claire who had met Morovia.

"Goodness," he said, becoming still. A minute or so elapsed—it was hard to tell.

Micaela lost herself in thought too. Then Rekke stood up, looking a little unsteady and just as pale as before. Nevertheless, he now seemed purposeful, and it sounded as if he were muttering *Claritas, claritas*, although she might have misheard.

There was hardly any clarity to be had here, but he was up to something and she stood up too and asked whether they should walk home to Grevgatan. He didn't seem to hear, instead standing there quite still with his gaze directed at the water.

"A thought occurs to me," he said. "Two thoughts, actually," he added, which made her smile—she couldn't help it.

She had missed those words, and she needed to hear them. It was as if a light that had gone out inside her had been lit again. She linked arms with Rekke and together they began to stroll toward Grevgatan just as the sun set over the city.

# TWENTY-FOUR

Julia turned onto Fredrikshovsgatan, just managing to avoid the uber-ambitious and uber-good-looking Lydia, who had recently got into Yale, which was something, she supposed.

She definitely wasn't up for meeting the old gang. She was done with their stupid fixation with status and all their bullshit about their amazing holidays and the parties they were going to over the summer. She loved a man who was above all that kind of stuff, and *he* loved her. He said so over and over, and she saw it in his eyes and felt it in his touch. It was just that . . . Why did he keep running off?

Like earlier, for example. He'd been just so wonderful but then a text had arrived on his phone and he'd said he had to go. That he needed to sort something out. He'd be back soon. Then he'd dressed without looking at her even once, as if he'd suddenly forgotten her. He left in his wake a void that she wasn't ready for, and she found herself sucked back into her old destructive thoughts.

She wasn't going to make anything of herself—she wouldn't stand a chance against all those Lydias. She lacked ambition and talent, and hadn't he hesitated when she'd asked if she was thin enough? She was increasingly sure of it, which was why she had gone out for a walk.

She wanted to burn off some calories and regain control—and it had helped.

But now, as she was approaching her flat on Karlaplan, the feelings of anxiety and unease returned. There was something else about him too, but she couldn't put her finger on it. It was as if he sometimes became someone else, someone who wasn't all kind and understanding but looked at her as if she were a thing rather than a person. She thought again of his back and the feeling it had given her, and she got it into her head that he hurt people. Reluctantly, she entered the door to her stairwell and got into the elevator to go up. I'm imagining it, she thought to herself. But she couldn't shake it off, and she thought about her own nails that might or might not have scratched that back. She shuddered and closed her eyes. When she opened them again, she had reached her floor and she looked around, disoriented. A second later she recoiled in fright. A shadow was moving toward her, and that shadow was holding something: a gun, she thought. A weapon.

When Rekke went into the living room and sat down on the sofa with a tea towel wrapped around his hand, Micaela remembered the first time she had met him. That had been a summer's day too. She and the rest of the detectives on the investigation—all the guys—had gone out to the big house in Djursholm where Rekke lived at the time to seek help with cracking a murder suspect during questioning.

But nothing had turned out as they had expected. Instead of a confession, they had been on the receiving end of a staggering evisceration and not long afterward the suspect had been released. It had been downright humiliating. Not that Rekke was unpleasant or even arrogant. He was just . . . better. Not only richer and more sophisticated, but smarter too.

Driving back afterward, the suppressed rage and jealousy had been almost palpable, and she had certainly not been free of those emotions either. It was as if Rekke and his very existence had reminded them all of what they lacked. Yet that was why she was here with him now; other forces had been awakened in her, such as the desire for the kind of clarity that characterised Rekke's observations.

She had picked up the scent of something that day, something she hadn't known she needed, and whenever people had expressed themselves stupidly or with logical shortcomings in the months that followed, she had often fantasised about what Rekke would have said. In that respect he was always present in her thoughts while remaining as unattainable as royalty.

Then—well, how to put it? Then the whole world had fallen on her head. She had seen him at a Tunnelbana station just as he was about to hurl himself in front of a train. A better person than she would surely have felt sympathy and pity for him. She had merely been furious that he—who had it all—wanted to end his life, and she had scolded him accordingly.

She had scolded the man she had never thought she could get close to, and ever since then she had oscillated between disappointment and admiration. She looked at him slumped on the sofa twitching his left leg nervously. He was worn out and a little dazed, but his eyes were shining. Outside on Strandvägen she could hear the buzz of Friday night.

"What were these thoughts that occurred to you?" she said.

Rekke gazed toward the studio-loft window.

"I was thinking of my old friend Herman Camphausen."

"Why him in particular?"

"Can I offer you something?" he said. "To make up for my hopelessness, or simply to celebrate that we are here again talking about an old investigation?"

She smiled. "Why not?"

"Then let us start with some white wine—I never did get around to drinking it," he said, waving his wrapped hand around. "Then we'll have a bite to eat."

"Sounds good," she said, watching him disappear off to the kitchen and return with the bottle she had seen on the table in there.

"It's no longer suitably chilled. I hope it will do nonetheless."

She held out her hands as if to say she couldn't care less.

"Herman and I knew each other as children," Rekke said. "Herman was a classical guitarist, but he was a bookworm too. A bibliophile and a collector—often historical works. Like me, Herman had met Gabor Morovia and been impressed. After all, no-one was progressing as quickly through the school system."

"So you both knew him," Micaela said.

"Regrettably so," Rekke said. "In poor Herman's case, it led to one of his finest books, a first edition of Gibbon's *The History of the Decline and Fall of the Roman Empire*—it's from the eighteenth century, you see, leather-bound in six volumes, costs a fortune and was as dear to him as his close friends—disappearing one day before turning up burned to a crisp outside the family home. *That* united us. We had a common enemy."

"So you had already been on the receiving end of Morovia's attentions by then?"

"I had. My cat, Ahasuerus . . ."

She tensed.

"You had a cat named Ahasuerus?"

"Indeed, yes. It was somewhat precocious and ridiculous, I agree. But that doesn't really matter anymore. What I was going to say was that Herman and I lost contact and only saw each other again much later on, at a reception hosted by the French embassy in Vienna. Herman was so bad at answering my questions about his life that I realised he must have become an intelligence officer, and I believe he eventually accepted that I knew things I should not. This was ten years ago or more. Russia was our new best friend and we all seemed to be falling into the reassuring embrace of liberal democracy, and I was a little curious about what he and all the other spies were going to do now that the Cold War was over. Would they all end up writing thrillers or going into consultancy? He replied—I remember this well—that Russia might have moved closer to the West, but that there was still much that was intact from the Communist era. The KGB was still around, even if they had changed a few letters in their name, and there was nothing to indicate that the organisation had become any kinder or more human. On the contrary, a marriage was taking place with the world of organised crime, and in that context he mentioned Gabor Morovia."

"In what way?" she said.

"He said Gabor was too close to Russian intelligence, especially the St. Petersburg office, and that he was helping to loot the country and hide assets in Switzerland and London. I suppose I must have been in a combative mood, because I said, 'Well, put him away then.' But all Herman did was squirm. I think he was embarrassed."

"For what reason?"

"Lack of success. He said that taking Morovia down was difficult. It was impossible to get people to testify. No-one dared to come forward, and those that did either disappeared or were murdered. Herman had made extensive use of witness-protection schemes, but that hadn't worked either. Those with close ties to the secret police usually spot the chinks in the armour of these programmes, but he said he was doing everything he could to improve the safety of those who dared to speak out. He said he was thinking creatively."

"Okay . . ." Micaela said thoughtfully.

"And those were the words that came back to me just now while we were sitting on that bench. They whispered something to me."

She looked intently at Rekke.

"What did they whisper?"

He topped up their wine glasses.

"That there may be an explanation for the peculiar supposition that Claire Lidman has risen from the dead to stride through a holiday snap clutching a book on chess."

"And what might that be?"

"Perhaps Claire Lidman knew something crucial about Morovia. Perhaps she was under serious threat and was offered a new, protected identity?"

"With the cover of being dead?"

"Yes, my thoughts are along those lines. The police—possibly with the assistance of the intelligence services—saw their chance when a number of burned bodies turned up, to give her the best protection there is. I'm aware of a couple of similar cases in the U.S. and Italy. But of course . . ." He sipped his wine, looking somewhat melancholic. "It's not an ideal solution to the problem. Especially not for Samuel," he said.

"What do you mean by that?"

"That kind of protection is normally offered to spouses too. You don't split them up unless there are special circumstances, or the exposed party has clear wishes in that regard."

"Such as Claire not wanting to bring Samuel with her to her new life?"

"I really would like to take a look at that photograph," he said, taking another mouthful of wine.

For the thousandth time, Micaela cursed Lindroos and wondered what he had seen in the photo.

Kaj Lindroos had made up his mind: he hadn't seen jack shit. He had just been out of sorts and pissed off with that stroppy Latina and had started seeing ghosts all over the shop. On his way home from work, he'd thought he'd caught a glimpse of a guy he'd arrested in a serious fraud case a few years back but who had gotten out pretty quickly due to lack of evidence and threatened to sue him. The whole city was full of shadows and phantoms. Without even glancing at the post on the doormat, he went over to the fridge and helped himself to a Heineken, but it was too insubstantial. He needed booze and so he settled on vodka instead—neat vodka, in an homage to Russian wartime strategy—without bothering to waste time on a glass. He grabbed the bottle and went to his study, where he thought he might call someone—a woman, preferably, ideally an old flame who was a little rough around the edges and not too sentimental, and who would help him to forget about all this crap. But curiosity and apprehension gained the upper hand, and he began to go through his desk drawers.

Tucked under a couple of insurance documents he found two photographs of Claire that he really should have returned to Samuel long ago, but there had been so many in circulation that he'd managed to hang on to them without any issues—and it hadn't been for strictly professional reasons, if he was honest. He was slightly bewitched by them—especially the one of Claire sitting on a white garden bench wearing a black polka dot cotton dress pulled up over her legs. Sometimes, when he wanted to unwind, he took the photo with him to bed and undid his trousers. He was only human, which was why he knew her face and body inside out, and also why he didn't think Samuel deserved her.

But just a second . . . Would he really dare to compare them? Fuck it—why the hell not? It was nothing. It couldn't be real. He pulled out the holiday snap from St. Mark's Square that he'd brought home from work and laid it on the desk next to the picture of Claire in the black polka dot dress and took a big slug of vodka. Let's see, he muttered to himself.

The first feeling that struck him was relief. The holiday snap was worse quality than he remembered. It wasn't fully in focus and there was nothing to suggest it might be Claire—nothing at all—except for that eerie feeling that had come over him again. So he drank some more and looked again, hoping to confirm that it was a completely different person. The woman in the photo, however, seemed to resemble Claire more and more, and in the end he did something he never could fully explain, even if it was mostly out of guilt—guilt over not handling the investigation as he should have.

He tore up the photograph—not just in half but into ten or twenty tiny pieces—but that didn't make the feelings disappear. Once again, he fell to thinking about Comisario Antonio Rivera and Claire's mother and sister at the mortuary in San Sebastián—about the sense of urgency and the suffocating, sweet stench of the body that broke down his resistance and drove him out of the building against his instincts as a police officer. He should have looked more closely. He should have done all sorts of things. He toyed anxiously with his mobile and wondered whether to get in touch with forensics. Surely they had expertise in this kind of thing. But he could hardly hand them a ripped-up photograph, and he really didn't feel like calling Comisario Rivera, and the mother was dead.

But the sister, Linda, with her G-cup boobs or whatever they'd been . . . Should he contact her? She lived in Stockholm nowadays. Why not? He just needed to drink a little more first and daydream a bit. What if he travelled to Venice for a bit of a break and to search for Claire? Who knew? Perhaps she'd be sitting in some hotel lobby when he came down one evening to order a dry martini. Maybe then they'd . . . He snorted, splattering some saliva and vodka onto the desk. That was enough James Bond stuff for one evening. Bottoms up, he said to himself as he took another slug and then dialled the sister's number. He was perhaps not entirely sober. On the other hand, he was a pro when it came to concealing that kind of thing.

"I'm sorry to bother you on a Friday evening. This is Inspector Lindroos," he said, awarding himself a promotion for some reason.

"Hello, Kaj," said the sister. "It's been a while. Has something happened?"

"No, no," he said. "Well, yes, actually. A recent photograph has been passed to us and it seems as if Claire might be—although of course it probably isn't her—visible in the background. That's why I'd like to know—"

"Are you joking?" she interrupted.

"Absolutely not," he said. "But I often think back to the identification in San Sebastián, and sometimes I wonder if you were keeping something from me."

"My God, have you been drinking?"

"Not really," he said.

"What kind of picture are you talking about?"

"It's just a regular holiday snap," he said, vainly attempting to put the torn pieces back together.

"And how in God's name would we have been able to keep anything from you? She's dead, Kaj. *Dead*. You and I both saw her, and I can't wrap my head around why you're calling me to rake this all up on a Friday night," she said, sounding upset, but there was something else there too, perhaps. He thought she sounded afraid—she wasn't just pissed off with a drunk cop, she was scared, and he sensed that her fear was doing the talking.

He had been deceived, although he had no idea what to do with that information except to empty the vodka bottle and resolve not to make any other stupid calls. Perhaps he should offer a few words to smooth things over with the sister. He really would be in the shit if she rang up Lars Hellner or one of his superiors.

"I'm sorry if I came over a bit abruptly. I've always liked you, Linda. You wouldn't by any chance feel like a drink to talk it over, would you? Like you said, it *is* Friday night."

He heard the click as she hung up and he kicked the desk, making the vodka bottle fall to the floor.

# TWENTY-FIVE

Had Claire been assaulted during her late-night meeting with the Hungarian investment company?

Samuel was furious at the mere thought of it. No-one had been able to read Claire like he could. He would never have missed something like that. It was true that she had come back in a state that night, but she had described in detail how she had fallen off her bike, and according to the cops there had been witnesses too. It was an accident—nothing more. He was certain of it. Well, almost certain. But then again ... he'd not looked into it *that* closely.

She'd left him without any explanation, so of course there had been goddamn loads he'd never understood, and sometimes he suspected that Claire had had something going on with the guy who owned that company, or at least that she'd had some kind of history with him. She'd radiated a kind of excitement prior to the meeting that had been difficult to interpret, and no matter how hard he pushed she wouldn't say anything about the guy. "Sweetie, I can't," was all she said. "I can't."

She was worryingly quiet and withdrawn. There was no getting away from it, and he hadn't got much more out of Lindroos after the fact, either. All the cop had said was that the proprietor had been looked into, questioned and ruled out, and while Samuel hadn't been satisfied with that he hadn't given it the attention it deserved.

The only thing he had done was contact a woman in Stockholm who worked for the company—something or other Kovács, if he remembered correctly. But she had been so kind and sympathetic that he'd been bowled over, especially when the woman had gotten in touch later to say she'd missed him at the funeral. "So you were there?" he'd asked. "Of course, Claire assisted us with a most elegant solution," the woman had said, adding many other superlatives along the way. Just how was it he'd got hold of her again? He couldn't remember, but Rebecka Wahlin—Claire's old colleague—would know, wouldn't she? He could contact her and get a number. He had to do something. He couldn't just sit there. He got up, pulled out his phone and made the call.

The shadow moved toward Julia and now she saw him—he really was holding something, and she took a few steps back in horror before realising it was flowers.

"Baby girl! Sorry I had to run off. I'm never going to leave you again," he said, with a dazzling smile.

She could barely believe it as she went into his embrace. *Flowers.* How incredibly considerate. He must have known that she was worried and dropped into a florist. No-one else she knew would do something like that. The whole world disappeared in his presence. She looked at the flowers and then up at him and had the same feeling as so often before.

"They're beautiful," she said.

"You should be given flowers every day," he said.

She kissed him, opened the front door and went to the kitchen to get a blue vase to put them in. He followed and pressed his body against her. He smelled of aftershave and something else with a little more bite. Man, she thought to herself. *Man.* She turned around and put her arms around his back—the same back that had prompted all those strange thoughts a little earlier—and slightly to her own surprise she said:

"Be rough with me."

She regretted it immediately, not that she hadn't meant it. The temptation had come from his body and his scent, an unexpected and contradictory force, but she was embarrassed to have exposed herself. He looked at her questioningly.

"Seriously?" he said.

She nodded boldly, glimpsing something new on his face. His eyes were suddenly empty, and he grasped her wrists so tightly that her hands went white. Not long after that, he was on top of her in bed, and though she had brief moments of panic, she shuddered with excitement—or at least, she told herself she did. Afterward, when she had cried out as much in pain as in lust, she wanted to get all the stupid thoughts she'd got from her father or had thought herself off her chest—all that nonsense that had only cropped up because she'd felt abandoned and like a failure.

"Pappa thinks you're bad for me."

He looked concerned for a moment. Then he said:

"Isn't that what all dads think? No-one is good enough for their little girl."

She could feel her wrists hurting.

"Yes, but he has these other ideas too. He spots some tiny detail on a body and draws planet-sized conclusions."

"Quite the detective then," he said, grinning.

"Definitely. People think he's, like, the smartest guy in the world because he's always doing that. But I promise you that in reality he doesn't understand anything. He'll say the dumbest things," she said, and he was listening to her in exactly the way she loved, and it gave her even more self-confidence.

She told him about Pappa's depression and his pill addiction, and he stroked her hair and neck and told her his dad had been the same: hunched over books and generally weak and worthless. But he'd dealt with it, he said, and she was struck by the fact that he'd had similar experiences, when she'd thought he came from a completely different world.

She spent the whole evening talking as if she were crafting a new life story for herself: a narrative in which her father was no longer the hero and she had slowly freed herself before ending up here with *him*, with Lucas, who was going to protect her from all the bad things.

Alicia Kovács slammed the car door shut and walked toward her house on Lidingö. Yet another day of mourning, and that was probably why she had been so enchanted when Rekke had played with such beauty that it would have reduced an angel to tears. He had resurrected a world lost to her, but she shouldn't have allowed herself to be seduced. She must not soften.

Rain had begun to fall. There was a wind coming off the sea as she disarmed the security alarm and went inside her large, detached house. She was occasionally still astounded by the luxury she was immersed in: any one of those paintings on the wall was worth more than her mother had earned in her whole life. None of the furniture lacked class—in fact, none of it was available to buy in any ordinary shop. But then again, as she often told herself, she'd had to pay with her soul.

She took off her jacket and high heels, went into the kitchen and took a bottle of white wine out of the chiller—not dissimilar to the one Rekke had offered her. She settled on the sofa that afforded her views of the garden and the pool as she downed her first glass.

She pictured the professor: his piercing blue eyes and long, small-boned hands. Rekke was simultaneously like Gabor and also his antithesis. He was perhaps even the very kind of person that Alicia had hoped Gabor would become—a thoughtful, sensitive intellectual who was able to grieve and didn't just strike back and avenge his disappointments.

Alicia knew better than anyone that Gabor had been abandoned by his mother as a young boy, losing all the privileges he had taken for granted. She knew Gabor believed the Rekkes to be responsible for his misfortunes, and that no penance could redress that injustice. She knew that since then it had been essential for him to be the smartest person in the room, and she also knew that the only person who posed any serious threat to him in that respect was Hans Rekke. She realised that Gabor both hated and admired him for it, but what she didn't know, which troubled her, was what he really wanted to do with him. That he had waited so long to hand over the necklace was surely a good sign. He wasn't always merciless. Sometimes he merely toyed with his enemies, and if she were honest, surely he would mourn Rekke if he wasn't there as a challenge to be savoured. If he didn't have someone he not only wanted to destroy but also to conquer intellectually.

Gabor had stepped into Alicia's life in the early eighties, bewitching her with his charm and acumen. There had been three of them back then—all young women, all shining lights in class, all loyal in the way that good girls often are to their teachers and mentors. They had barely noticed as the boundaries had shifted and they had eventually found themselves in a reality that should have been alien to them—although they soon got used to it, or at least *she* did. She even learned to love the game itself. Then again . . . what choice did she have? She was the one who had fallen pregnant; she was the winner. Well . . . The telephone rang.

She let it ring out while massaging her feet and downing another glass of wine. Far away outside a train was passing, and she was tempted to put on a CD—perhaps something by Liszt. *Liebesträume*—she had always loved it. The telephone rang again, and this time she picked up. It might be Gabor, but . . . No. Good God. Of all the old ghosts out there, it was Samuel Lidman. That could hardly be a coincidence. It had to be part of what had been brought to life by Rekke's inquiries.

"Good evening," she said. "It's been a long time, Samuel. How are you keeping these days?"

"Rebecka Wahlin gave me your number," he said hastily.

"Do give her my best."

"I will," he said. "But I also found out other things. Apparently, you already knew Claire."

She realised she had to be on her guard.

"That's right," she said. "It's a small world. We were in the same cohort at the London School of Economics."

"Were you friends?"

"I should say so," she said. "But it was no mean feat getting her to let her hair down. She was very ambitious on all levels—always putting in extra hours."

"But you must have spent some time together, right?"

"We went running a few times, and on one occasion I went with her to see a doctor. Her knee had started to give her real grief. Well, you know how it was for her."

"So you didn't play chess?"

He's after something, she thought to herself, but she couldn't understand what and she made sure to laugh in gentle amusement.

"Goodness gracious no, I wouldn't have dared. She was a master."

Not that she stood a chance against Gabor.

"Why do you ask?" she added.

"Because . . ."

Then Samuel said something so incomprehensible that she was barely able to take it in.

"I beg your pardon?" she said.

"The coffin they buried must have contained somebody else's corpse."

"What are you talking about?"

"Claire's alive. I've got proof."

She felt cold all over.

"I'm afraid you've lost me."

"But it's true," he said. "And she still plays chess and she's still working on the Sicilian Defence."

"Sicilian . . ." she managed to stutter before she swiftly regained her composure, an unpleasant memory coming to mind.

She did her best to filter her thoughts as Samuel told her about some strange holiday snap that had turned up, and as he did she thought about Gabor and what he had said over and over again at the time: *I don't like the way she died, nor the timing of the accident.*

"And you really think it's Claire in the photo?" she said.

"I'm certain of it," he said.

Absolute rot, she thought to herself. Samuel Lidman was known to have been driven mad by grief. Yet she felt increasingly uneasy—it seemed Gabor wasn't the only one to think the death was suspicious and far too convenient. She had herself speculated that the police might have staged Claire's death and used her to get to their organisation, but when nothing had happened with the passing of the years, her misgivings had waned. Then again, Gabor might know more—he might have kept things from her, just like the women he saw behind her back.

"Do you think I could take a look at that picture?" she said.

"Absolutely," Samuel Lidman said, sounding uncertain again, which reassured her a little, though she didn't intend to take any risks.

"Why don't you pop into our offices on Strandvägen tomorrow at nine o'clock?"

"Okay, that's great," he said, sounding almost hopeful.

She poured another glass of wine. If he's right, what a poor devil. What a poor, wretched devil.

# TWENTY-SIX

While they ate a late supper that Mrs. Hansson had cooked for them—butter-fried cod, new potatoes and ratatouille—Micaela outlined everything she knew about the case, while Rekke mostly sat and listened. Afterward, he stood up and paced restlessly back and forth across the kitchen.

"If I'm right..." he said.

"If Claire Lidman really has taken on a new identity?"

"Yes. Do you think Lindroos knows?"

"Surely not," she said.

He looked at her.

"What makes you say that?"

"I get the impression the investigation makes him feel touchy and inferior. He'd never be that bitter if he was in on a big secret."

"That seems a sensible deduction to me," he said. "But isn't it still a little peculiar that he kept the photo?"

"It was idiotic of me not to demand it back."

"Did he recognise her and get scared?"

"First and foremost, he's vain. He's nervous about *anything* that will put him in a bad light."

"So we can assume he's a little worried."

She nodded, suddenly realising that they were now talking about Claire Lidman as if she were definitely alive.

"Do you really believe it's her?" she asked.

Rekke stopped his penitential journey around the kitchen floor and looked at her.

"I believe in it as a hypothesis that merits examination, but you are naturally right that I have my own reasons for engaging with the matter."

"You have the necklace."

"Yes, indeed I do," he said. "On the other hand, what I'm wondering is . . ." He looked at her anxiously. "What is your role in all this?"

"My role?"

"You can't start playing games with Morovia just like that. He's genuinely dangerous."

"I'll cope," she said.

Rekke looked tense.

"Better than most, but that may not necessarily be enough. I want to keep you out of this."

Micaela considered whether to tell him about Lucas and Hugo and explain that she already had quite enough entanglements as it was, but she saw no reason to burden him with it. That was another story. It was her life.

"I saw Julia," she said.

He focused on her.

"She's met someone new," she said.

"Did she say who?"

"I got the feeling it was someone a bit grittier—someone from my neck of the woods, not yours," she said.

"That might not be far off the mark," he said.

"Yeah, it might not be," she said, somehow hurt, but then she thought about her own feelings of disorientation in both Husby and Östermalm.

"But that doesn't make things any easier," she added.

"She's lost weight," he said. "That worries me."

"It's not that bad," she said, not entirely truthfully, at which point he looked toward the window and seemed to want to say more, but stayed silent. She let him be for a while.

When he still said nothing, she asked:

"How do we proceed with Claire Lidman?"

Rekke sat down at the kitchen table again.

"I think we should leave her alone. Anyway, Micaela, aren't you supposed to be on holiday? Go away. Clear your head."

She shook her head.

"I'm staying," she said.

He paused for thought.

"In that case, I still think we should leave her alone."

"What makes you say that?"

"A woman who doesn't want to be found shouldn't be troubled unnecessarily."

"That's true," she said.

"And even if we were tempted, it wouldn't be easy. If she had been seen somewhere else we might have assumed she lived nearby, but in Venice..."

"Everyone's a tourist."

"She might just as well live in Japan as in Italy."

"But wouldn't it be at least a little bit exciting to give it a try?" Micaela smiled at the thought.

"Anyway, there's one thing about that photo that's come back to me," he said.

"What?" she said.

"Do you remember the slight twist in the woman's neck? One had the impression that the pupils were turning to the left, as if she was about to look over her shoulder."

"What do you think that might mean?"

"That she had someone with her. Perhaps she was checking whether her companions were keeping up. She seemed to be walking fast."

"Interesting point," she said.

"Perhaps."

"Then there's the question of whether your witness-protection theory stacks up," she said. "What could she have known about Morovia that would make her a person of interest to the police and intelligence services?"

Rekke moved his chair a little closer.

"I dare say they already knew each other," he said.

"What makes you say that?"

"Didn't you say that Claire was at the London School of Economics in the early 1980s?"

She nodded.

"I don't know as much about Morovia as I should," he said. "He's peculiarly absent online—I imagine he has people cleaning up after him all over the internet. He's very cautious and secretive, and I haven't gone exploring with the requisite energy, but I know that he was lecturing at the LSE at that particular point in time, and that he's always forged connections with talented people, and above all women who occupy the moral high ground. It's as if he loves to make Albert Speers of them all."

"What are you getting at?"

"Speer—Hitler's architect and Minister of Armaments—is sometimes thought of as a man who was destined for great things but had the misfortune to cross paths with a charismatic and evil person at a vulnerable point in his life. There but for the grace of God go we. I've always thought that a rather generous interpretation. Regardless, it came to mind when I met Alicia Kovács."

"Was she a woman who occupied the moral high ground?"

"Maybe once, maybe somewhere. But she wasn't like you." He looked at her.

"What am I like?"

"You wouldn't allow yourself to be shaped by a superior force."

She smiled. "That sounds like a compliment."

"It is a compliment."

I could offer many more, he thought to himself as he continued to study Micaela, smiling at first but then increasingly focused, and then he saw what he had already suspected. She averted her gaze, as if she realised what he had divined.

He wondered if silence wasn't the best option at this juncture.

"You've had a confrontation with your brother," he said.

"How could you possibly know that?"

If only you knew, he thought.

If only you knew.

---

Julia woke with a nasty feeling that she was unable to breathe. She opened her eyes. He had just turned toward the living room, as if he had heard something suspicious, and she listened too. A bus drove past on Karlaplan. A motorcycle accelerated in the distance. Otherwise it was silent. She put a hand to her throat.

She coughed, bringing up blood and mucus. God, she really felt like shit. I have to get up, she thought to herself. I have to stand on the balcony and get some fresh air. But she couldn't. She needed to lie completely still and get her breathing under control.

"I'm scared," she said without really meaning to, instantly afraid that she had exposed herself.

He had been wonderful all evening, listening to her and saying the right things, but she also knew that you had to be strong in his world and not whine. You weren't supposed to analyse everything like Pappa did—she liked that. But now that her whole body was closing in on itself, it wasn't as easy being tough.

"I'm not feeling too good," she said.

He turned over. The pale scar on his forehead flushed with colour. His eyes narrowed and she thought she saw something reptilian in them.

"In what way?" he said.

"My windpipe feels constricted."

He leaned forward and put his hands over her throat like a doctor examining her tonsils.

"Where does it feel sore?" he said.

"About where you've got your hands," she said, hoping he'd take a hint.

Instead, he seemed to press harder—or that was how it felt to her. Finally, he released his grip, and she took the chance to sit up in bed, unsure of what was really happening. Was she in danger? It wasn't just the nausea and her throat; there was something strange about his reaction. He seemed embarrassed.

"How are you?" she said.

"Good. Why?"

"I was just wondering," she said. "You seemed tense just now."

"I've got a lot on my plate."

"Like what?"

She really did want to know. She still knew far too little about him, but he didn't answer and that was probably for the best, given how she was feeling. Nonetheless, she was hurt when he stood up without saying a word. When he returned, he was clutching a beer—only one for himself, thankfully. Beer was a calorie bomb—though he might have asked her if she wanted anything while he was going through the fridge anyway . . . Her throat was parched, and her thirst became even more apparent when she watched him drinking greedily, almost aggressively.

"Be glad you don't have any siblings," he said.

"Why should I be glad about that?"

"Because when the bastards betray you, it hurts."

"Has someone betrayed you?"

He took another greedy gulp. The scar on his forehead furrowed and unfolded as if it were alive.

"Yes," he said.

"I'm sorry."

She caressed her throat, the pressure within refusing to ebb.

"What's happened?" she said.

He didn't reply.

"Wasn't it like that with your family too?" he said.

"How do you mean?"

"Didn't you say your Uncle Magnus was always going behind your dad's back?"

"Oh yeah, sure," she said. Was that really how she'd expressed it?

"And your dad is always forgiving him?"

"I'm not sure about that," she said. "But he's, like, accepted him."

"Do you know how your dad should handle it?"

"How?"

Something came whistling through the air. She didn't have time to react. Her cheek flared hot and her head was thrust to one side, and she felt pain and confusion in equal measure. What was happening? He'd smacked her face. But why? He just smiled and took another swig of beer.

"That's what he should do. Strike back. That way Magnus won't dare say shit."

She couldn't produce any words.

"Do you understand?" he said.

"Okay, I'll be sure to tell him," she said in a mumble, putting her hand to her cheek. Then she went to the bathroom and sat there shaking, wondering if she should call Pappa. She abandoned the idea. What could that possibly do apart from making everything worse? Anyway—she tried to reassure herself—it wasn't a big deal. It was just a joke. A way of demonstrating something. Right? Instead, she rose from the toilet seat and stood in front of the mirror for a long time, prodding her stomach, which was protruding again. She felt ugly and miserable and she thought to herself that she should travel far away and not come back for a long time.

# TWENTY-SEVEN

"How can you know that I've spoken to my brother?" said Micaela.

"I can see it in you," Rekke said, remembering when he had looked into Lucas's eyes and sensed something cold and bottomless within: the complete dark triad—psychopathy, narcissism, Machiavellianism.

But above all, he'd noticed how Micaela reacted to him. Her pupils shrank. Her jaw tensed; her shoulders pulled up toward her neck. Rekke had known from the moment he had first met Micaela that she was tormented by his existence. Lucas left marks on her face and changed the rhythm of her footsteps.

"That's creepy," she said.

"Not at all. We're conditioned in evolutionary terms to respond to threats. You've challenged him, haven't you?"

She nodded, and he looked at her. She was so very young, and attractive too, but she always seemed to age when she spoke about Lucas, and he guessed that had been the case for a long time—even back when she had thought she admired him.

"In what way?" he said.

"I've been naive," she said. "An idiot who turned a blind eye. But now I know that he's dealing drugs and using kids to push them—they're below the age of criminal responsibility. I've tried to find evidence—I've got a little obsessed over the last few weeks."

"Did anything in particular precipitate this?"

She paused for thought.

"Perhaps," she said. "I saw something. I followed him and hid in the woods down by Järvafältet. Lucas was pestering a kid in a quilted jacket and he suddenly pulled out a gun and pressed it into the guy's throat. He scared the living daylights out of him. But do you know what's worse?"

"No."

"That it felt routine—he'd done it before. I can't quite describe the shock. I started to see my life in a whole new way."

He put his hand on hers and looked into her anxious brown eyes, which seemed full of fight.

"It's just awful," she said. "Husby was pretty okay when I was growing up. I never saw it as some down-and-out suburb, but now the amphetamines, khat, ecstasy, cannabis and that crap you take—fentanyl—are all pouring in. We've had deaths. One boy was only fourteen. His name was Muhammad, in case you were wondering."

"I'm sorry."

She angrily pulled her hand away.

"Stop it," she snapped. "You know exactly what you're part of, and it's not made any better by the fact that you get yours from a doctor."

"No, perhaps not."

"Anyway," she said more gently, "ever since I saw Lucas pull that gun the pieces have fallen into place and instead of being passive like I was before, I've been actively trying to find people in Husby to testify against him."

"Not an altogether risk-free enterprise, I take it," he said.

"No, and I went too fast. But it just felt like something snapped. You know my papá?"

"The historian."

"Yeah. He was always putting books in front of me, and he wanted me to look out at the wider world. He hated Husby. He thought it was a homogeneous tower-block hell, a futuristic nightmare, and he always insisted that I was going to go to university and get out of there. It became important to me too. I was going to be an academic like him and move abroad. Or at least to Lund. But when I graduated sixth form . . ."

"With good grades, naturally."

"Yes, actually . . . Well, then I applied to the Police Academy."

"And chose to serve in Husby."

"Exactly, and sometimes I bumped into my old teachers. I could tell how disappointed they were, and I couldn't explain to them or myself why I was plodding about the place in uniform."

"But somewhere deep down, you knew."

"Yes, in some way or other it was all about Lucas."

"You wanted clarity."

"There were too many questions from my childhood gnawing away at me."

"For instance, the cause of your father's death."

"Yes, although there's a lot of stuff it's not worth raking through. There's no chance of getting answers this long afterward. I should have let my colleagues do their jobs. Now I've made everything worse and I've got some fuckwits on my case."

"More than just your brother?"

"Yes." She hesitated. "Today on my way back to Rebecka Wahlin's to take a look at her bookshelf, I ran into one of Lucas's errand boys. His name's Hugo."

"And Hugo gave you that lip?"

"He threatened me. Well, not just me. He said that someone close to me might get into trouble, and I got it into my head they might come for you, Hans. That's why I went cold when I saw the blood on the kitchen floor."

"I'm sure I'll survive," he said, smiling quietly.

But he once again had the uneasy feeling that a great threat was imminent.

# TWENTY-EIGHT

Of course it isn't Claire in the photograph. Of course it isn't her.

Alicia Kovács sounded not dissimilar to Inspector Kaj Lindroos, who had in a moment of weakness promoted himself to chief inspector. Unlike the drunken cop, Alicia was precise and methodical as she laid out one photograph of Claire after another on the desk.

To this day she still felt the odd stab of jealousy. Claire had something she and Sofia didn't. She was the picture of urbanity. She could go head to head with Gabor and question his conclusions. Claire was the star—the one everyone thought Gabor would choose. So what had happened?

Alicia rose from the desk, put her hand to her heart and listened to the sounds of the garden and road. The threat to her life seemed audible out there in the darkness: the seeds of something gruesome, a fire that would spread from the floor, up her feet and legs, slowly consuming her. No, that's nonsense, she muttered to herself.

Gabor would take care of her—he loved her. They were connected by a child and by a tragedy. Nothing would happen, nothing. Yet . . . there had been three of them: her, Claire and Sofia. Three women who had hovered around Gabor, infatuated. Three hopeful, young, happy people, each convinced that their future was bright and shining.

Alicia was now the only one still alive—at least she hoped she was, even if it sounded harsh when put that way. Sofia Rodriguez had been found dead in the smouldering remains of her house in Madrid, her body exhibiting signs of torture. Claire Lidman had burned when a petrol tanker had plunged off a vertiginous road in San Sebastián. Fire, fire, always fire, leaving scorched earth behind.

Alicia looked away from the window and went into the kitchen to open another bottle of wine and calm her nerves. But then she changed her mind—it would be unprofessional to drink more. She thought back to when they had been reunited with Claire in Stockholm in September 1990. She remembered the expectations lingering in the air, the secretaries bustling back and forth, the contract proposals handed over, Gabor adjusting his suit in front of the mirror and applying wax to his hair. It had been a big deal for him, and not just because he had the chance to take over all of Axel Larsson's assets and grow even richer at a time when everyone else was bleeding to death. It was a big deal for him to see Claire again. She was the missing link—the one he was most attracted to. But nothing had gone the way he had expected. Claire had arrived and Gabor had kissed her on both cheeks. She had reacted with unmistakable physical discomfort, reaching up to wipe away his kisses. She detested him and made no effort to conceal it. The whole thing was folly and it was going to go horribly wrong, Alicia realised that much immediately—but Gabor was determined to make out otherwise.

He flattered Claire, offering her champagne and suggesting a game of chess as a warm-up for their negotiations. Claire reluctantly agreed. Alicia watched from an armchair nearby, and it was immediately apparent that Claire had improved. She played Black with the Sicilian Defence and held out for a long time before Gabor crushed her and toppled her king with his little finger. "You've got a long way to go," he said. "You still can't take me on."

He had said it with a smile, almost tenderly, but Alicia had immediately understood the underlying threat, and shortly after that what she had feared had come to pass. Gabor had asked her to leave. He wanted to be alone with Claire. Alicia remembered the helpless look from Claire, her gaze darting about searching for ways out, and the door closing. She remembered her own footsteps descending the stairs, and the feelings of jealousy and horror. To this day, she had no idea what happened that night—except that it was something terrible.

She was able to tell the morning after from the shadow on Gabor's face and his body language, and she hadn't been surprised when Claire had disappeared a few weeks later. It was already on the cards, and although she had shed a tear over the news of her death, she hadn't been unprepared for it. Claire had sealed her fate the moment she had looked at Gabor with that icy hatred. That was just how it was. That was the reality Alicia had come to live with and had slowly accepted, especially after giving birth to Gabor's son and seeing how much he was capable of loving—and mourning. Gabor was still the most intelligent, interesting man she had ever met. The man who had opened up the world for her and made life shine like one big promise.

Further down, on the water, there was a boat moving through the darkness. She listened for sounds in the garden and checked her watch again.

Five past ten—too late to call. Gabor's evenings were considered sacred. But what the hell . . . She had a good reason, and a lot of questions. He picked up right away, sounding warm and friendly. Like the good Gabor—the one she was tied to.

"We forgot about Jan's birthday last week. He would have been nineteen, as you know," he said.

"I didn't think there was much to celebrate, but I sat on the terrace and lit a candle."

"That's good. Do you have anything more to tell me about Rekke?"

She paused for thought.

"He said thank you."

"Thank you?"

"For awakening him from his slumber." She couldn't remember if that was exactly how he had put it. "He was very broken."

"I don't care how broken he is; he must never be underestimated. Did he make any other observations?"

He saw my shame, she thought to herself. *For the guilty, there is always hope.*

"Not really," she said.

"Then he was holding back," he said. "He reads people like an open book."

Like you, Gabor, she thought. Like you.

"You admire him?" she said.

"He sees clearly. That fascinates me."

But mostly you hate him, she thought.

"Is there anything about Ida Aminoff's death that I need to know?" she asked. She held her breath.

"She seemed an interesting woman," he said. "A little undisciplined, but exciting."

*Did you kill her?*

"Why the sudden urge to return the necklace?" she said instead.

"He asked after me and I returned something."

"Come on, Gabor. Why?"

"I already knew he would approach us."

"Did you?"

"Yes, I received a tip-off, and since then I've done a little research and turned up some unexpected information. It is only a suspicion so far, but I am seeking confirmation. It has to do with Jan."

"Oh," she said, not daring to ask more.

She decided to get to the point of her call. "Samuel Lidman phoned."

She heard Gabor take a deep breath.

"Really?" he said. "Although that was to be expected, I suppose. What did he want?"

"He claims to have photographic evidence that Claire is alive and has been sighted in Venice."

Gabor didn't answer at once, breathing heavily.

But when he spoke, there was no seriousness, no stifled hatred in his voice as there was when he talked about Rekke—only amusement of a sort. Curiosity.

"Well, well . . ."

"Exactly. Sounds totally cuckoo. But I've taken the liberty of making an appointment with him tomorrow at nine o'clock, just to check it out."

"Push it back," said Gabor. "I'll fly to Stockholm and meet him. I might . . ." He hesitated. "Bring company for the trip."

She was surprised, although not by that. He was always showing up with new beauties and mistresses, but she hadn't expected that he would want to take the meeting in person. It was usually only the rich and powerful who were so honoured.

"May I ask why?"

"Because it would be interesting," he said.

"Can you make it for one?"

"I think so," he said.

"Who is the company?" she said bitterly. "Who are you making happy this time?"

"It's not what you think. I shall provide a detailed explanation, but there was something else I wanted to ask you first."

She bit her lip.

"I have undertaken the delicate task of examining Rekke's personal circumstances, and my findings were far more interesting than I had dared hope," he said.

"I see," she said nervously.

"It transpires that Rekke has a lodger—a young woman, a quick-witted girl, I should think. She's a police officer, and a very honest one. A fighter in many ways and not at all spoiled from birth like him."

Just as long as you don't go after her too, she thought to herself.

"I didn't meet her."

"No, I gathered that. But—and this is the good bit—she has a brother who feels threatened by her. Additionally, he hates Rekke and the man's influence over his sister. His name is Vargas too—Lucas Vargas. I've spoken to him a little and he seems open to suggestion."

*You mean he's willing to be bought.*

"Hasn't Rekke suffered enough?"

"He hasn't suffered like we have."

"What do you want me to do?" she said.

"Speak to the brother—a situation has arisen. And in the meantime I shall endeavour to have my reports confirmed."

"Yes, Gabor," she said. "Of course. But . . ."

She didn't finish her sentence, instead wishing him a good night. Then she got on with what she had promised to do. She rescheduled the meeting with Samuel Lidman and spoke at some length with Lucas Vargas, who surprised her with his charm and sense of humour. He was a little reminiscent of Gabor, albeit a more primitive version. Afterward, she called Morovia again, and while talking to him she stared vacantly into the darkness, thinking.

*Just what is it I'm doing? What am I playing at?*

# TWENTY-NINE

Rekke's phone vibrated, startling him, but there was no-one on the line and that seemed to make him pensive. After that, he called Julia. She was apparently asleep—it was ten to eleven in the evening—and he immediately apologised and hung up.

"Why did you call Julia?" said Micaela.

"I'm not quite sure."

"I can't let go of the fact that you got the necklace back in the middle of all this."

"What?" He nervously played with the mobile phone as if he wanted to make another call.

"The necklace you got back."

"Yes, it was rather dramatic."

"You said there were suspicious circumstances around Ida Aminoff's death from the get-go."

"Yes," he said.

He didn't seem particularly inclined to talk.

"What circumstances?"

"A red mark on her neck, as I said, just below the hairline."

"What did they make of it?"

"Well, it might have occurred when the necklace was torn off."

"Torn off?"

"Yes, possibly."

"Very suspicious if you ask me."

"On the other hand, she might have done it herself. It was always hard to take that necklace off. She never could do it alone, and she could become very careless and angry when intoxicated."

"And the official cause of death was an overdose, right?"

"Yes, suffocation by overdose. She had large amounts of opiates and amphetamines in her system. Her blood alcohol was 1.6 and ... she was thin. It was quite plausible that that was what killed her."

"But not guaranteed?"

He sat quietly, still toying with his mobile.

"According to the medical examiner it was. He said there were no signs of any other serious damage."

"What did *you* think?"

"I wasn't as convinced, but I had no real authority."

"Did you get to see the body?"

"Yes, but only briefly. At the medical examiner's premises in Solna. I flew back from Helsinki and insisted. They showed me out pretty quickly."

"Did you notice anything?"

He turned to face her.

"Perhaps one thing. I had done some reading and I did something irreverent. I turned her lips up." He appeared to be picturing it, grimacing momentarily. "I knew it was difficult—almost impossible—to tell whether a person had died from violent suffocation if she had been unconscious or sliding toward unconsciousness at the time of the murder. You have to look for tiny, tiny signs, if there are no marks from nails or fingers."

"Hadn't they done that?"

He smiled as if returning to the present.

"Not with the thoroughness that I would later come to regard as a virtue."

"What did you see under the lips?" she said.

"A minor bleed on the oral mucosa, something that might imply forced or desperate movements with the tongue and teeth, but it was so discreet that I allowed myself to be brushed aside by the medical examiner."

"But..."

"The thought occurred to me that a murder might have been committed under the cover of a serious medical episode, but I wasn't able to persuade the detectives and I was much too despondent and unsure of myself at the time to push it."

"So nobody else's DNA was found?"

"That technology wasn't available then."

"No other defensive wounds?"

"Just bruises on the shoulders, but they were assumed to have been caused earlier in the evening. There were, however, signs of a commotion in the flat. There was a smashed flowerpot on the floor. The police thought Ida had knocked it over herself."

"Was the flat otherwise tidy?"

"Yes and no. Ida's clothes were all over the place, as usual. But someone had recently vacuumed, and the bedside table and lamp had been carefully wiped down."

She looked at him in wonder.

"It's inconceivable that you of all people decided to drop it."

"Yes," he said. "I suppose it is. Perhaps I didn't want to, or feel up to, digging any further. But it's not impossible"—he smiled sadly—"that it was a little bit the same for me as it is for you with your brother."

"What do you mean?"

"I thought I had let go, but it affected my whole life."

"How?"

"I quit as a concert pianist and began to study psychology, taking an interest in witness statements and forensics."

"I see," she said, sipping from her glass. "Were there statements from the investigation that you consciously or unconsciously wanted to understand better?"

He brushed the hair back from his brow.

"Yes," he said. "There was one in particular that I didn't like."

"Whose?"

"William Fors's."

She started. "As in Nordbanken William Fors?"

"He wasn't a banker then. He was studying at the Stockholm School of Economics. But yes, one and the same."

"You think there's a connection with Claire Lidman's disappearance?"

"There's something about the sudden reappearance of the necklace that bothers me. There was a society wedding taking place on Djurgården the night Ida died. Everyone from my world was there—apart from me—and apparently no-one was worse behaved than Wille. He was boozing, bragging and trying to get off with Ida. Ida was mostly messing with him, but when she went home he followed her. She told him to go to hell, but he persisted, and soon they started bickering about the necklace. At least that's what he said."

"So Ida was still wearing it then?"

"Yes, and Wille complimented her on it, so he said, and wanted to know what it had cost. But she took that badly and said all sorts of things about wanting to throw it into the sea because she hated fuss and finery and cheap compliments."

"So that was where you got the idea?"

"It was, and in retrospect it feels like he wanted to spin the idea that Ida had gotten rid of it herself. Something about his statement rings increasingly false to me."

"Was Morovia in Stockholm that night?"

"I was unable to ascertain that, no matter how much I asked around. But now I thought I might . . ." He stood up.

"Look into it more closely?"

"Yes, as it happens. I have an inkling of a way in, and according to my dear colleague and lodger I should not overly mistrust my hunches."

He smiled at her and walked away clutching the phone again, a troubled expression spreading across his face.

Julia woke early, feeling hungry. She suppressed this by thinking of herself dancing lightly—ever so lightly—on a jetty by the sea, and once she had regained control of her impulses she was gripped by a mild euphoria which fluttered about like an impatient butterfly in the room. It was raining gently outside. Daylight seeped in under the bottom edge of the curtain, dripping onto the windowsill. She looked at him. He had finally spent the night with her instead of sneaking off like usual, but it hadn't really felt right and that wasn't just because of the smack. He had been stealing off to the stairwell the whole evening and all night, to talk on his phone. He said there was a minor emergency in the family—perhaps it was to do with the siblings he had mentioned. But she couldn't help feeling that there was more to it.

He was sleeping on his back, gently snoring, and she moved as far away from him as she could in the bed, overcome with unease at his big shoulders and powerful ribs. What should she do? She hadn't really been asleep last night when Pappa had called. She just hadn't wanted to pick up in front of *him*. It would have been a disaster if she'd said so much as a single word. No-one could see through her tone like her father. But perhaps she could pop out now and call him back? It would be good to hear his voice and talk a little. No, that wouldn't work. She could hardly tell him about the smack. Pappa would never understand, and it was really no big deal, was it? And *he* might be in a bad mood because of all the problems with his family...

She was sure it would all work out, and they'd had a good time during the night between all the calls. He had promised her a "super luxurious surprise" to make up for all the hassle. That weekend it was going to be just him and her and no phones—that was what he had said. It did sound nice. No. She was right. It would be a pity to ruin the mood now. She felt a hand on her shoulder. He had woken up and was favouring her with his biggest, loveliest smile—the one that could vanquish almost any worry.

"Good morning," he said.

She smiled and wondered whether she should kiss him just to show that nothing had really happened, but she settled for a "Good morning" too.

"My beautiful baby girl," he said.

She took a deep breath.

"What are we doing today?"

"Having a great time," he said. "Going to stay in a hotel. Do you like champagne?"

"I do," she said, though she felt no great enthusiasm—perhaps because of all the calories.

"I've just got a few calls to make. Then we'll pack and get out of here," he said.

"I have to see my dad first."

"Oh, come on," he said. "You don't even like him, not really. Now it's just you and me."

"Sure, okay," she said, smiling. "You and me."

Then she wrapped herself around him after all, even though it called for an unexpectedly great effort on her part.

# THIRTY

Samuel Lidman had arranged for a new copy of the holiday snap to be printed and was now in his Sunday best, freshly shaven, with his hair slicked back, having an early beer in a cheap boozer on Birger Jarlsgatan.

I can't do it, he muttered to himself. I can't do it. Of course, that wasn't what he meant. Perhaps it was an expression of the anxiety he felt ahead of his meeting with Alicia Kovács, or perhaps it was a reaction to what Rebecka Wahlin had told him about the chess book in the photo. Perhaps it was only then that he had really understood.

Rebecka's words had made it sink in that it really *was* Claire in the photo, and that Claire had not only abandoned him but she was still dressing elegantly and reading chess books as if he had never existed. The realisation was more than he could bear, so he ordered another beer and got sufficiently worked up that in the end he was pissed off with Micaela Vargas too. Apparently, she was the one who had worked out what the book in the picture was, and yet she hadn't told him—as if it was no concern of his. What a fucking nerve, he thought to himself as he pulled out his mobile and called her. He was taken aback by how excited she sounded.

"Hi, Samuel," she said. "I've been meaning to call you."

"Me too—" he began to say.

"We've discovered something," she interrupted.

"I know," he said angrily, and out spilled a furious torrent of words about how Claire's love of chess apparently far exceeded her love of him.

Micaela seemed to be waiting for him to finish.

"So was Lev Polugaevsky important to her?" she said.

"Huh? Yes . . ." he said. "Absolutely. She even preferred him to Kasparov."

"You don't remember anything else from the night when she met Gabor Morovia, do you?" she said.

He pictured it all again—her staggering in, pale and haggard, and disappearing into the bathroom, but unlike the other times he had recalled it he felt no warmth. Instead, he saw something perfidious in the face that she turned away from his kisses.

"She was a deceitful bitch," he snapped.

"I'm sorry?"

"She ruined my life."

"Yes, but . . ." Micaela said, clearly shocked.

He must have hung up after that. At any rate, Micaela was suddenly gone, and he stood up with a grimace and stumbled into the street with other memories flickering through his head, and just to screw with him Claire was naked and looked incredible in most of them. Instead of wanting to press himself close to her, all he wanted was to scream and shout, and he yanked a grey ladies' hat off a rack outside a shop.

"Hey, what do you think you're doing?" someone shouted.

"I hate hats," he said, making his way toward the Royal Dramatic and wondering how the hell he was going to kill time before his meeting with Alicia Kovács on Strandvägen.

Micaela was holding her mobile in her hand, looking quizzically at Rekke, who had just emerged from his study. He wore the same clothes as the day before—grey trousers and a black shirt that had become even more crumpled. He looked dazed—he'd evidently been up all night. Perhaps he'd even taken one of his downers. His hands trembled as he smoothed down his hair.

"I just spoke to Samuel Lidman," she said.

He looked at her. "What did he say?"

"He called Claire a deceitful bitch."

"I must say that doesn't seem very friendly."

"Would you please leave out the irony?" she said, angry that he wasn't taking it more seriously.

"Of course," said Rekke. "Do you want to talk about it?"

She glared at him.

"Now you sound like a damn psychologist."

"I *am* a damn psychologist," he said.

"And what do you have to say about it?" she said more amicably. "About our friendly strongman who's suddenly lost it."

Rekke gestured toward the sofa, which meant he wanted to sit down himself. She had noticed that early on: it was impossible for him to sit if she didn't too.

"It surprised me at an early juncture that the friendly strongman wasn't angrier when talking about the photo and Claire," he said.

"What do you mean?"

"He spoke as if he thought everything would resolve itself if only he found her, but such an encounter can hardly be expected to end well. A rupture of that ilk cannot be healed."

"Aren't you the pessimist? He just seemed so nice."

"That isn't always a good solution to a crisis."

"You mean he might explode or something? Or maybe . . ." she pondered, ". . . he already has?"

He shrugged. It was clearly not something he wished to speculate over, and she pictured the holiday snap once again—the woman sweeping through the crowds, chess book in hand.

"In the photo—you thought Claire wasn't alone in St. Mark's Square."

"That was my momentary guess."

"There might be a new man in her life. That wouldn't make things any easier."

"Of course, that is possible, but rather I wonder . . ."

Micaela leaned forward. "What?"

"Whether the woman's gaze wasn't slightly too anxious to be taken as meaning that."

"How can you see anxiety in that blurry photo?"

"I sensed something contradictory in her movements."

"You mentioned an old injury."

"There were other things too. Something both self-conscious and protective. You remember, right? A pigeon has flapped up and she has raised her hand to shield herself, but she also seems to be turning her body to peer somewhat anxiously over her shoulder."

"So you mean . . . ?"

"Rather than a man—a lover—behind her, I would guess a child, or another vulnerable individual."

Rebecka Wahlin's words about Claire looking pregnant before she disappeared came to mind, and a question took shape, but she realised at once that it was impossible to answer. Nevertheless, she put it into words:

"How old might the child be?"

To her surprise, Rekke took the question seriously.

"If we accept my basic premise—which is shaky—then I would guess twelve or thirteen."

She looked at him in amazement.

"Are you kidding?"

"She would surely be holding the hand of a younger child, especially somewhere like St. Mark's Square. A teenager would not be the cause of the same anxious expression."

"So that would be . . . ?"

Samuel's child, was what she wanted to say, but she didn't complete her sentence—it was much too early to speculate. Perhaps this was all a kind of daydream—the consequence of a sudden desire for a happy ending to the entire business.

"It would be a beautiful thing if Samuel got back both Claire and a child."

"You see," he said. "I have a troubling ability to awaken vain hopes."

Then he nodded to Micaela and returned to his study.

He paused for a moment to listen. Micaela too left the kitchen with that punctuated eighth pace that he liked so much. Her footsteps were a complete contrast to those of Ida Aminoff. If Micaela's sounded like an irregular—and unstoppable—march, then Ida's had been more of a meandering jazz solo. She seemed capable of disappearing in new and unexpected directions at any given moment, and that made all investigation into her very difficult. There was a constant unpredictability about her—the feeling that she really might have thrown priceless jewellery into the bay.

Rekke had spent the whole night reading his own notes on the inquiry, and it had been even worse than ploughing through old diaries. His flaws, his inability, stabbed like needles, and it had become even more incomprehensible that he had dropped it all. Crucial information was missing. That in itself did not necessarily mean that Ida had been murdered, but it remained very disagreeable that no-one knew what had happened during the final hours of her life. Ida had been lying on her back on the bed, one of her high-heel shoes still on her foot. Her right hand was resting on her throat as if she had been struggling to breathe. It was apparent from her face that she had suffered. The door was unlocked.

Someone might easily have sneaked in and killed her—or helped her to die—and taken the necklace. And that someone could have been Gabor or someone in league with him. One of the neighbours thought they'd heard footsteps early that morning, perhaps a commotion in the flat.

There was a whole catalogue of questionable fools who might have turned up at her place in the middle of the night, and it increasingly bothered Rekke that the most probable candidate went by the name of William Fors. Rekke had met him just days after Ida's death, in a city centre bar. Fors had been deeply troubled, almost impossible to talk to. He was clearly ashamed. In his notes from the meeting, Rekke had written:

> *Taciturn, fidgety, hardly a killer, but hiding something? He described how they parted ways outside the Nordic Museum. She stumbled away toward the Djurgårdsbron bridge, heading home to Torstenssonsgatan. "She looked exhausted," he said, ranting about how Ida threatened to throw the necklace into the water. He apologised again: "I should have left her alone. I knew she loved you, Hans."*

Rekke was ashamed by what he read. There was no precise observation there, nothing of value, and why on earth had he even bothered with that final sentence? He had his suspicions. Instead of answering his own question—was William hiding something?—or at least articulating why he had asked it, he had sought the only comfort available to him: Ida's love. Adolescence was an unforgivable condition, but his instincts had probably been sound. William hadn't told him everything. Could he speak to him again? Of course, he could do whatever he pleased, but how did one make a man talk about something he only wanted to forget? One gave him something for his trouble, of course. And he could no longer blame his own youthful innocence if he didn't pursue the matter.

Rekke stood up abruptly, firmly resolved to seek Fors out. Unfortunately, Ida's death wasn't the only thing worrying him, and on his way out of the study he thought about Julia and the call the night before. He pulled out his mobile and phoned her. There was no answer. He tried again and again, seized by the same sense of unease, before deciding to call on her in person. After all, surely it couldn't hurt to check if she was at home but ignoring her phone.

Julia studied herself in the mirror. She'd been told that they were off to Trosa to celebrate, and she felt full of expectation in spite of everything. But she wasn't happy with her appearance. She thought she looked childish. Her cheeks were puffy and her eyes looked like a doll's. As for her stomach? Bigger than ever. Her cheek was also aching. She had a bruise on her left cheekbone. So damn embarrassing. I'll have to come up with a good explanation for that, she thought as she emerged from the bathroom. She paused in the centre of the living-room floor, possessed by a premonition. Was he going to hit her again?

No, no, it was clearly just a one-off. But she should have made it clearer that it was horrible and scary. She murmured the fateful words *domestic violence*. Obviously, this wasn't domestic violence, but . . . She really should discuss it with him, maybe just to say that she didn't really get what he meant by it.

"Hey," she called out.

He didn't reply. He was on his mobile in the bedroom, and something in his movements—his tense arms—made her swallow what she wanted to say. Besides, why make a fuss now that they were off to stay in a hotel? She went over and pressed herself against him and happened to look down at his phone—it wasn't intentional, not in the slightest, but he took it as an act of espionage. He pushed her away and she was hurt. Still, she smiled.

"Are we going soon? I'm all packed and I've dolled myself up," she said, hoping for a compliment.

She didn't get so much as a glance—not even when she said a few kind words about him. All he did was mutter that he needed to take a call in the stairwell again, then they'd be off. He went down to the landing on the floor below, and although she knew she shouldn't, she eavesdropped for a while. He was speaking English. His pronunciation was surprisingly bad and uneducated, and she just had time to reflect on what different upbringings they must have had when she heard something that made her start. "I must have a guarantee that you won't hurt her," he said. Who wasn't going to hurt whom? Was this part of his family emergency? Or was he talking about her? She took another step out onto the landing and listened some more. He cleared his throat before saying: "Yes, yes, sounds great." Then he seemed to liven up. He laughed, saying "Wow, cool," and that ought perhaps to have provided reassurance, but there was something about that laugh that Julia didn't like—as if the person on the other end of the line wasn't in on the joke and would pay a price in due course. She tried to keep listening, but at that moment he moved away, so she went to the bathroom instead.

In a way, it was a curse. The more dissatisfied she was with her appearance, the more she was drawn to the mirror. She stood very close to it while she thought about those words . . . "A guarantee that you won't hurt her." Should she get out of there? She stood still, as if she were paralysed, applying concealer to the bruise on her cheek. Then she began to apply yet more make-up to the rest of her face, and as if that weren't enough, she inspected her stomach and her thighs again, pinching her skin with disgust. What was she playing at? It was humiliating. She should step aside and call Pappa.

She heard footsteps in the stairwell and emerged from the bathroom, looking at him anxiously but unable to read him. He walked past her into the kitchen and wrote something down on a Post-it that he then tore off and tucked into his trouser pocket.

Then he smiled and kissed her and she felt better—although not completely better, but calmer at least—and though she was still thinking about leaving, she did the last of the packing and went out to the elevator with him. On the way down, he pulled out his mobile again and made a solemn gesture with his hand.

"What are you doing?" she said.

"Turning off my phone. Now it's just you and me."

She turned off her mobile too, unsure how she actually felt about it, and maybe he realised that.

"I can't wait," he said, stroking her hair.

He smelled of aftershave.

"I can't wait either," she said.

He wrapped his arm around her waist and led her out to his Audi Cabriolet, which was parked directly outside in the street. It was a fine day without a cloud in the sky, and maybe it was going to be a wonderful weekend after all. There was already heat lingering in the air, and in the distance there was an orchestra playing. It seemed to be a day made for patriotic festivities.

She gazed down toward Narvavägen, taking in the big city one last time before they went on their way. She recoiled. Further down the street there was an unmistakable, tall figure in a black shirt approaching, and while she wanted to rush toward him and hug him and tell him everything that had happened, the instinct to flee took over.

"Let's get out of here," she said. "I think that's my dad down there."

"Where?" he said, more tensely than she would have liked.

"There," she said, pointing.

He suddenly seemed to be in a hurry. He opened the car door for her then got in behind the wheel and accelerated away so aggressively that it caused a lurch in her stomach.

# THIRTY-ONE

Decrepit old men—veterans of the Normandy invasion—on parade. They all looked a hundred years old. Some of them were in wheelchairs. Others were staggering along under their own steam. They should have been left at home with a blanket tucked around their legs.

On the Atlantic coast, the warships were lined up, while lower down on the grandstand sat the dignitaries, every single one of them, and that was in itself impressive. But good grief, he hated these kinds of ceremonies. There was something so pompous and mendacious about them it made him want to scream obscenities.

He supposed it wouldn't be long until the warplanes came thundering past overhead to meddle with his hangover. He'd been a fool to drink the day before, but it was all Hans's fault, of course. Well, his and Gabor Morovia's. The discomfort they had caused had compelled him to knock back beer after beer. Next time it would have to be wine, he thought to himself as he put a hand to his belly. He would pull through this. He wasn't one to despair. He was a fighter. Right now there was some very dull shit going on down there. President Chirac, who was seated next to Queen Elizabeth in the first row, rose to his feet. He was presumably going to hand out medals and God knew what else and give a speech that was about as controversial as saying amen in church. Why couldn't he nip off for a quick chaser? A beer to oil the wheels. It was hopeless.

He was crippled with anxiety. He looked around the grandstand. Where had Putin got to? Perhaps he resented acknowledging that the Allies had helped to defeat Hitler. Hang on . . . There he was. Up on the balcony with King Harald. Should he try to make contact? They'd spoken quite a bit when Putin had served as Yeltsin's prime minister, and he would surely be familiar with Morovia—they had probably helped each other to grow rich as they drained Mother Russia of her assets.

Kleeberger tapped him on the shoulder. What did he want now?

"Look how bald Chirac has got . . ." he said, the intent behind his comment clear as daylight.

He wanted to cure his own inferiority complex by finding fault with those more powerful than himself, and Magnus would ordinarily have played along. Yes, Schröder looks like a washed-up alkie. Yes, Berlusconi has been carved to bits by the surgeon's knife. Yes, Tarja Halonen is a lady—a school mistress. But right now he didn't feel up to it.

"I wouldn't say so," he said harshly, and regardless of his own feelings on the matter Gabor Morovia appeared in his mind's eye—Gabor bending down and doing something unthinkable.

Out in the street, Rekke encountered Mrs. Hansson lugging a pair of carrier bags from the small local supermarket, and he held the door open for her and asked how her gout was. She said she shouldn't complain but that she was *so* happy that Micaela had come back.

"Perhaps we'll have some order around the place now."

"Perhaps," he said.

"Are you off for a walk?"

"I was going to look in on Julia," he said, smiling back at her as if it were merely an innocent visit.

As soon as he was alone again, the feelings of unease returned and it didn't help when he tried to dismiss them as irrational. He remembered the spideriness of Julia's movements when she had withdrawn from him in the kitchen.

She's subject to a harder gaze now—hers or someone else's, he thought, and he looked toward an elderly man in a checked jacket passing on the other side of the street.

The man was walking slowly, and as he so often did, Rekke scrutinised his body to see what he could discern about his life, but this time it wasn't really that which interested him. It was his own focus on the details. It was uncanny in a way, wasn't it?

The more he stared at the man's feet—size forty-six, he guessed—the more the world around him disappeared and the bigger those feet seemed to be. Of course, he knew why. It was the brain's way of ensuring they didn't vanish from sight, but it was also a trick of the eye that changed the perspective, which was exactly what he assumed had happened to Julia. She looked at parts of her body so much that—in her eyes—they grew. It was part of an eating disorder's grim modus operandi, and once again he recalled the sound of her voice when he had called the evening before. Something was wrong—he could feel it—and so he hurried along the street.

The sound of an accelerating engine cut through the air from Karlaplan—a rising roar in the form of a major third, a glissando from A to C sharp. He looked up. A red sports car vanished from sight onto Karlavägen, which was nothing remarkable in itself. Östermalm was full of horny men who needed to steel and titillate their nerves with flashy cars. But something about the sound and sight of the receding vehicle made him feel ill at ease as he continued toward Julia's door.

In the elevator, he was able to detect the smell of aftershave and perfume. A couple—young, he thought—had stood here very recently. Feeling even more uneasy, he got off at the fifth floor and rang Julia's bell. As he had already suspected, no-one came to the door.

---

Micaela did a lap of the apartment and concluded that Rekke must be out. Concerned, she called Mrs. Hansson, who immediately reassured her. Rekke had simply popped out to see Julia, she said. He'd looked bright and summery.

"You're not leaving, are you?" she asked.

"I don't know," Micaela said.

"He needs you."

She was tempted to ask whether her own needs were even vaguely relevant in this context.

"I don't know whether I need him as much."

"But he stimulates you, doesn't he?"

"When he's got his nose above water. Otherwise, all he does is drive me to distraction."

"He drives us all to distraction. On the other hand, he sometimes makes us gasp too."

Micaela considered this.

"That's true."

"And you like him."

She didn't answer that.

"And perhaps I should add," Mrs. Hansson said, becoming somewhat cryptic, "that he's an incurable gentleman, in case you've ever wondered."

What a bore, Micaela thought.

"I don't think I want to hear about that," she said.

"My apologies."

She found herself thinking about something else entirely.

"You looked after Magnus and Hans when they were children. Do you remember a boy named Gabor Morovia?"

Mrs. Hansson took her time to reply.

"I'd better come up," she said. "I'd better come up."

# THIRTY-TWO

Rekke had keys for Julia's flat, but he would never enter without her permission—unlike his own mother when he'd been young. She had been wont to barge in and rummage around as if she had a divine right to do so, and ever since he had always been able to tell when someone had been in his room. He knew it before his senses became aware of what they were registering, and he had sworn to respect Julia's privacy. Yet...

He was a father, and fathers went against their principles all the time—it was part of the job. He unlocked the door and realised immediately from the smell of aftershave and perfume that Julia and the new boyfriend must only just have left the flat. They might very well have been the people being carried away with that engine noise—and if that were the case then he had both the pitch of his car and his scent. It was a start, and there was probably more in the flat—if he was going to start poking his nose in it. It was rigorously tidy, which seemed to tally with the stricter diet of late. *Ordo ducit ad ordinem.* With order comes order.

The bed was made, the dirty dishes in the kitchen had been loaded into the dishwasher, and the counter wiped down. Lying on the kitchen table were three days' copies of *Dagens Nyheter* in a neat stack next to a Post-it notepad. Okay, he thought to himself. Leave. Don't start searching boxes and hiding places. But then he looked at the kitchen table again and the Post-its and he spotted the faint impression of a longer word and two numbers—perhaps 52. Probably an address. He was able to make out a large H at the beginning and equally big b's and g's further in, and though he couldn't decipher it in full, he knew that Julia hadn't written it down. The author had been a male with a squiggly, unkempt handwriting style. Intriguing. He knew that a new handwriting method had been introduced into the Swedish curriculum in 1975, one that would supposedly produce more legible results with fewer embellishments. The g's, for instance, were no longer supposed to be joined to the next letter to avoid loops, but here the g definitely was, and there were no traces of the new style whatsoever. In other words, this meant that the writer—if he had been raised in Sweden—belonged to the preceding generation, which made him much older than Julia, though that wasn't necessarily a bad thing.

But it wasn't a good thing either. He grabbed the Post-it with the faint impressions and called his daughter—once again without reply.

Mrs. Hansson came up dressed smartly in white linen trousers and a navy-blue cashmere cardigan that seemed far too warm given the weather. She stood for a moment with her hands behind her back, looking serious, and then began to make a pot of tea.

"Has Hans started talking about Gabor Morovia?" she said.

"He's turned up in a cold case we're looking at," Micaela said.

Mrs. Hansson smiled cautiously.

"So you're working on a case again?"

"It would seem so."

"Oh, I am pleased! It'll do Hans the world of good. It was the same when he was a child: as soon as he had a mystery to ponder, he perked up."

The concerned expression resurfaced and she sat down on a kitchen chair. She seemed tired.

"How are you doing, Sigrid?" Micaela said.

"Oh you know," she said. "I'm not getting any younger, and I've had some dreadful experiences in my life. But I can't help wondering if the ones involving Morovia aren't among the worst of them."

Micaela sat down too.

"So you've met him?"

Mrs. Hansson ran her hand across her brow and blinked nervously.

"I buried the family cat after he burned it alive and I stood watch for several nights, terrified that he'd come back and do the same to the house. But I had met him before that too—when the family thought he was just another talented boy."

"But he wasn't?"

"Oh no," she said. She stood up to get the tea and set out some scones. "But it took a while for us to realise that. At first, all we knew was that Dr. Brandt encountered the boy at a chess tournament in Vienna and had been deeply impressed, almost smitten. He dreamed that Hans and Gabor would be friends and would compete with and measure themselves against each other. I sincerely believe his actions were well intentioned."

"I see."

"But it could only ever have gone badly. Hatred of the Rekkes had been passed to Gabor in his mother's milk."

"I've heard that," said Micaela.

"It was Harald Rekke—the boys' father—who realised the connection, but by then it was already too late, and you can't imagine the to-do that followed. Harald went to the police and social services, and he barged into the Hungarian embassy in Vienna. But by then Gabor no longer lived there and no-one would say where he had gone. Later on, we found out that Dr. Brandt of all people had helped him to secure a scholarship at a school in Bonn. Harald never forgave the doctor for that, and all contact with him was severed."

"Do you know what happened to Gabor Morovia after that?" said Micaela.

Mrs. Hansson acted as mother, pouring tea for them both.

"Since I'm the only one to have remained in touch with Dr. Brandt, I should think I know more than anyone else in the family," she said.

"Would you tell me about it?"

"I don't know," she said.

"What makes you say that?"

Mrs. Hansson finished her mouthful of scone.

"I've sought to protect Hans from that information."

"Why?"

"I've always been afraid that Gabor might come after him again, and I didn't want Hans to feel any sympathy whatsoever. It might make him weak."

"It sounds unlikely that he would feel sympathy for Morovia, given what happened."

Mrs. Hansson laughed in mild resignation.

"You never know with Hans. He'll adopt any lost soul going. Nothing human is alien to him. *Homo sum, humani nihil a me alienum puto,* as he says. But I'll tell you, Micaela—if you promise not to pass it straight on to him."

"I promise," she said, wondering whether she really meant it.

"Things went about as you'd expect for Morovia," Mrs. Hansson said. "He had a brilliant academic career and built a successful business, but something wasn't right. People close to him would disappear or die, and Dr. Brandt regretted ever getting involved with him. Then something happened that seemed to change everything."

"What was that?"

"Gabor was always embarking upon new love affairs, and his lawyers were kept busy dealing with accusations of assault. But there was a woman who stood by him through thick and thin—a compatriot who had been his student in London. Her name was Alicia Kovács, and she gave birth to his son—a beautiful boy, so they say, who excelled both academically and athletically. Gabor loved him so much that he wanted to make a break from the organised criminals he was involved with in Russia."

"Did he?"

"I don't know. All I know is that he acquired even more enemies. Sometime in the spring of 1994, a bomb was planted in his limousine in St. Petersburg, but they botched it and only half the car was blasted apart. Gabor survived with burns to his torso and legs. The son, Jan, didn't make it. He died in his father's arms, and from then on Gabor was completely merciless. Reportedly."

"Oh," Micaela said thoughtfully.

"And that worries me. The boy would have been the same age as Julia is now if he'd survived."

"But Morovia can hardly come after Hans for that."

"Perhaps not. But Gabor is fixated on him. Honestly, Micaela . . ." Mrs. Hansson put her hands to her lower back again.

"Yes?"

"I've been worried all these years that Morovia would find some reason to come after Hans again. He's the cruellest person I've ever met. Did I mention he tortured the cat before setting it alight?"

"No."

"And he was only twelve years old at the time, while today . . . Well, I barely want to tell you what I've heard. They say the best thing that can happen to witnesses who turn against him is a bullet to the head. They usually meet with the same fate as the cat."

"So I've gathered."

"He's absolutely terrible, Micaela. And so very intelligent—he's a genius in his own awful way. You have to promise me that Hans won't start another quarrel with Gabor Morovia."

"I'll try," Micaela said, as she heard Rekke's footsteps on the landing outside.

As Rekke entered he could tell from the serious tone in their voices that Mrs. Hansson and Micaela had been talking about him, but he didn't pay it any heed. He went into his study and examined the imprints in the yellow Post-it. There wasn't much to see. They hadn't pressed down very hard. He was able to make out *Hög*-something-*gatan 52*, and at the very beginning of the illegible bit there was a discernible ä. Högbärsgatan, perhaps? *Högbär*?

He wondered if *högbär*—"highberry"—was a name he didn't recognise, or perhaps an actual berry that had somehow passed him by. Or perhaps a misspelling? Högbergsgatan, however, was very real and located in the Södermalm neighbourhood. Number 52—he searched online—was home to the Maria Elementary School. That sounded innocent enough. Was he just being paranoid? What else did he have? A mark on Julia's wrist, something defiant in her gaze, her voice in the night, anxious and almost certainly lying, and the handwriting of a man who was over thirty and whose style implied delusions of grandeur. But graphology was hardly a science, and daughters told lies when they had gentlemen callers. Perhaps it was all just paternal mania. Matters were hardly improved by his aching chest and racing heart, while this heightened state of anxiety was sapping his concentration.

He was suffering from withdrawal and he really should swallow something or other, but he shied away from doing so. He should be a responsible parent. Although what help was he to Julia if he couldn't think clearly? None at all. Better capable than drug-free, he decided, rising to go to the bathroom. On his way there, he heard Micaela speaking on the phone.

She mentioned a meeting at one o'clock, and once she had hung up, he approached her. She looked as if she had been caught red-handed. There was a sheepish look in her eyes as she looked down at the floor.

"Did you catch Julia?" she said.

"No," he said. "She wasn't at home. Are you off too?"

"I'm going to see Claire Lidman's sister, Linda."

"Why?"

Mrs. Hansson was rattling about behind them. She was clattering about rather more than usual, occasionally pausing in her movements. There were sharp C's as she put the wine glasses into the dishwasher.

"I want confirmation that Claire is alive."

"Ah, a trifling matter."

"Rest assured that I'll read between the lines. I'm not just going to straight up ask her."

"Have you heard anything more?" he said.

"Kaj Lindroos called her last night and was apparently drunk and creepy."

"Had he been staring at that photograph for too long as well?"

"That's not encouraging."

"Care for company?"

She looked uncertain, and he realised she had found something out that she didn't want to share. Instinctively, he listened to Mrs. Hansson, as if hoping for more information from the notes emanating from her movements.

"But you'll probably do perfectly well on your own," he said.

"I don't know," she said.

"Oh, I'm sure you will," he said, patting her shoulder and wondering how best to occupy himself in the meantime.

He couldn't just wander about worrying about Julia. He had other business to attend to. He'd got back his necklace and spotted inconsistencies in William Fors's old witness statement—and he had a hunch about a connection, a direct line from Nordbanken's negotiations with Axel Larsson to Claire Lidman's disappearance. That was something substantial to deal with, rather than casting suspicion onto his daughter's boyfriends. He closed his eyes and then moved resolutely toward the bathroom, where he opened the medicine cabinet in an effort to repair himself a little.

# THIRTY-THREE

En route to the Normandy American Cemetery, Magnus spotted a middle-aged man with dark, curly hair whom he recognised but was unable to place.

Whoever it was was absurdly popular. Everyone wanted to greet him. Might it be some seldom-seen head of state he hadn't heard of? No, that was impossible. No-one was better informed than he. Then the penny dropped. The man in question was Tom Hanks. He snorted. *An actor. Run, Forrest, run,* he thought to himself as he pushed past. He couldn't handle the fawning over Hollywood stars. It was even worse with them than with royalty—everyone lost their wits. Everyone wanted to be in the picture.

Then again . . . there might be hope after all. He spotted a short, thin-haired figure with hollow cheeks who was indifferent to all the commotion. Or at least he was feigning indifference. It struck Magnus that this man also liked fawning, even if Tom Hanks was far too wimpy and liberal for his tastes. Putin—for Magnus had recognised him instantly—preferred action and muscles, the likes of Steven Seagal.

"Vladimir Vladimirovich!" Magnus called out a little too loudly, which caused unrest to spread through Putin's entourage—either because Magnus was moving too quickly or because he was expressing himself irreverently—so he added: "Herr Präsident," not only to add the title but because he knew Putin liked to show off his German.

"Magnus."

He couldn't help feeling flattered that this man—of all people—had addressed him by his first name. There was a bit of puff and swagger to be found in him too, if he were honest, and the familiar mode of address clearly made an impression. An opening appeared around Putin and a hand was extended—it was a brief handshake, but he noted that people were looking at them. Perhaps even Forrest Gump.

"How are you?" he said.

He received a smile, both vigilant and amused.

"I'm keeping busy."

"You look magnificent."

Putin made a face that suggested he had heard such words ad nauseam all day.

"And congratulations on your electoral success," Magnus said. "You didn't seem to have much competition?"

"That's history now."

"And new history is always being written. I was meaning to ask you about a mutual . . ." He hesitated. What was it he meant to say? Mutual friend . . . or *enemy*? There was so much that had been unclear since the bomb attack. "About an individual with whom we are both acquainted," he said.

"Who?"

"Gabor Morovia."

A cold wind swept across Putin's face and Magnus just had time to think that it was damn fortunate that he hadn't said "friend"—or even "acquaintance." Of course Putin hated Gabor. But a second later, the president was laughing it off, and then everyone else was grinning too, even if they had no idea what it was all about.

"You are having problems with him?" Putin said.

"I may be about to," Magnus replied with candour.

Putin leaned forward and gazed at him with an expression that it was impossible to interpret.

"Then shoot him."

A joke, of course. Nevertheless, Magnus felt his entire body shudder, and not just because it was incredible to hear these words from one of the most powerful men in the world. They reflected a secret dream of his—what a relief it would be if Gabor disappeared, taking his secrets with him to the grave. Perhaps that was why he replied in a manner rather unbecoming of a Swedish undersecretary:

"Can't you do the job for us?"

"We're working on it," Putin said, grinning again, and Magnus laughed ostentatiously just in case someone had overheard or, even worse, their exchange had been caught on tape.

But by then Putin and his entourage were already on the move again, and in a rare moment of weakness Magnus wondered whether he should serve up another compliment—perhaps something about the ice hockey game or the fishing trip. No . . . He still had some pride. After all, he wasn't like the idiots with Forrest Gump.

He slowed down and waited for Kleeberger and the prime minister, feeling in high spirits. It was damn lucky that Morovia didn't have Putin onside too. Otherwise, one might fear that the duo were best friends. Then again, equals didn't always attract. It was probably all connected to Gabor's son. Who would have dared do something like that to him other than a member of Putin's inner circle? He turned around to tell Kleeberger. Although . . . what business was it of Kleeberger's?

He resolved to keep it to himself as he quietly and thoughtfully moved on toward the monument, where President Bush was due to deliver his speech shortly.

Rekke had gone out and Micaela felt restless and curious. She was due to meet Linda Wilson at one o'clock, but with some time to kill she couldn't help sneaking into Rekke's study to find out what he had been doing all night.

He had most definitely been keeping busy. There was a mess of old case documents on his desk with illegible notes in the margins. She glanced at the top page. It appeared to be an excerpt from a police interview with William Fors:

> Fors stated that he was "a little drunk and crazy." He had received an inheritance and withdrawn a large sum of cash, and had the idea of rolling cigarettes using said banknotes. He also sprayed champagne at the walls and onto Ida Aminoff's dress. He insisted upon drinking out of her shoe and said he wanted to hire it for two thousand kronor. He can understand why she got angry. Nonetheless, he said that gave her no right to steal his wallet. Following repeated questioning, he admitted that he is not certain that she stole it. He stated that he may also have lost it. He was very intoxicated and "a little obsessed with her." She "looked like the Queen of Sheba or something like that with her necklace and I wanted her to pipe down." He also didn't harm her—all he did was chase her into the night. "Was that so strange?" he said. After all, she made everyone lose it a little. "I had a feeling something terrible might happen to her, the way she was carrying on," he added.

Surely it should say the way *he* was carrying on, Micaela thought. Damn it. Spraying champagne onto the walls and rolling cigarettes with thousand-kronor notes. She thought about the money she had given to Mamá, but also about Papá, who back in the day had doled out banknotes with guilty gravity, as if ashamed that he didn't have more of them. She left the room, slamming the door.

Rekke would just have to research that upper-class bollocks by himself, she thought as she slipped on her denim jacket and left. She might as well arrive early to see Linda Wilson.

There wasn't much traffic on the E4, and Lucas put his foot down. He got up to one hundred and forty kilometres per hour and glanced at

Julia. Her strawberry-blond hair was fluttering in the wind, and he reached out a hand toward her. She was so hot she was smoking. He should take her down to Husby. No offence to Natali—his girlfriend—but this girl was next level. Everyone would be so jealous. They'd all be like, Jesus, that's one hell of a chica Lucas has got himself. What Lucas wants, he gets.

On the other hand, he had to be careful. Julia came with temptations—like an expensive glass vase. He wanted to both own her and shatter her.

She was so fragile and beautiful that it made his fingers itch, and he'd already come close to crossing the line. Last night when she had been asleep and he had been studying her by the light seeping in under the blind, he had grabbed her by the throat and squeezed. There was something about it that just turned him on so fucking much—it made his stomach flutter. Thank goodness he had stopped in time—perhaps it hadn't just been Julia that he wanted to kill in that moment.

It had been Micaela too, and who could blame him? She was the one who'd sent him off the rails.

After all he'd done for her, she was trying to get him sent down. It was such a terrible betrayal, and if it hadn't been for Mamá and Vanessa he would have been first in line to strangle her—no-one would be able to claim she hadn't been warned. It was as if she were blind and deaf. She was going to mess everything up, whatever she did, and she definitely was not a cop who stuck to her job. She took advantage of every single thing she had ever seen or heard in their lives, and he needed to strike back.

He needed someone like Julia. But . . . she was mined territory, and going as far as hurting her for real was out of the question. It would be suicide. He'd have the whole world after him. Instead, the plan was to show how in love with him she was, and to get Micaela to realise that she couldn't challenge him. Things might happen. It was just that . . . he wasn't sure he could completely trust himself. Julia awakened something dark within him.

That slender neck, he thought to himself. That mouth. The face of a girl who had been given it all but who still—or perhaps that was why—trembled at the slightest thing. It was irresistible, wasn't it? And to top it all off . . . her old man. What a guy. No wonder he had enemies.

But the way this world worked was that your enemy's enemies were your friends, and he had spent the whole of the preceding evening talking to one hell of a charming lady lawyer who worked for a hotshot he'd talked to before, who had offered him money—lots of money—if they could join forces to apply pressure to Rekke. They wanted photos—nothing else—of him and Julia together. Material that would allow for arms to be twisted. In return Lucas would get to borrow their house in Trosa.

The house was apparently swanky as anything, and there would be champagne and food in the fridge. It looked like a good set-up—perhaps a little too good. But the lawyer—her name was Alicia—had promised to back him up legally if anything went awry. Although to be honest . . . there wouldn't be much she could do if he lost his self-control again like last night. He'd have to be careful—keep his hands in check. But that wouldn't be a problem, not really. This wasn't his first rodeo. Fuck it, he'd got out of all manner of binds just by being smarter than the rest. His self-confidence was brimming over as he briefly caught his own eye in the rear-view mirror. He was a handsome devil too—not to mention charming. He could get whoever he wanted, and no-one dared deceive him any longer. He'd made sure of that, and thinking about it—about everything he had accomplished—made him want to cross the line. As a reward. A trigger.

He put his foot down. The speedometer bounced up to one hundred and seventy, and Julia stiffened. It was as if the accelerator were connected to her nervous system.

"Do you mind slowing down?" she said.

"Sorry babe, I just got a bit excited," he said. It was true. He'd had all sorts of images in his head, and he grasped her wrist tightly the way he always liked to. If only you knew how precious you are, you spoiled brat, he thought, once again feeling that persistent temptation to scare her shitless.

# THIRTY-FOUR

Linda Wilson got down on her knees and prayed. *Dear Lord Jesus and Holy Mother of God.* But she stopped before long. Her back hurt, so she stretched out her arms. Her shoulders popped, which was an answer of sorts to her prayers. She'd been as tense as a bow for months, and no surprise...

Something terrible had happened to her sister, even if no-one was willing to spell it out, and likely as not no-one knew for certain either. There had been days when she had felt better and thought that the whole thing had been nothing more than a long spell of silence—the kind Claire had subjected them to many times during her life in exile. But today the fear had come back worse than ever. She'd had one troubling visit and was due another from a different police officer.

She stood up, reinforced at least by the fact that she hadn't become a slave to prayer. Given the complexity of the world and all the human destinies that God had to intervene in to satisfy one small wish, the logic underpinning it was unreasonable. Or that was what Claire had once said to her long ago, and they had laughed and promised each other not to pray anymore. She had kept that promise for a long time. If she had worshipped a god, then it had been Dionysus. She had drunk and lived as if there were no tomorrow.

Yet it didn't matter. When the crisis had come, religion had dug its claws into her again, and while she hadn't retained any of the good aspects of the Catholic faith, she'd been lumped with plenty of the rest: guilt; shame; feeling lost. Today it was worse than ever. She needed a drink—or three—but above all she needed a sign of life.

"Please, dear Claire, say something," she muttered as she went to make a gin and tonic. The kitchen was modern, having been renovated ten years earlier, but the flat was otherwise old-fashioned and filled with nineteenth-century furniture. Linda bought and sold Victorian antiques, though she didn't make much from it—quite the opposite, in fact. But she had money aplenty, nonetheless, and thank God for that. Claire had left behind more than necessary, because while she hadn't really died, a will had been drawn up just in case, which allowed Linda to live here in the city centre, not far from Östermalmstorg.

It was more than she could have expected when she was hopping between temporary roles in hospitality—and then signed off on permanent disability by the benefits office at just forty years of age because of her bad back. She shouldn't complain. She had become someone only by virtue of her sisterhood with Claire, but it had entailed other things too: a whole world of espionage with its encrypted messages, secret messengers and constant paranoia—and just when she had grown accustomed to that, something would happen—like now—and she'd feel like she was going crazy. She couldn't sleep, could barely think, and she hated Claire for that. She hated her and she loved her.

The doorbell rang. She swore. Not already. She'd barely had time to clear things away after Lars Hellner's visit. She went over to the hall mirror and sighed. She looked hollow-eyed and scared, or so she thought. Like an alcoholic, too. "Just a second," she shouted at the door. But at least she was decently dressed, she thought, looking at her pressed cotton trousers and ironed black blouse. She would probably be able to lie convincingly today, too. On that front no-one could find fault with her.

"Coming!" she said. "Coming."

Linda Wilson made Micaela feel small. She was tall and bulky with ravaged but beautiful facial features and large vivacious eyes. Claire was visible in her: a bigger, slightly older Claire, but still ... Linda Wilson had presence and a nervous, charming smile, and she lived as if she were marooned in another century. Hanging on the wall was a dark oil painting of Jesus just taken down from the cross, and there were antique dressers and chairs all over the place.

Micaela knew that the sisters' mother—who had married an English engineer who had left when they were still children—had lived the wild life in her younger years. After going through a detox programme for heroin addicts at a religious institution, she had converted to Catholicism and become increasingly orthodox and possibly more ascetic in her faith. Rebecka Wahlin was not the only one to say that she had been a destructive influence on the daughters in many ways.

"You have a lovely home," Micaela said.

"I'm not so sure about that," Linda said, before inviting Micaela to sit down in front of an open fire on a dark hardwood chair topped with a green cushion that was much too thin.

"I'm finding this very difficult," she said. "Just what is it you want?"

There was nothing aggressive about the question, but Micaela was still startled and she allowed herself to become entangled in a lengthy and not particularly convincing explanation that concluded with her encounter with Inspector Lindroos.

"You put some strange ideas into his head," Linda said.

"I'm sorry about that."

"Now he seems to think Claire might be alive. It's so damn twisted and disrespectful. You've no idea what this is bringing up. He even identified her himself in Spain."

Micaela nodded and feigned concern.

"You mentioned he was drunk?"

"Not sober at any rate," she said. "He tried to invite me out for a drink."

Micaela remembered the look she'd received when she had stepped into the police station on Bergsgatan.

"Isn't that what he always does?"

Linda smiled back at her rather unexpectedly.

"He tried to hit on you too?"

Micaela shrugged.

"Maybe I should have been flattered," Linda said. "I don't get many invitations of that kind these days. But let me be straight with you—this is not making me feel good."

"I can only apologise if I've triggered something painful," Micaela said.

Linda looked at her suspiciously.

"Have you come across rumours that Claire is alive before?" Micaela said.

"I've put up with Samuel for fourteen years, so yes."

"But not from anyone else?"

"No, I wouldn't say so."

Micaela heard the tiniest hitch in her voice, and speaking as neutrally as she could, she said:

"I'm interested in what happened before she disappeared."

"I suppose we all are."

"Well, what did happen?"

Linda Wilson looked offended.

"You'll know that better than I do. She was threatened and extorted."

"By whom?"

"By Axel Larsson, of course. And that Hungarian company. Cartaphilus."

"Did she ever talk about the owner, Gabor Morovia?" Micaela said, at which point a dark shadow crossed Linda Wilson's face, briefly but unmistakably.

"I'm not really sure," she said.

"But if you think about it?"

"Well, she mentioned him."

"In what way?"

"She said he was supportive at first. Caring. They had known each other at university. It was Morovia—before anyone else—who made her realise that there was going to be an economic crash. She . . . well, her estate, I suppose . . . made a lot of money from that insight. He saw things clearly."

*Clearly.*

"But then . . ."

"Things got tense. Claire was frightened of him."

"Did he attack her?"

"Something happened. She had stomach pains and nightmares, and she began looking over her shoulder in the street."

"Did she want to take him down?"

"I guess we'll never know the answer to that."

"But it was because of Morovia that she fled?"

"I dare say it was for all sorts of reasons."

"Because of Samuel too?"

Linda Wilson hesitated and glanced at her wristwatch. She evidently didn't like the turn the conversation had taken.

"A little, perhaps."

"What makes you say that?"

"It's great to be loved, but there are limits."

"But . . ." Micaela said.

"But what?"

"Just leaving him without a word of explanation. That's harsh."

"Maybe she didn't see any other way out," Linda said in a voice that deepened, making her other answers seem no more than hollow phrases empty of meaning. It was as if she had suddenly and unintentionally stumbled over something that was close to the truth. Micaela wondered how to proceed.

"She only wrote a single postcard to Samuel before she . . . died." Micaela intentionally dwelled on that last word. "But I wonder . . . did she write more to you?"

"Not even a line," she said.

"But she was writing a long letter just before her disappearance, wasn't she?"

"According to Samuel. But it never arrived, and as you know your colleagues did everything they could to find it. The post office even launched their own inquiry. I've been waiting for it ever since."

"Did she always write long letters?"

Linda Wilson smiled enigmatically.

"She wanted to be my mum."

"Is that so?"

"Yes, never mind that she was the little sister. But I guess you can understand it in a way. Our own mother wasn't much to write home about."

"In what way?"

"Almost every way. She gave us enough guilt to last a lifetime. Claire was keen to adopt the role of the sensible one in the family from an early age, while I . . ."

"While you?"

"Went off the rails instead."

"That's another solution."

"It is, and the more I messed up, the more talented Claire became. My weakness made her strong."

Micaela thought about Mamá and her other brother, Simón, who had spent their whole lives dealing with setbacks by giving in, while she had gritted her teeth and fought even harder.

"That sounds familiar," she said.

Linda Wilson scrutinised her.

"But the other way around, right?" said Linda.

"I suppose so. Although I've been pretty cheerless too."

Linda looked at her with a hesitant smile.

"Then you'll have to do something about it."

"I'm working on it." She pulled herself together. "So there was nothing particular—as far as you know—that Claire had on Gabor Morovia? Something that he had reason to fear?"

"I don't know," said Linda. "Maybe."

"You mean she hinted at something?"

"Yes, in a way."

Linda Wilson looked alert, or even frightened. It was hard to say which.

"Perhaps it's best you tell me?"

"She had a friend who died—her house burned down in Madrid the same autumn Claire disappeared," Linda said.

"Sofia . . ."

"That's right. Rodriguez. You've heard about it? They studied together and they were both close to Morovia. They worshipped him, I think. But then Sofia wanted to free herself, and she ended up whispering into the ear of the Spanish police. I suppose I shouldn't be telling you this."

"Why not?"

Linda hesitated.

"Because I don't really know much about it. But this much I can say: Sofia Rodriguez was found in her bed in the charred remains of her house. There were signs that the fire had started at her feet and spread up. They thought she'd been bound. The position of her hands indicated that much."

"As if she'd been tortured."

"Yes."

"And Claire thought Morovia had done it?"

"She never said as much, but that was how I took it."

Micaela leaned forward and said significantly:

"And Lindroos and his team obviously looked at it in detail."

Linda Wilson looked back at her with flint in her eyes.

"Not Lindroos, exactly."

"But the others did, right?"

Linda Wilson peered toward the kitchen. She seemed to be thinking intently about something.

"I heard you're collaborating with a professor who can interpret impossible clues and invisible signs."

Micaela was at once on her guard.

"You're changing the subject," she said.

"Actually, I'm sticking to it. I'm just trying to think. I could ask someone to give you a ring. I can't help wondering whether they're already considering it."

"Who?"

Linda's hands moved across her thighs.

"I can't say."

"But you're worried about something, aren't you?" said Micaela.

"Maybe."

"Do you want to talk about it?"

"I want you to leave."

"What?"

Micaela struggled to process the sudden change in tone.

"Why?"

"Because I do. Perhaps we'll speak again, but right now I'd like to be alone."

Micaela wondered whether there was anything she could say that would enable her to stay.

"This holiday snap with the woman . . ." she said.

Linda Wilson stood up.

"I don't want to hear about it."

"Rekke—the professor I'm working with—thinks the woman is anxiously looking over her shoulder for someone just behind her. Do you have any idea who that might be?"

"Thanks for coming," Linda said.

She held out her hand. Micaela stood up as well, reflecting that it probably was time to leave. She had the feeling that some sort of decision was being reached.

Rekke called Julia. Her phone was switched off. He swore. Instead, he texted his ex-wife, Lovisa. Maybe it was just him that Julia didn't want to talk to? Perhaps she preferred her chilly mother to her nervous father? The cool indifference as opposed to the suffocating anxiety . . .

He was walking restlessly around Djurgården. There were people strolling everywhere with their children, seemingly carefree. He was on the main tourist drag by Skansen, the Hasselbacken restaurant and the Gröna Lund amusement park. The sun was beating down and he was becoming increasingly sweaty and uncomfortable. Högbergsgatan 52. Might it be an address anywhere other than Stockholm? He would check that as soon as he got home. First, he needed to devise a strategy if he really was going to call William Fors.

He was certain that there was more to the story than Wille's excesses and all his frightful nonsense. Indeed, his readiness to immediately admit what a pretentious idiot he'd been that evening was suspicious in itself. Wille Fors was not the type to casually admit to embarrassments and mistakes. Not back then, nor in the years that followed.

In fact, he seemed to prefer to show what a sincere soul he was. There were also contradictions in his statement—oddities that were clearer now that years had passed and Rekke was no longer blinded by youthful incomprehension. Morovia presumably had something on him. Nordbanken's behaviour during the negotiations over Axel Larsson's assets indicated as much. Rekke needed to choose his words wisely and demonstrate that he was an expert in interrogation techniques in practice too. Although if he were honest . . . he had no idea how he was going to pull this off. The withdrawal symptoms were making him feel miserable.

On the other hand, Wille would probably not be in fine fettle himself. The job offers were hardly rolling in these days. But that thirty million kronor parachute they'd given him was presumably keeping him afloat, and he was no doubt still blessed with his car salesman's charm.

It would just have to be the way it was. He pulled out his mobile and dialled.

"Fors," said a voice on the line.

"Wille," he said. "It's Hans Rekke."

"Hans," said Fors.

It didn't seem that this was the most welcome phone call he had ever received, and Rekke wondered whether he should attempt to rally him a little. Happy bankers were more loquacious. But he couldn't bring himself to.

"I'm sorry to trouble you, but I think we need to discuss Claire Lidman and Ida Aminoff."

The call evidently wasn't improving for Fors.

"You mean they have something to do with each other?"

"Rather unexpectedly, yes. The same men were circling them—albeit with an interval of fifteen years."

"Which men would they be?"

"You and Gabor Morovia. Perhaps you're friends?"

"Certainly not."

He seemed shocked by the suggestion.

"Of course, you're right. One does not become friends with Morovia that easily. But perhaps he's whispered instructions into your ear?"

"Now you're insulting me."

"Perhaps a little."

"I don't know any more than what I told you and the police at the time. I don't understand why you're phoning me after all these years."

"Do you remember Ida's necklace?"

"Well, yes, of course," Fors said, troubled.

"You were the last person to see it on her neck."

"I hardly think so," Wille said, colliding with something in the background. It sounded like a lamp.

*"Nostri nervi loquuntur."*

"What?"

"Our nerves speak. But what I was going to say was that the necklace was torn off. It was wrenched from her neck with a brutality whose magnitude I only now understand."

"What do you mean, *only now*?" Wille seemed shaken.

"The mark on her neck," said Rekke. "It was always there as a point of concern—a missing link. But it wasn't taken seriously enough. It was too superficial a wound, a notch that wasn't more than a few millimetres in depth and didn't seem to correlate with the thickness of the necklace. But the detectives forgot two things: the necklace could have been torn off post mortem, and it could have been done quickly with two hands distributing the pressure."

"What are you getting at?"

"That I've identified a new scenario, William. I can make out the contours of it in the police interviews with you. Right from the off, you wanted to plant the idea that Ida had gotten rid of the necklace herself. You had an agenda, William."

"I've no idea what you're talking about."

"I should say you do. I know you lied, and provided you didn't kill her, I promise to spare you. But if you don't help me, I shall come after you with everything I've got."

"Are you threatening me, Hans?"

"It certainly seems so. I must say I'm a little surprised. I'm usually much too polite. I think we should meet right away."

"No, no, I can't."

"Of course you can. I'm going to pop down to the KMK and sip a couple of espressos. Be there as quickly as you can," Rekke said, reflecting that he wasn't quite so useless at this after all.

Samuel was walking along Strandvägen thinking about Claire. He was no longer angry or bitter, but thoughtful, as if there was something new about her he wanted to understand. He had met her at a party in Bromma almost fifteen years before. He'd been invited at the last minute, mostly out of politeness because he had custom-built a couple of coffee tables for the host—a rather arrogant executive at the Alfred Berg fund. Consequently, he had felt lost at the party. There had been no-one but hotshots and financiers in attendance, and he was keeping out of the way in the garden when she came up to him with a cautious smile and said something along the lines of: "I can't stand it here either."

It had been disarming and nicely put, but it hadn't reassured him.

She had taken his breath away with her beauty, and he had mostly concentrated on not coming across as awkward. But then something had happened. God had sent an idiot to help him—a man in a pinstriped suit with slicked-back hair, who waved his hands around before spilling a glass of red wine down her white dress. That was all it had taken for him to seize the initiative. He grabbed hold of the man and shook him like a rag doll over the lawn.

"Apologise *now* and offer to pay for her dry cleaning," he said with a sudden air of authority.

The man had mumbled a pitiful apology before beating a hasty retreat. The truly marvellous thing, however, was Claire's gaze. She looked at him with longing, nothing else, and not long afterward she took him by the hand and led him away. She hurried as if it were urgent, and of all the things he could describe about their departure there was one thing he remembered better than anything. He was no longer awkward. In fact, he took centre stage. He became funnier and wittier than ever, intoxicated, and not only by his own feelings. Claire understood him so quickly and so intuitively that the words came by themselves, which was why Claire hadn't been the only person to step into his life that evening.

He had caught sight of himself and a part of his personality that he hadn't known existed—and after that it had all gone so strangely fast. The very first night, when Claire was entwined with him, she had said with sudden gravity:

"Will you be kind to me?"

"Always," he said. "Always."

He solemnly swore it, and he had always regarded it as the start of their pact—their secret agreement. But now, hurrying along Strandvägen, he sensed for the first time another invisible presence in that bed: the shadow of another man who hadn't been kind, and who had in some respect been a backdrop to Samuel's path through life thereafter.

He stopped. Was that what he was? A contrast? An interval between storms, a person who in all other contexts would have been too kind and dull, but who fit into her life at that particular moment? He raised his gaze and looked toward the water. There were lots of people about, and the Swedish flag adorned the buses and trams. Was it the National Day? He didn't care. He kept walking until he spotted Professor Rekke further ahead in the crowd.

Should he rush over and ask about all the new things they had found out? No, the professor seemed to be in a hurry, so instead Samuel took the photograph out of his pocket. Had he really just been a respite for Claire—a stop on her journey? He refused to believe it. He gazed up at the street numbers on Strandvägen. It should be just here, but there wasn't a sign and only after inspecting the façade did he spot the name *Adler advokatkontor* in discreet lettering. He pressed the intercom button. A camera was following his movements. The door opened with a muffled buzz. He climbed a curving staircase, looking around nervously.

This was a grand place and he struggled to maintain good posture. Don't hunch your shoulders, he told himself, trying to find something to lend him strength, but it was no easy task. The room, furniture and art on the walls all made him feel small, and matters were not improved by the young woman who received him at reception. She was extremely chic—barely thirty, tall, beautiful and wearing a grey and green suit. Her eyes were friendly and welcoming.

"Mr. Lidman? Welcome," she said in English.

"Yes, good afternoon. I have an appointment with Alicia Kovács," he said, thrusting out his chest.

"I think there are a few others who would like to talk with you, but I'm afraid we're running a little late. Can I get you anything?"

"I'll take a glass of wine, please," he said, wondering whether it was impudent or even a sign of alcoholism.

It was only one o'clock, after all, and presumably they no longer drank in the middle of the day at posh offices, and it was no doubt apparent that he'd already knocked back a couple of beers, though if it was then the woman didn't let on.

"Bordeaux, Bourgogne, Chablis Premier Cru?" she asked with the same warm smile.

He couldn't help being vulgar.

"Whichever's the strongest."

She was silent for a moment before giggling, and he too managed to laugh along with her in a relatively light-hearted manner, regaining some of his self-respect.

"I'm not quite sure. But I'll check if you like," she said.

"Go for it," he said, smiling.

Once the woman had disappeared with soft footsteps, he looked around again. Above him hung a crystal chandelier. Two in fact. The walls were lined with walnut bookcases filled with leather-bound volumes, and there were several paintings that looked as if they had cost a pretty penny at auction. To the right there was a small black marble table on which stood a chessboard with finely chiselled pieces laid out on it. Might Alicia Kovács know something about Claire? Might it be as simple as there being someone with the answers just around the corner in his own city?

The young woman returned briskly.

"The strongest I could find was an Amarone. It's fourteen percent," she said.

"Thanks, that's great," he said, unable to sound as light in tone anymore.

In fact, he was embarrassed, and he found himself drinking two or three nervous gulps as though to underline that his quip about the alcohol content was deadly serious. Shortly thereafter, the woman returned and said he could go up one floor.

"Professor Morovia is expecting you."

*Professor Morovia.* Samuel's whole body tensed, and he thought again about the words Claire had whispered to him: "Will you be kind to me?"

# THIRTY-FIVE

Magnus couldn't be bothered to listen, and since he was sitting a long way back, he sneaked away despite having nothing else to do. He just wanted to get away and get to the sea that was so strangely calm down there—but there were soldiers and guards everywhere, and Bush's nasal voice interrupted his own thoughts.

The president was talking about D-Day, and it didn't take long for him to get onto his favourite topic: prayer. He was talking about the blessings offered to the soldiers landing here some sixty years earlier by their fellow Americans back home, and how God had been with them, somehow. Bollocks, Magnus muttered. Republican chicanery. Then again—he kicked a stone on the gravel path—it was a move that still worked. If you couldn't change the gun laws or sort out the war in Iraq, you could always offer your prayers. It was cheap, and it sounded kind of fancy. He might try it himself sometime when speaking in the U.S.

Above, in the clear sky, a helicopter circled before disappearing along the coast. Along an avenue, a couple of young men in white trousers and caps were smoking. They looked slightly more rebellious than the other tense tin soldiers lined up in rows with their straight backs. Magnus walked down toward them, feeling a little guilty, like a troublemaking schoolboy who had escaped the headmaster's speech, and it didn't help matters that his hangover had gotten worse.

He thought about his encounter with Putin. It was strange, wasn't it? On the other hand, Putin was a snake. He was mafioso. It had taken a while for Magnus to see through him, and he wasn't the only one in that respect. Bush himself had blurted out not long ago: "I looked the man in the eye. I was able to get a sense of his soul," as if that soul was both fine and reliable. But in the course of the last year, there had been no mistaking who Putin really was. He had set about crushing the media and turning every news outlet into a mouthpiece for propaganda, but above all he had challenged and threatened the oligarchs, making them both loyal and fearful. It had been a master stroke to arrest Khodorkovsky—the richest one of all. No-one was safe, no matter how many billions they had amassed. Was it during that process that Morovia and Putin had become enemies? Or perhaps . . . Well, surely they must have been already? Magnus was again reminded of the bomb planted in Gabor's limousine that had killed his son. Not a prudent thing—and that was putting it mildly—to do to a man who was already predisposed toward revenge and dangerous to boot.

It was all very disturbing—and what did Hans know about it? Likely as not, far too much, but . . . in the past when Magnus had fished around the topic, he had in fact got the impression that the opposite was true, as if Gabor was something Hans had dropped and moved on from. But ignorance and innocence were not things one could pin one's hopes on in the long term with him. Goodness gracious no, what a hopeless person he was—and couldn't that damned president cease his croaking? It was impossible to think while he was harping on. Blah blah blah . . . We stand united. Yes, well, we'll see how that works out. Had Bush strengthened his Texas accent? Of course he had. Magnus knew it was yet more chicanery. When the president wanted to be the tough guy and resonate with the grassroots, he sounded more like a cowboy. But who cared? And what was he, Magnus, going to do about Morovia? Stick his head in the sand? Flee? Of course not. Keep your enemies close, he thought to himself, so that you can determine how much danger you're in.

He hesitated for a second or two. Then he pulled out his phone with a complete contempt for death that both frightened and excited him and called Gabor.

Samuel heard a telephone ringing in the distance as he climbed the stairs to the floor above, where he entered a large room with a terrace overlooking Strandvägen and Nybroviken. Beside a large oak desk there was a middle-aged man standing with his back to him. The man looked fit and wore a well-tailored grey suit. He had thick, dark hair and he was focused on his mobile.

He seemed to be amused by what he saw, and that reinforced the impression of someone who was very pleased with himself. The man turned around and Samuel gasped.

It was as if he had expected to see a demon—the manifestation of everything that had hurt Claire so much. But Morovia's face was beautiful and friendly, which defused Samuel's anger, and he sensed immediately that it wouldn't be easy to stand up for himself against a man like this.

"Samuel Lidman, I presume," Morovia said in English in a deep and sonorous voice. "I've heard a lot of good things about you."

"Is that so?" Samuel said, trying to meet Morovia's gaze, which was no mean feat either. His eyes seemed to shift in colour, and were able to simultaneously see past and through him.

"Oh yes, indeed," Morovia said. "And not just your bench press and deadlift records either. I've seen your cabinet making. You have an eye for detail. You're a passionate man, and you chose the best of them for your bride."

"Thank you," Samuel said. "But then I was left alone, too."

"As we all are eventually," Morovia said, looking at him more closely now. "By the by, aren't you and I . . ." He fell silent.

"What?" Samuel said nervously.

"Rather alike—and I'm not referring merely to the fact that we both take care of our bodies. I'm thinking more of our features and colouring. Most of all, our lips."

"I don't know," Samuel said, surprised by the observation. "But you flatter me."

And when it came to it, Morovia was doing just that. He stood there looking so elegant and dignified with his intelligent eyes and his luminescent charisma, and Samuel couldn't help being affected at the comparison.

"On the contrary, it is I who am gratified. It truly is a pleasure to meet you, Mr. Lidman," Morovia said.

Samuel made an effort to retain some degree of composure. He had to understand what this was all about, and he couldn't allow himself to be manipulated.

"What's this about?" he said. "Do you have information about my wife?"

Morovia looked out the window.

"Claire has told me so much about you."

Blood rushed to Samuel's head.

"When was that?" he said.

Morovia came closer to him with that same friendly smile, but his body language was completely different now. Something about him had become threatening, and Samuel took a step back in fright.

"Have a seat," Morovia said, pointing to a brown armchair in front of the desk.

Samuel sat down while Morovia took a seat adjacent to him. His gaze was concentrated, seemingly more monochromatic now.

"I keep myself informed," he said, and now there was something unpleasant about the smile.

"Is she alive?"

"It would seem so. You had a photo, did you not?"

Samuel became even more uneasy.

"Why would you accept it without even having seen the photo?" he said.

"I have my reasons for believing it—but why don't we take a look at the picture before we discuss the matter? I may be able to help you."

"Why would you do that?"

"You and I share experiences in common."

"Such as?"

"Claire has betrayed us both. Badly."

"She hasn't . . ." he said, before realising he could be wrong.

No-one could escape the fact that Claire had left him in a cruel way, and he didn't dare or didn't want to ask how Claire had betrayed Morovia. He wanted to show the photograph first, so he put his hand into his inside pocket. A feeling that something definitive and fateful was taking place settled upon him as he handed over the print. Morovia took it. His body tensed. He squinted at it—and continued to do so for some time. It was somehow excruciating.

"Interesting," Morovia said at last. "Although somewhat unfortunate."

Samuel did not ask why it should be deemed so.

All he said was: "So you can see it's her?"

Morovia didn't answer—the only thing audible was a faint whistle as he exhaled. He turned the photograph, studying it from all angles.

"Strange," he said when he was done.

"So you agree it's her?"

"I do. Are there more pictures on the same roll of film?"

"What? No . . . How do you mean?" Samuel said.

"There's someone missing from the photo."

"Who?"

Morovia looked at him, his gaze icy cold.

"No-one you need to know about—not right now. But I would be grateful for the information—it would lend me greater clarity."

"In what way?"

"In a number of ways, both chronological and causal. I also recognise the book in her hand."

Samuel recoiled. "What do you mean?"

"I too have held it."

"Polugaevsky's *Sicilian Love*?" Samuel stammered.

"Exactly. The Sicilian Defence has been important to us both. We have memories associated with it. Did Rekke make that observation?"

"I think so. How can you have held—"

"What else did Rekke see in the photo?" Morovia said, interrupting him as if he hadn't heard him or even noticed the tension in the air. The photograph which had made him tense for a moment now seemed to amuse him.

"Have you seen Claire?" Samuel said.

"What else did Rekke see in the photo?" Morovia repeated.

Samuel didn't want to reply. He wanted answers to a thousand questions, but instead here he was in the hands of this terrifying man. I'll have to do as he wishes, at least to begin with, he told himself.

"He spotted that the woman had a damaged meniscus, just like Claire, and that she had a particular aura about her. What was it he said? Where I go, life goes."

"Is that a Marilyn Monroe quotation?"

"I don't know," Samuel said.

"Well, it doesn't matter now. One does not meet such people often."

"Which people?"

"Like Rekke. People are mostly blind. But some see. It is as if they live in another kind of world, where the details speak instead of being mere props."

"You have to tell me if . . ." Samuel tried to say, but something about Morovia made him once again fall silent.

"What do you make of Rekke's companion—Vargas?"

He could barely comprehend the question.

"Micaela Vargas—what is your view on her?" Morovia said.

Anger flared up in him. "Why are we talking about her when we're faced with the fact that Claire is alive?"

"I shall answer your questions, Mr. Lidman. But first I wish for you to tell me about Vargas."

"I don't know what to say. You have to understand—"

"I have always been intrigued by Rekke's choice of women," Morovia said, interrupting Samuel's reaction, unmoved. "They often possess something essential that he lacks, and I am constantly drawn to them too, but I have been unable to get a grip on Vargas. Of all the women he might have chosen, why collaborate with her in particular? I do not understand."

Samuel rose to his feet, now beside himself.

"Stop it!" he shouted. "I don't give a damn about Vargas. I don't give a damn why Rekke is working with her. What do you know about Claire?"

Morovia glanced back at the photograph before answering calmly.

"Just like you, I took the news of her death particularly poorly. It was rather clumsily handled, no? I realised early on that she was being protected from me. It's because of me that this entire charade has been staged—but I have always had my ways. I managed to find her after a few years, and my intentions at that time were not good—nor were hers, for that matter. But we still managed to establish a decent—albeit strained—relationship before I chanced upon something that happens to pertain to you."

Samuel sat down again, gaping.

"My God—where is she now?"

Morovia gazed at him with a smile that did not look altogether unfriendly.

"Do you want to see her?"

"Yes, of course! My God!" Samuel spat out the words, completely out of his mind.

"Then I shall tell her. For you see, Samuel Anders Benjamin Lidman, she never loved me—not even in those early days when I offered her the world. *You* were her great love."

Morovia's words broke across Samuel like a wave, and he sat still, afraid to move.

"Just what is it you're saying?"

"It's you whom she has loved all along."

Samuel's cheeks flushed. His heart pounded.

"But why hasn't she contacted me?"

Morovia looked at him in a manner that, if not exactly sympathetic, suggested intense interest.

"Because she has been unable to do so, and because I have not wanted her to. It was a delicate situation."

"You mean to say it's your fault?"

Samuel barely knew what he was saying.

"I wouldn't put it in such terms," Morovia said coldly. "If the responsibility had been solely mine, then Claire would no longer have been a problem, but she was playing both sides in a manner that was rather impressive, and shamefully I allowed myself to be fooled. But all that is behind us now, and I am convinced that she is at last ready to see you, provided you listen to me."

"I'm listening."

Samuel hated the pleading, pitiful note in his voice, but he could no longer help it. "What do I have to do?"

"You must be on my side, Samuel. You must not speak to the police—or Rekke."

"Okay," Samuel said uncertainly.

"Good. Alicia Kovács will telephone—but now it is time for you to go. I have an important call to take."

"No," Samuel said. "There must be more."

All the same, he managed to content himself with that. He needed to process what he had heard, and as he staggered out into the sunshine feeling suddenly happy, or at least hopeful, he kept thinking over and over: *She loves me. She loves me.*

Magnus cadged a cigarette from the soldiers who were smoking and was about to engage them in conversation when his mobile buzzed. It was Gabor returning his call, and it made his heart jump. He decided not to pick up. It had been a mistake to call, a mistake to concern himself with Gabor's existence at all. But in the end, after six or seven rings, he caved. Morovia said he was glad to hear his voice; he had been meaning to call for a while.

"What's that going on in the background?"

Magnus held the phone aloft.

"Is that President Bush?"

Magnus explained that he was in Arromanches in Normandy for the sixtieth anniversary of D-Day, at which point Gabor began to laugh wildly, as if Magnus had told him he was at the circus.

"And you're calling me in the middle of his speech?"

"You find that disrespectful?"

"Not at all," said Gabor. "It's you, Magnus. You're a caricature of yourself."

"What do you mean by that?"

"You love power, but you love mocking its pomp and circumstance even more."

Magnus laughed in a somewhat strained way.

"I just ran into Vladimir Vladimirovich," he said.

"Putin?"

"Indeed."

"And it made your blood sing."

"What are you talking about?"

"Your brother pops his opiates. Your drug of choice is power. Putin gave you the courage to call your enemy, no?"

"Bullshit," Magnus said, but he knew Gabor was right.

When Putin had addressed him by his first name and they had joked and hobnobbed almost as equals, he had felt invincible for a brief spell and it had made him foolhardy. That was the truth, and he was ashamed.

"You should be on your guard with that one. He wants to see you shot," he said.

"Was that why you called?"

"No," Magnus said, swallowing. "What I wanted to say was . . . Hans is digging into Ida Aminoff's death again."

Morovia fell silent and for a moment Magnus thought that Gabor was as frightened as he was at the prospect, but after a second or two he simply laughed again.

"I thought you were going to bring me news, Magnus."

"So you already knew."

"You might say I precipitated it."

Magnus took a moment to ponder this.

"How?"

"I returned a modest trifle to him. But I should think it began with his interest in Claire Lidman."

Magnus coughed. Claire Lidman was something he had helped Gabor with, which should count in his favour.

"I saved you from her," he said.

"I saved myself from her, but I thank you for your contribution."

Magnus tried to change the subject. "We have a mutual interest in stopping Hans."

"Do we?"

Morovia sounded sarcastic. Magnus bit his lip.

"I am actually more interested in something else entirely," Gabor said. "I have been looking into it for some time, but I have been unable to obtain a definitive answer and it is not my wish to pass judgement without evidence."

Magnus took a deep breath.

"Out with it then."

"It concerns Hans's old chum, Herman Camphausen. You remember Herman, don't you?"

Magnus remembered Herman very well—a fearful bookworm who had toughened up later in life and become an intelligence officer with the Bundesnachrichtendienst in Berlin, where he fought organised crime with any means he could.

"What about him?" he said.

"He's always admired Hans."

"I'm sure he has."

"Quite, and I am curious as to whether Herman asked your brother for assistance back in '94."

"Why that year in particular?" Magnus asked.

"Why indeed?" Morovia said with a rhetorical flourish. "Perhaps because a number of imbeciles in the Western intelligence services at the time believed Russia to be a splendid new friend and gave the KGB—or whatever they called themselves back then—high-grade information."

Magnus felt the discomfort crawling under his skin.

"But more specifically," Morovia went on, "I want to know if Herman involved Hans in the investigation into the murder of Chabarov in Berlin."

Magnus was now genuinely scared.

"How am I supposed to know that?"

"Because, Magnus, you've always found out everything about Hans. For that simple reason."

Magnus's whole body tensed in concentration.

"That's not true," he said.

"What a pity."

An icy chill had descended over Morovia's voice.

"Then again," Magnus said, "even if I could find out, why would I tell you?"

"Out of self-preservation, naturally. If you give me that information, then I shall remain your friend."

"And if I don't?"

"Then I may whisper things into certain ears."

Magnus stared in the direction of President Bush, who had just finished his speech.

"I was a fool to call," he muttered.

"Not at all. You read my thoughts," said Gabor.

Magnus hung up, resolving to forsake global politics and go home at once.

# THIRTY-SIX

Micaela took the elevator down from Linda Wilson's and emerged onto Nybrogatan. As she reached Östermalmstorg, a text message arrived. It was from Natali—Lucas's girlfriend—and she thought she knew exactly what it was about. Natali was going to try the soft approach: leave Lucas alone for the sake of the family. Why fight when you can take care of each other?

She'd heard it all before, and it wasn't a bad tactic. It was definitely more effective than threats and violence, and it was the kind of plea that had made her waver from the start. But as it turned out, that wasn't it at all.

Natali was wondering where Lucas was. She said she was worried. *Jealous*. It was a striking admission. Natali never showed weakness, and her loyalty to Lucas was unwavering, but all of a sudden she was *jealous*. Well, let her be. She ignored the message, thinking instead about Claire Lidman and her sister's reaction when she had mentioned Morovia. Had that been fear on Linda's face? And what had she meant when she'd said someone would be in touch?

She surveyed the city, wondering whether she should try and take some time off—or at least sit down to think it all over. She could even give Vanessa a call, or get in touch with Jonas Beijer and apologise for her hysterical call about Rekke.

She made her way up Riddargatan, past the Hedvig Eleonora Church, feeling once again that she didn't belong in this neighbourhood. On the other hand, Husby was little better, given what had happened. Her mobile rang—Natali, no doubt.

In fact, it was from an unknown number and she answered hesitantly. It was Superintendent Lars Hellner from the Eco Crime Office at the National Criminal Police. There was urgency in his voice, and she got the impression he was about to impart something worrying or shocking.

"Where are you?" he said.

"I'm on Riddargatan. Why do you ask?"

"Excellent," he said in a lighter tone of voice. "Make your way down toward Grevgatan and look out for a rather short, skinny man in his sixties. He's wearing a pair of cheap sunglasses he picked up at the petrol station to avoid the damn sunlight. Incidentally, you bumped into him recently. He took more notice of you than you realised."

"What's this about?"

"I've been looking for you. I was just up at Professor Rekke's place, but you had both fled the field. But there . . . ah, how serendipitous . . . I can see you on the phone talking to a short old man."

She hung up. Further down the street she spotted a man in a pale-grey shirt carrying a rather large grey briefcase. He had a narrow, blotchy face, but seemed otherwise youthful; he had a spring in his step, and in reality he wasn't all that short or skinny. On the other hand, he really was wearing a pair of round sunglasses that looked a bit eccentric on him. He took them off and waved at her in apparent amusement. He was probably right that they had met recently. She couldn't work out who he was until he came closer and proffered his hand. He was the man who had stepped into the office and interrupted her and Lindroos the afternoon before.

"You," she said.

"Quite: me. You left a most exhausted inspector feeling very much off-kilter. You must have brought him something."

"Yes," she said hesitantly.

"How did you get on with Linda? She was awfully nervous about you coming."

She stopped, surprised.

"How do you know about that?"

"I've been in contact with her all day," he said.

She began to walk again, thoughtfully this time.

"Why?"

"Lindroos called her yesterday and ranted on about some new photograph of Claire Lidman in Venice."

"I heard that."

"It interests me very much for a number of reasons. You wouldn't happen to have a copy?"

Micaela's body tensed.

"Afraid not," she said.

Hellner gazed at her in disappointment.

"That's a shame. I've only seen parts of the photo so far. I tried to put it together this morning, but there are pieces missing."

"How come?"

At once she became intensely focused.

"Well, I've been around to Lindroos's too. I haven't exactly been slacking, if that's what you're thinking. But the damn fool had ripped the photograph up into a thousand pieces in some sort of panic attack."

"That doesn't sound very sensible."

"No, and that alone piqued my interest. I couldn't believe he would have done that if he hadn't seen something in it. The investigation is an open wound for him, you see. He feels betrayed, and I'm guessing he's always suspected there was something going on there that we never let him in on."

"And that is indeed the case, is it?"

The amused, somewhat quizzical expression on the superintendent's face disappeared and Micaela looked away, across Riddargatan.

"I meant to discuss it with Rekke," he said. "I have got non-disclosure agreements that I'd like you both to sign. You see, I'm in a very tricky situation here."

She had time to envisage multiple *tricky situations* before she replied.

"What do you mean?"

"I find myself urgently in need of a tracer and I gather that Rekke can read people and places like an open book."

"I guess, sometimes," she said, smiling a little. "Other times, all he does is doubt himself. He could do with a little more self-belief."

"Sherlock Holmes without the bravado, in other words."

"Something like that," she said, smiling again. "What do you want to ask him about?"

"The photograph. The timing of when it was taken makes this all very interesting, and I wonder whether . . ." He hesitated. "You don't have a special number for him, do you? Apart from his mobile."

She shook her head.

"I think he's taking a meeting."

"The thing is, you see, we're somewhat depleted," the superintendent said. "The investigation was closed quite some time ago—we can thank the pack of crooks in the government for that. What's more, there are rather a lot of people in my immediate vicinity whom I don't trust. And like I said, we need help from someone who knows how to do jigsaws—your efforts around that soccer ref have passed into myth down our way. That's why I thought . . ."

His eyes sparkled with a hint of devilry.

"You thought what?"

She leaned forward instinctively, as if he were about to impart a big secret to her.

"That I might perhaps be a little incautious."

Good, she thought. Good.

"The situation has been turned on its head," Hellner said. "But if I do decide to spill the beans, then you and Rekke need to know that you can't tell anyone else what you hear. In fact, I'll put you away if you do."

"Understood," she said.

"Splendid. Well, in that case, I've got a document for you to sign, and some other technical mumbo-jumbo too." He rummaged through his briefcase. "One of these," he said, showing her a grey metal box. "An acoustic safe box for our mobiles."

"Of course," she said, pulling her phone out.

At that moment, it rang. This time it actually was Natali, and Micaela looked at Hellner, who shrugged as if to say, *Take it, but then that's the last of it.*

"Hi, Natali, I'm kind of busy," she said. "Can I call you back later?"

Natali didn't seem to hear her, plunging straight in and telling her that Lucas hadn't come home that night and that she thought he'd met a girl, some little posh girl, "probably a teenager." She'd heard him on the phone—it had been an awful call, she said. Micaela took a step to one side so that Hellner wouldn't overhear.

"Did it seem serious or what?"

"No," she said. "More like a mean game. It doesn't seem to be doing him any good, and lately I'm sorry to say I've been afraid, Micaela. For the first time he's scaring me."

"Lucas would never do anything to you," Micaela said.

"I'm not afraid for my own sake," Natali said.

"Then who do you think is going to end up getting hurt?"

"When he was talking to that girl, he did a weird movement with his hand as if he was breaking a bird's neck or something. It was nasty, Micaela, and I think this is all to do with the two of you fighting. That's what's made him lose it completely. Can't you talk to him?"

"Sure, I'll try."

"But don't tell him we talked."

"I promise. I'll be in touch. I've got something else to handle right now. Take care," she said in a voice she had probably never used with Natali before.

She turned back to Superintendent Hellner. He was looking at her, concerned, and seemed on the point of asking what the call had been about, but he refrained and instead took her phone and slipped it into his lock box. Then they began to stroll down toward Strandvägen and the water.

"Your colleague Jonas Beijer sends his best, by the way," Hellner said. "He sometimes helps us out. He said you're a good cop, but that everyone on the murder squad in Solna bitches about Rekke. Do you understand why?"

She thought about this.

"It's hard to deal with someone who sees more clearly than the rest of us. No-one wants to feel stupid," she said.

Hellner laughed, but quickly became serious again, and although Micaela understood that what she was going to hear was new and perhaps shocking, it was Natali who was on her mind.

What had she just told her?

Perhaps it was all a mistake. Lucas had misgivings—and not just because of his throbbing desire to terrify Julia. He'd received conflicting information from Alicia, the lawyer he'd been communicating with.

She didn't seem to know what she wanted either. Having pulled into a petrol station at the exit for Gnesta, where he'd called her as agreed, he'd been told that she was awaiting orders—some kind of confirmation. Lucas was to stand by for the time being and not do anything stupid. He fumed. This was weapons-grade bullshit.

He was doing what she wanted. And who the fuck did she think she was anyway, giving him orders? But just as he was about to say as much and hang up, the call was put through and that guy he'd spoken to briefly before came onto the line. The words stuck in his throat. Something about that voice made him mutter "Sure, sure" like a schoolboy, and when he emerged from the shop and saw Julia sitting in the passenger seat with her big, nervous eyes he was even more pissed off. He slammed the car door shut. The voice had diminished him. Who the hell did the guy think he was?

"What were you doing?" said Julia.

"Nothing," he said, passing her a Cola Light he'd grabbed from the chiller inside.

"Did you call someone? I could do with—"

"No," he said, interrupting her. "I was just taking a slash."

He pulled back out onto the motorway, drumming the wheel furiously as he began to think about Micaela again. If things went up shit creek then it was her fault—no-one else's.

Rekke was sitting in the café of the KMK—the Royal Motorboat Club—when William Fors came striding along the footpath. Life seemed to have been kind to him. He appeared to be just as stuck-up as before, with his plus-fours and sailing jacket and the rest of it. Nothing about him suggested that he was in a tight spot, and perhaps he didn't realise he was. *Beati pauperes spiritu*, blessed in spirit are the poor.

Rekke, on the other hand, had nothing to be cocksure about either. There was no doubting who spent his days in the sun and who spent them indoors gazing inside himself. William also seemed to take note of this with a degree of satisfaction.

"Hans," he said, sitting down. "What's happened to you? The last time I saw you, you were giving a talk in the Aula Magna at Stockholm University, and we were all gaping at your wisdom."

"Kind of you to remind me of my better days. You, however, appear to be living your best life."

"I can't complain. The markets are rising and my handicap is falling."

"Magnificent. Who could ask for more? And that means you'll be able to hold your own in the event that I attempt to take you down," he said, managing to shake the man at least a little.

William glanced anxiously down toward the water.

"Why are you raking all this up again?" he muttered. "This whole business was laid to rest long ago."

Rekke ran his hand over his hair and looked William in the eye.

"Laid to rest?" he said. "The unsolved murder of the person whom I loved most on earth. How could that ever be laid to rest or forgotten?"

"I didn't mean to hurt you, Hans. But you're saying it's an unsolved murder? I thought it was an overdose."

Rekke deliberately remained silent for a while.

"It was an unsolved murder all along," he said at last. "I just couldn't see that clearly at the time. But above all, I missed the very nub of the story—the disturbing star around which the entire business orbited."

"What do you mean?"

"The pearl necklace I bought her."

William twitched restlessly.

"It was never found?" he said.

"I conducted endless searches and contacted all the leading dealers in oriental pearls of that kind, but I had no success. I did, however, learn something: if a necklace like that *had* come onto the market, the connoisseurs would have heard about it. The information would have reached me. I realised that whoever had taken it must have kept it as a trophy—as a souvenir. That person—I always envisaged him to be a man—was very probably well-off. Otherwise, the temptation to liquidate it would surely have become too great. I spent a long time crafting a profile of the perpetrator. Who keeps such a fateful and valuable item at home year after year? Did they look at it regularly, with a modicum of pleasure, recalling the moment she died? I always imagined it to be so, and I thought—despite the red mark on the neck, or perhaps precisely because the mark was so indistinct—that the necklace had been removed from Ida's neck with care. I pictured a kind of sensuality in the action—a thief's solemnity, a gentle desecration—but now . . ."

He grasped Fors by the wrist.

"Yes?" William said nervously.

". . . I've realised I was wrong. You can see for yourself."

Rekke took the necklace from his pocket and laid it on the table. There was a shimmer upon it, a light that seemed to hail from a different era. The pearls, reflecting the sunlight, hinted at all the colours of the rainbow, and for a moment it became clear to Rekke why he had bought something so exclusive. The piece of jewellery still made him catch his breath, and there was no doubt that it also moved Fors.

"Beautiful, isn't it?"

William looked around anxiously, as if Rekke had set down contraband on the table.

"Yes, very," he muttered.

"But this is what I wanted to show you: look at the clasp." Rekke turned the necklace around and passed it over. "It's robust in quality, no? Yet it's broken."

William nodded and pushed the necklace away.

"You don't want to examine it yourself?"

He shook his head.

"Okay, but this clasp here . . . you see . . . it broke. What does that indicate?"

"I don't know," William said, looking away.

"It indicates violence, and what usually precedes violence?"

William Fors looked down at the table.

"Aggression," he said, speaking in a low voice again.

"Indeed, not to mention violence. Violence is preceded by violence, and I spotted a wound on Ida's oral mucosa whose import I did not initially recognise. She tried to open her mouth for air. I'm sure she had her own difficulties given the alcohol and opiates in her system, but she was helped to suffocate. I can see that clearly now, and I cannot abide the fact that you lied to me at the time."

"I didn't lie," William said, glancing pleadingly toward the waitress as if she might be able to save him, but the young girl with the pageboy haircut seemed completely oblivious.

"It's hard being invisible, Wille. Nor is it easy being overly visible. No problem—I shall order for you. What would you like?"

"Some water and a cappuccino will be fine, Hans."

"Some water and a cappuccino, if you please!" Rekke called out.

The waitress reacted immediately and set to work on the order.

"You haven't lost your authority. I'm impressed," William said, perhaps in an attempt to lighten the mood. "But as I said . . ."

"I read your police interview transcripts last night, and you put your foot in it."

William began to toy with the necklace.

"In what way?"

"You said that Ida didn't want to feel like the Empress of China."

William ran his hand nervously over his face.

"Ah, yes. Of course. She said that. You know what she was like. Completely damn..."

He stopped, afraid to say something unflattering, at which point Rekke leaned forward and fixed his gaze on him.

"Quite, Wille. I *do* know what she was like. I dare say that's why I believed you—believed that she really might have thrown the necklace into the bay—but now that I've read the file again, I see that your words are false. They differ from other witness statements from that night."

"Why would I lie about something like that?"

"I should say it was to provide an alternate explanation for why the necklace went missing—and no, don't say a word. Don't offer any moronic excuses."

"I shan't."

"Good, because if you killed her and stole her necklace then I intend to crush you. I shall not relent until I have proven it and you are behind bars. But if you saw something that you are keeping quiet about because you are scared, or because you promised to keep your mouth shut, then I shall protect you as if you were my most important ally. All I'm after is the man who grasped the necklace in his hand and pulled."

"I saw your brother."

"What?"

Rekke had, of course, heard him, but he couldn't take it in. Magnus had hoodwinked him so many times and plotted against him even more frequently, but the idea that he was involved in the death of Ida Aminoff was more than he could countenance. He fixed his gaze on William Fors's face to try to assess the value of this revelation.

"Nothing," William said, clearly regretting his words.

"Peculiar," said Rekke. "I thought you just said you saw my brother."

"Yes, but..."

Rekke took a deep breath, fully aware that he must not allow himself to be carried away.

"I'm thinking of Claire Lidman," he said.

"Claire Lidman?" Wille parroted, conspicuously baffled by the sudden change of course.

"Indeed," Rekke said with all the coolness he could summon. "I wonder what you had to do with her disappearance?"

Wille looked even more horrified.

"I didn't have . . ." he said in a stammer.

"Are you sure? Those who lie during one police investigation might easily be suspected of doing the same in another."

"You wouldn't dare to accuse me of that."

"Oh, I dare, Wille. But I can protect you too."

"Not from this."

Rekke scrutinised him.

"Is it that bad?"

"It is."

Rekke managed to produce a smile.

"I may be a detective of sorts, but I am not a policeman or a lawyer, troubled by anything as insignificant as perjury or the rights of the accused. If you didn't kill Claire or Ida, then I might even be able to rely upon my psychologist's duty of confidentiality to my patients. On the other hand . . ."

"What?"

"If you don't tell me, Wille, then I will be a bloodhound. I will dig it all up anyway, and I will not be anything like as kind."

"You are not yourself, Hans."

"No, indeed. Murder of those I love suppresses the friendliness in my nature. You didn't go straight home after parting ways with Ida."

"I did go straight home," Wille said defensively.

"Really?"

"I lived on Styrmansgatan back then, and I can remember barely being able to unlock the door."

"You were drunk?"

"As a skunk. The place was a damn mess and I was totally hammered."

"So what happened?"

"I sat down on the edge of the bed and began ringing around girls I'd been with. One of those drunken things, you know. One starts desperately calling people."

"Not *one*, Wille. You!"

"Okay, me. Should I continue, or do you want to moralise some more?"

"Continue."

"But I require undertakings. I don't want to read about this or be called upon by the police or any other palaver like that."

"I've invoked my duty of confidentiality and that's sacred to me—you, on the other hand, have to actually talk. That's part of our agreement, no?"

"Yes, fine, but in my own time."

Rekke nodded. "Certainly. So what happened?" he said.

"What do you want me to say?" Fors said. "When no-one answered or the ones who did told me to go to hell, I headed back out. I don't think I had any plan at all. I suppose I must just have hoped something would turn up, and I probably spent a good hour wandering about, but I ended up on Torstenssonsgatan and stood there outside the door to Ida's stairwell like a fool."

"You just stood there."

"I guess I called out 'Ida, Ida, I'm sorry' or something like that. 'Let's just talk about it—let me come in.' I was pathetic, Hans. I won't mince my words about that. But then all of a sudden the door flew open and someone came out. It was a young man in a dark jacket, and I could tell right away from his body language that something had happened to him. He seemed to tumble out, and I shouted something like 'Hello? Hello?' and that was when he turned around, and I saw it was Magnus. Damn it, Hans, I promise I've never seen him like that, ever. He seemed completely shattered and he walked toward me, not completely steady on his feet—not because he was drunk but because he was shaken—and I can't really remember what he said, except for one thing. 'You weren't here,' he said. 'You weren't here.'"

"And you agreed, just like that," said Rekke.

"I didn't touch her. I have no idea what happened to her. You promised you'd be on my side, Hans."

"Provided you're telling the truth," Rekke said, glancing up and seeing—to his surprise—Micaela making toward Nobelgatan with a short, rather authoritative gentleman wearing round sunglasses.

# THIRTY-SEVEN

The sky had become overcast, and there weren't as many people out and about. The footpath crunched beneath their feet. Above them were the elegant diplomatic residences, fenced off and sometimes fit with bars across the windows. Micaela glanced at Superintendent Hellner. He had been diffident and thoughtful for some time, but now he cleared his throat as if about to make a speech—or a confession.

"Just a year or so ago, it would have been unthinkable for me to take a walk like this with you to talk about Claire Lidman, but as I said, the situation has changed."

"What's happened?"

He smiled melancholically and took off his sunglasses.

"Unfortunately, you could say that we no longer have anything to fear," he said. "What we had feared has already happened, and now what we want to do is reach out, rather vainly hoping for help."

"I'm not sure I understand."

"You aren't supposed to. Perhaps we should wait until we can track Rekke down?"

"Why don't you give me the basics?"

He stopped and shook his head.

"No," he said. "Let's wait—I'll only have to repeat myself. But okay... well, there you have it... not even I am particularly consistent anymore."

"Consistency is overrated," she said.

He laughed in resignation.

"Well, to keep it short and sweet: Claire Lidman is alive. But I suppose you've already worked that out. Or to put it another way: we *hope* she's alive. The last sign of life we received from her was in March this year, shortly before that photograph was taken."

A jolt of tension ran through Micaela.

"Then what happened?"

"She simply disappeared. None of our contacts have been able to reach her, and that makes us very concerned, but we already knew thanks to CCTV and eyewitnesses that she had been in Venice, which is most unlike her. She would never usually visit public locations like that. But perhaps it's best if I start from the beginning—briefly."

Micaela nodded, and Hellner slowed down and lowered his voice.

"And Rekke already knows this, so I suppose I can tell you too. In the late 1980s, we resolved to take vigorous action against organised crime. To our dismay, we had observed an increasing willingness to accept—even among serious finance houses and banks—the proceeds of criminal activities. I dare say most of them took it because money was money. That was very much the spirit of the times. But others were afraid—and with good reason. People were being killed and going missing, and very few people were being held accountable. It was a poison within society, and the government issued us with a directive to deal with it. It was an early pan-European project. There were six or seven national police bodies across Europe—depending how you counted—who were working together, and we were immediately given resources and muscle. There was only one question: where to start? Should we go after the minnows and work our way up, or instead start with a big scalp and get a lot of attention from the off? We decided on the latter, and there was one name that came up right away."

"Gabor Morovia."

"Exactly. He was perfect: good-looking, sharp, a mathematician, and in bed with power—with people like Putin—even if Putin back then was nothing more than a humble KGB operative in Dresden. But Morovia had an incredible backstory, and of all the crooks we were looking at, he had the highest concentration of people around him who tended to disappear. Many were burned or tortured to death. We all felt incredibly motivated: we were going to put the bastard away. At the same time, we were warned we didn't stand a chance. He was said to have powerful protectors everywhere."

"Such as the Swedish state," she said.

"Yes, but I'll get to that later. As we entered the nineties and autumn came, the Morovia case was designated a priority project at the highest level, and we were presented with an unexpected opening. I'm sure you can work out what. Claire Lidman approached us at the National Criminal Police and said she wanted to talk. I was the first to meet with her."

"What did she have on him?"

"She was shaken. It was early in the morning, and I don't think she could have slept much. She struggled to stay seated, her neck was clearly sore. She didn't say it in as many words, and it didn't seem to be something she wanted to talk about, but I had the strong impression that she'd been subjected to something that had provoked her into action. I could tell she was furious."

"What did she have to tell you?"

"What she knew. She brought documents: notes, diaries, lists of names. But above all—and this was crucial—she had information that would prove one of her friends from her college days in London had been murdered in Madrid."

"Sofia Rodriguez."

"Quite. And once we realised that we could substantiate her story, we knew we had him."

"Sounds promising," said Micaela.

"Exactly," he said. "It was a big deal—a real breakthrough. At the same time, we realised the risk we were exposing her to, and we started work to protect Claire and her husband."

"So Samuel was part of the equation from the start?"

"Oh yes, we had no intention of separating them, and that was the last thing Claire wanted. She loved Samuel—she told us over and over that she couldn't manage without him."

"Yet he didn't go with her."

"No, she was suddenly panic-stricken and did a complete about-turn. It was incomprehensible to us, and we had a number of crisis summits with her, but she refused to budge. Only afterward, when we worked with our Spanish colleagues to stage her death, did we understand."

"What?"

"She was expecting."

"So it was true then?"

They passed a large red-brick house. Two women were sitting on a balcony, laughing.

"Exactly. She was pregnant," Hellner said. "But she didn't know who the father was. Most likely, of course, it was Samuel, in which case it was nothing but good news. A happy event. Claire and Samuel had been trying for a baby for some time, and she had been longing for good news, something new to live for. But there was a risk—a small one, she thought—that it might be Morovia's child, and that would be disastrous, she said. We thought so too. So you can understand..."

"She was filled with hope and dread all at once."

"Yes, and as the weeks went by and she both wanted and didn't want to get an abortion... It wasn't easy for her, poor thing. Nevertheless, we had some wonderful times. We had placed Claire in a safe house, a small cottage in the Alps near the Austrian border. There were guards, of course, and one of us investigators was always there too. I stayed there a few times. In the evenings, we'd drink tea and play chess—or rather, she schooled me in chess—and we'd have serious conversations about life. It tormented her that Samuel believed her to be dead, and I remember being worried that she might contact him. Everything had to be approached with the utmost caution."

"Of course."

"But I was also making careful plans for how to facilitate a reunion—because it had to be Samuel's baby. It just had to be. That was what Claire kept saying, and she eventually convinced the rest of us too, and we all began to dream of a happy ending. We were looking forward to a husband and wife being reunited around a little baby, and we discussed at length how to extract Samuel and explain his disappearance. It was quite an enterprise in every respect."

"But it wasn't Samuel's son?"

Hellner looked at her with an expression that made Micaela hope that it had been.

"We were all very relieved after the birth," he said. "I'll never forget the call from Claire. She sounded so happy," the superintendent added, looking toward the square bulk of the National Museum of Science and Technology.

When Rekke saw Micaela vanishing toward Nobelgatan, he felt a pang of longing, and perhaps of regret. He should have been better with her. Then he turned resolutely back to William Fors.

"Continue," he said.

"I went home—that was it. And the next day I heard in the evening that Ida was dead. I was watching the news on TV. About half an hour after that, Magnus was at my door. He didn't look much better than before—I don't think he'd slept a wink. In his hand he had an envelope stuffed with photos that had been sent to him by messenger. He laid them out on my kitchen table. They were grainy—they'd been taken in the dark with a telephoto lens—and it took me a while before I realised what they were. A series of photographs showing Magnus emerging from Ida's stairwell on Torstenssonsgatan, and it was apparent that he was upset and shocked—just as I'd seen in person. Magnus laid out the pictures one by one across the table until..."

"You appeared in one too."

"Yes, in one of the photographs I was talking to him, and while I might not have looked shocked, I looked as though I had something to hide. I was scared. There was already talk of suspicious circumstances. I asked who had taken the pictures. Magnus wouldn't say. It was best I didn't know, he said. 'If I'm going to stay quiet about this, then at least I need to know what's happened here,' I said angrily. He'd been called in the middle of the night. Someone—he didn't say who—had phoned him and told him that something serious had happened to his brother."

"To me?"

"Yes, you, Hans. The voice told him it was a matter of urgency and gave the address on Torstenssonsgatan, so Magnus had raced off. He told me he had no idea that was where Ida lived. He'd just run off into the night, and when he arrived, he'd found Ida dead in bed, and that was apparently the whole reason for the phone call. Someone wanted him to see her and to make him complicit."

For a brief time, Rekke couldn't take in what William Fors was saying. All he could see before him was Magnus—Magnus in the days when you couldn't even see the conniver in him. Instead, there was only a self-conscious young man who never came to his brother's concerts because he couldn't bear to be in his shadow. Had that person—that almost pathetic big brother who still didn't know what he wanted to do with his unyielding desire to get ahead in life—been carrying a secret of that magnitude around all this time? It was barely comprehensible, but it had to be true, it *sounded* true, well—Rekke pulled himself together and slipped the necklace back into his pocket—it sounded like a half-truth.

"There aren't many people we know who would place a call like that," he said.

"No, perhaps not. But I didn't know him then. All I was told was that he was merciless and dangerous, and I kept my mouth shut through all of it. I'm sorry, Hans."

"It's inconceivable that I didn't have a presentiment of what you were hiding from me."

"You weren't the acclaimed Professor Rekke then."

I was blind and deaf, he thought to himself.

"Then those pictures turned up again, I suppose?"

William Fors winced.

"How can you possibly know that?"

"Something made you fold in your negotiations with Axel Larsson."

William Fors looked down at his hands.

"Well, yes. You're right, of course. Morovia's colleague Alicia Kovács reminded us about them."

"So my Ida played an unwelcome role even in that matter, and ensured the state lost out on billions."

"We fought back pretty well in the end."

"Well yes, you had Claire Lidman."

"We were a team fighting for what was ours."

Rekke brushed his hand across his brow.

"Yours to plunder."

"I did what I could," Fors said quietly.

"Did you?"

"Cartaphilus had a good reputation at the time."

"But you knew the true lay of the land. *Necessitas non omnes corrumpit.*"

"What?"

"Necessity does not corrupt everyone, William. You already had it in you. Go away and wallow in your agonies. I intend to contact my brother, because there is something missing from your account."

Rekke stood up. At that moment, he received a text message from Micaela and spotted that he had missed several calls.

## THIRTY-EIGHT

At 03:52 on July 23, 1991, high in the Alps near Garmisch-Partenkirchen, Claire Lidman, née Wilson, was delivered of a son who did not make a sound.

The room was ominously quiet. Only the movements of the midwife, Hanna, were audible, and no child cried, nor even whimpered. He's dead, she thought. Claire found this perfectly plausible, and not just as a moral consequence. She had sensed it from Hanna's strained smile and nervous footsteps, and if she were honest, hadn't the contractions felt more like the pains of hell than the torments of purgatory?

Had her body realised from the start that it was birthing something dead and lifeless, or semi-monstrous? It had hurt in a way that surely could not be healthy or natural, and now she closed her eyes and tried to disappear into her exhaustion—into the fact that the worst pain was now gone. But there was no forgetting. No mercy. The creature, the child—the small dead thing—was laid on her. It was a greeting and a farewell all at once. I killed you, she thought. I put my desire for revenge over life and love. Forgive me, Holy Mother of God.

But just when her despair was at its worst, she felt movement—a hand grasping at her skin, and shallow, rapid breaths. She opened her eyes. Dare she look?

"It's a boy," said Hanna. "A healthy boy who's had a bit of a bumpy landing, but he'll get over it. He has a good colour."

"So he's going to survive?"

"Yes, Claire. Congratulations."

She tried to understand and to feel joyful, but before it had sunk in, everything that had kept her awake at night came back to her. Who was he? The son of the kindest person she had ever met?

Or of the most evil?

"Who does he look like?" she said.

"He looks like you."

That was no answer. It was a cop-out, and so she lowered her chin and gazed down at the baby, gently shifting him on her chest. He was heavy, she thought to herself. That was promising. She thought about Samuel's weight on her breast. She remembered his scent and his arms around her, recalling an entire lost world she had exchanged—well, for what? For nothing? She was poking about in everything that had hurt her so badly. Then she peered at the creature—the baby, the boy—and what a strange little person he was. Wrinkled, slender-limbed, looking up intently and panting like someone just rescued from drowning. She closed her eyes again.

The image of the boy lingered on her retinas, merging with her memories. That's no Morovia, she thought. There was a thrill of joy that she immediately wanted to suppress. Don't jump to hasty conclusions, she thought. Babies are alien beings. But as she looked more closely, she was increasingly convinced. She recognised Samuel's brow and lips. She drew the boy close to her. The child's heartbeat seemed to rise and fall in time with her own. She lay still, completely exhausted, breathing oh so deeply and imagining how she would phone Samuel and make all that was broken whole again.

Is this me? That wasn't a new question for Julia. She had wondered the same thing many times over the last year, and there was nothing strange about that. She was growing older and seeking a new identity, while weighing up her old self against the new, mature one.

It looked like it was going to be a glorious day. There wasn't a cloud in the sky and Lucas was driving slowly as he looked for the right address. He was calmer now, and she was also feeling better. Perhaps the surroundings were helping. It was picturesque and idyllic here, populated with old wooden cabins with small gardens. This was the Sweden of old, an Astrid Lindgren world. She turned on the radio for the news. The National Day was being marked across the country. There was uproar about the Sweden Democrats, a rather xenophobic political party. There was a brief obituary for Ronald Reagan, who had died the day before. She heard him say "Tear down this wall." Now President Bush was giving a speech in Normandy. Lucas turned it off.

"I can't stand that shit," he said.

"I'm trying to keep up," she said quietly.

Lucas didn't reply. She thought about Pappa: how he would be engrossed in the newspapers each morning and how his gaze sometimes rose—he was always willing to discuss the state of the world or to modestly pontificate. She really did need to call him.

"Lucas, can I have my phone, please?"

"I thought we said we weren't going to have our mobiles on?"

"But you made a call."

She hated the submissive tone of her voice.

"Later. Right now I need to find the place."

He was crawling along, looking around, but then he nodded to himself, pulled over and turned off the engine. Had they arrived? The house before them was most definitely not a hotel, but it was bigger than all the other houses on the street. Its wooden façade had been freshly painted in white and there was an expanse of decking, and that question recurred to her: *Is this me? Someone who isn't allowed to listen to the news.* Further away, a woman was laughing in an adjacent garden. Something about that laughter hurt her—as though it belonged to a world she had been severed from. At that moment, Lucas got out of the car.

His back was broad and menacing as she watched him bend down beside the doors to a double garage. He retrieved a pair of keys from underneath a green flowerpot. He beckoned to her, and she got out with excessively eager movements, as if she had succumbed to a new and invisible force, although perhaps she was trying extra hard to please him right now so she could get her phone back. Above them, on the exterior of the house, there was a grey camera. It resembled a cold, vacant eye.

Lucas rolled his shoulders and stretched. She followed close behind as he opened the door and stepped inside. She looked around. What kind of interior decor was this? It was hardly decor at all. Impersonal and airy, although still a little luxurious—like an airport lounge.

They went into a brand-new kitchen and then out onto another deck that overlooked a secluded garden featuring a swimming pool and jacuzzi.

"I thought we were staying at a hotel?" she said.

"This is better—a whole house to ourselves."

It didn't feel better at all, and she thought about the conversation she'd overheard that morning.

"But why are we here?" she said.

He looked at her as if her words had hurt him, but then he perked up and came toward her.

"If it's no good we can go somewhere else."

She almost got the impression that he wanted her to say: okay then, let's get out of here. Nonetheless, she shook her head and said she was sure it would be fine.

"Then I'll get our bags and we can change and have a dip," he said.

She had no inclination whatsoever to swim, but she didn't want to be boring or a contrarian bitch. She wanted her phone back. So she simply nodded as he disappeared off. When he returned, he seemed more at ease. With a smirk he unzipped his holdall and pulled out a pair of blue swimming trunks. If he really had been unsure just now, it was no longer obvious. He changed right in front of her—for a few moments he was completely naked as he stood at the edge of the pool.

She felt like a prude as she went into the kitchen to put on the bikini she'd bought the year before in Nice. It was too big, and for the third time she asked herself: Is this me? Then she stepped back outside into the sun. Lucas smiled at her and threw himself into the water with a brutal, slightly reckless movement.

Julia cautiously climbed in, afraid her bikini top might slip off if she jumped. The water was cold, and she was standing on the bottom on tiptoe when Lucas swam into her and pressed her against the side of the pool, and while she let him kiss her and grab her rear, she found herself wishing she wasn't there. She even began to listen for footsteps—the sound of someone who might interrupt them.

Micaela and Superintendent Lars Hellner continued to walk along the water toward Djurgården.

"So it was Samuel's baby?" she said.

"That's what we thought," Hellner said. "That's what we told ourselves. But we couldn't say for sure, and Claire didn't want to do a paternity test. 'It's Samuel's boy,' was all she said. 'I can feel it in my heart.' But she didn't get in touch with Samuel, and she put off our work on the prosecution case. She generally said one thing and did another. The only obvious positive was that she was forming a strong bond with her son, and I can't say I've got much experience of that. I never had children of my own. I realise it's an incredibly special thing and no-one doubted that Claire felt lonely and vulnerable and needed to connect with someone. And yet, Micaela, yet . . ."

"What?"

"She crossed the line. She became completely engrossed in her son. He was to be named Jakob—that was Samuel's middle name. She went crazy over him, constantly sitting with him pressed to her body, kissing his cheeks. It was beautiful—an archetype. But we were worried about losing focus and momentum, especially since . . ."

He hesitated. A runner was approaching—a small, tired-looking man in late middle age, panting toward them. Further away toward Djurgården, the woods around the path became denser.

"Yes?" she said, once the runner had passed.

"We didn't feel we were receiving the same backup as before."

"In what way?"

"The National Police Chief was beginning to waver, but not of his own volition. Someone higher up the chain was whispering in his ear—one of the few people in government circles who knew what we were up to, and unfortunately there was logic to that. If we nailed Morovia then it would be revealed not only that the Swedish state-owned bank had had dealings with organised crime, but that it had actually folded in a tussle over billions that belonged to the taxpayer, and we became increasingly worried about the future of the investigation. By the winter of 1993 we'd reached a dead end. We were going nowhere and Claire was pulling away from us with her little boy, and—I'm ashamed to say this—we got laxer in our oversight. We had moved her south by then, to a small village outside Limena in northern Italy—she was staying in a house we'd rented from a German publisher. She would occasionally go out shopping on her own. There was a small store a few kilometres away—in the middle of nowhere—and I suppose some genius thought it was risk-free. Well, not to mention—and there are embarrassing indications that this was the case—that she had probably nagged for it. 'I can't take it, I have to get some air,' is what she was always saying. And the boy, Jakob . . . My God. That was a whole story in its own right. He was walking before other children learn to crawl, and he would not settle even for a moment. It was like keeping track of a cat. No, a fox."

"Whose child was he?" Micaela said impatiently.

"Don't get ahead of yourself. Anyway, to say something in mitigation for those Italian bodyguards: Claire didn't look the same as before. She'd changed her hair colour, she had a new look, a new identity and a new way of talking, and she was rarely out and about on her own."

"But that was all it took."

"Yes, I'm afraid so. Disaster struck and after that there was no going back. The investigation was dead in the water."

"So what actually happened?"

Lars Hellner smiled, despite the fact that he was talking about a disaster, as if he were enjoying having the upper hand in this interaction. It annoyed her and she gestured to indicate he should continue. He didn't answer her question. Instead, he raised his briefcase and pulled the lock box out.

"I want Rekke there when I tell you. I've already said far too much. Why don't we try calling him again?"

She nodded and took her phone and stared at it. She had two missed calls from Natali, and that left her thoughtful, momentarily forgetting all about Hellner and his story. Natali's words came back to her. A little posh girl, she had said. Lucas was seeing someone else. A young girl. There were a million beautiful young girls out there, but . . . Hugo had come up to her stirring things. "Someone you like might get hurt."

Could it be Julia? No. Julia came from another world. She had just graduated from sixth form. She would never fall for a man fifteen years her senior and a criminal to boot. Then again . . . Julia had changed her look and met someone new. It was worth looking into. She called Rekke as she had been asked, but he didn't pick up. She turned to Hellner with a shake of her head.

"Not there?"

"No, but he should get in touch soon," she said, finding herself thinking about Vanessa.

Vanessa picked up on gossip faster than the wind. Might she know? Micaela stepped aside to call her. Vanessa answered the phone with a brash "Darling!" as if there hadn't even been the slightest discord between them.

"Hey gorgeous," Micaela said. "Just a quickie: is Lucas giving the benefit to anyone else?"

Vanessa hesitated. "I shouldn't say."

Damn it, Micaela thought to herself.

"Come on!"

"He's seeing some young upper-class chick, Hugo says. Lives somewhere up your way."

"By Karlaplan?"

"Something like that. She's an art student or some other bullshit like that. Totally left field."

Micaela's body stiffened and she looked toward Hellner in horror.

"Hey, what's going on?" Vanessa said, sensing the change in atmosphere.

"I'll call later," Micaela said, hanging up.

Then she muttered an apology before making off back toward town. Hellner called out to her and she considered turning around. She'd been initiated into a big secret. It was unprofessional to leg it after that, and there was nothing to suggest that Julia was in immediate danger.

Surely Lucas wouldn't hurt her for no reason. He probably only wanted to apply pressure on his meddling sister and get her to give in—but this was Rekke's daughter and it was all Micaela's fault. She remembered what Natali had said about Lucas's hands. *As if he was breaking a bird's neck*. Could he really be so stupid as to hurt Julia? And what was she going to tell Rekke?

Maybe nothing. Not yet. Not until she knew more. She pulled out her phone and rang Julia, and at the same time she spotted that Hellner was running to catch up with her.

"What are you doing?" he called out.

She couldn't care less about him right now. Julia's mobile was off—so was Lucas's. Shit. Shit! What was going on? She turned around and told Hellner that she was going to find Rekke and return as soon as possible. Then she picked up the pace. The American embassy loomed above her with its soulless architecture. She tugged her denim jacket closer to her body. For Christ's sake—she'd been pissed off with Rekke for being hopeless. Now her own actions had put his daughter in danger! This was on another level, and without thinking too hard about it she fired off a text to him, nothing specific, just a few words to say they needed to talk right away, even if she didn't know what she would say. Perhaps something about Claire Lidman and Lars Hellner. Only time would tell. But first of all . . . she had to act. If something had happened to Julia, she would never forgive herself. She stopped abruptly. A couple of pigeons flapped around her legs.

What should she do? She wanted to shout: Do whatever you want, Lucas. Beat me to a pulp if you like—but don't you fucking dare touch Julia. She texted him: *I'll stop digging dirt on you. All you have to do is leave Julia Rekke alone.* It wasn't perfect. It might provoke him. But all the same she wanted to document it. In any case, a promise was unlikely to cut it. Lucas would doubtless demand guarantees. She waved the pigeons away.

It was concerning that their phones were off. It might mean that Lucas didn't want anyone to track them down—or perhaps that he was planning something. Or was she just being paranoid? Maybe, but this was Julia. She couldn't take any chances. It occurred to her that Lucas must have turned his phone off *somewhere*, and that it might give an indication of what he was up to. A moment later she dialled Jonas Beijer's number. Things were certainly not as uncomplicated between them as they had once been, but Jonas was still always flirtatious and caring, and he had an important role in the serious crime squad in Solna. He should be able to help. Sure enough he picked up, sounding cheery as ever.

"Did you find Rekke?" he said.

She cut right to the chase.

"Right now, I need help with something else."

"Okay," he said. "I'm listening."

"It's about Lucas. My brother. I need to find out which tower his mobile was last picked up by."

"Want to tell me why?"

"No, not yet."

An awkward silence.

"You've got to be kidding."

"Please don't be difficult, Jonas. I'm up shit creek."

He seemed to think it over.

"Okay," he said. "But fuck me, it won't be easy. You know just as well as I do that these guys are changing burners all the time."

"Just have a look."

"I'll give it a try, but only because it's you," he said, at which point she considered saying something friendly and grateful. But, yet again, she was unable to wrap up her conversation. Just like the last time she'd been speaking to Jonas, she spotted Rekke up ahead, walking toward her with a rather absent-minded and gloomy expression.

# THIRTY-NINE

Magnus was about to board the plane to Stockholm when Hans's old friend Herman Camphausen rang on a secure line. Magnus had sought him out as soon as he had hung up with Morovia, hinting that it was urgent, which had been indiscreet. It raised expectations about what he had to cough up.

"Herman," he said nervously, dropping out of the line at the gate. "It's been a long time. How have you been keeping?"

"My curiosity is always piqued when such a busy gentleman calls," Herman said. "I'm currently looking at a photo on the AFP wires depicting you and Putin. You seemed to be getting along handsomely."

For a moment, Magnus regained his self-confidence. *You and Putin.* That didn't sound too bad, all things considered. In fact, he'd be damned if he came cap in hand to ask for information. He would flirt with this intelligence buffoon and coax it out of him.

"We were talking about Morovia," he said.

"My goodness."

He felt even more empowered. How easy it was to alter the balance of power, he mused, making sure he kept Herman hanging on a little longer, just to be safe.

"Exactly—it was our topic du jour," he said somewhat jocularly.

"What did Putin have to say?"

Magnus considered whether to concoct something particularly titillating now that there was photographic evidence of his encounter.

"Putin wants him shot."

Herman Camphausen gave a polite laugh.

"It seems incredible you would get something like that out of him."

"We were joking, but there was an underlying seriousness," he said. "And I thought it would be good for you to know, if you're going to try to nab your nemesis at last."

"It's not news that Morovia and the Kremlin have fallen out," Herman said, seeming more cautious now.

"Indeed. Ever since the murder of Chabarov, I suppose?" Magnus said. He might as well mention the elephant in the room at once. "But Morovia has come to life too. He contacted me and was quite threatening."

"Are you hoping to play them off against each other?"

"No, no, I . . ." He made an effort to sound more serious. "I'm just concerned. Concerned that Morovia will set his sights on Hans again."

They were waving to him from the desk. He made a dismissive gesture in reply.

"Has something new happened?" Herman said, sounding more serious too.

Magnus thought he might as well chance it.

"I'm afraid Morovia knows that Hans assisted you in the Chabarov investigation."

Herman didn't reply at once, leaving a silence Magnus tried hard to interpret.

"I can't comment on that, Magnus, and your brother can't either. But . . ."

"Yes?"

He closed his eyes.

"If Morovia has got that into his head, then Hans needs protection—or to be moved to a secure location."

That was confirmation, he told himself. It had to be. Suddenly he was keen to ring off.

"I see," he said. "Look, Herman, I have to get on my plane now. They're waving rather insistently at me. Let's keep in touch. And let's get Morovia once and for all."

"You're not up to something again, are you?" said Herman.

Magnus demurred.

"What? No, absolutely not. I'll ensure Hans gets to safety. I'll be in touch," he said, hanging up and thinking he should do just as he had said: warn Hans.

But as he rummaged for his boarding pass and passport, he reflected that while family was everything—blood was thicker than water, and so on—self-preservation was even more important. He proceeded to send an encrypted message to Morovia to say that Hans had indeed consulted on the Chabarov case, then he got onto the plane. He promised himself that he would contact Hans as soon as he arrived.

Julia floundered and struggled. Lucas had grabbed her harder than he'd meant to. He was frustrated, so he pulled her under the water—not for long, not long at all—but she went nuts. It degenerated into an absolute fucking circus, and he had to help her out of the pool and hold her while she coughed and panted.

"Take it easy—you're turning me on," he said.

"I swallowed a lot of water," she managed to say, adjusting her bikini top, which had ridden up. He stared at her breasts.

Fuck, she was skinny. Her ribs were visible, her back curved like a cat's, and he was overcome by the desire to strike her again. He just wanted to punish her for being so damn annoying. Perhaps she noticed, because she recoiled and, instead of hitting her, he toppled a sun lounger onto the ground with a crash, at which point she screamed as if she had seen a mouse. Spoiled brat, he thought, as he held her firmly and reluctantly spat out a few words of kindness, even managing a "sorry." Anything to calm her down. He was so sick of it all. He just knew he was going to do something dumb any moment now.

And if he did, well, it would be Micaela's fault. She wanted to ruin his life, and yet he'd done everything for her—he'd even saved her from Papá. Papá had been a pathetic wretch in his final years, just sitting there, grumpily writing his damn notes: *I'm worried about you, Lucas. Where are you getting your money from?* It was none of his business. He should have been happy that someone was bringing money in, full stop. He was lax too. He let Micaela run around all the time, and he was always whining: *Your nature worries me, Lucas,* he wrote. *Don't you care about human decency at all?*

Toward the end, he had tried to keep Lucas away from Micaela as much as possible. He saw it as his duty to separate her from her brother. That crossed every line there was. Who was actually taking care of the family? Not Papá. It was him—Lucas—the only real man of the house, and what he'd done he'd been forced to do. No more, no less. An opportunity had presented itself early that winter's morning, and he'd taken it. He had that ability, and sometimes, even long afterward, he would withdraw into himself and picture it unfolding. It was so easy—verging on elegant—just a nudge, a quick movement, and then a fall. Not even a cry.

In a way, he came into being in that moment. He was reborn when he sent his father over the balustrade. Afterward, he drove all the books in the flat to the dump, repainted and hung new wallpaper, and laid down his own code to live by in which no-one was more important than Micaela. It was the two of them against the world, and yet . . . fuck it. That damn bitch had betrayed him in the worst possible way. He was wrenched back into the present, and perhaps in his fury he'd squeezed Julia a little too tightly.

"Let go of me," she snapped. She was kicking his legs.

He was shocked. Here was an anger he'd not had a whiff of before. There was some backbone to her all of a sudden, and he let go and went to get a towel. He draped it around her shoulders, apologised again—achieving in the process some kind of new personal record for apologies—and gently patted her dry. She let him, and he wondered whether to go inside and get the champagne that was supposedly in the fridge. If he was going to take a photo and send it to Micaela, it'd be good if they looked happy and in love. That would have the best effect. But he didn't have time to get anything. Julia's body tensed, as she pricked up her ears eagerly.

What had caught her attention? He couldn't hear anything, but he'd already noticed that Julia had a kind of superpower. She perceived things early, put two and two together far quicker than anyone he had ever met, and . . . he could hear it now as well. There was a car on the road outside. It stopped. The driver turned the engine off. Shit, shit, shit. Surely no-one was coming here? They'd promised to leave them alone. On the other hand . . . they'd talked about a message. Some kind of confirmation. Had something happened? He cursed himself for ever taking their damn money. Wait, wait. What was happening? The front door had been opened. They might at least have rung the bell. Now they heard footsteps, and it bugged him that Julia seemed to be expectant rather than frightened. Did she want to be saved from him?

"I'll take care of it," he said.

Linda Wilson was cracking up—that was how it felt. She turned off her mobile. That was quite enough for one day. She couldn't bear to talk to anyone else, not even Claire if—by some miracle—she were to show up unannounced.

Linda hadn't heard a word from her in months, although there was nothing unusual about that in itself. They'd never been in close contact—partly for security reasons, and partly because time just slipped past. But it felt different now, and she could tell from Hellner that something was badly wrong. She's dead, she thought to herself. And it's my fault.

Linda had been furious for a long time that Claire had given it all up—including their relationship—to take down a man who had actually done her the world of good. Gabor Morovia had propelled Claire into his gilded world and helped her secure a job and make her fortune. Why take down someone like that? She just couldn't understand it, and only when it was too late did she know any better. There were things that simply couldn't go unpunished. There were things you had to put a stop to, even if you paid with your own life and liberty.

The last time she'd been in contact with Claire—with the whole procedure and rigmarole that required—her sister had been en route to Venice. She'd been summoned there somehow. Issued an ultimatum. An order. But she hadn't wanted to give any details. Nevertheless, Linda understood right away that it was an important journey. Claire would never otherwise visit that kind of tourist destination. She kept herself out of the way. Linda had waited for a report on the trip with bated breath, but no signs of life had been forthcoming and an alert had been triggered. A huge effort had been initiated in secret. But they had been unable to turn up anything more than blurry CCTV footage and vague witness statements.

The best Linda could hope for was that Claire no longer trusted her police contacts and had gone to ground. Not that she believed that. Something dreadful had happened, and for the thousandth time she wondered how things could have gone so badly wrong.

It had all started—that much she knew—with the group at the London School of Economics: Alicia, Claire and Sofia. Three girls that Linda was so jealous of she was fit to burst. They appeared to have it all: they were hot, brainy and full of ambition, and they had a charismatic genius—a wealthy Hungarian superstar mathematician—opening doors for them and introducing them to the financial elite. It looked as if they were living the dream, and there were moments over the course of those years when Linda had wished something would happen to Claire. Her sister seemed to be getting far too much, while Linda seemed to be condemned to a life in the margins. Then again . . . Claire should have envied Linda and the blissful simplicity of her existence. While she'd been hopping from one waitressing job to another, Claire was being drawn—step by step—into a life of crime. She had signed a contract with the devil, and there was no way out except the way the stunningly beautiful Sofia Rodriguez had taken—death and hellfire. Oh my Lord, how ashamed she was. She had behaved unforgivably. But with Claire gone she had lost her only true support in life, and no-one could explain to her—at least not with the appropriate conviction—why it was so necessary. She couldn't help but regard it as selfish—evil, almost—and she thought particularly of that mortuary in San Sebastián.

She would never forget the charred woman on the steel table. The suffocating stench—the whole damn charade they were forced to take part in. She hated it from the very first moment. She almost wished it were Claire who was dead. At the time, she seemed to deserve it. Well, perhaps Linda really did want revenge for her sister's direct and uncompromising nature.

She supposed she had also dreamed—and this was the awful thought—of being seen as a person with agency by the man who had bewitched her sister. Perhaps that was why she had allowed herself to be manipulated so easily. That must have been it, yes. Yes. A hundred times over. She should have raised the alarm when he turned up behind her one day on Sibyllegatan. Only slowly did it dawn on her who he was. He was completely different from what she had imagined. There was sorrow writ on his face, with its gentle features and green eyes, and he'd been plainly dressed in jeans and a leather jacket. He looked just like a regular guy, only a little more handsome, more considerate than the rest, and without doubt he *saw* her. He made her feel special.

"You're actually the more interesting of the two of you," he said, buying her a drink in a small joint nearby, and it was there that she'd noticed his voice. It lulled her into a sense of security and drew her in, but actually she hadn't said that much. She didn't even have to say that Claire wasn't dead. Morovia already seemed to know she was alive, and it wasn't as if Linda knew much beyond that. Hellner and the others had been careful not to tell her too much. Yet she still apparently provided a clue of sorts.

Morovia must have put two and two together—they said he was a genius. The knowledge of what had escaped from her that day was something she could barely live with, but things were the way they were. She had to accept it. Now she had to make up for it as best she could, and make sure that Claire was returned to safety. Oh Holy Mother of God, how difficult it all was.

# FORTY

There were moments that portended the disaster. While living outside Limena in northern Italy, Claire sometimes went out unescorted by her bodyguards to go to a general store along a road between cornfields in the middle of nowhere. Her son, Jakob, was barely three years old and thin as a rake. He was behind the curve when it came to height and weight, but well ahead in every other respect: speech, motor skills, cognition.

She was indescribably proud of him. Today she had dressed him in shorts and an azure shirt. The shop occupied a yellow-brick building with white-framed windows. It sold not only food but also clothing, toys and garden items. Jakob skipped inside. Every step was an adventure for him at that time. As usual they chatted with Francesca, the young daughter of the owner, who was whiling her life away at the register, and as usual they left hand-in-hand.

The carrier bags were heavy, and Claire's knee hurt, but it was a wonderful, cloudless day and it felt fantastic to be out without the bodyguards and their eye-rolling at her child's whims and high jinks. There were no warning signs anywhere, and what happened wasn't in itself dramatic—at least, not obviously.

Jakob took a bouncy ball out of his pocket along with a chocolate bar in a red wrapper—the haul of a petty thief but presented in such a wide-eyed and happy manner that he couldn't have grasped the meaning of the act. Nevertheless, she slapped him.

Jakob was so stunned that he didn't even run away, just stood there with his lower lip trembling, and it was a while before she dared to acknowledge what had happened.

It wasn't the theft, it was Jakob's gaze and his smile when he had pulled out his spoils, and the fact that in that moment his face was not at all reminiscent of Samuel's but instead reminded her of what she wanted to forget—Gabor smiling threateningly at her and telling her to undress and stand completely still by the mirror. Gabor whispering that she would burn like Sofia if she betrayed him. A series of terrifying recollections were triggered by one single smile from a little boy she loved, and once he'd awoken from his petrification, she let him run away.

Claire watched him vanish in a small cloud of dust as she sank to her knees, dropping the carrier bags onto the gravel road.

Rekke was coming toward Micaela, passing the diplomatic residences overlooking the water. There was a purposefulness to his steps. He's himself again, she thought, or at least on the way up, and that would have been great were it not for the fact that she was going to send him back down into darkness again. How was she even going to put it into words? *Lucas, my brother, is seeing your daughter...*

She decided to put it off. After all, there was nothing they could do about it. They had to locate them first. She resolved to keep her mouth shut for the time being and await an update from Jonas Beijer. Perhaps there was no rush after all. Lucas only wanted her to stop rooting around in his life, which meant that threats—rather than fully fledged crimes—were his best tactic. Things would be fine until he got in touch. She looked down at the ground.

It was just . . . she had no idea what emotions a girl like Julia might arouse in him. Lust, hubris, anger, jealousy, the desire to possess her? Or to crush her?

"Hello there," she said.

Rekke looked rather wild, she reflected. The whites of his eyes were bloodshot, and his right fist was clenched. He was about to say something when his mobile buzzed. He looked at the display in surprise and made a nervous gesture with his hand. "I have to take this," he said, stepping aside. She heard him speaking German and saw his expression become even grimmer. When he returned, his gaze was no longer as focused—he looked past her toward the water, and in a way, she was grateful for that.

"You texted me?" he said.

She wanted to ask him about the call he'd just received.

"I met a superintendent from the National Criminal Police," she said, "who wants you to sign a non-disclosure agreement. He's been working on the Claire Lidman investigation for years."

Rekke turned toward her, his thoughts seemingly elsewhere. His fist was still clenched.

"So she's really alive?" he said.

"She was in March, at any rate. I think the superintendent—Lars Hellner's his name—wants to hire you to find out what's happened."

Rekke nodded absently at her.

"Indeed," he said. "But first I must get hold of my brother Magnus."

"What for?"

"I barely know what to say," he said. "I've just been informed that I should seek out a safe location. Magnus has . . . I can hardly grasp it."

He looked almost shocked but then he peered along the footpath and seemed to perk up—somewhat irrationally, she thought.

"But look . . ." he said. "It's your Superintendent Hellner with his briefcase and sunglasses and the rest of it. Seems like you left him suddenly."

Micaela didn't ask how he knew that the man in the distance was

Hellner, let alone how he knew that she had ditched him in a rush. She waved guiltily at the policeman and pointed at Rekke as if she had found what she had been looking for, and Hellner beamed and approached them before bowing slightly.

"What an honour," he said. "I've heard a great deal about you."

Lars Hellner was not exaggerating. He had heard a lot about Rekke: his name had cropped up every now and then over the last fifteen years. Hellner had wanted to involve him in their work from an early stage, but Rekke was ultimately regarded as an inappropriate resource, who was—at least in some people's eyes—not entirely reliable. Nevertheless, the professor had made a very significant contribution to the investigation without their knowledge, and this had only come to their attention very late in the day. A high-ranking official in German intelligence had consulted him off his own back—and it had apparently been a success. Rekke had seen a whole world in a set of footprints in the ashes. Those in the know still talked about it, but unfortunately none of it had mattered in the end. The battle was lost anyway, and they were forced to let go of Claire. She was left to fend for herself—more or less—and after that no-one knew which side she was on, although it was hardly likely it was that of the law. It was all very regrettable, and her son . . . Hellner didn't want to think about that. They should have taken better care of them.

"I mean it. It truly is a pleasure to meet you—a tremendous honour," he said.

"The pleasure is all mine," the professor replied, smiling somewhat anxiously. "The perturbing issue we face is that Claire is not the only one to have been betrayed. It would appear I have been too. So, if I am to try to help you, we must make haste."

"Of course, of course," Hellner said, beginning to rummage nervously through his briefcase.

# FORTY-ONE

Disaster struck on an unusually hot day when the sun was at its highest in the sky. Claire had started trading stocks and derivatives under her new identity, as well as investing in property. But above all she was a mother. Jakob was almost pathologically attached to her, and would react strongly to sounds, light, smells and changes in tone and facial expression.

"Mamma, are you angry with me?" he would ask all the time, even though she was never angry with him, except for that one time she had struck him.

He would react to the tiniest shift in her gaze or expression, and he would do jigsaws with a manic energy and play constantly with chess pieces. She loved him desperately, but sometimes he really drove her crazy. On this particular day, as she was on her way to the general store—once again unaccompanied by her bodyguards—he was walking so close to her that she had to keep looking at her feet to ensure she didn't trip over him.

Francesca was at the register, hair down and the top buttons on her blouse undone. She couldn't have been more than twenty and she was good for business. Men would make extra purchases just to linger in her presence, and each and every one of them thought she was in love with him in particular. However, she seemed most eager to talk to Claire—who now went by the name Sara. Francesca knew nothing about her—no-one in the area did, and what little they thought they knew was false and contrived. Nevertheless, Francesca had realised that Claire was a woman of substance, and she always lit up when she approached.

However, on this particular day there was something furtive and secretive about her. She blushed when Claire stepped forward.

"What's up with you?" said Claire.

"I'm not allowed to say anything."

"Don't, then."

"There's a man looking for you. A rich, handsome man."

Francesca shivered with excitement as she said it, and perhaps she expected a shiver in reply—or at least a sign of curiosity or anticipation. Claire merely nodded. "Well, how about that?" Then she paid for her purchases and left quite calmly, but she must have grasped Jakob's hand too tightly.

"Ouch!" he said.

"Sorry," she muttered without letting go, and she juggled with her mobile and her pager.

She should have called her bodyguards right away to raise the alarm. Instead, she walked along the road, her mind paralysed, realising they would have to move again. They had stayed put for too long. The sun was scorching her neck. Her back was damp with perspiration. A tractor drove past and she upped her pace, so much so that Jakob had to scurry alongside her.

"What's wrong, Mamma? What's wrong?" he said.

"Nothing," she said reassuringly. "We just need to hurry up a bit."

She lifted him onto her shoulders. He was still so strangely light. He tugged nervously at her hair—as if she were a steed—as she surveyed the road ahead. Not far ahead was the stream and the hill and from there it was just a left toward the woods and up the hill and they would be back home. It would all be fine. She triggered an alert on her pager—the bodyguards would be there within a few minutes.

She patted Jakob on the leg and told him to stop messing about with her hair.

From behind them there came the sound of a car with a quiet engine. It was driving slowly, so she waited for it to overtake them—she even gestured to encourage it to pass. But it continued to crawl behind them like a predator waiting to strike. She took Jakob off her shoulders and prepared to hurl herself into the ditch with him and roll into the field.

A moment later, the car stopped. A door opened and closed again; there was the sound of footsteps approaching them and she was reluctant to turn around. It wasn't until Jakob asked, "Mamma, who is it?" that she looked at the figure coming toward them. He was the same as ever—at least upon first sight. He wore a khaki-coloured linen suit, a white shirt and a hat—like a gangster in a movie—and he looked at her with his green, mesmeric eyes.

"Am I going to die?" she said in English.

"Yes, my friend," he said.

He drew a pistol from a holster concealed by his jacket, which was at least some consolation, she reflected. He wasn't going to burn her slowly.

"How did you find us?" she said.

"I never believed that accident you fabricated," he said. He put a hand to his chest. "I could feel in my heart that you were alive, but as you can see it took me a while to find you. I've had to expend considerable effort. They hid you well."

"He's your son."

He didn't seem to hear. Instead, he stared toward the cornfield, raising his weapon and focusing on her chest as if that was where he was going to take aim. His shoes were surprisingly grubby, and there was sweat glistening on his brow and chin. His lips were cracked and dry, and he hadn't shaved for a day or two. Perhaps he too was suffering from inner tumult—he appeared to have aged.

His hand, however, was steady and his steps were purposeful, and she drew Jakob close even though she probably should have pushed him as far away as possible.

"He's your son," she said again.

"I no longer have a son," he said.

"Look at him, Gabor. He's yours."

She still wasn't completely certain—still hoped some days that the opposite was true—but now she took the opportunity to let it all out.

"He's got no-one but me, and he's yours, you damned beast."

Gabor didn't look at Jakob—it was as if he didn't want to see him or be influenced by him—but then he lowered his gaze, only briefly at first, then for longer, studying the boy more intently, and then something happened to him. A shadow crept across his face. His eyes became shiny, his expression confused. Tears began to trickle down his cheeks and his hand shook.

"I lost my boy," he said. "He died in my arms, and no-one can . . ."

He fell silent, lowering the gun and aiming it at Jakob instead. She just had time to scream before the shot was fired. It was followed by a terrible silence.

Julia was listening to the approaching footsteps. At first, she had welcomed them. Lucas had been frightening her and she was relieved at the interruption—but now she was worried. Who came in without knocking? Then she heaved a sigh of relief. A friendly and reassuring-looking man in a grey suit was coming toward her, a smile playing across his lips. Was he the owner of the house? Perhaps there had been some kind of mix-up with the rental? She glanced over her shoulder at Lucas.

Lucas seemed to be confused too, and she wrapped herself in her towel and looked up at the man, who raised an eyebrow before vanishing inside and then returning with a bathrobe that he handed to her. She momentarily hesitated to put it on. The whole situation felt strange. Nevertheless, she wrapped herself up in it. It was too big, but it made her feel warm and she said thank you. The man replied in English.

"Not at all. It was my pleasure."

He sat down on one of the sun loungers next to her.

"Er, sorry, but who are you?" she said.

"I happened to be passing," he said.

That was a peculiar answer, and she glanced again at Lucas, who seemed to be annoyed for some reason. What was going on? She felt increasingly uneasy.

"I don't understand," she said.

The man exuded charisma and when he spoke his voice almost possessed her. He replied calmly:

"I'm very sorry to have bothered you. Allow me to explain. But perhaps first I must..."

He too looked toward Lucas. Then he apologised before standing up and going over to speak with him in a low voice. Julia heard nothing that passed between them. Instead, she waited, hoping that something good was happening. All the same, she was concerned that Lucas seemed so angry.

"Sorry," the man said when he returned. "How are you?"

He settled back down on the sun lounger. He was wearing an expensive wristwatch and she saw that he had clearly defined veins.

"Better. But I really do need my phone."

The man scrutinised her intently, smiling sadly.

"Then we must make sure you get it. Have you seen the young lady's mobile phone?" he said loudly.

Lucas merely shook his head, even though he'd taken it from her because they were going to have a "fantastic weekend" together. She wanted to scream: Just give it back. Don't be such a dick. But instead, she felt increasingly confused about the entire situation, and she asked politely whether she might borrow the man's phone.

"Naturally," he said.

"I need to call my dad," she clarified, when the man didn't make any move toward his pockets.

"You think he may be worried?"

"I'm pretty sure he is," she said. "Do you have kids yourself?"

She had no idea why she had asked that question. Perhaps it was a way of getting a better grasp of the man and figuring out why he hadn't given her his phone right away. She looked at him more closely. He looked elegant in his suit. His thick black hair was slicked back with a centre parting, and his features were distinct and clean-cut, albeit asymmetrical in a way she couldn't quite put her finger on, but perhaps it was something about the eyes in particular... They seemed to be different colours, which gave a rather contradictory impression. He was about Pappa's age. Perhaps he reminded her a little of him: he had that same penetrating gaze, and the same melancholy eyes, although his smile wasn't as warm—but then again, how could it be?

"I had two boys," he said.

She wondered whether she should ask what had happened to them, or whether she should just pretend not to have heard and ask for the phone again.

"But not anymore?" she said.

"I lost them."

"I'm sorry. What happened?"

She should have kept her trap shut, but the question had just spilled out—whether out of politeness or curiosity, or simply because she felt it was important to know.

"One of them died in a bombing," the man said.

She recoiled. "Oh my God."

"He was named Jan and he was the most astonishing boy imaginable. He was only nine years old, but he was already a master of karate and judo. I had taught him."

"So he was a fighter."

She tried to smile.

"Yes," the man said with exaggerated seriousness. "He was strong and self-confident."

"And your other son?" she said.

"He was never like Jan."

"What happened to him?"

"I'm not sure you would understand. He was weak. I know your father."

"You do?"

It had upset her to hear him refer to his other son as weak.

She was even less happy about the fact that he knew Pappa.

"Yes," he said. "We go back a long way."

"How come?"

"Our parents knew each other. But his father—your grandfather, that is—crushed my father. He never recovered."

"I'm sorry about that," she said.

"Then we met as children. Your father had a tutor who wanted us to compete and measure ourselves against each other."

Julia swallowed and looked over at Lucas.

"Were you able to measure up to him?" she said.

The man appeared to be amused by the question.

"I was, but he gave me the runaround. I've always been fascinated by him. Have you inherited any of his abilities?"

She shook her head nervously.

"No," she said. "I'm just an ordinary girl."

"You may have to prove otherwise."

"What do you mean by that?"

He didn't reply. He pulled out his phone and she briefly forgot about the unpleasantness behind his cryptic remark. Maybe she really was going to get to ring Pappa. But the man didn't give her the mobile—instead he read a text that had arrived.

"Can I borrow the phone?" she said.

He gazed at her with a new, excited look in his eyes.

"I should like to have had your father here," he said. "But it might have got rather complicated."

There was something unsettling about the way he said that.

"What do you mean?"

He didn't answer immediately.

"I would like him to see."

She didn't know what Pappa would get to see. She didn't even want to guess. Instead, she concentrated on the situation at hand, as if her life depended on what she noticed and understood about the situation, and she realised two things at once.

There was a schism between Lucas and the man. That was becoming increasingly clear as Lucas dressed by the pool, his body language sullen and hostile. She might be able to turn them against each other, which might give her the chance to sneak away. But it worried her that she'd heard other footsteps outside.

The second thought was that there was something crucial concealed in the man's story about his sons. She even got it into her head that it had to do with her and Pappa, and instead of asking for the phone again she said calmly:

"What happened to your other son? The weak one."

# FORTY-TWO

The shot seemed to have burst her eardrums. She looked into the sky. The sun was blazing. It suddenly felt mercilessly hot. In the distance, she heard the sound of people screaming—perhaps they were reacting to the gunshot. There was the smell of manure and scorched earth, and she told herself: Don't look down, not yet. Let me have hope for just one more second. But then she heard something—not much, just an inhalation of breath, and a whimper—and she realised she was still holding on to Jakob.

She could feel his hand in hers, and she looked down at him. He was still standing. He was deathly pale and utterly dumbfounded, but he was still alive, and she fell to her knees and ran her hands over his body to find where he was bleeding. The bullet must have hit him somewhere. He was obviously injured. Life seemed to be draining out of him, but she couldn't find anything and only then did she glance up at Gabor. He was still clutching his pistol. The barrel was smoking.

He nodded his head as if to confirm something she didn't understand, and in that moment, she felt a weight against her body, an impact. Jakob collapsed against her, and she caught him in her arms before he hit the ground.

"Call an ambulance!" she cried out.

"There's no need," Gabor said.

"Why didn't you shoot me instead?" she said.

"I was . . ."

"You were what? What the hell were you?"

"Angry because he was alive and Jan wasn't. I lost it. I was losing it."

"What do you mean, *losing it*," she yelled, pulling Jakob's top off. She continued to search for gunshot wounds.

She still couldn't find anything—except that the boy had wet himself and it was running down his calves.

"I fired into the ground," Gabor said, re-holstering his gun.

The blood returned to his face and he looked her in the eye—not with his usual assurance, but still with an air of control. He said something she didn't catch.

"What?" she said.

"As you see, I will always find you. The slightest word from you and I'll shoot you both," he said. "Or I'll let you burn."

She didn't answer. Instead, she lowered her gaze and repeated her son's name until the boy opened his eyes and life returned and the landscape regained some colour. "Mamma," he mumbled, and she pressed him against her, and although all she wanted was to lose herself in that moment, she was conscious of Gabor's presence with every passing second, and she kept wondering: What should I say to him? What should I say?

"I'll never testify against you. I swear on the boy's life. Maybe I can even help you by telling you what the police know. And if you want . . . if it would help . . ."

She didn't know what she was spewing out—more or less anything she thought might preserve their lives.

"Yes, Claire?"

"If you ever want to meet up with him—to see the result of what you did to me—then that could be arranged. He's a wonderful boy."

"He's skinny and slight and not at all like my . . ."

Gabor seemed to lose his train of thought again, and she regretted what she had just said, but she was in such a state she would have promised her own arms and legs just to protect her son.

"I'll get him to eat, I promise. You'll be proud of him," she said, and Gabor nodded and came closer.

She bent down. He sank to his knees as well and caressed Jakob on the cheek with his index finger—the same finger that had just squeezed the trigger. He spoke in the language of children:

"Aren't you a fine boy? That was quite a bang, wasn't it?"

Then he got up and left. Claire remembered his footsteps receding, the car door slamming shut, and Jakob's heart pounding against her chest, but then she pulled herself together and picked Jakob up and set him on her shoulders. On the way home, she encountered her bodyguards hurrying toward her.

When would she say something? Soon. It had to be soon. She just needed to wait for Jonas Beijer to call back, and maybe get in touch with Lucas to find out what he wanted. Rekke and Hellner were deep in conversation. Hellner's body language showed that he had far greater respect for Rekke than he did for her. He was tense, keenly aware, interrupting himself at the slightest sign of an interjection from the professor.

"When did you abandon the investigation into Morovia?" said Rekke.

"We finally threw in the towel in 1994. We no longer had support from upstairs and we weren't getting any help whatsoever from Claire. She'd retracted what she'd previously told us."

"Why?"

Lars Hellner looked around and caught sight of a bench further along the path, down by the water—the same one that Rekke and Micaela had sat on the evening before.

"Why don't we sit?" he said.

They strode over to the bench. The superintendent stowed their mobiles in his lock box. He waited for a middle-aged woman walking two dachshunds on leads to pass by.

"To be quite honest, I think we kicked Claire into Morovia's arms," he said finally. "When we couldn't protect her, she had no other option than to seek refuge with him. There was, I suppose, a dark logic to it. If we couldn't keep her safe, then she had to ally herself with her enemy."

"So Morovia tracked her down?" said Rekke.

"Yes, although we didn't cotton on to that right away. All we knew was that something awful had happened to them. The boy stopped talking for a while, and Claire pulled away from us—she was clearly shaken. But neither of them would say what had happened, and it wasn't long before Claire asked us to slacken the reins and cut back on the protection detail."

"And did you?"

"In the end we did, but not because of her demand. We obtained evidence that she was secretly in contact with Morovia, which meant there was no point protecting her from someone she was voluntarily involved with."

Micaela interjected.

"Why did Morovia spare Claire when he was so merciless to everyone else who betrayed him?"

Hellner turned to her.

"Because of the boy," he said. "I can see no other reason. Perhaps that's a weak point of his, and I suppose it's not so difficult to imagine. He'd just lost a son in a bombing and then suddenly a new boy shows up and Claire says he's his. It must have felt like a miracle, to say the least."

"So the boy is Morovia's?"

"Morovia certainly assumed paternity for the time being, and met the boy and gave him expensive gifts. That much we know from our sources. But he maintained the strictest secrecy around it. Not even those closest to him were aware of it."

"But then something happened?"

"Claire started a new life in many ways, becoming a successful financial analyst once again. She bought properties in Germany and France. She seemed quite contented on the few occasions I met her. She'd grown wealthy and radiated a new power and assurance, but it was clear there was also something bothering her, and she didn't want to return to Sweden. I'm fairly certain that Morovia had something on her, and we noticed that the boy—Jakob—wasn't in a good place either. I know Claire was trying to keep him away from Morovia as much as possible, but sometimes he summoned them, and they dared not refuse. I'd wager something along those lines happened in March this year: Claire and Jakob travelled to Venice; Morovia has a house on the Grand Canal. There was nothing to indicate that there was anything out of the ordinary about the trip—it seemed to be no more than one of Morovia's sporadic meetings with his son. But Claire went missing in Venice—vanished into thin air."

"On what date was that?" said Micaela.

"Twenty-second of March, which is why the photo you handed over to Lindroos is so important to us. It may be one of the final signs of life we have from her."

Micaela pictured the holiday snap.

"What other leads do you have?" she said.

"That's what I was going to show you. I'd like to know if you can gather more than we can. But first . . ." Hellner turned back to Rekke again and paused while another dog walker passed. "I need to ask you something else, professor."

Rekke looked at him self-consciously.

"You said you had been betrayed?"

"I'm apparently part of a chain of events that led to the death of Morovia's son," Rekke said.

"That's a rather drastic way of putting it," said Hellner.

"I'm simply looking at it from Morovia's point of view. I wasn't previously aware of it."

"Surely all you did was help to solve the murder of Andrei Chabarov in Berlin?" the superintendent said.

Rekke shrugged.

"Who was Chabarov?" said Micaela.

Rekke turned to her.

"He was a *silovik*, as we said back in those days, a businessman—well, a gangster really—with KGB ties. He was close to the ruling classes in St. Petersburg, including Putin, and tremendously aggressive toward the oligarchs and their new-found wealth. He was found dead in February 1994—in a warehouse in east Berlin. The body was distorted and charred. He'd bitten off his own tongue before he died, and clearly he had suffered terribly. At the time, I was working on a book about interrogation techniques in times of war. I'd learned a fair bit about torture, and I was foolish enough to agree to help my old friend Herman Camphausen when he approached me to ask if I would assist with the investigation."

"The same Herman you mentioned earlier?"

"Yes," he said. "But I didn't really do much. Herman already had suspicions about who the killer was, and I merely confirmed them. I examined the pictures and the forensic evidence. There wasn't much to go on. They had cleaned up pretty thoroughly. But around ten metres from the crime scene there were three footprints preserved in the dust and ash, and I focused my efforts on those."

"What did you find?" said Hellner.

"I saw that the left foot had tilted slightly inwards. The impression was light and soft, while the right shoe in the third and final print had been pressed down with unusual force as if to compensate for the lightness of the first two. It was a pattern I had seen before."

"Where?"

"Beside the bushes outside our house in Vienna, when I was eleven or twelve years old. The feet were smaller then, and the stride wasn't as long. But the characteristics were still clear, and I simply told Herman: 'It looks like Morovia.' That was it. He nodded and disappeared, and I forgot all about it. Well, actually, I actively repressed it. But now . . ." He glanced up toward Nobelgatan above them. "I just received a telephone call from Herman, who said that our conclusion in the investigation was leaked to the security services in St. Petersburg. And someone there—whether directly or indirectly tied to the organisation—appears to have taken matters into their own hands. With disastrous consequences," Rekke said, looking as if he was about to stand up.

"Yes, most unfortunate," Hellner said, also looking troubled and quite clearly worried that Rekke would up and leave. "But . . . what do you both say? Why don't we take a look at the traces of Claire and her son?"

Rekke seemed decidedly reluctant to undertake the task. He gazed toward the water. Micaela thought about Lucas and Julia—her brother and Rekke's daughter.

"Sorry," she said. "I need my phone again."

"My God," Hellner said. "I thought I had your undivided attention at least briefly, but fine . . ." He took the mobile out of the lock box. Micaela reassured him that it would only be a brief call and walked up toward Nobelgatan to ring Jonas Beijer. It was a while before he answered. He sounded annoyed and stressed. But yes, he did have the information. Lucas's phone had last been tracked by a mast outside Järna, south-west of Stockholm.

"Before that he was in Tumba, Salem and Pershagen, so I'd guess he's heading south on the E4. But after that we've got nothing," he said.

She digested the information and concluded she might as well push her luck.

"Can you search for footage of his car too? It's an Audi Cabriolet. Using the traffic cameras? I really need to figure out where he's gone."

Jonas didn't answer at first.

"This is no small thing you're asking, given you haven't even outlined any suspicions that a crime has been committed," he said.

"Please," she said. "I'll do anything."

"I'll do what I can."

She hung up and went back to the bench firmly resolved to tell Rekke exactly what was going on, but Lars Hellner didn't appear to have bothered waiting for her. He had taken a laptop out of his briefcase and was now showing Rekke surveillance images from Venice. Rekke, on the other hand, seemed to be struggling to take it all in—his body language still suggested he wanted to stride away.

Then he was shown a brief video clip, and at that point he froze. Micaela decided to postpone the announcement just a little longer.

# FORTY-THREE

What they saw on Lars Hellner's laptop was a grainy video of Claire captured on CCTV in St. Mark's Square in Venice at 18:22 on the twenty-second of March that year.

The recording had most likely captured the moments just after she had been immortalised in Erik Lundberg's holiday snap. But if the Claire in the photograph had looked like she was bursting with life—or however Rekke had expressed it—she now seemed anxious.

It looked like she was saying a few words to a boy who was thirteen years old, according to the superintendent, but seemed younger, with his big, nervous eyes and dark curly hair. He was slender-limbed and scrawny, and in the brief video—it was just six seconds long—he shook his head, as if Claire had said something to him that he didn't want to hear. There was something poignant and vulnerable about his entire being, and he seemed uncomfortable in his clothes—a pale suit with a blue shirt. He was breathing heavily, as though he'd been running, or at least hurrying—and he stood still for a few moments before Claire pulled him out of shot.

"What do you make of it?" Hellner said, turning to Rekke.

"I'm not quite sure," Rekke said. "But it looks worrying. She seems to feel hunted. What's more . . . Can you rewind? I want to take a look at something."

They watched the clip again, and Rekke became animated. He was not necessarily happy, but he was lively and alert—as if a thousand thoughts were crossing his mind at once.

"They're speaking English to each other, aren't they? I'm fairly certain Claire is saying, 'We'll leave the car.' Have you found a car or vehicle that might be tied to her?"

"No vehicle in the area was registered to her or rented in her new name—Sara Miller—and we don't have any pictures of her arriving in Venice. She must have been extremely careful."

Rekke ran a hand through his hair.

"Have you checked cars that were towed from parking lots around Venice in the days after her disappearance, or any that were left parked for too long?" he asked.

"We tried, but we haven't got anywhere. It's quite a job, as you can imagine."

"Indeed, but it's quite an investigation too, is it not?" Rekke said. "Would you show me those pictures again?" he added.

"Of course," Hellner said, retrieving the photographs he had shown while Micaela was gone: six shots taken from different angles over the course of a few minutes.

"Have you noticed the recurring motif?"

Lars Hellner paused for thought.

"Not really—well, except for him."

He pointed to a young man in black trousers and a spotted, almost leopard-patterned shirt, who could be glimpsed behind Jakob in one of the photos.

"He's in two of them," Hellner said.

"Three, if we count his back here," Rekke said, putting his finger on another of the photos—it was definitely him, even if there wasn't much of him in sight.

He was hidden by the same group of Japanese tourists depicted in the holiday snap; Micaela was able to recognise him by his shoulders and the rather feminine way he had raised his left hand. The man's hair was bleached. The ends closest to the crown were darker, and he was perhaps not all that young—thirty-five or maybe even forty. He had an earring, and he was good-looking and he knew it. He was smiling, and seemingly pleased with himself. He looked like a gay tourist. It was hard to believe he had anything to do with Claire. The only potentially suspicious thing about him was that he was looking at her son, but there could be many reasons for that. The boy was drawing stares with his suit and his slender, anxious figure.

"He's looking at Jakob," she said. "Possibly covetously."

"Yes, and I assume he hasn't yet been spotted," Rekke said. "But that's not what I'm thinking. Look at this guy." Rekke picked up one of the photographs. "Do you see his right hand and thumb? It's curved—it doesn't look quite natural."

Hellner peered at the man's hand with intense interest.

"You're right," he said. "I hadn't noticed that before."

Rekke closed his eyes briefly.

"Do you have a pen?" he said. "Or something thin and oblong? That will do nicely, thank you."

He slipped the biro Hellner had handed him inside his sleeve so that it lay along his forearm and held it there by letting the pen rest against his bent thumb.

"Good grief," said Hellner. "That's exactly it. The man's hiding something. Could it be a weapon? A knife?"

"Yes, it could. It's just possible—although it's hard to see—to discern something black, like part of a handle, pressing against the thumb. And you're right, Micaela. I don't like the way the man is looking at the boy either. It troubles me."

"It's not good."

"My advice to you is to find this man. I have no idea how far your facial-recognition software has come on in recent years, but with a little luck you should be able to find him in other CCTV images and locate an address as a starting point—and you might even catch up with him to stage an *examen rigorosum*."

"I beg your pardon?"

"A tough interrogation. He has something to tell, and the boy . . . Such a small child, after all. I wonder . . . There's something characteristic about his . . ."

He didn't finish his sentence, suddenly preoccupied. After a few moments, he pulled himself together and asked for the return of his phone as well. He stepped aside just as Micaela had done, and while she couldn't hear much of what he said, she realised he was calling his brother. Meanwhile, she and Hellner returned to the surveillance photographs to try and understand the observations Rekke had made about the boy, but they couldn't work out what he was referring to and simply discussed in general terms how to find the man with the bleached hair.

When Rekke had finished his phone call, he returned to them wearing a grave expression—almost one of shock—although he was still his usual polite self.

"I do sincerely apologise," he said. "I'd be most grateful if you would send an encrypted file to me containing the pictures and as much other material as you can. However, I regret that I must now leave."

"No, you can't," Hellner said, shaking his head. "I have more things I need to consult you about."

"I'm sorry," Rekke said, proffering his hand and looking Hellner in the eye.

Then he nodded to Micaela to indicate that she should follow him, which flattered her a little. She was an inevitable part of his life. They walked back toward town, and though Rekke was once again lost in thought and he most definitely did not need any more problems, she decided it could no longer be put off.

"You were worried about Julia's new boyfriend," she said.

"Yes, indeed."

"I'm afraid it's my brother Lucas," she said. She had no idea how he would react, but she instinctively took a step away from him.

"What?" he said.

"I'm so sorry."

He stood still for a while in the same petrified state as before.

"Do we know where they are?" he said.

She told him what had happened and what Jonas Beijer had said. He didn't reply. He remained in the same position, muttering something that sounded like an address, but he didn't explain himself and he said nothing about the shocking fact that his daughter had gotten together with her gangster of a brother. It was as if he had seen it coming, and the only clear sign that he had absorbed the news at all was that he quickened his pace. She had to jog to keep up.

"Just so you know," she said. "I've texted Lucas to say I'll drop all my inquiries into his affairs. He has no reason to hurt her."

Rekke didn't reply. He just kept walking until he reached the door to his stairwell. He tapped in the code, and together they got into the elevator, and she saw that he was in a trance-like state of concentration, soaking up every detail inside the elevator. He bent down. He examined a piece of gravel that had been tracked in on someone's shoe. He picked it up and weighed it in his hand. Then he stood up, slid open the door and announced they had visitors. Micaela could smell perfume on the landing, and she opened the front door rather gingerly. Mrs. Hansson came toward them, her expression apologetic.

"Your mother is here," she said, turning to Rekke.

"I know," he said, not seeming to care.

He went straight to his computer, where he entered a few phrases into the search engine, even as a pair of high heels clicked toward them. There was something summoning about those footsteps: power, Micaela thought to herself, authority, but also reproach. A moment later, she was standing there—the woman about whom Micaela had heard so much, the one who had pulled Rekke out of school to transform him into a concert pianist and a world star, and who had long fought his efforts to seek out his natural habitat: logic and empirical analysis.

"Hans," she said sternly.

Rekke didn't even look up, but Micaela stared at her, entranced. She was perhaps seventy-five years old, yet she was youthful, slim and straight-backed. She wore her hair up and was dressed in riding boots, a tightly buttoned blue blouse and a pair of equally tight trousers. Micaela instinctively found herself wanting to improve her posture—or simply curtsey, as if she had been graced with a visit from the powers that be. The woman was nearly six feet tall and still beautiful, rather like Hans but with a sterner aura. She resembled an aged and strictly drilled ballerina, with her sharp cheekbones and big attentive eyes.

"Aren't you even going to greet me, Hans?" she said.

"Hello, Mamma," he said. "Did you catch any perch?"

"What? Oh, yes. Two. How on earth could you know that?"

"The gravel you tracked in with you is from the path down to the bait shop out in the country, and I can't recall you ever having any other business there except procuring a landing net for your perch."

"My God, are you manic again?"

He has no choice, Micaela thought to herself.

"I am purposeful," he said. "Allow me to introduce Micaela. My friend and lodger."

The woman, Elisabeth Rekke, née von Bülow, inspected Micaela from head to foot and was very clearly displeased. It took a hawk's eye to understand that, something Micaela happened to possess at that moment—she was able to distinguish the feigned benevolence from the hidden contempt.

"Finally, my dear," Elisabeth Rekke said, extending her hand. "I've heard so much about you."

Micaela nodded, wondering if she should return the compliment. She settled for a "nice to meet you."

"You're a delightful young lady. I adore your face. But once Hans has time and takes a break from his nonsense, he should take you out and dress you up a little. We have a slightly different sense of fashion here in Östermalm."

"Above all we're apparently prejudiced and condescending," Rekke said. "But it's good to see you, Mother." He raised his gaze to her. "And I'm proud that you managed to clean the net yourself this time. Did Lottie have the day off?"

Elisabeth Rekke looked down at her hands.

"Hmm? Not at all. But I could hardly let her do it herself. The net was in the most appalling tangle. Vivian Sparre just rang and was very worked up about the fact that there is a photograph circulating on the internet in which Magnus is smirking at President Putin. I must say, I feel he could exhibit a little more dignity."

"If only you knew," Rekke murmured, standing up with a baleful look. "I'm ever so sorry, Mamma, but I must rush off. Was there any particular reason you dropped by?"

"For goodness' sake! Does there have to be a reason, Hans? I've been worried, and you don't answer when I telephone. I still can't believe you gave up your career. You could have been anything."

"You too, Mamma. But it's not too late. Once we have a little spare time, Micaela and I will take you out and add a little extra zest to your attire. After all, the fashions are slightly different now we're in the twenty-first century. Did you know that the necklace I gave to Ida Aminoff has been returned to me?"

"Do not mention that dreadful person. I really do think you should reconcile with Lovisa this instant."

*"Vare, Vare, redde mihi legiones meas,"* Rekke murmured, before disappearing off to start rummaging through drawers and coat pockets and bureaus and under heaps of clothes, initially maintaining his grim-faced composure.

But before long, his entire being had been overcome by some unknown force. His hand began to tremble. His gaze was wandering, and he flapped about the flat overturning all he saw, while his mother and Mrs. Hansson circled him almost as if locked in a dance. Micaela was fairly certain this was a scene that had unfolded many times before.

"My God, what are you looking for, Hans?" Elisabeth Rekke said.

"The car keys?" said Mrs. Hansson.

"Indeed, yes," said Rekke.

"I've hidden them from you, Hans. I don't think you've been in a fit state to drive recently and if I'm quite honest, Hans, you probably shouldn't get behind the wheel right now either."

"I have no choice, Sigrid. Please be so kind as to give them to me now," he said in a voice that rang out with such agitated authority that Mrs. Hansson merely nodded submissively and went off to retrieve them.

Rekke told Micaela to come with him and they hastened away as the two ladies continued to protest. "We're going to Trosa," he said as the elevator began its descent.

# FORTY-FOUR

Damn it all to hell. He should have called Hans before he got on the plane. Now *he* had called first and caught him on the hop. He was emerging from the terminal at Arlanda, his jacket slung over his shoulder and his undone tie hanging down his chest like a narrow scarf. He felt like a lousy person, which wasn't that usual for him. But things were bad. In order to save his own skin, he had put his brother in serious danger, and that was crossing a line in the sand—even for him. Good God, how had this happened?

The whole world had come crashing down around him. He strode out of the arrivals hall and got into a taxi. He snapped at the driver to take him to Grevgatan. It would be best if he saw Hans face to face and engaged in some damage limitation as best as he could. Not that there was much to be done at this stage. Well, there was . . . He rang his contact at the Security Service and explained the situation, asking them to keep an eye on Hans and provide him with a protection detail. He felt better afterward, although only for a few seconds.

The conversation with his brother had been very brief and he had done most of the talking, but Hans had still managed to say—with an eerie chill in his voice—that he had found out more about Ida Aminoff's death, and that was a horror unto itself.

"What? No, forget about it. It's none of your business."

He glowered at the taxi driver—an older man with long sideburns—who had asked what the matter was. Being stuck in a cab like any other Tom, Dick or Harry was pure hell. He should have requested a car from the ministry, but he'd felt guilty and not as powerful as usual, and worse, now there were traffic jams everywhere. He was about to explode. Memories were washing over him—memories of that distant, shitty wedding on Djurgården full of morons spraying champagne and ripping clothes. It was a caricature of an upper-class event. He had been obliged to drink to cope with it, and he had gotten home late. He had just drifted off, still in his clothes, when the telephone had rung. He remembered reaching out toward the bedside table and picking up the receiver.

It was Gabor Morovia. He sounded agitated, which should have made Magnus suspicious right away. Gabor never got upset. His only mode was cold calculation, and it took a while for Magnus to understand what he was saying. Apparently Gabor was also in Stockholm and he was apologising, which was actually even stranger. Gabor was not one for apologies. But he said he had acted unfairly, that he'd taken things too far with Hans.

"Isn't Hans in Helsinki?" said Magnus.

"No, and he's in a bad way," Gabor said. "I need help." Doubtless Magnus should have seen through that too, but he was groggy and still drunk and he was not closely acquainted with Hans's touring schedule. The Helsinki concert might just as well have been the day before or the day before that, and he supposed it might not hurt to help out—he needed brownie points with his brother. So he rushed off to the address that Gabor had given him: 6 Torstenssonsgatan. He made his way there as if in a dream. Part of him still seemed to be asleep as he tapped in the code to unlock the main door and climbed two flights of stairs.

There was a black high-heeled shoe lying on the landing. That was a little strange, but he didn't give it much thought. He had come from a party where people had been throwing clothes about, and without bothering to pick up the shoe, he rang the bell. Morovia opened the door, looking neat and tidy and clean-shaven, as if his day had just begun rather than nearing its end.

"What's happened?" said Magnus.

Gabor didn't reply. Instead, he let Magnus in, closed the door and pointed to a large double bed to the right. Ida Aminoff was lying on her back in her glittering necklace. Despite the fact that she was clearly unwell, she looked somehow mutinous. Her black dress was pulled up above her thighs, and one of her legs—the one that still had a shoe on it—was lying on the bed while the other was hanging off the edge.

The dress was unbuttoned at the chest and she was breathing heavily, her right hand at her throat. She seemed to be confused and tormented, and was mumbling something about Hans, an apology, he thought, and "I love him," words that sounded rather more desperate than loving. "Help me, please . . ." she breathed. By then Magnus had already spun on his heel in a frantic movement.

"We have to call a doctor."

Gabor gazed back at him with the same collected calm as he had at the door.

"Calm yourself. It's just a little too much booze and opiates. I thought you might help me sort her out. I've got naloxone with me—that'll ease the breathing difficulties," he said, which sounded promising, but something was obviously wrong.

If Gabor could help her then why hadn't he done so already—and why had he called someone who knew nothing about overdoses or breathing difficulties?

"What are you doing?" Magnus said angrily. "What's this all about?"

"I'm helping her," Gabor said, putting his hand into his inside pocket as if to pull out the medicine, but it was just a distraction.

A moment later Magnus sank to his knees, was gasping for air. The blow seemed to have come out of nowhere. Nevertheless, he knew right away that he wasn't the one in danger. That was Ida. Bent double on the floor, he gazed at her and reached out a hand while Gabor leaned over her and kissed her, groping her breasts and between her legs. It seemed a dreadful violation. Ida tried desperately to shake him off, but she was too far gone. Magnus staggered back to his feet, took a fresh blow and went down again, and only when he had pulled himself together a little did he see Gabor bending over her, covering her nose and mouth and holding on.

It didn't last long. It couldn't have. Magnus hadn't even managed to stand before Ida's body contorted, and in that jolt there was something unbearable. The motion itself was brief and silent, but still thoroughly eerie, and when Magnus finally made it over to the bed, her face had changed. It had taken on a new and distressing expression, and she was no longer breathing. She was dead—and Magnus did not know what he did after that. Only that he took a swing at Gabor. But he didn't stand a chance, and he was perhaps more beside himself than angry, and for a few crazy seconds after he had allowed himself to be overpowered, Gabor had held him in an insane embrace as he whispered:

"We're bound together now, Magnus. Now we advance or fall as one."

Gabor might as well have stuck a knife in his back. When—shortly thereafter—Magnus stumbled out of the flat for want of alternatives and bumped into William Fors in the dawn light, he didn't think it was possible to survive such an experience. He didn't think anything would ever be the same again. But the days had passed, and months had turned to years. Somehow, life went on, especially once the police investigation ruled that it was an overdose. Hans—to the extent that he was able to engage with it—was constantly seeking to trace events back to the wedding party. But there was nothing there, merely illusory hints. Gabor had remained out of sight the whole evening, and afterward he knew just how to keep his blackmail victims onside. Slowly Magnus had formed a connection with Morovia; he convinced himself that it was merely a temporary connection, but they continued to give and take, linked by a frightful memory.

That had been their reality for a long time, and he had thought the danger was over. Of course, that was naive. Hans was Hans. He could unravel *anything*, even from a distance of decades. Magnus gazed out of the window, feeling increasingly impatient. Ever so slowly they were approaching Östermalm. His phone rang. It was Kleeberger, who presumably wondered where he'd got to. Magnus couldn't bring himself to answer. He thought instead of Putin, of all people. Let the bastard shoot Morovia, he thought. What was stopping him?

It was taking an utterly hopeless amount of time. Everywhere there were red lights, one-way streets, dawdling pedestrians and senile drivers. Why the hell should he put up with it? Putin would probably have cleansed the city. But up ahead was Grevgatan—at last—the small stub leading down to Strandvägen. Magnus was rehearsing what he would say to his brother, when the taxi driver slammed on the brakes. He swore.

They had come close to colliding with some moron. A second later he saw that the moron in question was Hans along with his Latina maid, or whatever she was.

# FORTY-FIVE

Rekke could have splurged on a fancier ride, she thought to herself, but she guessed things worked a little differently around here from the way they did out in Husby.

In Husby, the car was the thing. If you were going to show you had made it in life, then you did it with some serious wheels. As far as Rekke was concerned, it was a petty concern. He didn't even know what model it was. "Volvo," was all he said, and he pulled out of the underground parking lot with the same kind of jerky neurotic movements he had just exhibited in the flat, in the process almost T-boning a taxi.

"Calm down," said Micaela.

But calm was the last thing Rekke became. He floored the brakes and leaped out of the car, and Micaela was convinced that he was going to start a brawl with the driver, regardless of how out of keeping that was with his character—but it wasn't the narrowly averted collision he was angry about. It was his brother, who was sitting in the back seat of the taxi and who immediately got out and stood on the sidewalk. Rekke glared at him furiously. Magnus waved his right arm and muttered something about protection.

"I don't need protecting, but I have a daughter too. Or had you forgotten that?"

Magnus looked at him in horror.

"Has something happened to Julia?"

"I hope not."

"I'm terribly sorry, and I never meant—"

Rekke cut him off.

"I've already foreseen all your excuses. I cannot bring myself to listen to them now, but as soon as I have time, I want to know exactly how Morovia gained influence over you. Then I shall give thought to . . ." Rekke fell silent and looked toward Micaela in the car.

"Yes?" Magnus said. "What?"

Rekke seemed to want to say something fraught with consequence, such as: *what your punishment will be, Magnus*. But he didn't have time to say anything. At that moment the door to his stairwell opened and Elisabeth Rekke emerged in all her grandeur, which hardly made Magnus feel any better.

"What the hell?" he muttered. "You're dragging Mamma into this?"

Rekke gazed absent-mindedly at his mother, then turned back to Magnus.

"I'm happy to drag the whole world in. If something happens to Julia, I shall devote my life to crushing you *and* Morovia."

Magnus looked at his mother as if seeking her assistance instead.

"But I love Julia! Tell me what I can do."

"My God, what's the matter with Julia?" Elisabeth Rekke called to them as she approached.

Rekke did not even glance at her. Instead, he stared deep into Magnus's eyes.

"You can move out of the way, Magnus. Keep your mobile close."

"Yes, of course," he said.

Rekke got back into the car and drove away. Neither he nor Micaela said a word; they were both preoccupied with apprehensions and alternate plans. But once they were on the motorway and Rekke had put his foot down and the sky seemed to be darkening, Micaela could no longer contain herself. She spoke quietly and doggedly:

"I have a hard time believing that Lucas would hurt Julia. He just wants to apply pressure to me," she said. "He has no reason to hurt her."

Rekke glanced at her.

"What makes you say that?" he said.

She paused for thought. Why had she said it?

"Because when Lucas does something awful, he's always thought it through," she said. "I think we can remain calm until we hear from him. He's not impulsive."

"Is that really true?" Rekke said, and she immediately realised that he was right—at least in part.

Lucas was not nearly as controlled as he liked to claim—it was only after the fact that he always had a good explanation to hand. He was a ticking time bomb in so many ways. Yet she didn't want to agree with Rekke.

"He hasn't got a record," she said. "He's always made sure not to do anything stupid."

Rekke muttered something.

"Or are you worried that he might be in league with Morovia?"

"Yes," he said. "I am."

"Lucas hates it when other people interfere, especially guys like Morovia. He wants to be in control of everything himself."

"You're forgetting one thing," he said. "Lucas isn't as smart as his sister." He gave her a melancholy smile. "Morovia is drawn to young people like Lucas. He senses their desire to be seen and turns their heads. And then he drowns them in money."

Micaela swallowed hard.

"So you really think they're collaborating somehow?"

"I'm afraid so," he said. "I found an address in Trosa, and just before we left, I looked it up. The house in question is owned by a Swiss trust, which troubles me. Although I may be wrong. I hope I'm wrong."

He fell silent, grasping the steering wheel, and she too was quiet—

unable to think of anything to say. She had never seen him drive before, and she was able to examine him in a new way. He was such a contradictory person. There was immense habitude in his movements, but also an increasing number of signs that he was crumbling within. His left hand kept running up and down his torso, and he rummaged through the various compartments and slots in the front of the car before moving to his pockets and eventually pulling out a small pill that he examined before swallowing it.

"You're on a comedown," she said.

He nodded.

"Should I drive?"

"No, it's good for me to occupy myself with something."

She patted him on the shoulder.

"And in the midst of it all, Claire Lidman seems to be alive," she said.

"Yes, hopefully," he said.

"Although you were troubled by the man with the bleached hair in the surveillance images, weren't you?"

He nodded, seemingly reluctant to go into detail, but she couldn't stop now that she had started.

"And Claire's son, Jakob. You saw something in him too, didn't you?"

"Perhaps," he said.

Christ, he was being difficult all of a sudden.

"What did you see?"

He muttered as if to himself:

"Something. But also that he's a talented boy—naturally—who's just witnessed something dramatic and tumultuous."

"How were you able to tell that?"

"From his arms, his eyebrows, his way of seeing the world, his way of pressing together his knees. Just as soon..." he hesitated, "... as I've got Julia back home, I shall take a closer look to make certain. A thought occurs to me."

"Why do you have to be so cryptic?"

"I think I can fool myself."

She studied him as he continued to search for more pills that she suspected he would not find.

"So it was Morovia who killed Ida?"

"It would seem so."

"And Magnus knew about it?"

"I believe he was a witness."

She took this in.

"We should throttle our brothers," she said.

Rekke smiled reluctantly and pushed the accelerator further toward the floor, drumming all his fingers on the wheel like a wild virtuoso. He made it sound as if there were an entire small orchestra of drums thundering along the motorway.

That morning—the twenty-second of March—Claire stood in front of the mirror for a long time, and despite the warmth in the air she put on a new red coat she'd had tailored in London. It wasn't just for her that she had made lavish purchases. She had bought Jakob a linen suit and dressed him in a freshly pressed white shirt and a loosely knotted tie. He might be small and fragile, but he could also look grown-up and too sweet for words with his serious face. In any case, it would do no harm for him to be as handsome as possible. There was something unsettling in the air.

Morovia's invitation had been as gracious as ever. *I request the pleasure of your company for lunch and festivities at my home in Venice*, it had said on the handwritten card. But it had been a long time since all three of them had met, and none of what she recalled from the most recent encounter in Paris was good. Gabor had been openly hostile and had even tugged at Jakob's hair without justification.

Of course, the whole thing had been an insane arrangement from the very start, but it was the only way out she could see. If you couldn't escape your enemy, then you had to ally yourself with him. It had been an act of desperation—nothing more or less—and of course she knew that Gabor was keeping tabs on them, and that he would never need to threaten her again. The threat was there anyway, in every step, every breath, in the constant presence of the memory from the Italian cornfield.

She slipped some underwear, toiletries and a book into her bag. She didn't bother to pack more. Cool-headed, she expected to return that same evening, or to stop at a hotel on the way home. She went into the hallway and called to Jakob. He emerged reluctantly and together they stepped out into the chilly morning and got into the car. It was an unassuming Passat that she had rented with a fake driver's licence issued to her by Gabor's men. She and Jakob spent their springs not far from Rosenheim in Bavaria, so they drove from there through Austria and into Italy, making for Venice. She thought she had done a good job of masking her worries on the drive, but she began to suspect that Jakob was doing the same thing.

When they parked in the parking lot at Santa Croce, the apprehension was visible in his eyes.

"Hurry up, darling," she said.

Jakob was walking ever so slowly, his arms folded. When she turned around to urge him to hurry up, she mis-stepped. Her old knee injury twinged and she had to lean against a wall. He came over to her.

"Why don't we drive home again?" he said.

She looked at him tenderly. Jakob was thirteen by now and not excessively short, but he was still slight, with big dark eyes and curly black hair. He was not doing nearly as well at school as she had expected. He was in a world of his own, and he seemed to have no friends to speak of. He mostly stayed at home with his computer and his games. He would still ask constantly: "Are you angry with me, Mamma?" He was often anxious, and things were constantly breaking in his hands—or getting lost.

"What's the matter?" he said.

"My knee's just a little sore, that's all."

"You're afraid of him, aren't you?"

"No," she said. "I'm not afraid. But let's make sure it's a short visit."

Then they walked close together toward the quay, which was not far away. Sitting on a bench there was Ricardo Bruni in a brown leather jacket, puffing away on a cigarette. She had always liked Ricardo—he was a break from the homogeneity of the macho men and pretty young women who surrounded Gabor. Ricardo was openly gay and very chatty, and unlike Gabor he uttered nothing but kind words to Jakob. Nevertheless, Claire had felt uneasy about him too on recent occasions, perhaps because of the way that he had looked at Jakob.

"Quickly, quickly," Ricardo said as they approached.

Claire and Jakob ducked as they stepped down into the smart launch waiting for them, and then quickly went below deck. They were not allowed to show themselves on the journey, but she had no desire to either. It was a quarter past two in the afternoon. She watched Jakob tenderly. No matter how uncomfortable he was, he couldn't help but look around, wide-eyed. Poor boy. A life on the run hadn't overloaded him with sensory experiences. And it was incredibly beautiful out there. As they sailed along the Grand Canal, the houses lining it were reflected in the water. It was like entering a kaleidoscope. They passed tourist boats and gondolas and slipped under bridges and arches. In the distance, the domes of St. Mark's Basilica rose into the sky, and she thought of Samuel and her old life and of her sister, Linda.

They disembarked onto Gabor's jetty, quickly entered the house and climbed two flights of stairs. Gabor was waiting for them in a large, church-like room with frescoes, and she noticed right away that he didn't even glance at Jakob. He was only courting her eyes, and she grew increasingly nervous. When he helped her out of the red coat, she made a careless movement. The chess book she had brought with her fell out of her bag. Gabor picked it up and pointed to the title.

"Sicilian Love?"

She snatched it back—it was none of his business.

"Interesting," he said.

"What do you want?" she said.

He didn't reply. Instead, he smiled coolly and looked at Jakob for the first time. His eyes filled with what she thought was disgust, and that frightened her. She kept the boy close to her while Gabor led them onto the terrace, where there was a long table already laid with plates of shellfish, burrata, bruschetta, prosciutto and a profusion of other Italian aperitivi, as well as champagne. Ricardo had come out too and he poured a glass of it for her.

"I'm not drinking today," she said. "I have to drive home."

"Really?" Gabor said, with a hint of a threat in his voice, at which point Claire took Jakob's hand, resolving to be strong.

She straightened her dress and sat down with her back to the canal and the city beyond. It was half past two in the afternoon on the twenty-second of March 2004 and in a few hours she would be captured in a holiday snap.

# FORTY-SIX

Jonas Beijer called. He had pulled out all the stops. Lucas's Audi had been seen entering Trosa, and that confirmed what Rekke had thought ever since he'd picked up a faint impression in Julia's flat. "Högbergsgatan," he said. "Let's go and have a look." She nodded, wondering whether she should call to see whether her colleagues in uniform were ready to intervene, but decided to wait.

She still didn't believe that Lucas would harm Julia, and she couldn't conceive of the idea that he had involved a man like Morovia in his private affairs. Truth be told, she even thought they should leave Lucas and Julia alone. They might only trigger something if they barged in on their date.

Besides, she had no gun. She never carried her service weapon when off duty, and what would Rekke be able to do if Lucas lost it? Not a thing. No-one stood a chance against Lucas in close combat—everyone in Husby knew that—and it wouldn't surprise her in the slightest if Lucas had a gun stashed somewhere in his car.

"We should wait until we get some kind of message from Lucas," she said. "I must have texted him at least ten times by now. He'll answer soon."

Rekke nodded, searching the car yet again for pills. It had already started to drizzle, but now the rain came down properly, and she switched on the windshield wipers for him. Rekke mimicked their sound—*tick, tack*—with perfect pitch and said it was like a metronome for his thoughts. He said nothing else after that and, each wrapped up in their own thoughts, they glided into the town of Trosa. She had never been there before, but she had heard it was something of a middle-class paradise—a holiday town with old wooden houses lining narrow canals. Down the road she saw two girls around Julia's age walking along the sidewalk engaged in lively conversation.

"I'm sorry..." she said.

"What...?"

He looked at her in confusion, as if he had been far, far away in his thoughts.

"For dragging you into this."

"I should say we've quite competently dragged each other into this," he said.

"But you have a child; that makes it worse."

"Yes," he said. "That makes it worse."

They wended their way to the address in question, and it didn't take long for her to see they had found the right place. Lucas's Audi was parked outside, but there were also other cars—a Mercedes and a Land Rover—and that worried her. Should she raise the alarm with Jonas? No, it was too soon—to her knowledge no crime had yet been committed. And, of course, there were always fancy cars on a street like this. She supposed all the damned fools around here were rich.

Then again, she couldn't help being tense—and she was annoyed at Rekke, who parked carelessly and got out without closing the door properly; the seatbelt got in the way. However, his powers of observation compensated for his shortcomings as a driver. He scrutinised the vehicles and the house with a sharp eye. He crouched down by the metre-wide path leading to the front door and inspected the ground.

She could tell that several people had passed along it recently, but there were many footprints and they were so faint that she could not detect anything more precise from them. She looked at Rekke.

He stood up, his body even more tense now.

"You were in contact with a colleague."

"Yes," she said.

"Perhaps you should let him know that we're about to enter the house?"

"We're definitely not going in," she said. "There seems to be a lot of people in there. But . . . Fine, I'll contact him."

She walked away and texted Jonas Beijer with a brief explanation and the address. Then she turned back to Rekke. He was standing right by the door and peering down again at the footprints in the gravel. He was even paler now.

"You're probably right," he said.

"About what?"

"That we shouldn't go in. I can see prints left by five people—one of them is Julia. The other four are men, but that's not really what troubles me. Rather . . ." He fell silent and pointed rather vaguely at the ground. "It's that left foot," he said. "The tilt and twist. I'm sorry, Micaela."

"No," she said.

But it was already too late. Rekke wrenched open the door. She swore to herself. She was certain it was a mistake, but what was done was done and nothing had happened for that matter. The house was silent, until she called out, "Hello? This is the police. We're coming in!" which made her just as much of a fool as he was. Damn it, what were they doing? This could only end badly.

Her heart pounding, she looked around. A staircase led to the upper floor, while to her left there was an impersonal-looking living room. But there were no footsteps to be heard, nothing to indicate that there was anyone inside, despite those footprints on the path, and once again Rekke crouched. He examined the floor and ran his index finger across the parquet.

He turned left and entered the living room. Micaela was still unable to discern any sign of people in the house—there were no bags or clothes, no mess—but ahead of her there was another room, and that was when she heard something. It was someone breathing, someone who must have been standing still because she hadn't perceived any movement, so she called out again:

"Hello?"

"Sis."

His voice was deeper than usual, and perhaps more bitter too, and a moment later she heard his footsteps. He moved quickly, and when she saw him he barely resembled the controlled, collected Lucas she knew. He was angry and his face was bright red, and he came straight up to her and grasped her arm tightly.

"What are you doing here?"

He looked toward Rekke and then glanced hastily over his shoulder. Something had happened in this house—that much was apparent—but she couldn't understand what, and she tried vainly to release herself from his grip.

"Where's Julia?" she said.

"How the hell did you know we were here? Did those muppets blab?" he said, glancing further back into the house.

What muppets? she thought. But she kept that to herself. She needed to understand, and she furiously yanked herself loose before he could shove her aside. It looked like Lucas was on the brink of losing it at any moment.

"What's happened?" she said.

"I haven't touched her, and if anything's happened it's because of you. You've messed it all up."

She pushed him aside to make her way into the kitchen, but apparently that was all it took for Lucas to lose his temper. He struck her face, and she gave as good as she got. She raised her fists. In that moment, he didn't frighten her in the slightest. She was completely focused on continuing further into the house and finding Julia. And then something happened that she couldn't immediately take in. Lucas was slammed against the wall, and there in front of him was Rekke.

For a few seconds the men eyeballed each other, and it didn't really surprise her that Lucas quickly settled into the contest. That kind of showdown was his lifeblood, and the sensible outcome would obviously be for Rekke to back down and calm the situation using his intellect. Instead, he opted for the worst possible strategy. He lectured Lucas.

"Do not touch her," he said. Micaela realised right away that it was all about to explode, especially when Rekke added: "Move."

Lucas had retreated and was now barring the way into the kitchen.

"Or what?" he snarled.

"You'll be surprised," Rekke said, shifting his gaze away from him. "Julia!" he called into the house.

"Pappa!" said a voice that seemed to come from outside in the garden.

"What's going to surprise me, professor?" Lucas said threateningly.

Rekke didn't reply. He merely walked toward the kitchen, completely beside himself at the sound of Julia's vice, and he didn't care that Lucas was blocking his path. He shoved him out of the way, and that was an even worse idea. Lucas flipped and lunged at Rekke with violent force, and all Micaela had time to think in that moment was that it was just as she'd thought in the car. Lucas had never lost a fight. That's what everyone said. It wasn't just because he was both fit and violent. He lacked the measure of hesitation that was present in others. He always took aim at the weakest point when he struck. Sure enough, Rekke tumbled to the floor, seemingly defenceless, and Micaela leaped forward to intervene, but then something odd happened. Rekke was transformed. It was something she would remember for a long time.

# FORTY-SEVEN

Claire had known it all along. It was absurd to seek protection from the man who had wanted to kill them. Yet there had been a dark logic to it. She had sensed it that time on the gravel road outside Limena. There was a life insurance policy right there in the voice that had broken, in the trembling hand, in the entire violent storm of emotions that had contrasted so sharply with his ordinary coldness.

A son—a replacement for the one he had lost—could keep them alive, and for a long time she thought she was right. Gabor had shown a new, more human side with Jakob, and his hostility toward her had disappeared, or at least been on hiatus. But nothing lasted forever. A tinge of disappointment was increasingly visible in Gabor's eyes when he looked at the boy—he was always comparing him with Jan, and never in Jakob's favour.

If Jan had been strong, athletic and outgoing, then Jakob was anything but those things: he was fragile, slender and withdrawn, and it had only got worse with the passing years. His flaws multiplied, while the mythical sheen around the deceased son was amplified, and now that they had arrived in Venice and taken their seats on the terrace, there seemed to be nothing left but pure contempt. Gabor looked at

Jakob with revulsion. Claire wanted to grab her fork and stab it through his hand.

"He's better than you," she snapped.

"Who?" Gabor said, pretending not to understand.

"Jakob," she said.

"*Him*," he said, spitting the word out. "He's only fit to perform certain practical tasks, at best. Basic carpentry perhaps. And I should imagine he's too nervous even for that."

"Don't speak like that in front of him," she said, taking the boy's hand under the table.

Gabor indicated that he wanted more champagne. Ricardo rushed over and poured.

"I shall speak however I wish," Gabor said. "The boy is useless at sport and does not understand any of the high art forms, least of all mathematics."

"You don't know anything about him."

"He's a coward."

"He's not been feeling well—is that so strange, given the childhood you've ensured he's had?"

"My son wouldn't feel unwell. He would pull himself together. I remember Jan . . ."

"I don't fucking care about Jan," she said, looking at Jakob, who was staring straight down at his thighs. "*We're* here now, Gabor, so why don't you tell us why you asked us to come? Otherwise, we'll leave at once. We aren't going to sit here and be insulted."

"Three times you have betrayed me, Claire. Three. You are in no position to make demands."

She felt a pang of terror.

"How do you reach that conclusion?" she said.

"I took a strand of hair from him when we last met."

"What?" she said in confusion.

"I took a strand of hair and sent it to a lab in Berlin. The hair was compared to a strand of my own."

"What are you saying?" she said, beside herself.

"You took advantage of me."

"He's your son, Gabor."

"I liked the boy at first. I was so despondent at the time that I fooled myself—I saw similarities that never existed. But then, Claire, my vision became clear and I discovered the pitifulness of his being, his weakness of character. Look at him. He can't even look us in the eye. He's squirming like an eel."

"Don't talk like that."

Gabor drained his glass.

"He's not mine, Claire," he said. "I received confirmation a few weeks ago."

Claire was unable to digest this, let alone to rejoice as she would have done in so many other situations. Instead, all she saw was the impending danger.

"That can't be possible," she said. "I've seen..."

"Yes, what is it you've seen?"

She looked at Jakob, who was compulsively gazing down at the floor.

"You. In him."

"I'm not there. You deceived me."

"I was convinced, Gabor. Convinced."

"But now we know, and let's not forget, Claire, that you went to the police. I'll never forgive that."

"What are you going to do?"

"I haven't decided yet."

She gripped Jakob's hand.

"No?"

"No," he said, suddenly smiling with what almost constituted charm. "Do you know what I'm thinking about?"

She shook her head.

"Your book, Claire."

"What book?"

"Polugaevsky. *Sicilian Love*. It made me remember our old games."

She looked around anxiously.

"I always defeated you," he said. "But I think often of that evening in Stockholm."

"When you raped me?"

"When we played chess," he said. "You came close to defeating me."

"I'm not so sure."

"But you gambled hard on winning."

"Perhaps," she said.

"And you want to do that now as well. You want to get out of the bind you've ended up in—and win."

She swallowed.

Gabor sat back contentedly and waved to the men waiting on them.

"All I want, Gabor, is to leave. I want you to leave us alone," she said.

"So I should just quietly sit here waiting for you to stab me in the back again, Claire?"

"I would never go to the police again. You know that. I'll do anything to protect my boy."

Gabor fixed his gaze on her.

"Did you know that the Kremlin are after me too? Putin has a personal interest in it. A food taster has to check everything I eat. I'm constantly on the alert, wondering which dangers I need to eliminate. I don't take any risks."

"I'm not Putin," she said. "I'm completely harmless."

"Are you really? Aren't you, in fact, rather more dangerous than most? But fine . . . Perhaps I will give you a chance, nonetheless. By way of thanks for the dreams you once evoked in me. I thought we might decide your fate in a game of chess."

She gripped Jakob's hand even tighter.

"I don't want to, Gabor."

"My dear Claire," he said. "You're in no position to quibble." He barked: "Kristof!"

Kristof was another of his closest henchmen—a young, toned man with a look of brutality in his eyes and a faint scar below his lower lip. While he didn't really frighten her any more than Ricardo, he had none of the duality of his colleague. No matter how hard she looked, she could find nothing kind or gentle about him.

"Conjure us a chessboard, Kristof. The most beautiful you can find."

Kristof vanished, and the fear began to constrict her neck like a rope. Gabor loved cruel games. Rumour had it that he had let one of his victims in St. Petersburg roll a die for their life.

"What are we playing for—specifically?" she said.

"You two," he said. "Your freedom."

"I don't want to."

"I'm afraid it has already begun."

She closed her eyes.

"Okay," she said. "But if I win, you'll leave us alone."

He smiled confidently.

"Yes," he said.

"And if it's a draw?"

"Then one of you will have your freedom."

"I don't want to, Gabor," she said in horror. "I can't."

"You shouldn't have betrayed me," he said.

Shortly thereafter, Kristof returned and cleared the end of the table before folding back the tablecloth, setting out a chessboard and putting the pieces in their places. The unease in the air intensified. Kristof looked tense. Ricardo and the others were exchanging curious glances, and she realised there was no point in protesting further.

Instead she was overcome by sudden concentration as she wondered whether she might have a chance. An opportunity to surprise him. She had always kept detailed chess notes, and in her many hours of solitude since her flight from Sweden she had reviewed her old games against Morovia—always with Jakob by her side, just as he was now.

"I'd like to play Black," she said.

"Goodness—you want to give me an advantage?"

He rotated the board.

"Or is this all about some Sicilian tricks you've picked up from Polugaevsky's book?" he said.

"I have learned a thing or two," she said with a strained smile as she surveyed the board.

The pieces were exquisite: beautifully carved Chinese figures with individual features and friendly faces—except for the queens, who looked murderous.

"So if I win you'll let us go," she said.

"Yes," he said. "We shall take our leave."

"And we won't have to look over our shoulders or be afraid?"

"As long as you don't think of crossing me, then yes, you have my word. Now let us begin," he said.

She nodded, not wholly understanding what she was embarking upon, but she supposed she couldn't help but play. She'd always had a feeling that it was possible to defeat Gabor, and perhaps that time might be now, when her whole body was screaming to be free of him.

He opened with pawn to e4. Her immediate response was pawn to c5. Then they continued, without a clock or any other rules of conduct.

Gabor's face changed, jaw clenched, and she had expected nothing less. He wants to crush me, she thought to herself. He wants to show his superiority before he destroys me, and she focused as hard as she could on the board in front of her, but she was soon surprised by something else altogether. Jakob, who had spent the entire conversation looking down at the floor, had now raised his gaze and was contemplating the pieces with the same intensity she was, and it occurred to her that this was something she had seen before, but there was no time to think about it now. She had to focus.

Gabor was playing in an increasingly aggressive and unorthodox way, and it was going to be hard—harder than she could ever have imagined, and while she knew she shouldn't let her mind wander, she thought about Samuel.

Samuel Lidman was back at the gym, tightening his weightlifting belt. Today was leg day. He hated leg days. Regardless, he didn't want to hold back. As usual, he was intending to pile it on so hard it almost broke him, and if anyone asked why, he wouldn't be able to explain, except that a routine was a routine and that was what he'd always done.

As in his younger and better days, he started with heavy squats. He added one hundred and fifty kilos to the pole and positioned himself wide-legged beneath the frame. It's time, he thought to himself. Suck it up and hope your knees and veins hold up. He heaved the whole damned lot up and snorted so hard saliva splashed out while the pole swayed on his shoulders. So damn heavy. He gasped for breath and was about to go on with his activity when the mobile in his bag rang.

Don't stop, he thought to himself. Don't hope. Then again . . . He remembered what Morovia had said. *She loves you.* He brushed aside the thought. Stop dreaming. Total nonsense. Of course it can't be Claire. Why would she come back after all these years, just because he'd seen her in a photo? It was ridiculous. It was absurd. Blast. He'd already lost his concentration. He staggered forward a couple of paces, but that was apparently more than he could manage. His vision darkened. His legs gave way and only with a desperate movement did he manage to hurl the pole away against the wall and the mirrors.

There was a deafening crash. Glass shattered and he fell to one side while the pole bounced around as if it had taken on a life of its own, and he supposed he had injured himself. His thigh was burning—perhaps his head too—and there were people running from all directions, but all he cared about was the phone in his bag, and as he lay on the floor he rummaged until he found it and bellowed at everyone that he was fine.

He just needed to check something. Get lost, all of you, he said, as he stared at the mobile. The number was familiar. That was at once ominous and hopeful. Then he understood. It was Alicia Kovács. With a supreme effort, he stood up and shoved people out of his way as he limped outside to call back. His heart was pounding. Maybe there's something there after all, he thought. Why else would she call?

"Alicia Kovács," a voice on the line said.

"You called?" he said.

"My goodness, are you alright? You're panting."

"I'm at the gym," he said. "What's this about?"

Alicia Kovács fell silent and that feeling intensified. Something had happened. Something big. He didn't know whether it was good or bad, but it was something, and he loosened his belt and tried to control his breathing and the pain. He closed his eyes.

"I've spoken to someone who is very eager to see you," Kovács said. *It's happening, it's really happening.*

"Claire," he said.

"I don't want to say anything—not on the phone—but if you can be at the office in an hour, I can bring you together. You'll have a lot to talk about."

"Yes, of course," he managed to stammer, feeling that he needed to find a bathroom mirror to smarten up.

He needed to look more handsome than ever—no matter how much his damn thigh and head hurt.

# FORTY-EIGHT

Lucas leaped at Rekke. He slammed into him with violent force and pummelled him with his fists. It went quickly. Lucas was aggressive and muscular, but Rekke was lanky and middle-aged and a little unsteady, and he took a blow to the face and another to his shoulder which propelled him backwards.

He parried the third blow and stepped to one side, which was when he underwent a transformation. His whole body seemed to become alert and ready, and he adopted a stance that appeared rehearsed, his hands tensed at his sides. His gaze roamed, as if absorbing information, and his left leg twitched just as it did when he performed his analyses.

Lucas must have felt the change. He hesitated before resuming his attack, and this time he was dogged and vigilant, like a boxer probing for a weakness. He jumped about, striking suddenly, and that should have paid off because he was fast and explosive—but he immediately encountered a problem.

Rekke moved to the side and struck back, grabbing Lucas's arm while simultaneously extending his own right leg and turning his body so he was able to get a grip.

Then he pulled, and there wasn't even a moment when things hung in the balance. Lucas hit the floor with a deafening crash. Micaela could hardly believe it. It felt impossible.

The wrong person was on their back and the wrong person was standing over them, ready to do it all again.

"What the hell?" Lucas muttered.

"Quite," said Rekke. "Anger blinds us. *Ira nos caecos facit.*"

Lucas stood up, provoked by the Latin and his opponent's tone. Rekke let him get to his feet and regain his balance before felling him with a new throw, and this time Lucas hit his head hard. It wasn't serious, but he was clearly stunned, and when he finally tried to stand up, he swayed before collapsing again.

"You're strong," Rekke said, as if offering advice. "But you're much too impulsive and predictable. Your attacks are preceded by a twitching of your shoulders. Your body gives you away—I'd say you need to work on that—and at present you're dazed and a little groggy and I mean to exploit that."

Rekke pulled Lucas off the floor and pressed him against the wall. "Julia," he began. But then another change took place. Rekke froze, paying close attention to the room, and let go of Lucas. Micaela was worried he was making himself vulnerable, although Lucas also seemed to have noticed something—and now she too could hear footsteps and a faint wheezing sound accompanying them.

"G and now an F sharp," Rekke said, and then the man Micaela had heard so much about, and who had already become a mythical force in her consciousness, was standing right there.

"I'm impressed, Hans," he said. "You've kept yourself active. I bid you welcome. I must say, I didn't expect you to find the place, but as usual you have surprised me."

"Let go of my daughter or I'll kill you."

"Will you really?" Morovia said with a smile, before turning to Micaela. At that point she became truly afraid.

He gazed at her like a predator observing its prey, and behind him two men stepped forward holding guns. She immediately recognised one of them. He was the man with the bleached hair they'd seen in the pictures from Venice.

Claire surveyed the board. She could secure a draw without too much trouble, but that was out of the question. One of them would lose their freedom and perhaps their life. Gabor had said that much. It was horrifying. She would have to summon her winning instincts and play the game of her life. She closed her eyes for a brief second.

When she opened them again, she saw the board through eyes that seemed to glow, and she was suddenly eager—and even rancorous. She was going to crush him, nothing less, and a moment later she saw an opportunity—a brilliant move, she thought. She would advance with her knight and establish a double-edged threat to Gabor's rook and bishop. She took hold of the piece. Just then, she received a nip to the side. It was Jakob. He had been acting strange since the game began, staring at the board with glassy eyes. It was not easy for her to understand what he was up to. She knew he was always interested in her games, but he could hardly keep up at this level—perhaps he was just trying to cope with the tension in the atmosphere.

"Yes, sweetheart? What is it?"

He didn't reply. He glanced meaningfully at the board and gripped the hand which was holding the knight. Should she ask for a break to see how he was doing? No, she needed to concentrate on the game and seize her chance—her opportunity to gain the upper hand. She gently shook off his hand and made to make her move, at which point Jakob uttered the first word he'd said during the game.

"No," he said.

Morovia's face assumed an expression of sarcasm.

"Is he trying to help?"

She looked quizzically at Jakob.

"By all means let him try, so that we can bring this to a timely end," Gabor said.

"It's you and I who are playing, Gabor," she said. "Don't involve the boy."

"See—not even you believe in him. You know he's worthless."

"Beast," she muttered, on the brink of hurling herself at him, but she managed to contain herself just in time. "He's far more intelligent than your judo-kicking little bully boy," she said instead.

Gabor's eyes sparkled with anger.

"Don't you dare," he said.

"I dare far more than you think. And I trust my boy. Jakob, help me out here."

Jakob lowered his gaze, deeply uncomfortable with the attention, but he did say something, although neither of them heard what it was.

"I'm sorry, what did you say?"

"You should retreat the queen to b4," he mumbled, and she smiled tenderly at him while wondering what on earth she was playing at.

Should she really embarrass the boy like that? Retreating with the queen would ruin her opportunity to gain the upper hand. Nevertheless, she did just as he said, perhaps to avoid admitting Gabor was right. She wanted to demonstrate that she believed in Jakob, though she swore silently at the fact that she had allowed herself to be provoked. The move might cost her victory and perhaps her life.

Samuel was standing in front of the mirror in the gym doing his best to look handsome—but it wasn't going well. He must have scratched his cheek as he fell. He had a mark just below his left eye and it reinforced his reddish, somewhat boozed-up air.

Additionally, the left-hand side of his face—this was the worst bit—had sagged more than the right. He looked lopsided, didn't he? Not to mention old.

Faced with the prospect of seeing Claire, he found all the things he had given little thought to over recent years were now painful to behold. His upper body, on the other hand . . . He took off his jacket and stood there in just his shirt. Below the neck he still looked thirty. Claire should be impressed by that at least. He combed back his hair to conceal the bald patch that had become visible on the crown of his head.

Then he set off. The sun was beating down after the rain. It was a glorious day and he felt inescapable hope. What if he really did get to see her? What would he say? Not a single unkind word, he decided. He would be understanding. She had hurt him terribly, but he would not judge her. He would listen and put himself in her shoes. There had to be an explanation.

He upped his pace, remembering her more clearly than he had done for many years. She stood before him without the sense of injury that always surrounded her in his memories. Soon after that, he became anxious. Perhaps he would be punished for harbouring such bright and hopeful thoughts. He looked down at the sidewalk and his legs and noticed he was limping. Beads of sweat formed on his brow and under his shirt. He shouldn't arrive sweat-sodden, or worse, smelling of perspiration.

Claire was sensitive to smells. He laughed nervously. It wouldn't boil down to a few drops of sweat, but then again you never know. It could be the little things that made the difference, and when a taxi drove past—he was by then on Odenplan—he hailed it, got in and tried to calm his thoughts. *Made the difference to what . . . ?* He needed to cool it. Did he really think she would suddenly come back after fourteen years? Those hopes were insane. He didn't know anything. Nothing at all. It might not even be Claire. Or more to the point, it would be a miracle if it was. Then again . . . You'll have a lot to talk about. That was what Alicia Kovács had said. It had to be Claire. He clasped his hands and prayed, just as Claire had done in moments of vulnerability. *Dear Lord Jesus and Holy Mother of God, let it be Claire.*

The taxi drove along Birger Jarlsgatan and turned onto Strandvägen. He asked the driver to stop a couple of hundred metres before his destination so that he could prepare himself. He checked his watch. He was much too early, but surely they would understand? He couldn't arrive punctually when his whole life was at stake. He hurried to the door and entered the law firm's office with his chest thrust out, and there he once again encountered the girl who had brought him the glass of Amarone. She looked at him in alarm and he was perceptive enough to understand why. He probably looked wild.

"I'm sorry I'm so early," he said.

The girl looked at the clock on the wall and replied rather abruptly, "Yes, you are," which irritated him. Fortunately, she received an immediate reprimand. Alicia Kovács came down the stairs, beaming at him, and said it didn't matter at all, it was quite alright.

"Your visitor is here," she said.

"Where?" he said.

"Up in Gabor's office, where you were last time," she said, and he was led upstairs and into the room, his heart pounding, limping even more heavily.

Just before he stepped through the door, he closed his eyes, and when he opened them, his gaze wandered around the room without being able to understand what he was seeing.

# FORTY-NINE

Micaela had, for some reason, imagined Morovia to be like Rekke—tall, angular, intense, but darker, not only in colour but also in outlook—and she hadn't been altogether wrong. He was shorter and more powerfully built, with a soft, almost feminine stride and artful, elegant movements. He wore a grey three-piece suit with a scarf around his neck. His face was beautiful and quite pale, but his hair was thick and black and his gaze was piercing—just like Rekke's.

His eyes shifted in colour, and his lips were rounded and sensual, while the rest of him seemed distinct and angular, and regardless of whether or not Micaela wanted it, he made an overwhelming impression. He seemed to take over the whole room. Nothing in his eyes betrayed surprise at the fact that Lucas was lying on the floor in humiliation, although presumably he didn't care about that—she barely did either. It was as if the world were narrowing and trembling in anticipation of his encounter with Rekke.

"Hans, if only you knew how I have longed to see you in such a state of accomplished concentration again," Morovia said, and Micaela felt it right away—it was a feeling deep in her chest.

There really was something hypnotic about his voice and his charisma. Rekke, however, not only neglected to reply but gazed past Morovia toward the men behind him and the kitchen beyond. Naturally he urgently needed an overview of the situation in its entirety, but it still felt like a blatant provocation. He didn't even look at Morovia. His body seemed to want to show how much he hated him.

"Don't you want to answer?" Morovia said.

"All I'm interested in is speaking to my daughter."

Morovia took another step toward him.

"I'm afraid we'll have to do this my way," he said. "And in the event that anyone else were to barge in here, then it's safe to say that things would not go well for her."

He looked at Micaela before smiling again.

"I see," she said.

He proffered a hand. She took it reluctantly, unsure where to look, but Morovia turned straight back to Rekke.

"I must congratulate you on an intriguing choice of partner. Not exactly from your own circles, eh?"

"You know, you can talk *to* me as well," she said.

"Naturally. But you must understand that my dialogue is fundamentally with Hans, which is why I address him directly. I might add that what is happening to Julia is my responsibility. I assume the burden of guilt from your brother Lucas."

"Take me to her," Rekke said, interrupting but keeping his gaze averted from Morovia.

"Are you challenging me?"

"I'll do whatever it takes to get her back."

"Regrettably, that is rather a lot," Moravia said. "But let us see her first—she is a most beautiful and sensitive girl, isn't she?"

Rekke didn't answer that either. Instead, all he did was look around as they entered the large kitchen, which led onto a terrace, and then he recoiled. Outside the window by the pool, Julia was crouched down, swaddled in a large, blue bathrobe. She was lashed to two metal eyelets on the ground. She was pale and frightened. Standing next to her was the man with the bleached hair. He was holding a gun, and on the paved floor beside the pool there was a grey jerrycan and a video camera—both of which gave Micaela a chill.

"Julia," Rekke said as he rushed toward her.

"Pappa," she said. "I'm sorry."

"It's my fault—no-one else's," he said.

"More like it's mine," Micaela muttered as Rekke advanced with open arms.

He was stopped by the man with the gun, and seemingly he had decided not to fight for now. Instead, he stared furiously toward Morovia, who was smiling with the same self-assurance as before as he held out his hands.

"Perhaps not the most epic stage I have ever sourced but it will have to do, and I have always thought about—"

"Oh, do shut up, Gabor," Rekke said. "Just say what you want instead."

"I want revenge, Hans. Isn't it obvious? But first, I want to thank you. Enemies make us alert and keep us feeling alive. We need each other so as not to lose our edge, no?"

"Spare me your philosophy of power nonsense."

Gabor shook his head as if he found Rekke's dismissal almost touching.

"Consider it a chance, Hans. Nothing is predestined. There is always hope. Seize it, and speak to me. You know, I think occasionally of your cat."

"I'm sure you do," Rekke said.

"It helped me to find my way home. Many have burned since then. But your cat was the first. Do you know what I've often thought?"

Rekke didn't reply. He merely smiled bitterly toward Julia, muttering yet another apology.

"I've often reflected on the fact that you named the cat Ahasuerus," Morovia said. "It was projection, was it not? You were Ahasuerus. Condemned to wander for eternity and see through everything. Condemned to seek clarity but only ever find new darkness. Condemned to solve mysteries, while always realising that the question is more interesting than the answer, the riddle more shimmering than its solution."

"You really are a fool."

"But you found love along the way. I'll give you that. You had your Ida, and then . . ." He glanced at Julia. "The whims of fate brought you a child at the same time as me, and I should guess you love your daughter like I loved my son Jan."

"I am sorry about what happened, Gabor," Rekke said, looking Morovia in the eye for the first time.

"Thank you, Hans. So it would seem you do care, a little? That's almost touching. Of course, it is all much too late."

"It's never too late to doubt your intentions."

Rekke's voice cracked.

"Oh yes," Morovia said. "But before we devote ourselves to Julia, I'd like for us to continue our conversation. Think of it as a gift of a few minutes to you and your companion. You *are* looking for Claire Lidman, I take it?"

"I'm doing nothing other than saving my daughter," Rekke said.

"Allow me to correct myself," Gabor said. "You *were* looking for Claire Lidman before life became focused on another issue. Let me tell you about her. I shall see to Julia for the time being, I promise. Ricardo, would you give her some water and painkillers? Do ask her whether she would like anything to eat . . ."

Rekke threw another anxious glance toward his daughter. "It'll be alright, my dear. I'll get us out of this."

Gabor beamed, as if he were pleased with Rekke's statement.

"You absolutely can," he said. "I shall give you a chance. I gave Claire one and she took it, even if . . . Well, I shan't ruin the story for you. Let me start from the beginning. Or perhaps you would prefer to hear about Ida first?"

"All I want to hear about is what I have to do to get Julia out of here."

Gabor Morovia took a step forward and looked down at his hands.

There was an eye-catching signet ring with a black stone on his little finger.

"You are looking at my ring, I take it? It is in memory of Jan—his time of death is inscribed inside it. A quarter past three on the afternoon of February twenty-third. He was nine years old, and his final words were 'Sorry, father,' as if he were somehow complicit." Morovia turned back toward Rekke. "I think you would have liked him. But..." He nodded at Rekke, who had not taken his eyes off Julia. "I shouldn't bore you with my own pain—I must concentrate on yours, both that which you have and that which shall be meted out to you."

"Damn you to hell."

"Very well. If you don't want to hear about Ida or Claire then allow me to answer your question. Is there anything you can do? Give me something significant in place of your daughter and I will consider the matter."

"Take my life instead," said Rekke.

"*Your life?*" Morovia laughed theatrically. "A hero's words. But that won't do. Whom shall I play with once you're gone? No, Hans, you'll have to offer me something better than that. Give me secrets. What did you say to Herman Camphausen to make him come after me? And who leaked the information to Putin's assassins?"

Rekke ran a hand through his hair.

"I didn't tell Herman anything that he didn't already know," he said. "And I don't know who the leak was, but I shouldn't think it would make any difference. You never truly take revenge, Gabor. You merely seek pretexts to cause pain and awaken what is dead inside you. Revenge is but a chimera to mask your sadism. But there is one thing I can give you."

"What is that, Hans? Pray tell."

"Compassion, Gabor. You are trying to heal your wound, but instead all you do is dig deeper into it. *Veritas odium parit.* And you find nothing except more hatred."

Morovia snorted.

"Don't forget that I've seen you fight, Hans. I've heard you play.

I've looked into your eyes as you threw me out of your dressing room. There is just as much hatred festering away in you. I can see it now, and I know you've always yearned to compete with me."

Rekke took another couple of steps toward Julia.

"You know less than you think, Gabor. Like all little tyrants, you merely project your own perversions. You have no idea what I'm thinking right now. Your arrogance makes you vulnerable," he said, giving Micaela a look. It was a look of exhortation, and a moment later all hell broke loose.

Rekke kicked the gun out of the blond man's hand and threw him down into the pool in a swift movement. Then he turned toward Morovia, battle-ready. It looked as if he had stepped in front of a mirror. With lightning speed, Morovia imitated his attacking stance, and for a second the men seemed prepared to throw themselves at each other, but Micaela didn't have time to stop and stare. She rushed for the gun, some ten metres or so away on the side of the pool, though she never made it. Julia shouted out in desperation.

"Behind you!"

She swung around. The second of Morovia's men—a powerfully built man with cold eyes—was aiming his weapon at her. Micaela was rooted to the spot for a couple of seconds as she searched for ways out. Then Julia cried out again.

"Lucas!"

Where the hell was he? There. Now she saw him. In the kitchen. His body was contorted as if he wanted to move in two different directions at once. He didn't respond to Julia's cry. He looked both irresolute and furious.

"Help us! Surely you're not on the same side as these morons?" Julia said, which wasn't such a bad idea.

It wasn't Lucas's style to tie up beautiful young women and threaten to kill them, but Lucas—the cowardly bastard—was just standing there, seemingly confused, and then he disappeared. He slipped away with a profanity on his lips, and that was the very moment when Morovia launched a new attack on Rekke that made him stagger backwards.

It was immediately apparent that Gabor was the stronger and quicker of the two, the one who had seriously and purposefully devoted himself to the martial arts.

The situation very quickly seemed completely hopeless, especially when the blond man heaved himself out of the pool, soaked through, and bent down to retrieve his gun from the paving.

But Rekke seemed to be looking for options, and he stepped back, nodding at Julia. Then he lashed out in a movement he must have rehearsed and kicked the pistol out of the man's hand before attacking Morovia with a series of blows and kicks. Morovia's face shone almost lustfully, as if he were absolutely convinced he was going to win. He struck back and it looked like a dance, as if it had been choreographed.

Micaela stepped forward and headbutted the blond man, but in the ruckus that followed they both ended up in the pool. Unable to do anything about the situation, she saw Morovia give Rekke a fierce kick to the stomach that made him bend double.

Then something inconceivable happened. She should have predicted it, but it still shocked her to her core. The other man—the one with the cold eyes who had trained his pistol on her—stepped forward, and upon Morovia's signal he grabbed the jerrycan next to Julia. He unscrewed the cap and raised it deliberately before dowsing Julia with the contents. Despite the shouts and screams lingering in the air and the general state of chaos, nothing was clearer in that moment than the unmistakable smell of petrol.

Claire had lost the initiative when she had moved her queen back, and she was doing all she could to repair the damage she thought the move had caused, but as she was getting to grips with the new position, she saw something on Gabor's face. It wasn't much—just a shift in his eyes—but something was quite clearly bothering him, and suddenly she knew what it was. She had upset his plan. Well, actually, Jakob had.

His move had saved her from a trap on the right flank. The thought made her blood sing and suddenly she got into the swing of it. It was as if all the work she had put in during those solitary evenings was suddenly paying off, and at every moment she saw intuitively what she needed to do.

Her brain was in overdrive like never before. While she quickly moved her pieces Gabor took his time, and yet she still predicted his moves. She was in command, and no matter how she looked at it, she couldn't see a way out for him—it was over. She considered saying: do you give up? But she was afraid of his reaction.

She had no idea how he would take a loss, but she couldn't back down now. He had promised her their freedom if she won, and she continued to play with increasing mania. The whole world disappeared. All she saw was the board, and she picked up the pace even more. She could see that she was going to go all the way with her pawn and promote it to a queen. There was no doubt about it: it was over.

"I'll give you a draw," he said.

She looked at Gabor, perplexed.

"Are you joking?" she said. "You're losing. Surely you must see that?"

Gabor pretended not to hear, and instead of looking her in the eye he turned toward Jakob with an expression of dissatisfaction.

"I never lose," he said.

She didn't know what to say, but made an effort not to lose her temper.

"Show some dignity and take it like a man, Gabor. You're a better player than me, but this time you weren't good enough." She gestured toward the pieces to illustrate how hopeless his position was. "And you promised me . . ." she said.

Gabor held up his hand to stop her and she fell silent, trying to understand what was going on.

"Besides, you've received help," he said. "That's cheating under all the rules of the game."

She could hardly believe her ears.

"I enlisted the help of the boy you called useless—at your initiative."

Gabor stared toward the canal, adjusting his collar.

"He *is* useless," he said.

She made an effort to sit still.

"You have no right to say that," she said.

"But it's the truth. Look at him. He can't even look people in the eye. He stutters and squirms. He's an oddball, Claire, and nothing else. And weak."

"Strong enough to see through your chess game."

Her cheeks flushed.

"He's pathetic."

"You don't know him," she said, no longer able to control her own voice.

"I'm just doing what I must. Besides, our game is over. You are free to go."

She looked at him, her mouth dry and her heart racing.

"So you acknowledge your defeat?"

"It was a draw. You only win half a point."

Stay calm, she thought. This is a critical moment. Don't blow it.

"We can sit down and analyse our positions if you like," she said.

"I have no inclination to do so," he said, beginning to pick up the pieces.

"No," she cried out, putting her hand on his.

He clearly disliked the contact and pushed her hand away. Then he stood, and she saw no way out other than to stand up too, but even though she gestured toward Jakob he remained where he was, with his legs crossed as if tied up in knots.

"As I said, look at him," said Gabor.

"Monster," she snapped, but that too was the wrong tactic.

The word only seemed to make Gabor calmer. Apparently, she could defeat him at chess, but she would never win in this kind of psychological contest, and indeed, he was smiling at her as if he were the perfect host dealing with a guest who had said something out of line.

"It was delightful of you both to come, but I really must be getting on now. Allow me to get your coat and bag. Are you able to see to your son, or shall I ask Ricardo to assist?"

"He'll be just fine," she said, helping Jakob up.

He was more brazen than she had expected. He straightened his back and accompanied her to the vault-like room, where she retrieved her bag and coat.

Gabor extended his hand.

She took it and looked him in the eyes. His smile was almost melancholy. If she hadn't known better, she might have interpreted it as friendly.

"You'll leave us alone now? Are we safe?"

"Farewell, Claire," he said, without letting go of her hand. "And farewell, Jakob."

It was plain that he hadn't answered her question, and she wondered whether to ask it again. Instead she nodded, turned on her heel and took Jakob by the hand before descending the curved staircase with feverish, rather reckless strides. The chess book fell out of her bag again. Gabor moved quickly to pick it up.

"Perhaps you don't need this. You have evidently studied it very closely," he said, and that was—she supposed—the closest she was going to come to an acknowledgement that she had defeated him, but she didn't comment. She merely took the book in her right hand and beat a retreat toward St. Mark's Square with Jakob.

# FIFTY

Samuel was so set on meeting Claire that he couldn't fathom what he was looking at. What he had imagined merged into one with what stood before him—something incomprehensible, a kind of angelic figure with wiry arms that was shifting in and out of focus, blending into the sunlight that was streaming through the window.

Once Samuel had gotten his breathing under control and blinked a couple of times, he realised it was a young boy with curly hair and big, nervous eyes. The kid was wearing a crumpled beige suit which fit perfectly but seemed far too grown-up for him. The suit and his apprehensive posture reinforced the impression that he was just a small child, despite his height. His head was swaying back and forth, and his right foot was entwined with his left, making his whole body seem unsteady, as if he might topple over at any moment.

"Who are you?" the boy said in English, and when Samuel didn't reply at once, he continued. "They said it was important for me to meet you, but they wouldn't say any more. Do you know where Mum is? She disappeared and they say they don't know where she is, but I think they're lying. They say you know her. She would never just disappear unless something serious had happened."

The words poured out of him, and Samuel wanted to turn on his heel. He was angry because the boy wasn't Claire. He felt like the victim of a terrible betrayal, and if he had followed his instincts in that moment he would have bellowed at the boy and left, slamming the door behind him. But he was level-headed enough to realise that was heartless. The boy was just as distressed as he was. Tears were filling his eyes. He was squirming like a snake, and in a moment of strange reflection Samuel got it into his head that the boy was the mirror image of himself. Of his own despair.

"Who's your mother?" he said.

"Sara Miller," came the reply.

The boy took a hesitant step toward him. He seemed to be on the verge of falling headlong onto the floor. Samuel stood ready to catch him.

"What?" he said. "Who?"

"I've been living with an old man," the boy said, as if he hadn't heard the question. "I haven't been to school since March, and no-one has explained anything to me. All they've said is that I have to wait and see. But then this morning..."

He was growing paler.

"I think you should sit down," Samuel said, before helping him to the same armchair that Morovia had been sitting in just a few hours earlier.

Samuel sat down next to him, wondering if he should summon Alicia Kovács. It felt as if the boy needed help.

"What happened this morning?" he said.

"They told me I was going to the airport. I barely had time to pack, and I flew on a private jet. I saw Pap"—he changed his mind—"Morovia at the front. But he didn't want to talk to me. He looked at me as if I'd disappointed him."

"Is Morovia your father?"

"No, but I thought so for a long time. My mother used to tell me to call him that, but I think she was scared. She let him see me because that would make us safer."

"And your mother's name is Sara Miller?"

The boy's head swayed again, and Samuel had the feeling he was on the verge of breaking down.

"Sometimes she's called Claire too. She used to be called that."

"My God," Samuel said.

"Do you know her?"

"I was her husband," he said, before correcting himself. "I *am* her husband."

"Her husband?"

The boy seemed even more disoriented.

"Your mother and I were married," Samuel said, making an effort to remain matter-of-fact. "But she disappeared, and I believed for many years that she was dead. I'm guessing she was in hiding..."

"From Morovia," the boy said, suddenly sounding calmer—and older.

"Probably, yes," Samuel said. He could feel a thousand questions take shape in his head, but he kept them to himself. Despite his disappointment moments earlier, he didn't want to ruin something that felt valuable, as if it were some kind of replacement for Claire.

"I loved her," he said.

The boy seemed to be thinking something over.

"Are you the strong one?" he said. "Who can fix everything?"

"I don't know whether I can fix much anymore. But I am pretty strong."

Samuel did an awkward front double bicep pose.

"Everyone says I should work out," the boy said. "Morovia calls me weak."

"You look good to me."

"No." It was said with such melancholy that Samuel was overcome by the impulse to take him by the hands.

"What's all this nonsense?" he said. "That's how everyone feels when they've had a tough time. You end up seeing yourself as worthless, but actually..."

"Mamma's told me about you," the boy said, interjecting.

"Has she?"

Samuel flinched. He didn't want to hear about it. Things had gone too fast. He couldn't understand how he was suddenly talking to the boy with such familiarity. It was an escape, he thought to himself. A way to get away from all the questions searing his insides: Where was Claire? What was going on?

"She said she never learned to cook because you took care of everything. She said she felt like she was disabled."

"I'm sorry if I made her feel disabled."

"I think she meant it in a nice way."

Samuel felt a lump in his throat.

"What happened to your mother?"

"We were in Venice," the boy said.

Samuel leaned forward, his whole body tense.

"What were you doing there?"

"We were visiting . . . Morovia," the boy said with a grimace of distaste.

"What happened?" Samuel said.

"We ate and they began playing chess. It seemed important—like they were playing for something important. My mother said it was our freedom."

"Your freedom?"

"Yes. Mamma was really tense, as if her life depended on it, and she was about to fall into a trap, but I helped her a little. She regained the upper hand."

Samuel looked at the boy as if he had misheard.

"You helped? I've never heard of anyone who could help Claire to play chess."

"I recognised the game—it sort of reminded me of Capablanca's game against Marotti in London in 1922."

Samuel looked at him in amazement.

"You know that kind of stuff?"

"Yes," the boy said gravely, without any hint of pride. "I haven't had much to do, and I've never really had any friends. I study old chess matches and play against myself."

"Against yourself..."

"And sometimes against a chess computer."

Samuel swallowed.

"You must be a genius. You don't help Claire. You just sit back and admire her."

The boy smiled sadly, and sounding ever so grown-up again he said:

"She has some shortcomings."

Samuel smiled back sadly.

"That's true. She does. What happened?"

"She was only six moves from checkmate when Morovia stopped playing and offered her a draw."

"He didn't want to lose?"

The boy glanced towards the window.

"No," he said. "Things turned really weird and Morovia said all sorts of horrible things."

"Like what?"

"Do I have to tell you?"

"No."

"Then we left. Mamma was in a real hurry."

"And you were in St. Mark's Square?"

"St. Mark's Square?"

"I saw a photo of her."

"Did you? Well, I don't know any places there. Mamma was very upset and walking quickly. There were lots of old buildings and loads of people and birds, and somehow I ended up lagging behind and suddenly I heard someone calling my name. It was one of Morovia's men—he's called Ricardo..."

He was clearly struggling to talk about it, and his head began to sway again.

"And?" said Samuel.

"I stopped. I thought we must have forgotten something. And when

I was going to run to Mamma again I couldn't find her anymore. She was gone and I shouted for all I was worth and once I heard her crying out 'Jakob! Jakob!' But I couldn't tell where the voice was coming from. I just ran around and around for hours, asking for her and trying to call her, but she was gone."

"My God," Samuel said. He felt a fresh impulse to grasp the boy's hands, but he remained still on his chair. "What happened then?"

"Morovia showed up and said that Mamma had been forced to go away, but I didn't believe him, and I kicked him and fought and tore at him and yelled that I hated him, and then he just left and other people came and got me and I had to live with a nice lady in Milan. But I don't think she could stand me. I broke things and tried to escape several times and I got handed over to an old man who said he was related to Morovia and his two servants."

"Then you flew here?"

"Yes, I was sure I was going to see Mamma again in the end. Didn't you live here in Sweden?"

"Yes, that's right—not far from here."

"But I've been in this office for hours now and she still hasn't come. What should I do?"

Samuel had no idea what the boy should do, but in that moment he saw something strange in the boy's eyes and the corners of his mouth that made him feel dizzy. No, it was ridiculous. It was new and idiotic wishful thinking, and he never did have time to follow it to its conclusion. The door opened and Alicia Kovács entered, looking as if she were going through her own inner drama too. She was pale. Her eyes were distressed.

"I think it would be best if you both leave now," she said.

Samuel stood up.

"What do you mean?"

"I'm worried," she said quietly. "Go somewhere safe. He's in the worst of moods."

Who? Samuel wondered. Who was in the worst of moods? But he

didn't really need to ask. He understood, and he took the boy by the hand and left.

Julia knew immediately that it was petrol. The whole world became motionless, and she blinked desperately to prevent it from getting into her eyes, but something in her began to act, or in the absence of opportunities for action began to think, to focus. She looked up at the man who had emptied the can over her. He wore a green cotton jacket and was muscular, his gaze cold, but his hands were trembling, which she thought was a good thing. He was under pressure and had too many things to deal with: his gun, which he had tucked into his holster, the chaos ensuing around him, and what he had pulled out of his jeans pocket and was fumbling with. It was a small, metallic object that flashed like silver, and the sight of it made her struggle wildly. It was a lighter.

She was going to burn any moment now, and she did all she could not to convulse in terror. She tried to continue thinking clearly, to work out if she might be able to tear herself loose and get into the pool, but there wasn't time. The man made a terrifying movement with his fingers. It was going to happen, and while deep down she knew that both Pappa and Micaela were screaming, she heard something else. It was Morovia's hypnotic voice. He spoke quietly and solemnly in a low vibrato and with a faint whistle as he exhaled.

"Hans, I want you to see her burn like my Jan. I want us to share that pain."

It was so inconceivable that it felt as if the fire had already taken hold of her. She made a new, violent attempt to move, but she was stuck. Then she saw something strange. Pappa stood up and raised his arm as if he were about to wave or say goodbye. Then he took a step back a metre or so, while Morovia positioned himself in front of him, ready to attack. But that wasn't all that happened. Everywhere, at ultra-rapid speed and with terrifying clarity, she saw movements, shifts, threats and the hope of salvation. Micaela got out of the pool, a gun was aimed at her, someone else emerged from the water. It foreshadowed what was about to happen, and no matter how little she wanted to see it, there was no doubt about it: Morovia and his men had the upper hand. It was three on two, and they had guns and a lighter.

But then Pappa and Micaela both made violent lunges in her direction. A second later, a shot was fired. There was a splash in the water and she couldn't quite grasp what was happening—only that Pappa was fighting Morovia and Micaela was rushing toward her and then there was the terrifying sound of something metallic hitting the ground. Was it the lighter? Would she burn?

She only knew that shots were being fired and someone was shouting, "For fuck's sake, stop! Let her go!" and she jumped, convinced that it was the police, coming to their rescue, but she was wrong. It wasn't a police officer. It was Lucas who emerged into the garden with a gun in his hand and something deranged in his gaze.

# FIFTY-ONE

Claire thought she saw a familiar face in the crowd, and that worried her. Nevertheless, she quickly pushed the thought away. There were other, more pressing things to worry about. She was convinced that Gabor would follow them. She had to reach safety.

There was a police station not far away on the Rampa Santa Chiara. She had already checked that. She would contact Lars Hellner in Stockholm. He would sort all this out, she thought to herself as she hurried past a group of Japanese tourists listening attentively to their guide. A southern European man immediately next to them whistled at her, and she raised her head proudly to indicate she was indifferent to all attention. Was Jakob still keeping up? It would be a nightmare to lose him. She turned around. A pigeon flapped past her and she heard the click of a camera. She heaved a sigh of relief. Jakob was close behind.

"How are you doing, sweetheart?"

"Why are we in such a hurry?" he said.

"I'm just a bit stressed out, but it's all fine now. Come on, my sweet," she said, extending her hand toward him.

He didn't want to take it. That was new. He no longer wanted to walk hand-in-hand with his mother, which she considered a little worrying, and she slowed her pace. She smiled at him as if they were out on a perfectly innocent adventure, but she couldn't calm herself down and of course Jakob noticed that.

"Was it wrong to beat him?" he said.

"On the contrary," she said. "People like that need to lose occasionally, and he promised us..."

"Freedom," he said.

"Yes," she said, wondering once again just what Gabor had meant, but pushing that thought away too.

She had to hurry. She had to get to the police station. She looked around hastily. In front of her stood one of those poor men painted gold pretending to be a statue to earn a few euros. What a job, she thought as she collided with someone. She didn't think it was her fault. She apologised nonetheless and then she took a bump diagonally from behind—it was a violent, unpleasant blow that hurt her side. Rage coursed through her.

Instead of remonstrating, she turned to look for Jakob. She couldn't see him, and overcome with panic, she called out loudly as she felt something wet and sticky under her dress. She put a hand to her hip. Good God—she was bleeding. She would have to deal with that later. First she had to find Jakob, but when she began to run she staggered and two arms quickly and firmly led her through a doorway immediately to her left. There she collapsed, and as her world went black, she was carried away.

Micaela threw herself headlong to the ground, convinced they were doomed. They had no chance, and now there was a gun aimed at her. She might die, but first she was going to get Julia in the water. That was the only thing occupying her thoughts until something clattered onto the ground. She didn't understand what it was—there was such a commotion—but then she saw it clearly. It was the lighter. The flame flared after a moment's delay, and she rolled over and lay right on top of it, not caring whether she would burn herself.

Shots rang out in the air and she winced, thinking she must have been hit this time. They could hardly miss. She was just lying there, completely defenceless. But she had obviously smothered the flame and she could feel the lighter under her chest. At the same time, there were footsteps approaching. Would she be executed like a dog, shot in the neck? When she looked up, she couldn't fathom what was going on.

The man in the green jacket who had been holding the lighter had sunk down to his knees, his hands to his stomach, but that wasn't all. The man from the footage in Venice had just got out of the pool, but now he staggered away and once again fell into the water. It was a complete reversal of fortunes, and now she saw that her brother was standing by the door to the kitchen, a pistol in his hand.

"Dickheads," he muttered, aiming the gun at Morovia, who was reeling backwards after a fresh blow from Rekke.

"Lucas," she said.

"Sis," he said, getting closer, and she realised that it was not clear what would happen next.

Lucas had saved them and shot their assailants, but for him it wasn't as simple as friend or foe. There was no doubt about it: Morovia had betrayed him and done something truly terrible that had not been part of their agreement, but no-one had humiliated him more than Rekke. It was Rekke he hated most of all, and she could see in his eyes that he had completely lost control.

He trained the gun here and there before he eventually aimed it at Rekke.

"Shoot him," Morovia said loudly.

"No," Rekke said, taking a step forward. "You're wiser than that, Lucas."

He thrust his chest outwards as if exposing himself to a shot. Micaela inhaled sharply. She wasn't sure that was the right strategy. Lucas had his finger on the trigger.

"You started all this," Lucas said furiously. "You messed my sister up with your fucking psychologist bullshit."

Rekke took another step forward, seemingly quite calm, and Micaela was terrified that it might provoke her brother.

"That's entirely possible," Rekke said. "But think rationally about this. Right now, you're our hero. That will speak in your favour. *Fortes fortuna adiuvat.* Fortune favours the bold. If you shoot me then things become more complicated."

"I won't say a word against you if you leave Pappa alone," Julia said.

"I'll stop digging dirt on you," Micaela said, afraid she could promise anything she liked and it wouldn't help.

The reminder of what she had done seemed to make Lucas even more furious. Nevertheless, he muttered:

"You gotta, sis."

"I promise," she said.

Lucas nodded. He seemed to have regained his self-control. He aimed the gun at Morovia, who was standing stock-still with a face that shone with hatred and arrogance. Moments later, Rekke put a hand to his ear and muttered *di, do*. It sounded as if he were mimicking a police siren with perfect pitch.

Cars were approaching. Rekke staggered forward, untied the ropes binding Julia's hands and feet and removed the petrol-sodden robe. Micaela and Lucas—in a sudden and unexpected alliance—watched Morovia, vigilantly following his every movement.

A minute or so after that, Security Service officers flooded the garden, with a red-faced Magnus Rekke in tow. He seemed ill at ease and avoided looking his brother in the eye. But Hans didn't care about Magnus either. He was fully occupied seeing to Julia, and before long the house was a maelstrom as even more police officers descended upon it. The place was suddenly crawling with cops, and Micaela, Rekke and Julia left without even glancing at Morovia and his wounded lieutenants.

It was late in the afternoon of the sixth of June, and Micaela saw that Samuel Lidman had called her six times.

# FIFTY-TWO

Micaela emerged from the Catholic Cathedral on Folkungagatan wearing a black dress that chafed. It was the twelfth of July and most people she knew were on holiday, although she herself was back on duty and had no shortage of things to do.

It had been a conventional, rather protracted ceremony. Nevertheless, she had been moved, even though she had never met the woman being buried. Perhaps that was mostly because Samuel Lidman had been sitting at the very front with a thirteen-year-old boy he had just met, but who stayed close to him as if Samuel were already the boy's entire world.

The remains of Claire Lidman had been found three weeks earlier in the waters of Lake Garda and had been repatriated to Stockholm. It had not been certain that there would be a Catholic service given Claire's wavering faith, but Linda Wilson had pulled rank as her sister and it had ended up being a beautiful ceremony. The priest had refrained from hyperbole, and the music had been lovely. Micaela was glad she had come. She gazed toward the square at Medborgarplatsen and nodded at Rebecka Wahlin as she slipped past her wearing something absurdly modish that made Micaela's dress feel even shabbier and cheaper than before. She allowed her gaze to continue wandering.

Then she approached the boy, Jakob, who had hidden himself behind Samuel's broad-shouldered back. He was wearing a black linen suit and clutching a red rose that he had forgotten to put on the coffin. He looked as if he wished he was far away from there.

"Hi, Jakob," she said. "I'm so sorry."

She knew it wasn't easy to get him to talk, and she had only meant to offer her condolences and then go home.

The boy fidgeted. "Isn't the professor here?" he said.

"No, something came up," she said, annoyed with Rekke—he had been on his way to the ceremony with her but had suddenly returned home instead.

Some bullshit or other with Magnus, she thought.

"I wanted to ask him something," Jakob said.

"What was that?" she said.

"Samuel said the professor saw something specific in those photos of me from Venice."

She smiled. "He noticed your earlobes, Jakob. They're attached. They join straight up with your cheek, just like Samuel's."

The boy paused for thought.

"So he understood something that it took Morovia a DNA test to figure out."

She shrugged.

"He wasn't sure—he comes up with all sorts of things. He's becoming manic again."

"What does that mean?"

"He runs around and draws all sorts of conclusions. Sometimes he sees right through things. Other times, he goes completely off the rails."

While the boy processed that, Micaela put a hand on his shoulder. Then she hugged Samuel and watched father and son disappear together. Those two needed each other, she reflected. They were both equally uncomfortable and odd, with their wavering gazes and reluctance to make eye contact.

She checked her watch and realised she had time to pop in to Grevgatan before she needed to go to work. She made haste toward Slussen to catch the Tunnelbana home. Her phone rang as she was walking up Götgatsbacken. It was Mamá. Micaela answered reluctantly. Her mother had been harping on a lot lately about Lucas being pushed too hard in questioning "when he was the big hero and all," and Micaela couldn't bring herself to say that Lucas had gotten off ridiculously lightly given the circumstances. It was a damn disgrace, and that was the truth.

"Yes, Mamá," she said. "What is it?"

She needn't have bothered asking.

"I can't believe they're turning the screws on your brother like that while the real villain gets off scot-free."

"Morovia isn't getting off at all," she said. "He's going down with bells on."

"But he's got a lot of fancy lawyers. And didn't Berlusconi—of all people!—defend him?"

"I didn't know about that."

"That's what the world is like. The rich get off while people like us get taken down."

"You're simplifying things, Mamá."

"I'm just saying what it feels like to an outsider. Vanessa feels the same way. I just saw her at Dolores's. You wouldn't believe how gorgeous she looks with her new hairdo. It wouldn't do any harm if you—"

"I'm hanging up now."

"Sorry, I'm babbling. I get nervous talking to you now you've gone up in the world."

"Stop it."

Micaela turned toward the Tunnelbana station.

"But I'm proud, mostly. I'm so pleased you've got back together with your count."

"He's a count now, is he?"

"Well, I'm still waiting for an invitation. You can't imagine how many interesting things I have to say. But what I was really getting at, cariña..."

"Yes," she said irritably.

"... is that because of all this, Lucas barely has time to visit. Not that I really need it. I've just finished a wonderful painting that I'm sure I'll be able to sell. By the way, how's the young girl? Is she feeling better?"

"How much do you need?"

"Not much, not much at all. About the same as last time, when you were in such a tearing hurry."

"I'll come tomorrow after work," Micaela said as she hung up, and she descended the stairs into the station blissfully unaware that her mother was at least right about one thing.

The doorbell rang. "Finally," Rekke muttered to himself. Magnus was two hours late and had been unreachable on the telephone or by email, which was a source of apprehension. But it was actually Julia. He beamed at her and embraced her.

"You look beautiful," he said, and it was true in so many respects.

Julia was dressed casually in cotton trousers and a navy blouse, and she was no longer as skinny.

"You, however, seem fucked up," she said.

"What? No—I am simply worried about you, as always. Do come in, so that I may envelop you in my nervous affection. Have you eaten lunch?"

"You were expecting someone else, weren't you?"

He explained that his brother was on the way, but that Magnus had been greatly delayed.

"Then it's hardly good news he's bringing, is it?" she said.

Good for him, perhaps, but not necessarily me, he thought as he went to the kitchen.

He opened the fridge to see what he had to offer.

"You should nail him," Julia said, sitting down at the table.

Rekke grimaced.

"Magnus is going to be called as a witness in Morovia's trial, and it will do him a great deal of harm. I'll settle for that for the time being."

And for the truth, he thought to himself. The best possible version of it.

"But he's hiding something?"

"True."

"And he's ashamed."

"I suppose we have to consider that progress," he said, trying to work out what he had caught sight of in the fridge. Something or other made by Mrs. Hansson, of course. Was it lasagne? Or moussaka?

"How about this most delicious and decidedly low-calorie delight?" he said, showing it to her.

"I'm not hungry," she said.

"Are you sure?"

He pricked his ears.

"The elevator is coming," he said.

"Is it Magnus?"

He listened to the steps exiting the elevator.

"It's Micaela," he said. "With her punctuated eighth tempo. And . . . Magnus. They've arrived together."

"That's weird," said Julia.

"What? Hmm, yes."

He lost his focus, feeling in his gut that those footsteps were the bearers of bad news.

# FIFTY-THREE

Magnus was unusually cool when Micaela bumped into him outside, but that was hardly a surprise, given what they now knew about him. Still, she thought he might have made more of an effort—if only out of self-preservation. He didn't have anything to gain from treating her like shit.

"What have you been up to?" he said.

He eyed her scruffy black dress and she decided to give as good as she got.

"I've been at Claire Lidman's funeral. What have you been up to?" she said, making him wince as if she'd stirred up something unpleasant within him, which was at least something.

What was more, he was nervously looking over his shoulder as if afraid he had been followed, and when she looked too, she did indeed spot a woman in early middle age gazing sternly at them. The woman was good-looking and wore a striking green velvet jacket and a black skirt with silver buttons and a slit, but she seemed nervous and immediately looked away when Micaela met her gaze. "Bitch," Magnus muttered as he tapped in the code and they both entered. When they stepped into the elevator, it was even more apparent how troubled he was. He was breathing heavily and muttering profanities, and she wondered if she should say something, but she decided she didn't give a damn. She emerged from the elevator a few steps ahead of him. Rekke opened the door while holding a dish containing some kind of gratin. Julia was visible beyond him.

"Micaela, I really would like to hear about the funeral," he said. "But first, Magnus, you must tell us what has happened."

"I could do with a beer first."

Rekke looked as if he was considering whether Magnus had earned one. Then he nodded and went into the kitchen and set the dish down on the counter before taking two Peronis from the fridge. He handed both to Magnus and asked him to sit down.

"Now," he said.

"I don't think it's advisable for Julia to be present," Magnus said.

"I'm definitely staying," said Julia.

"Perhaps it would be better if I came back later."

Rekke took out a bottle opener and a glass and poured Magnus his beer.

"It would most certainly not be better," he said. "You should be glad you aren't behind bars. I speak to Herman Camphausen on a daily basis now, and I know all too well what you've done. But first: out with whatever it is you have to say. Julia is going to remain exactly where she is."

Magnus downed his beer and wiped his lips.

"Russia has requested the extradition of Morovia," he said.

"I heard that."

"Quite. And there has been tremendous pressure applied, and—entre nous—there have been certain negotiations about Russian gas, and I have in no way been involved."

"Of course not," Rekke said sarcastically. "You are but a humble undersecretary."

"Of course, we didn't agree to it. There are crimes on Swedish soil that must be investigated first."

"But . . . ?"

Rekke drummed his fingers on the table.

"We agreed to let Russian investigators question Morovia, and as part of that he was moved to a more secure location. Well, to a location that was deemed to be more secure, and in connection with that . . ."

Magnus fell silent and poured more beer into his glass, his eyelids fluttering nervously.

"Out with it."

"Of course . . . I'll try. We don't yet have any clarity on the incident, and the media are still in the dark. But I would guess it was a combination of blackmail and bribery. Two police officers and a prison officer are now in custody."

"Damn it—has he escaped?"

Micaela almost screamed.

"More like he bought his way out," Magnus said, avoiding her gaze. "I'm terribly sorry. Interpol has issued an alert, and we'll naturally make arrangements for protection of some kind for you, although I doubt Morovia will dare to return here."

"Bullshit," Micaela said. "He'll be even more determined to seek revenge."

"We're taking the necessary precautions," Magnus muttered.

Rekke was silent. They all were. They were all at a sudden loss for words; it felt like the calm before a storm. When Rekke finally spoke, he sounded calm and collected.

"How convenient that you should be spared the trouble of giving evidence at the trial," he said, almost in a whisper.

"I would have liked . . ." Magnus said tentatively.

"You most certainly would not have liked," Rekke said, interrupting. "Now drink up and be gone to lick your wounds. We must take care of Julia."

"I don't need taking care of."

"No, of course not. But we also have . . ."

"Another visitor," Julia said.

Micaela looked at them in confusion.

"Do we?" she said.

"Indeed," Rekke said. "*Click, clack.* A woman of about forty, I should guess, a somewhat nervous gait, but light-bodied. She has already turned away once, but she's returning now. She's worried about something."

"I think I saw her in the street," said Micaela.

Magnus stood up and muttered something about needing to be on his way to "deal with this mess." Then he nodded and made an attempt to embrace Julia, but she pulled away from him. He smiled awkwardly and walked toward the door.

It was not his finest exit but even if he looked downhearted and humiliated from behind, there was a secret smile on his lips. He figured he had gotten off lightly. He didn't bother to greet the woman outside the door. He beat a retreat into the elevator, glad to be out of there while his brother came to receive his visitor.

It was one o'clock and Micaela needed to be on her way to work, but she decided to linger and see what the woman wanted. There was something strange about her.

She was—as Rekke had guessed—about forty, or perhaps a little younger, and dressed—as Micaela had noted earlier—in extremely elegant clothing, as if she were on her way to a party. She wore her hair up, fastened at the crown of her head, and this accentuated her distinctive features. Although her body was agile, her movements were jerky and indecisive. She seemed to be in a state of distress, and fixed her gaze on Rekke as she offered a firm handshake.

"I'm sorry to bother you. I've come in the middle of something, haven't I?" she said, glancing at Julia and Micaela.

Rekke smiled kindly and invited her to sit down.

"On the contrary," he said. "You've come at just the right moment. We could all do with something else to think about. Was your lunch cut short?"

The woman stared at Rekke, perplexed.

"How do you know?"

"You're dressed as if you wish to make an impression on someone, and it's lunchtime. But above all, it's apparent that you have just heard something upsetting. Was it about your ex-husband?"

The woman looked dumbfounded.

"My God—has he called you?"

"Not at all," he said. "I can see from your finger that you've recently removed your wedding ring, and it was just a guess on my part. I am—quite frankly—a little manic at present, and dysregulated too, although for quite different reasons from you. But let's not get ahead of ourselves. Why have you sought us out?"

"I've heard about you, Professor Rekke," the woman said. "And you too, Micaela," she added somewhat apologetically. "They say you can solve problems, and I'm embroiled in the most peculiar episode with . . . well, my ex-husband, as you said, and just now I heard something completely insane. You'll have to forgive me. It's going to sound as if it's come straight from the pages of a detective novel."

Rekke glanced at Micaela, who smiled kindly at the woman.

"I think that sounds like a good start," he said, his left leg beginning to twitch.

## ACKNOWLEDGEMENTS

My thanks to Jessica Bab, my agent through thick and thin, Eva Bergman, my skilled editor, and Eva Gedin, my keen-eyed publisher. Thanks also to my good friend Johan Norberg, copy editor Åsa Sandzén and forensic pathologist Eva Rudd.

And thank you to Anne and the children.